A LIFE LESS ORDINARY

ALSO BY CHRISTOPHER NUTTALL

The Royal Sorceress
Bookworm

A LIFE LESS ORDINARY

CHRISTOPHER NUTTALL

Elsewhen Press

A Life Less Ordinary
First published in Great Britain by Elsewhen Press, 2013
An imprint of Alnpete Limited

Elsewhen Press, PO Box 757, Dartford, Kent DA2 7TQ
www.elsewhen.co.uk

British Library Cataloguing in Publication Data.
A catalogue record for this book is available from the British Library.

ISBN 978-1-908168-23-8 Print edition
ISBN 978-1-908168-33-7 eBook edition

Printed and bound by CPI Group (UK) Ltd, Croydon, CR0 4YY

To Aisha

Prologue

Magic didn't go out of this world. It just went sideways. You don't see it, but we are there, hidden in the corner of your eye. If you have the gift, or you believe in us, you will find us. You will enter a world of magic, of witches and wizards, sorcerers and necromancers, dragons and demons, elves and fairies. You will enter a world where the powerless of the dull mundane world take on new forms, where an ugly duckling can become a swan, where the great powers of Heaven and Hell – and all the many realms in-between – interact with frail humans and their world.

If you search for us, you will find us. Just don't blame us if you don't like what you find.

My name is my own, a secret shared only with my nearest and dearest. Names have power, even in the mundane world. In the magical world, to know a person's name is to have power over them. Never ask a magician what his name is; ever. Always ask what a person would like to be called.

You can call me Dizzy.

This is my story.

CHAPTER ONE

Where to begin, I wonder?

Where to begin?

I still remember my first meeting with Master Revels, even now, so many years after the fact. Even as an old woman, that day – the day that my life changed forever – continues to haunt me. If I hadn't followed him, my life would have been very different; happy and distant and small. Or perhaps I am just fooling myself.

I was eighteen when I left school in Edinburgh, many years ago. I hadn't paid enough attention while I had the chance, so I left my formal education with only a handful of awards, hardly enough to get into a good university. My mother – my father, of whom I prefer not to speak, had left us while I was a baby – looked at me, saw the waste I had made of my life, and ordered me to get out of hers. I moved in with a boyfriend and thought that I would never look back.

It turned out that there were few positions for unqualified teens in Edinburgh. I signed on at the dole and was pushed towards a series of positions that were, in effect, menial work. I scrubbed dishes and changed beds at old folks homes, I cooked and cleaned at a simple cafe and spent far too much time living hand to mouth. My first boyfriend finally got tired of me and kicked me out of his flat, leaving me out on the streets. Three of my girlfriends, who had set up a communal flat, allowed me to stay with them in exchange for paying a share of the rent. My second boyfriend – a drug addict I should have known better than to allow anywhere near me – wanted me to go into prostitution to pay the bills. I got out of that one quick and, with some help from a friend, managed to find an entry-level position at a famous shopping centre. It was dull, with absolutely no hope of promotion, but I thought that it would be permanent. The economic crash came along and suddenly I found my position threatened. The manager, a tight-fisted bastard, cut salaries all round, apart from himself, of course. He was being paid enough in his salary to keep us all working, but the rest of us had to survive on minimum wage. I didn't quit, because I had no choice. I had to keep working for the slave driver.

Edinburgh is a remarkable city, for those of you unlucky enough never to have visited. My first memory was seeing blue lights surrounding Edinburgh Castle, although my mother used to tell me that I was just imagining it. It was always hard to tell my memories from my imagination as I grew older, something that I never fully understood until I met Master Revels. The only relaxation I had – I couldn't afford to do things like going to the pictures or anything else that cost money – was walking through the city. One day, my sole day off in the entire week, I was walking through the Royal Mile when I saw Master Revels for the first time. I didn't know who he was, of course. Not then.

You may not have seen one of his posters, so I will describe him for you. He was a tall man, handsome in a bland sort of way, with a strong chin. He always wore a black suit, a white shirt and a top hat, something that he used to distract attention from his face. Even after I got to know him, I always found it hard to imagine him without his outfit; it was, in many ways, a case of clothes making the man. His face was pale, although never as inhumanly pale as his posters suggested, and his eyes were bright blue. His black hair – so black that people suspected that it came out of a bottle – seemed to glimmer in the sunlight.

It wasn't his face or his outfit that attracted my attention, however; it was the creature resting on his shoulder. It was riding like a parrot would ride on a pirate's shoulder, yet it was larger and stranger than any parrot, rather like a cross between a lizard and a peacock. I turned as he walked past, unaware of my scrutiny, and just stared at him. The creature should have been drawing attention from everyone, yet no one seemed to notice. No one apart from me.

For a moment, I thought that it was a puppet of some kind, just before it moved and turned to look at me. It wasn't just convincing, it was so *real* that I found myself believing in it completely. Almost unaware of what I was doing, heedless of my surroundings or of any manners my mother might have drummed into me over the years, I turned to follow the strange man and his remarkable beast. He was walking upwards, towards the castle, when he turned into a side alley I couldn't recall ever having seen before. I was still following him, almost in a daze, when I walked right into him. The shock of the collision brought me back to my senses.

"Good afternoon, my dear," the man said. He had a voice that sounded almost aristocratic, although without the underlying assumption of servility on my part. He didn't sound angry, much to my relief, just curious. "Do you have some reason to be following me?"

It honestly didn't occur to me to try to lie to him. "Sir," I said, "what is that creature on your shoulder?"

His eyes widened with genuine surprise. "You can see her?"

The creature, as if it was aware that we were speaking about her, seemed to turn to look at me again. Up close, it was easy to see how weird it truly was. She had the strangest golden eyes, so bright and understanding, as if she had looked upon all the sin of the world and forgiven one and all. Her scales, a strange shade of green, seemed to flicker as she stood up on his shoulder and – I found myself transfixed, unable to move – spread her wings. I hadn't realised until then, but I was looking at a tiny green dragon.

"Yes," I said. He hadn't taken his eyes off my face. It was a scrutiny that seemed to look deep into my very soul. "What is she?"

He ignored my question. "How often do you see creatures that are not supposed to exist?"

I looked up at him, puzzled. "I thought I saw a unicorn once, when I was a child," I said. The memory of the visit to the safari park, one of the few good memories from my childhood, still resounded within my head. "Why...?"

"I think that you had better come with me," the man said. He turned and led the way down the alleyway. "Coming?"

Prudence suggested that I should run, that I should try to get away from the weirdo and his strange pet dragon, but I had never been one for listening to prudence. Besides, the look in the dragon's eyes seemed to convince me that, whatever happened, I would be safe. I gathered myself and followed him through a maze of tiny alleys that I had never known existed, before we stopped outside a stone door. It looked so old that I wondered if we were going into the castle itself, before he pushed it open and waved me inside. The room we entered was large enough to be a ballroom, covered with endless heaps of trinkets and junk. I found myself staring as we passed a mountain of older books, many written in languages I didn't recognise, and found a tiny kitchen at one end of the room. The man pushed the dragon impatiently and she flew into the air, flapping over towards me. Before I could react, she settled on my shoulder and winked at me.

Whatever doubts I had kept, I lost them when I felt the dragon's skin. It was hot, yet not hot enough to be uncomfortable, moving with a strange beating motion. It felt almost like holding a scaly hamster, with the same rapidly beating heart and twitching eyes, although none of my pet hamsters had ever looked so wise. I stroked her gently and she crooned in pleasure, a deep sound that seemed to hum in my ear.

"I'm sorry about the mess," the man said, sounding unconcerned. He passed me a cup of tea and I sipped gratefully, surprised to discover that he'd made it exactly how I liked it. The dragon emitted a sharp noise and he flushed, almost embarrassed. "I am called Revels, Master Revels to my adoring public."

I smiled. "My name is..."

He held up a hand before I could complete the sentence. "If you're going to be involved in my world, and it seems that you are, you need to keep one thing in mind," he said. "Do *not* give anyone your real name, for names have power.

Pick a name for yourself, something you can be called, and stick to it."

I thought about it. "Be careful what you choose," Revels added. "The name you choose is going to have its own effect on you."

"My friends used to call me Dizzy," I said. It felt right, somehow. "Will that do?"

Revels gave me a very vague look. "The choice, my dear, is yours," he said, affecting a bored tone. "If it feels good, use it; if not, choose a different one."

I cleared my throat. "And now we're on assumed names terms," I said, "just what is going on?"

Revels smiled. "It is really quite simple," he said. "You have a gift, just like me and a handful of other people around the world, the gift of magic. Welcome to the magical world."

I stared at him. Somehow, it was impossible to disbelieve him. "Are you saying that there's a magical world out there, like Harry..."

"Don't get me started on those books," Revels interrupted, annoyed. "It doesn't work anything like that."

I wanted to ask more questions, but somehow I refrained. "Those of us who have real magic tend to stay out of sight," Revels continued, taking my silence for an invitation to continue. Most of the world is simply unable to see magic or anything touched by magic, such as Fiona there." He waved a hand at the dragon, still perched on my shoulder. "A horde of dragons could fly over Edinburgh and all the mundane population of the world would see would be dark clouds covering the sky. Everyone is so busy looking for humdrum explanations for everything that they miss the magic."

He grinned up at me, his eyes glittering with light. "But you saw the magic," he said. He waved a hand through the air and a rainbow appeared out of nowhere, shimmering in the air before it faded away into nothingness. "Welcome to the world."

I felt strange, almost...dizzy. I had never felt as if I really belonged anywhere, but now, sitting with this strange older man and his pet dragon, I felt as if I were home. We relaxed together, sipping our tea, and somehow it felt perfect. The dragon flew off my shoulder and somewhere into the distance, suddenly calling my attention to the fact that the room was impossibly big. How could anyone have shaved out so much space in Edinburgh? The room seemed to be larger than the castle itself.

"So," I said, tearing my eyes away from the piles of items on the floor. Some looked like junk still; others looked as if they were interesting and perhaps even valuable. "What do we do now?"

Revels grinned at me, removing his hat and reaching inside. Somehow, I wasn't surprised to see his arm go so far in, right up to the shoulder. He reached around inside the hat and eventually pulled out a smaller hat, which opened up at his touch. It was another black top hat. He passed it to me and started digging around again, producing a silver ring and a tiny knife made out of crystal. Could it be diamond? I took them in some bemusement, feeling a tingle running down my spine as I touched the ring.

"Does this mean we're engaged now?"

He didn't smile at my weak sally. "There are no coincidences in the world of magic," he said, seriously. "I need a new apprentice; you need a master to train you in the art of magic. I think that we were intended to meet and become acquainted." His voice darkened. "Will you do me the honour of becoming my apprentice?"

I stared down at the ring, feeling it tingling. The knife didn't feel so...magical, yet there was a curious deadness around it, something that felt weird to my touch. The top hat fitted perfectly. Why, I wondered, was I not surprised?

"I don't know," I admitted, finally. "What happens if I say no?"

Revels looked surprised, but answered the question. "You walk out of that door and never see me again," he said. "Your magic may fade away without proper direction, or you may grow and develop on your own, or you may find yourself a victim of...darker magicians. Later, once you develop your powers, you may decide to leave me and strike out alone."

He smiled at my expression. "Go take a look at yourself in the mirror over there," he said, pointing to a mirror that was large enough to show my entire body. "You might be pleasantly surprised."

I did as I was bid and looked into the mirror. I saw myself; tall, brown-haired, with pale skin and dark brown eyes. My breasts were smaller than I would have preferred – my second boyfriend had seriously proposed a boob job, which I couldn't have paid for without his help – but on the whole I was rather pleased with my appearance. An observer would hardly guess that I spent six days out of seven slaving for one of those soulless corporations raping the planet, pretending to smile at a boss who made normal assholes seem bland by comparison. My shirt and skirt were worn to make me seem carefree...

My appearance changed, suddenly. I saw myself naked and yelped aloud, looking down to check that I was still wearing clothes. When I looked up again, I saw myself wearing the same suit and top hat that Revels was wearing, which rapidly shifted to a traditional witch's outfit, complete with broom and bubbling cauldron. My appearance shifted again and again, some interesting, some absurd and some downright slutty. I looked away from the mirror and back towards him. He was smiling, clearly in no doubt as to what I would choose.

And he was right. I had wasted my life in the mundane world. I didn't have a hope of finding a proper job, not one that would allow me to grow and develop into someone important. Perhaps, as a magician, I could be something remarkable; even if there were dangers, surely it was worthwhile. I touched the top hat and smiled at the feel of the felt against my fingertips. Even if there was a price to be paid, I would gladly pay it, just for the chance to be something else. If I was being honest with myself, I hated my life.

"As my apprentice, I will teach you how to master the powers you have," Revels said, answering my unspoken question. "In exchange, you will help me carry out the more complex spells and do other duties for me. Cooking and cleaning, mainly; I just don't have the time and aptitude to actually do the work and wasting magic on cleaning is a bad idea. And, as my lovely assistant, you will get a share in the proceeds from every show."

I didn't understand until a few days later just what he had meant. Most of the magical community, those who weren't powerful enough to maintain a permanent separation from the mundane world, tended to hide in plain sight. They were stage magicians, performing their arts in public, showing the general public real magic and getting paid for it. The mundane world never truly realised that they were seeing actual magic, for they all *knew* that magic didn't exist. The next time you go watch a stage magician at work, wonder how the trick is really done. You might be looking at a real magician.

"That sounds wonderful," I said, sincerely. "What should I tell my employer?"

"You don't have to tell them anything," Revels assured me. "If you agree to learn from me, I will see to it that no one questions your absence. Your employer will take on a new person without ever quite knowing what has happened to you. Your flatmates will find someone else to take your place." I shrugged. I'd been sleeping on the sofa for the last couple of months, an uncomfortable position at the best of times. "You will just blur out of the mundane world, part of it yet never truly involved."

The dragon flew back towards me and landed neatly on my shoulder. I reached up absently and stroked the back of her neck, almost as one would stroke a cat. The dragon hummed and pushed closer to me, a long snake-like tongue flickering out to lick at my ear. I didn't flinch. Somehow, I was sure that the dragon wouldn't harm me. In fact, I was sure that it was more intelligent than it seemed.

Revels smiled at my expression. "It's your choice," he said, gently. He wasn't trying to pressure me into anything. "A life of magic, of wonders and terrors you can barely begin to imagine, or a return to the mundane world of boredom, where you were sleepwalking through life. What do you choose?"

"I accept," I said, holding out my hand. He took it in a surprisingly gentle grip and shook it firmly. "This looks like the start of a beautiful friendship."

CHAPTER TWO

I'd had the idea that I'd be learning magic from dawn till dusk. How wrong I was.

"You know, you could help with this," I grumbled to Fiona. The tiny dragon was perched, parrot-like, on top of a massive pile of books. "How am I meant to sort all of them out by myself?"

"You start at the beginning and go on to the end, where you stop," Fiona said. One red eye winked at me. "See? It's easy when you know how."

I glared at the dragon and stared down at the books. There were thousands of them – perhaps millions – in a room that was large enough to hold a football field. Most of the books looked old, yet there was very little damage, suggesting the presence of a preservation spell. Fiona had explained when we'd been left alone to get on with it that the owners of the magical apartment had been gathering books for hundreds of years. Looking down at them, I was prepared to believe that they'd just scooped up everything they could, dumped them in the chamber and never come back to read them. It was easy to believe.

Some of the books were written in English, with titles that ran from *Dangerous Potions* to *Demon Summoning for Women*. Others were written in French, or Latin, or what looked like a strange combination of Chinese and Arabic writing. I couldn't even begin to divine what they might contain; hell, I wasn't even sure how to catalogue them, let alone put them into something reassembling a proper order. I had never realised just how much hard work went on behind the scenes in a library.

"Tell me something," I said. "What would the Master say

if we went back to him and told him that it was hopeless?"

Fiona pretended to consider. "It isn't hopeless," she said, finally. "You might take most of a year sorting the books – longer, as you wouldn't be here all the time – but you could do it. I don't think the Master would like that very much."

"Oh," I said, bleakly. "And what would he do?"

"Well...he could shout at you a bit," Fiona said. That didn't sound too bad. "That's magical shouting, of course; what he called you might become real. Or he could turn you into a frog and leave you that way for a while, or perhaps settle for punishing you in a more traditional style, or..."

"I get the message," I said. I bent down and picked up a handful of English books. I had pretty much decided to separate out the English books – which I could read, if not very well – from the remainder of the collection. I could at least put them in order before I went to Master Revels and explained that I couldn't sort the remainder of the collection. Holding the books, I looked around for somewhere to put them, but there was nowhere apart from back on the floor. The few tables in the room were covered in books. It looked like a library that had been torn apart by a hurricane, scattering the books everywhere. "Where am I supposed to shelve them?"

Fiona snickered. "It's only a vague suggestion, but what about on the shelf?"

I counted to ten under my breath. "There are nowhere near enough shelves in this room to hold all of these books," I said, in what I hoped was a calm and composed voice. I didn't want my frustration leaking out into the atmosphere. "Where am I supposed to get more?"

The little dragon fluttered through the air towards the shelves. "These are magical shelves," Fiona said, in tones that suggested that she thought I was stupid. "All you have to do is put the books on them and allow them to extend to the size required."

"Oh," I said. I walked over to one of the shelves – it was barely larger than I – and pulled some of the books off it. A moment later, I found myself on the floor as dozens of books spilled off the shelves, knocking me down as they fell.

There was a sound rather like a snap and I looked up to see that one of the shelves had completely vanished. My chest hurt after the books had landed on me. I crawled out from under the pile of books and swore. "Now what do I do?"

"I don't think that that is how you do it," Fiona said, dryly. The dragon peered down at the pile of books. "You just broke the spell holding the shelf together."

I glared at the dragon, who – for once – decided to explain. "The original magician crafted a spell that created a pocket dimension for his books," Fiona said. "You could put an entire library onto a single shelf if you knew the key. Instead, you collapsed the spell and every book held within the pocket dimension was unceremoniously tossed out – onto you."

"I had noticed," I said, as I rubbed myself. I was going to be covered in bruises tomorrow. It was funny how I'd never realised that a book could be used as a deadly weapon before. "Now what do we do?"

Fiona smiled a dragonish smile. "Well," she said, "you could go see the Master and explain what happened and ask him to help...but perhaps he might turn you into something for a few hours, just to make the point about tampering with something you don't understand. Just don't let him turn you into a rabbit. I love eating rabbits."

I shuddered. "What will happen if I touch the next shelf?"

Fiona took to the air and floated over towards a safer perch. "I'll watch from a safe distance as you try," she said, dryly. "This is a magical library. Sometimes the books read you."

Something went *click* in my mind. "This is a magical library," I repeated. "Does that mean that, somewhere in here, there is a spell to create those...pocket dimensions?"

"Of course," Fiona said. "Do you know a magician who would willingly give up a book once it had fallen into his hands?"

I only knew one magician - Master Revels – but I could see her point. There were thousands of books just lying around in the library, suggesting that no one had ever cleaned it out and removed any of the older and less useful books from the collection. Actually, it made a great deal of sense. Knowledge is power, after all, and I could see magicians gathering hundreds of books to themselves, rather than filing them away in a public library.

"All right," I said. Part of my mind was saying that I shouldn't even be thinking about it, but it was drowned out by the thought of having to spend months sorting the books. "How do I find the spell?"

Fiona gave a hint of a shrug. For a dragon, her body language was very human. "You could start with the open spell book," she suggested, waving one wing towards the table near the door. "Or you could just pick up a spell book at random and see what you find."

I walked over towards the table, limping slightly, and looked down at the book. It had a palpable sense of age – it looked like a volume produced by a monk in a monastery, rather than a mass-produced modern book – and felt oddly warm to the touch. I found out later that it was impossible to actually mass-produce magical books. The strange rules binding magic made it impossible, although a considerable amount of common knowledge could be stored in more modern books or computers. I didn't know that at the time, of course. If someone should happen to write down a magical spell, they are effectively casting it. The implications are nastier than they sound.

The book opened at my touch and I started to read through the pages. There was a spell promising beauty untold to the woman who chanted it at full moon. It was tempting, but I had no idea how long it would be until full moon. There was a spell for cursing your enemies and giving them bad luck for a year and a day. I was thinking about my ex for several minutes before I hastily turned the page and moved on to the next spell. It talked about summoning invisible servants who would work for you, in exchange for a tiny drop of blood. The ritual involved in summoning them made me blush.

"Try the rear of the book," Fiona advised. "The more complex spells won't be held at the front of the book. They'll be weighed down by the less dangerous spells."

I flicked through the book and finally located a spell for creating pocket dimensions that could be spelled to me, or spelled to anyone who happened to be in the area. I could see a use for the former right away. I could create my own private dimension and not have to worry about carrying a bag or anything else ever again. Or – and I smiled at the thought, even though I would never put it into practice – I could use it to steal from shops and they would never have the slightest idea of what had happened.

The spell didn't look that complex, not even compared to some of the others in the earlier part of the book. I picked up the spellbook – in my hands, it felt light and yet surprisingly warm – and walked back over to the shelves. The pile of fallen books had shifted slightly, but they seemed disinclined to jump back onto the shelves. I wasn't too surprised. There was little room for the books to fit.

"Be careful," Fiona said, as I studied the words of the spell. They were written out phonically, allowing me to pronounce them correctly – or so I hoped. I had no idea what would happen if I mispronounced even one of the words. "You have to keep an image of what you want to happen in your mind at all times."

That wasn't quite as easy as it sounded. I started the spell and then was distracted as a thought burst into my mind, making it hard to concentrate. She'd told me not to think of anything else, so I naturally *did* think of something else, anything else. I felt a rising wave of frustration and forced it down, taking deep breaths to calm myself. There was no hurry. Even if it worked, I would still have to start shelving the books and that would take days, perhaps weeks. My breathing slowed to a crawl – I could hear my heartbeat pounding away – and I focused, concentrating on precisely what I wanted to happen. I wanted a pocket dimension, one anyone could use, one that wouldn't break when I removed a book...slowly, the image grew and settled in my mind. I opened my mouth and chanted the spell aloud.

I felt a sudden tingle running up my spine, which grew rapidly into a thunderstorm. Energy seemed to be crawling all over me, like the touch of an unwelcome or unwanted lover. I could barely move as the forces played over me – I was suddenly aware of just how vulnerable I was – and I almost panicked. Only the thought of losing control now, with so much magic in the air, kept me focused. The forces I had unleashed could tear me apart like paper if I lost my concentration. And then it was over. I keeled over and collapsed on the ground.

"You seem to have succeeded," Fiona commented, archly. The tiny dragon fluttered down to my side and rubbed her scaly head against my cheek. She felt hot to the touch. I pulled myself up into a sitting position and looked up at the shelves. Where the shelves had been there was now a faint blur, as if many different images were fighting for supremacy. I looked closer and understood. Hundreds of thousands of shelves were positioned within the pocket dimension, awaiting my touch. "It wasn't too bad for a first effort."

I frowned. The original shelves had been neater than mine. "How long will it last?"

Fiona snorted, producing an impressive gout of flame from her snout. "How long do you want them to last?"

"Forever," I said. I paused. I had been thinking of forever, hadn't I? "Will they last forever?"

"Well, I'm only a mere sorcerer's familiar, but I'm fairly sure that they will last a good long time," Fiona said. "You ought to be proud of yourself."

I couldn't help myself. I burst out laughing. I had been so scared and yet...I had succeeded. It had worked beautifully. I was so proud of myself.

"Thank you," I said, and meant it. "Now what do I do?"

A thought struck me and I walked back to the table, carrying the spellbook under my arm. I flicked through the pages again until I located the one I wanted, the one advising how to summon invisible servants. As I read through the spell again, it occurred to me that Master Revels might have given me the task as a test, one to see if I could learn to use the magic in the library to get the job done quicker and more efficiently. Fiona looked doubtful as I explained my brainwave to her, but I ignored her doubts. I was sure that I was right.

The spell was clearly written out and actually seemed to be less complex than the pocket dimension spell. I had to strip down to bare skin, squat on the floor and recite the spell aloud, with no room for error. I didn't understand the nakedness at the time, although I learned later that such rituals were often more about preparing the magician rather than part of the spell itself. The trick lay in separating what was truly vital from what wasn't – and research into the subject rarely led to a long and happy life. I cast a doubtful look at Fiona – reminded myself that she wasn't human and was female anyway – and started to undress. Halfway through, it struck me to wonder what Master Revels would think if he walked in on me, but I told myself that he would understand. It was necessary for the ritual, after all.

Fiona fluttered down to the table, her unblinking red eyes fixed on me. "Are you sure about this?"

I nodded, positioned the spellbook on my bare knees, and began.

This time, the tingle came quicker, followed rapidly by a wave of power that rapidly took on shape and form. I saw enough to understand why the servants were normally invisible to human eyes; looking at what I saw out of the corner of my eye, it was clear that prolonged contact would be bad for my sanity. I squeezed my eyes closed, yet I could feel them, a burning presence all around me.

It was hard, suddenly, to speak, but I forced out the words. "I bind and command you by a drop of my blood," I said. I held out my thumb, inviting them to suck on it. The spellbook had assured me that they could only take what they were permitted to take. "I order you to sort the books and shelve them into my pocket dimension."

There was a dull rumble, like distant thunder, but nothing else.

"I command you," I said. They hadn't taken anything from my thumb. A cold presentiment of disaster started to make its way down my spine. "I offer you my..."

It all happened very quickly. Suddenly, tiny fingers were running all over me, pinching and slapping at my body. I felt them reaching for my hairs and pulling at them, one by one, as others slapped at my private parts or my face. I screamed in pain as hands started to form around my neck and started to squeeze...

"Enough," a voice snapped. A blast of power shone, just for a second, though the air and the pinching stopped. "Get thee gone from this place."

There was a second blast of power and I opened my eyes. Master Revels was standing there, staring down at me. He didn't seem aware of my nakedness, but I didn't like the look in his eye. He looked angry. Somehow, I didn't blame him. I closed my eyes and awaited the worst.

"Stand up," he said, calmly. I opened my eyes and stood up. My body was covered in tiny scratches, some dripping blood onto the floor. I was surprised that there wasn't more pain. "What did you learn from that?"

It was hard to think and focus, but somehow I managed. "I learned that I shouldn't play with fire," I croaked. It hurt to speak. I touched my throat and my hand came away bloody. "What went wrong?"

Master Revels didn't seem to notice my discomfort. "There are spells that cannot be written down safely," he said, calmly. Fiona fluttered down to land on his shoulder. "When they are written down, there are always sections left unwritten, or rewritten to make the spell less dangerous. Never – ever – take anything for granted in the magical world."

He snorted. "Go have a shower" – he'd shown me where the showers were the first day I'd spent with him – "and look at yourself in the mirror. The scars will fade slowly, so don't forget."

"I won't," I promised, and meant it. It could have been a great deal worse.

***

The mirror was magical. It showed me almost as a holographic image, rotating me around so I could inspect myself from all angles. I was covered in bumps and bruises, with scars running down from my hairline to my knees. The little creatures had left me marked for a very long time. I washed, wincing as the water fell into my scratches, and swore never to try that again. I had come far too close to death.

On the other hand, I told myself, one spell had succeeded perfectly.

Perhaps I had a future as a magician after all.

CHAPTER THREE

"So tell me," Master Revels said. "What do you think of your costume?"

"I think they will all be looking at me," I groused. If I had seen the costume before agreeing to serve as his assistant, I might have had second thoughts. "No one will be looking at you at all."

"That's the point," Master Revels said, evilly. "I wouldn't want them looking closely enough to realise that the puppet has no strings."

I scowled as I examined myself in the mirror. The outfit gave new meanings to the word *revealing*. I looked rather like a demented cheerleader. My breasts were covered by a sequined tunic that drew attention to them, while my shorts – also sequined – were so tight that anyone watching would be convinced that they were painted on. They didn't feel uncomfortable, but they were so tight that I was half-convinced that I wasn't wearing anything to cover my rear. The tiny glamour that Master Revels had given me would obscure my features, yet also give me an air of beauty that would ensure that all eyes were turned to me. And I was barefooted. It didn't seem fair somehow.

Master Revels himself wore a black suit with a white shirt and a top hat. He looked far more like a typical stage magician, even down to the silver-topped cane he carried in one hand. I knew that his cane was, at least in part, a magic wand and he could produce anything he wanted from his top hat, but anyone else looking at him would only see a stage magician. I never understood why he wanted to show off on stage – I like to think that it was a uniquely male attribute – even though few would realise that there was real magic being displayed.

"Come on," he said, holding out a hand. I pulled on a pair of sandals and took it, reluctantly. A moment later, we were standing outside his house, near the castle. As he had promised, we were surrounded by hundreds of people wearing their own strange costumes; even I, wearing so little that I was almost naked, passed unnoticed. I saw a dozen men wearing kilts and carrying claymores, several men dressed up as famous cartoon characters and a woman wearing what looked like the world's largest hat, covered in fruit. There were small donkeys, a horse and even a giant dog, all carrying small children up and down the Royal Mile.

I had to smile. The Edinburgh Festival Fringe is the world's largest performing arts festival and it is held right here in Edinburgh. Hundreds of thousands of people from all over the world come to see the shows, even though it isn't quite as spectacular as Mardi Gras or some of the other festivals held around the world. Master Revels had been quite right. We could walk down the roads wearing only top hats to cover our privates and no one would actually notice, even without the glamour covering our presence. The entire magical world could walk out in the night and few would realise that they were in the presence of something unearthly. I watched a team of flamenco dancers from Latin America go dancing past and concealed a smile. We were definitely dressed conservatively for the area.

It was strange, but Edinburgh itself seemed to have taken on a new appearance after the time I'd spent in the magical chambers. The entire city seemed to shine with a strange blue glow, with certain areas marked out more clearly than others. The castle seemed to shine the brightest, but I could see a dozen others within the Royal Mile and another down towards the Grassmarket. It was weird, yet I was starting to understand that there were actually two cities, a magical Edinburgh co-existing with the dull mundane city. The more I looked, the more I saw, from strange creatures jumping from shadow to shadow to a glowing statue that seemed to dominate part of the city.

"That man volunteered to remain on guard for the rest of

his life," Master Revels commented, when I asked him. "The magical community lent him some of their strength and placed him there on guard. No one can invade Edinburgh while he remains there, a silent sentinel in the night."

I shivered as we walked past the statue. I could make out, now, the fine traces of magic that had turned a man into a statue. I wondered, suddenly, just how he was feeling. Was he aware of time passing while he remained frozen, or was he in a form of suspended animation? If I had been frozen like that for so long – the plaque at the base of the statue claimed that it had been there since the 1700s – I would have gone mad.

Master Revels had hired a medium-sized hall for his performance. He might not have been numbered among the greatest of the stage magicians – if only they knew – but he had a solid reputation and the crowds were already flocking into the hall. We slipped unnoticed through the crowds and into the hall, where Master Revels checked the equipment and reminded me of my role. We'd spent part of the last week – or so I thought; it was hard to measure time inside a magical house – rehearsing. I peeked out onto the stage and saw several boxes, a set of mirrors and even a tiny cage, with a rather bemused hamster squatting inside it. Beyond that, there was a large dog that seemed to wink at me. I had always wanted a pet dog, but my mother had refused, believing that I couldn't be trusted to take care of a large animal.

I could hear the sound of the crowd as they filed into the hall and took their seats. They sounded happy and good-natured, but I couldn't help feeling sheer terror at the thought of performing in front of them. I wasn't even going to do much and yet I was still terrified! Master Revels seemed to take it all in his stride. He checked his appearance, winked at me, and strode out onto the stage. I hesitated, realised that the curtain hadn't risen, and followed him, taking the place I'd been promised. I struck an absurd pose and he waved a finger at me.

"Ladies and gentlemen," a voice proclaimed. It took me a

second to realise that Master Revels was speaking into a hidden microphone. "I present to you the world's greatest magician - Master Revels!"

The curtain rose and a single spotlight shone down on his position, so bright that no one would be able to see me against the darkness. It was a neat bit of misdirection. Hardly anyone would know that I was there, even though I was wearing a silly outfit and standing right in front of them. There was a roar of approval from the crowd, including a group of drunken teenagers who waved glasses of beer in the air. I blanched, glad that no one could see me, and then swallowed hard. I knew what was coming.

"Welcome, one and all," Master Revels said. His voice seemed to boom out, effortlessly drowning out the noise of the crowd. "And, if you please, a big round of applause for my lovely assistant, the fair Dizzy!"

A spotlight shone down on me. The crowd roared its approval, the drunken young men loudest of all. I would have blushed, but instead I managed to smile. My costume suddenly made a great deal more sense. With the spotlight burning down, there were flashes of lights illuminating my body, drawing attention from all over the room.

"And now...we will begin," Master Revels proclaimed. He took off his top hat, bowed to the audience, and placed it down on the table. "Take a look at the table. There is nothing underneath; there is nothing on top, apart from the hat! And yet..."

He paused, dramatically. "Wait...I bet you don't trust me," he added. "I bet you think I have a trick up my sleeve." The crowd burst into laughter. "I need a victim...I'm sorry, I meant volunteer. I need a volunteer from the audience to prove that I have nothing up my sleeves."

There was a long pause, and then a young girl – barely older than twelve – was pushed onto the stage by her mother. There was a round of applause as I took her hand and escorted her over to the table, where she knelt and walked under the table, before picking up the hat and reaching deep into it. There was nothing there.

"It's empty," she said, disappointed.

"So it is," Master Revels said. He looked up at the watching audience. "A big hand for Charlotte, if you please!"

There was another round of applause as the girl was helped back into the audience. "And now," Master Revels added, "we will begin."

He clicked his fingers together, holding them over the hat. The crowd grew silent as they watched. He pressed his fingertips together, allowing a tiny trickle of glitter to fall into the hat, before he reached in...and in...and in. His entire arm seemed to go into the hat. There were some gasps, but most of the audience was still watching silently. Master Revels struggled, as if he were trying to hang onto something that didn't want to be caught, and then he pulled his hand out in one convulsive motion. A large green snake poured out of the hat and coiled itself on the stage, hissing nastily.

"Oh dear," Master Revels announced, dramatically. He pointed to a bulge in the snake's skin. "Slither has eaten my rabbit!"

The crowd roared with laughter, although a few nervous eyes were watching the snake. Slither's head was moving from side to side, as if he was deciding which of us would make the next meal. I hated snakes on general principles, but Slither looked truly unpleasant. His golden eyes were too knowing to belong to just a mere animal.

"I think I'd better rescue Mr Fluffy before he is digested," Master Revels continued. He snapped his fingers and there was a flash of light. Slither reared back, hissing angrily, just before the rabbit burst out of his mouth and onto the table. The crowd cheered, some with relief. The rabbit peered at them all disdainfully and jumped back into the hat. "And he's gone. I guess he doesn't like being eaten."

He lowered his voice, aiming it towards the youngest children in the room. "It's a jungle in there," he said. Slither, in the meantime, had sighted the hamster and reared up, clearly intending to have the small rodent for dinner instead. Master Revels stood up, reached into the hamster cage and rescued the cowering creature. "Shall we teach Slither a lesson, children?"

There was a general shout of approval. "All right," Master Revels said. "Lets!"

He placed the hamster down on the stage and waved to the snake. Slither turned and started to advance towards the hamster, just before Master Revels clicked his fingers. The hamster suddenly grew until it was the size of a large dog. Hamsters are cute and cuddly when they're small, but when they're large they look alarming. Those teeth are very sharp. The hamster started to advance on the snake, which turned and headed back to the top hat, rearing up and throwing itself back inside. The hamster followed and, a moment later, the hat started to shake as if the two were fighting. To the astonishment of the crowd, Master Revels picked up the hat and put it back on his head as if he didn't have a care in the world.

The next few tricks were simpler, but the crowd ate them up and begged for more. He used magic to read minds and predict the future. He used his wand to send me flying through the air with the greatest of ease. He created vast illusions to order, allowing the younger members of the audience to choose the illusions, just to show them that it was no trick. One audience member even wanted an image of a naked girl, so Master Revels created it – with her private parts neatly covered with black CENSORED signs. The audience nearly wet themselves laughing.

I was starting to understand the subtle magic he was weaving at the same time. The crowd were seeing real magic, yet his magic was convincing them that there was a mundane explanation, no matter how far-fetched. A small boy stood up while I was flying and proclaimed that it was all done with wires. His mother pulled him down, but not quickly enough to save him from the laughter of the crowd. They all believed him and yet they didn't believe.

"So," Master Revels said, finally. "For my second to last trick...I need a volunteer." He looked over at the boy who had shouted out. "How would you like to be sawn in half?"

"You bet," the boy said, scrambling to his feet. "It's a trick and I will expose you as soon as I see it."

I took the boy's hand as he climbed onto the stage. He

was about twelve years old, although I guessed that he hadn't been through puberty yet as he paid no attention to my costume. He was slightly overweight, with big glasses and a spotty face. I deduced that he was picked on at school, probably for being able to count to eleven without having to take off his shoes. His hand felt greasy and sweaty to the touch and I realised that, despite his brave appearance, the boy was a little nervous.

"If you will climb into the box, my dear George," Master Revels said cheerfully, "we can start sawing you in half."

The box itself looked rather like a coffin, although it was covered in stars and magical symbols. The boy looked surprised at how Master Revels had known his name, although he then looked down at the badge he was wearing and relaxed. I held his hand as the lid came down, for it was clear that he was growing more than a little nervous. It had been obvious, the moment he opened the box, that there was no hidden compartment, nor was there room for him to pull up his legs.

"As you can see," Master Revels continued, "this is a real saw. I normally use it for cutting down trees. Tonight, we are going to use it to cut a boy in half!"

There was a roar of applause as he started to saw into the box. It looked impressive, even though I knew the trick. The saw went through into the open area – George held my hand tightly as it seemed to go through his body – and then down through the bottom end. Master Revels opened the box and George fell out, seemingly intact.

"I told you it was a trick," George thundered. He jumped in the air with delight. "I didn't feel a thing and..."

The crowd burst out laughing. George hadn't realised it, but every time he jumped into the air, his torso literally parted in two. He *had* been cut in half. The only thing keeping him alive was Master Revels and his magic. George didn't realise it at all and kept jumping in the air, utterly unable to understand why everyone was laughing at him. He kept screaming that it was a trick and every time he jumped, he put the lie to his own words.

"Look down," Master Revels suggested. George did and

saw the cut. Before he could scream, Master Revels tapped him on the head and nodded to me. "My lovely assistant will heal him with a kiss!"

I leaned down and kissed George on the forehead, cancelling the spell that had cut him in two. George, much to his relief, was allowed to go back into the audience, no longer parted at the middle. I had to keep the laughter off my own face. It was so absurd. The audience loved it.

"And now, the final trick," Master Revels concluded. "I will make my own assistant disappear from this box!"

As before, he invited a couple of people from the audience to inspect the box. One of them was a teenage boy more interested in staring at me than at the box, but the other was an older man who tapped away at it before finally concluding that there was no way out. Master Revels waved to me and I stepped inside a box no larger than the Doctor's TARDIS, at least on the outside. There was a feeling of disorientation and I found myself stepping out of the box's twin, backstage.

"She's gone," Master Revels declared, in mock horror. His voice became remarkably melodramatic. "She's gone and she's stealing all my money!"

I smiled as the audience's roar grew louder and the curtain started to come down. Master Revels had explained that there would be two or three curtain calls, but I wouldn't have to be there for any of them. I found a seat and sat down, suddenly feeling inhumanly tired. I had never wanted a life on the stage.

"Well, hello," a voice said, from behind me. I jumped up and spun around. "The Black Rod has found himself a new assistant."

The figure was, at first, hidden in the gloom. As she stepped forward, I felt my eyes widening in disbelief. Even at the Fringe, she was unusual. She was tall, with long dark hair and eyes so dark that they sent a chill down my spine. She wore a long white dress, cut in a Grecian style that seemed almost to be a part of her. Her skin was inhumanly pale.

"You may call me Circe," she said. I was frozen, unable to

move, as she advanced towards me. One long finger reached out and touched me on the forehead. Her touch was cold, as if her fingers were made of ice. "Woman to frog."

CHAPTER FOUR

Before I could react, I felt a hammer blow at the back of my neck. My vision seemed to twist and fade, even as my entire body *shifted*. I felt, just for a second, as if I was melting and falling...and then my sense of perspective changed. The backroom seemed suddenly so much larger. The woman – Circe, she had called herself – was a walking giant. I could see right up her dress. It would have been hilarious under other circumstances, yet I had no idea what had happened to me. Something warm and soft landed on my head and I jumped. I jumped halfway across the room.

I caught sight of myself in a mirror and recoiled in horror. I was a frog! Or maybe I was a toad; I didn't know the difference between the two. I was small, green and warty, with eerie eyes. I opened my mouth, intending to scream, but all that came out was a frog-like noise. My ears seemed to have changed as well – I could suddenly hear so much better than before – yet everything sounded odd in the room. I had an overwhelming urge to seek fresh water and swim away from the terrifying surroundings...

Sheer panic brought me back to myself. One of the books I had glanced at while sorting out the piles of books had talked about animal transformations. The thinking mind might remain the same, even if a person had been transformed into a worm or a slug, but the unthinking mind would change along with the body. A transfigured person might lose themselves and end up becoming whatever they'd been transformed into. If I failed to keep hold of myself, I realised, I might end up falling into the frog's mind and dying. All that would be left would be a frog that couldn't remember being a woman.

I hopped across the room back towards Circe, who laughed at me as I came closer. If there was one consolation to being a frog, it was that the frog was far more athletic than I had ever been in my entire life. One jump took me halfway across the room. Circe's laughter grew darker and she held up a hand, somehow effortlessly deflecting me and sending me spinning across the room. Somehow, the shock helped me to focus my mind, rather than pushing my mind to collapse into the frog and vanish. It dawned on me that I could still hear cheers from the stage and that Master Revels was still working the crowd. I could go ask him for help, yet...would he recognise me as a frog? Circe had vanished somehow, leaving me alone. Would he realise that I was his apprentice or would he think I was just a pest who had somehow gotten into the building. Edinburgh was infested with wild creatures that somehow eked out an existence in the shadow of man. Only three weeks ago, I'd seen a fox sniffing through a litter bin...

My thoughts were treacherous. Every time I accepted – or came close to accepting – that I was a frog, I took one more step towards becoming a frog permanently. I tried to concentrate on being human, yet it was hard. There was no sense that I was crippled, or even in the wrong body. I imagined that men and women who wanted to change sex felt crippled in their original bodies, but the frog's body felt natural and right. I hopped again, hoping to catch sight of Circe, but she had vanished. I wondered if I should follow her out onto the streets – if she had gone out onto the streets – before realising that no one in the mundane world would know that I was human. I'd probably end up getting eaten by a cat or squashed by a bus.

An overwhelming feeling of despair washed over me. I couldn't escape; I might as well seek out a pond and spend the rest of my days croaking on a lily pad. Sheer anger blew the despair away – how could someone do that to me – yet it seemed impossible to focus on returning to human form. I had no idea how to cast a counter-spell or even how to attract Master Revels backstage so he could help me. I wished that Fiona was there, someone who could bridge the gap between animal and human, or...

I stopped, thinking hard. I hadn't paid close attention to the book on animal transformations, but it had talked about mirrors reflecting the true state of the soul. I hopped across the room – the body still felt natural, damn it – and towards the mirrors Master Revels had left there from one of his earlier acts. Or maybe they weren't his. I didn't know and didn't care. All I cared about was looking in them and seeing whatever I saw. I saw a small green frog, staring nervously into the mirror, and felt the despair washing up again. I was trapped.

Or was I? The magical world is never in plain sight. Master Revels had been clear on that point. A person without any magical talent – a mundane, in other words – would never be able to see magic properly, even if it was right in front of him. His mind would explain it away as a trick, just as George had done back on stage, or his eyes would simply miss it completely. I looked back into the mirror and saw the frog looking back at me...and something snapped inside my mind. I closed my eyes, feeling anger washing over me, and concentrated on my human form. I was human, I told myself, time and time again; I was human.

I opened my eyes. I was staring into a misty image of a naked human female. The image grew sharper and clearer until I saw my own face looking back at me. I recoiled in astonishment and fell over backwards, landing on my bare bottom. I was naked, but I was human again. Cool rationality asserted itself and I realised that when I'd been transformed for the first time, my clothes, designed for a human, would have simply fallen off. I yelped in delight and astonishment. I had broken the curse!

"I didn't realise that you hated your outfit that much," Master Revels said, from behind me. I yelped again and brought up my hands to cover my private parts. He looked away politely and flicked his cane, sending my clothes flying through the air towards me. I picked them up and slowly put them on. "I wondered what had happened to you."

I started to shake, now that it was over. "She turned me into a frog," I said, between gasps. I had never panicked before, yet now I was on the verge of breaking down. "I was a frog!"

Master Revels gave me a vague look. "I see," he said, calmly. I got the feeling that very little would ever bother him. I later learned that he had faced down a thousand devils and demons and after that mundane human problems could hardly bother him. "Who transformed you into a frog?"

"She said she was called Circe," I said, and blurted out the rest of the explanation. Master Revels listened politely, showing few signs of interest. I was starting to wonder if such transformations were more common than they seemed. How many people went missing every year, dropping out of the mundane world and vanishing completely? "Who *is* she?"

"She claims to be the goddess herself," Master Revels said, dispassionately. "If you believe her story, long ago she was confined on an island and allowed to prey on any settlers who landed on her territory. The Gods themselves had confined her because she was too dangerous for them to tolerate. Every time someone landed on the island, they would be wined and dined by her, before she turned them into an animal and added them to her flock of pets. Eventually, she was able to escape the island and start wandering through the magical world."

I remembered watching a TV show about her now. "She turned...I can't remember his name, but he was played by Homer Simpson...she turned his men into pigs and he ate them all before she could stop him."

Master Revels snorted. "The original version of the story has her turning a sailor's crew into pigs, but their leader – Odysseus - was aided by one of the Greek Gods, who gave him advice that allowed him to beat her and convince Circe to join his side," he said. "I don't think he ate his crewmen, seeing as they were able to leave the island safely once her power was broken."

"Oh," I said. I wasn't about to admit that I'd had very little time to read about the Greek Gods. "And now she walks the world turning people into frogs."

"Amongst other things," Master Revels said. He picked up his hat and turned to the door. "We'd better start heading home. Fiona will be worried."

"Wait," I said. "Tell me...is there nothing that can be done about her?"

Master Revels looked back at me. "What do you mean?"

"The next person she targets might not be able to break the spell," I insisted, as I stood up. It felt colder now, somehow, although that might have been just because my clothes had fallen off. I didn't appear to have suffered any permanent damage, but I resolved to wait and see if I felt an impulse to start grabbing at flies with my tongue. "Can't we stop her?"

"Think about it," Master Revels said. "She may or may not be a goddess, but she is extremely powerful. Who would want to get on her bad side by trying to curb her activities?"

I closed my eyes. "Besides," he added, "normally she goes after people who thoroughly deserve it. She gains some of her power that way. You were just the exception that proves the rule."

He opened the door and swept out, inviting me to follow. I hesitated, still shaking inwardly, before I somehow managed to start walking through the door and out into the streets. Darkness had fallen, but the city was still illuminated by both magical and mundane lighting, casting an eerie sheen over the buildings. I looked up towards the castle and blinked in surprise; if anything, the magical haze surrounding it, utterly invisible to most of the city's residents, had grown brighter.

"Come on," Master Revels said, firmly. He strode away, back towards his house, not looking back to see if I was following him. I shook my head and walked after him, feeling the cool air blowing against my exposed midriff and legs. I was aware of glances, of men looking at me, yet somehow it was easy to ignore them. Being turned into a frog, if only for a few minutes, had put the world in perspective.

As I walked, I became even more aware of how many

people cast long shadows into the magical world. They seemed to be out in force now that the sun had set, from a man I was convinced was a vampire to a very strange man with long legs and a tiny body. He looked like a daddy-long-legs given human form, I decided, after reminding myself that it was rude to stare. A stream of ghosts walked down past the castle, following a ghostly tour group that was showing foreigners around Edinburgh. I wondered if any of the tourists could see the real ghosts before deciding that it was unlikely. They would have run all the way down the Royal Mile if they could see the headless woman pulling faces at them. I was so distracted that I didn't notice the more mundane danger behind me until a hand fell on my shoulder.

I recognised them instantly. They were the drunken men from the stage show, now even drunker and clearly intent on some action. One of them pawed at me and I slapped him away, but another was trying to grab hold of me somewhere delicate. I reached inside me for the magic and pushed it at them, trying to push them away, yet it was unfocused and unprepared. They blinked, but clearly dismissed it as the wind.

"Now," one of the drunkards said. His breath smelt of alcohol, yet he seemed to be marginally less drunk than his companions. "You're going to dance for us and then..."

He broke off. I saw his skin melt and jumped back sharply, wondering if I'd somehow killed him – killed them all – with magic. He opened his mouth to scream, but his body melted away before any sound could come out, leaving him falling forward onto all fours. His clothes tore and fell off his body, falling to the ground, revealing a man transforming into a pig. I looked up, already sure of what I would see. Circe was standing there, lowering her arms to her side. Just by smiling, she made me feel frumpy and ugly. All of the drunkards were becoming pigs.

I found my voice. "Why?"

"They were pigs inside," Circe said. Now I knew more about her, I could hear an eerie timeless note in her voice. Her shadow didn't seem to correspond to her human form.

"And now their outside matches their inside."

She clicked her fingers and the pigs trouped up behind her. I wondered if they knew what had happened to them, or if they intended to try to fight. It seemed otherwise; they lined themselves up like good little pigs, waiting to walk away with their new mistress. Circe bowed to me, waved her hand and turned and walked away, leaving me staring after her in disbelief. It was a miracle that none of the mundane humans could see her or what she'd just done to the would-be muggers. How could they not see her?

"Give my regards to your Master," Circe called, and walked off into the shadows. They came alive and swallowed her and the pigs up, leaving me alone. I turned and fled, running blindly through the streets back towards where Master Revels and Fiona were waiting for me. As I ran, heads turned and eyes followed me, but no one reached out to bar my way. I ran into the house and closed the door behind me, still shaking. How many people survived two encounters with Circe in one day?

I caught at Master Revels as he peered down at me. "Teach me how to fight," I said. "I need to know."

"Yes," Master Revels agreed. "You certainly do."

***

After the encounter with Circe, my training took on a more focused nature, although Master Revels insisted on grounding me in all forms of magic. I learned how to cast small spells that used tiny amount of magic, although the more powerful spells remained beyond me for the moment. Master Revels explained that all new magicians were poor at casting powerful spells at first, although the more talented could sometimes cast them in times of desperate need. I needed to work on developing my reserves and using them to power my magic. It was like a muscle, Fiona added; the more I used it, the more I could do with it.

As the days passed, I also learned how to study and use a spellbook safely. Master Revels, after reminding me about what happened when I had used a spell without checking it first, helped me to learn how to work out what was missing and how to fill it in without accidentally causing a disaster, or killing myself. Magic tended to work by natural selection, he warned; stupid magicians rarely remained alive very long. I was taught to always ward myself against anything getting out of control, just to limit how badly I could be hurt by an accident or my own stupidity.

"Respect magic or you will end up burned," Master Revels said, at the end of every session. I nodded in understanding. I'd been studying some of the more complex charms and all of them had at least some danger for the unwary user. A charm to gain the seeming of another person – one that would be far more convincing than a simple glamour – could become permanent if due care was not observed.

Fiona had her own pithy comment. "It is like playing with fire," the dragon observed, "except you can get burned before you light the match."

A month after I started studying in earnest, Master Revels led me through the corridors and down into a small room. It looked alarmingly like a cell, although there were no chains or barred windows. Light seemed to flicker out of nowhere, casting eerie shadows over the stone walls. There was, naturally, a big wooden door blocking all escape.

"All you have to do," Master Revels said, "is get out, escape from this room before lunchtime."

Without further ado, he pushed me into the chamber and locked the door behind me. I looked around, but I didn't see anything to worry about, apart from the fact the light was failing. I muttered a spell under my breath and generated a globe of light that lit up the entire room. A moment later, it started failing too. I reached out, opening my senses in the manner I'd been taught, and realised that the walls were literally sucking all of the magic out of the air. They might not be able to drain me, yet...I cast every spell I could think of, only to see them all fade away. Desperately, I looked down at the door. It had remained resolutely solid...

"Oh," I said, in dawning realisation. The lock was exposed and I could pick it! I pulled a pen from my pocket and used it to twist the knob, finally opening the bolt and allowing me to leave the room. Laughing, I ran back up the stairs and into the dining room. "I made it!"

"The moral of that story," Master Revels observed, "is that magic isn't the answer to everything."

He chuckled as he waved a hand and my plate filled up with bacon and eggs. "Eat up," he urged. "I thought you would like to go on a trip this afternoon."

CHAPTER FIVE

When I'd been a schoolgirl, I had practically haunted the West Port and the bookshops hidden away there. They brought back images of a bygone age, before the internet and massive chains of bookstores had taken their trade away. I loved them dearly, for they were cheap, comprehensive and their owners actually knew something about books. And now, not entirely to my surprise, they were glowing with magical light. I wanted to go look into them and see what new wonders had been revealed, but Master Revels was keen to walk onwards towards the Grassmarket. Reluctantly, I followed.

The Grassmarket is set within a hollow and is actually lower than most of the surrounding area of Edinburgh. Once, long ago, it was a market in truth, but now the modern world has passed it by. There are a handful of shops and cafes that had spilled out onto the pavement, yet most of the area's charm is long gone. I watched as the tourists stared up towards the castle – which dominated the skyline – and took hundreds of photographs. I wondered if any of them saw the magical field surrounding the castle. Even in daytime, I could see the haze glowing against the sun.

"So," Master Revels said. He touched my cheek, gently, but firmly pointing me down towards the bridge at the end. "What do you see?"

I scowled, realising that it was another test. The Grassmarket didn't look very busy, apart from the tourists and a single piper droning away, massacring *The Flower of Scotland*. I looked from one end to the other and then realised that I was wasting my time. I should be looking *beyond*. It was hard to focus with the piper blaring away in the background, but somehow I managed to peer into the magical world. A moment later, the market opened up before us.

"My god," I said, in awe. I'd seen how magic could be used to fit an entire castle into a small house before, but this was fantastic. "This is the real market?"

Master Revels nodded. "We stand here between the worlds," he said, seriously. He gave my hand a squeeze as I stumbled back against him. "Many of the other worlds have points that intersect this location in space and time. This is neutral ground. No one, not even the most powerful and dangerous of the Great Powers, would dare to pick a fight here. The market itself would rise up against them."

He took my hand and led me into the market. There were stalls and people everywhere. Here, where the mundane world couldn't see them, most of them had dropped their glamour-spells and walked uncovered, allowing everyone with the right eyes to see them. I saw goblins, elves, fairies and a strange creature that looked like an eyeball floating without any visible means of support. Even more surprising, when I had finished staring at the creature, was the small goblin lady walking beside it, as if they were a married pair. A massive humanoid wolf walked past them and I lost sight of the odd couple in the crowd. I looked up as a shadow fell over the market, only to see a dragon flying overhead. Fiona was tiny, but this one was larger than a train. Its bright red eyes gazed down on the humans and humanoids below as if it were considering dinner. Master Revels seemed unconcerned by the possibility and so I tried to force myself to ignore it. It wasn't easy.

I saw, standing in a private circle, a couple dancing to the beat of an inaudible tune. The man was the darkest man I had ever seen, wearing a white suit and a dignified expression that seemed to contrast oddly with the joy of his partner. The woman was as pale as a ghost, with a long dark dress and very dark hair. Her face was suffused with joy. They were dancing together, completely unaware of the outside world. I felt a twinge of envy. They were happy in their own way.

"No one knows who they are," Master Revels said, when I asked. He looked oddly pensive at the thought. "They have been dancing for far longer than I have been alive. The magic around them won't let anyone interfere with the revels."

He shrugged, dispassionately. "There are three basic rules to remember here," he added, as we reached another strange statue. It was of an angel, with stone wings and a sad expression, from what little of it I could see. The angel's hands were permanently covering its face. "Be extremely polite to everyone you meet here, don't steal anything and don't start any fights." He smiled as he passed me a pouch of gold coins. "If you want to buy something, you can – but make sure you bargain first."

I looked up at him, surprised. "You're not going to stay with me?"

"I have other business to see to," Master Revels explained. "Don't worry; remember the rules and you will be safe here. This is neutral ground."

He turned and walked off towards the castle, leaving me standing on my own. I was tempted to follow him, but I had to admit that the idea of an afternoon spent exploring the market was rather more tempting. Besides, it had been months since I'd had any money to spend on myself and I wanted to enjoy it. It was impossible to tell just how large the market actually was, yet I was sure I'd find something I wanted. I grinned to myself and started to explore, heading towards the animal sounds in the distance. I just hoped that I wouldn't bump into Circe again.

There were thousands of animals in a number of stalls, ranging from common pets to more exotic creatures, some of which I only vaguely recognised. One store was selling gnomes, baby basilisks and even a handful of talking animals, which had apparently travelled to our world to escape some great catastrophe in their own world. An oversized mouse caught sight of me and started to explain that they'd been enslaved and needed to buy themselves free. I was horrified, but what could I do? The storeowner was demanding a vast sum of money for even one talking mouse.

"I'm sorry," I said, and walked on to the next section. At first sight, it was a butcher's market, but they were offering eye of newt and tongue of frog, along with hundreds of other ingredients I recognised were needed for spells of one kind or another. One sealed jar claimed to contain Gorgon eyes, harvested at great personal risk. A young buyer opened the jar without goggles and was instantly turned to stone. I recoiled, turned my back and walked away. There was nothing I could do for him.

The book stalls seemed more promising at first, although it didn't take long to realise that they weren't selling anything I hadn't already seen in the library back home. Most of the books were fairly basic spellbooks, copied out by hand; anything really interesting or unique would probably be offered privately to the people with the money or power to pay for it. I picked one of the rarer books up and examined it, but shook my head when I saw the price. I had nowhere near that much money.

A hand caught at my dress, catching my attention. "Can I have some of your blood, lady?"

I stared down in astonishment and horror. The speaker was a young boy – he couldn't be more than seven years old – with fangs growing out of his mouth. His pale skin and red eyes told the full story. Somehow, he'd been bitten by a vampire and survived the experience, making the transition from human to vampire without problems. I had no idea why he was begging at first and then I remembered what Master Revels had said. The market was neutral ground and no one, not even a starving vampire, would willingly take the risk of breaking that truce. And if he was a vampire, no matter how old he looked, it was a fair bet that he was a great deal older.

"No," I said, firmly. The vampire gazed up into my eyes and I felt my resolve starting to weaken. One of the books I had read had talked about vampires. A vampire had considerable powers to influence a human mind, even if the vampire in question hadn't drawn on the person's blood. Once they had sucked some of their blood, the person would become a slave, to all intents and purposes. I shook my head angrily, pushing away the compulsion that threatened to overwhelm my mind. "No!"

The vampire turned and walked off. I resisted the urge to stick a stake through its back and walked in the other direction, heading towards the sound of a man calling out for bids. There was a large tent, marked with a sign promising auctions today, so I entered. I saw, to my horror, a family standing on the stage, wearing nothing apart from iron collars around their necks. Their eyes were bleak and hopeless.

"And now, ladies and gentlemen," the barker was saying, "we have a family enslaved for a lucky winner! One man, a proven hard worker; one woman, a proven cook; one son, a promising worker in the future...and last, but not least, a daughter with many promising charms, if you know what I mean!" There was a roar of laughter from the crowd. I looked up at the daughter – she couldn't have been much younger than me – and stared in dismay. The iron collar around her neck kept her rooted to the spot and would force her to obey orders, whatever the orders were. I felt sick. Whatever they had done, if they had done anything to deserve punishment, they didn't deserve to be enslaved.

I turned and fled out of the tent as the bids started to rise higher and higher. I wondered if I should try to bid myself, just so I could free them, but I doubted I had anything like enough money to bid on even one of them. Master Revels might have the sort of money needed to buy slaves, yet I had no idea where to find him. I tried to push the image of the girl's helpless face out of my mind and walked over to one of the eateries. I needed something to eat, if only to take my mind off the slaves. The cook – a humanoid creature with six arms and four legs – waved at me. I wandered over to the counter and sat down, examining the menu. There was very little that was familiar, so I found myself ordering a burger and chips. It was in front of me almost before I sat down at the table, a great steaming burger and a massive pile of chips. It tasted far better than anything I'd had in the mundane world.

"Hi," a voice said. I didn't look up from my burger. I hadn't realised how hungry I was until I'd taken the first bite. "Can I join you?"

I looked up in some surprise. There were only a handful of customers in the store and there were plenty of other seats. The man in front of me was...I stared. He was tall, and patrician, with long blond hair and very fine cheekbones. I couldn't put my finger on it, but there was something about him that was overwhelmingly sexy. I swallowed hard. Whatever it was, however he did it, I wanted to roll over and spread my legs for him. And he knew it. I could have drowned in those eyes forever. If there was such a thing as love at first sight, this was it; no, maybe not love, but certainly lust at first sight. I had never felt such feelings before...

And they might not be natural.

"Of course," I said, swallowing again. "What is your...ah, what would you like to be called?"

"It always gets the newcomers that way," the man said, as he sat down in front of me and helped himself to a chip. I couldn't find the urge to argue. "You may call me Cardonel."

I frowned as I took another bite of my burger. It helped to keep my mind off him and his body and the two of us...I pushed that thought aside, angrily. If he was using magic to manipulate me, I wasn't going to fall for it. Besides, he was too handsome to be true; the more I looked at him, the more I was sure that he was covered by a glamour-spell of some kind. There was something about his ears that didn't seem quite right.

"You may call me Dizzy," I said, slowly. The lust wasn't diminishing even though I was sure that it was a spell. If anything, it was growing stronger. His smile – oh god, those cheekbones – was overpowering. "I..."

"You're the one who escaped one of *her* spells," Cardonel said, flatly. His smile seemed to grow more powerful as I finished my burger and gave serious thought to ordering another one. "Did you think that that would go unnoticed?"

"Circe?" I asked, surprised. Who *was* this man...if he was a man? Maybe *what* was he would be a better question. "It wasn't exactly easy."

Cardonel's eyes widened. "There are very few human magicians who could have broken one of her curses," he said. "And you're not even afraid to say her name!"

He leaned forward. "Do you have any idea just how...interesting that makes you?"

I caught myself before I could lean forward and kiss his lips. His voice just sent shivers of lust down my spine. I was certain now that I was being manipulated, yet that didn't make resisting it any easier. And if he was scared to say her name out loud...if she was who she claimed to be, she would be able to hear her name spoken, wherever she was. Someone so powerful had to daunt the entire magical community.

"And your Master is one of the most famous magicians in the world," Cardonel continued. "You're going to be something remarkable if you don't kill yourself first. You're going to be really special."

He was still leaning forward until I leaned back, angrily. Whatever I was feeling, whatever the cause of it, I wasn't going to allow those feelings to push me into doing something that I would regret. I still wanted to start panting for him, or worse, yet now I understood it better I could control it. Or so I told myself.

"But you need to ask yourself a question," Cardonel said, apparently unbothered by my unspoken refusal to get hot and sweaty with him. "What is your master, really?"

I looked up, sharply. "Why are you talking to me?"

"Let's just say that I have your best interests at heart," Cardonel said, sincerely. At least he sounded sincere, but I had to remind myself that he could be using a glamour-spell to project whatever feelings he wanted to project into the air. "You're a newcomer to a very dangerous world, one with more potential than actual training. You have to understand just where you stand."

"Oh," I said. My head was a mess. I wanted to leave, now, yet something kept me in my seat. It might have been a spell of some kind, or it might just have been my curiosity.

Even if I couldn't trust Cardonel any further than I could throw him, I wanted to hear what he had to say. Or perhaps he was *making* me want to hear what he had to say. "And where, may I ask, do I stand?"

"In the middle," Cardonel said. He looked down at me. "You need to ask your master just what he is and where he stands. It won't be long before everyone has to choose a side. I hope you choose wisely."

"Thank you," I said, sourly. "And what are you going to do now?"

He leaned forward, so close that his lips were almost brushing mine. "We could go out together," he whispered. His voice was touching off all the glands in my body. I knew he was bad news and yet I couldn't help a sudden surge of arousal. "I could show you strange pleasures and wonders that you would never find for yourself. We could have an evening to remember and then do it all again, and again, and again."

"Doubtless," a new voice said. "However, Dizzy has her own obligations at the moment."

I looked up, breaking free of the near-kiss. Master Revels was standing there, leaning on his cane. His eyes were very cold as they stared at Cardonel, who flinched before he could help himself. I realised that Cardonel had been right, at least to some extent. I *was* caught in the middle.

"I suggest that you find someone else to bother," Master Revels said, calmly. "Dizzy and I have other work to do."

Cardonel bowed and pressed my hand, just for a moment. "I will see you for our date," he said, and headed off into the market. He turned when he was at a safe distance and waved. "Somewhere nice and new for us both, I think."

Master Revels watched him stride away. "You should know better than to talk to strangers, even in the mundane world," he said. "Here...it can be very dangerous."

I stared at him. There was something in his expression that I didn't like. "Why...?"

"Your new friend isn't human," Master Revels said. "Well...not *completely* human. Didn't you see the ears? Your friend is a half-elf. They're dangerous."

He shrugged and turned back to me. "Come on," he said, before I could ask any more questions. "We have a job to do."

With that, he led the way out of the market and I followed him.

CHAPTER SIX

"So," I said, as we returned to the mundane world. "What is a half-elf when it is at home?"

Master Revels ignored my question. As soon as the market faded away into whatever pocket dimension it occupied, he started to walk towards the Mound as fast as he could. I followed him like a lost sheep, wondering just what had gotten into his head. We were crossing the Royal Mile by the time he slowed down and started to walk towards the New Town. I was somehow unsurprised to realised that the glow of magic was dimmer towards the newer regions of Edinburgh, while the Old Town glowed brightly even in daylight.

"All right," I said, as we reached Princes Street. "Why didn't you like me talking to that man?"

"He isn't a man," Master Revels answered. "He's a half-elf. You cannot – ever – trust an elf."

I frowned, puzzled. Now I was away from his presence, my thoughts were a confused jumble. I had felt attracted to him, yet...there had been a real person under that glamour, one that had been impressed with me and had tried to warn me about my teacher. How much of that, I asked myself, had been the glamour-spell surrounding him? There was no way to know. Glamour-spells were subtle magic, so subtle that plenty of people in the mundane world had some ability to use them, without knowing what they were doing.

He turned to face me. "Listen to me," he said, sharply. "Elves are *dangerous*. They're a society so different from ours that the only reason we imagine that we have things in common is because of the fact they look humanoid. They do things that make no sense to us because their culture is entirely unlike ours. You cannot trust one to act with anything you consider a sense of morality. And they are composed of raw magic, not flesh and blood. You cannot trust them, ever!"

"So you keep saying," I said, slowly. It sounded racist to me, yet...I knew almost nothing about the elves. "If they're that bad, where do half-elves come from?"

Master Revels snorted. "I hope I don't have to tell you about the birds and the bees," he said, dryly. I flushed and he laughed. "Somewhere in the past, an elf thought it would be funny to seduce a human maiden and get her pregnant. There was probably pain or trickery involved, because elves think that that is hilarious. Perhaps his father posed as the woman's husband or perhaps he used magic to rape her. She would have died in childbirth so there is no way to know for sure."

I stared. "She would have died?"

"Elves are composed of raw magic," Master Revels reminded me, patiently. "A human body isn't built to contain that kind of magic. Even the most powerful witch in the world couldn't have warded herself to ensure her survival. The child would be safe because the magic and flesh would have bound themselves together in the womb, but the mother...the mother would wind up dead, leaving a child behind."

"And the father doesn't take care of the child?"

"The elves would not accept the spawn of any interracial mating," Master Revels said, flatly. "Your new friend isn't a pureblood elf and so he would not be accepted by the elves in their homeland. I guess that he spends most of his time on the fringes of the magical world and rarely has anything to do with pureblood elves. They'd walk all over him if they knew he existed."

He snorted. "When they discover what they are – because the elves don't try to hide it from their half-breed children – most of them walk completely into the mundane world and abandon their other halves," he added. "There's more magic in humanity's bloodline than you might expect. There's even a school of thought that suggests that humanity's magicians are descended from half-breeds. No one knows for sure."

"And no one takes care of them?" I asked, astonished. "Why are they just abandoned?"

"Like I said, most people don't trust elves," Master Revels said. "You cannot trust them, ever."

"But why can't you trust them?" I asked. I knew that I was pushing it, but I wanted to know why elves were so untrustworthy, even half-elves. "What is wrong with them?"

Master Revels sighed. "Have you ever felt the urge to murder someone, or to do something you really shouldn't do?"

"Yes," I said, puzzled. A long time ago, I had fought the temptation to push one of my playmates off a wall after we'd been arguing over whose turn it was to have the CD we'd bought by combining our funds. I couldn't even remember the band's name now. "Why...?"

"Elves are creatures of pure impulse," Master Revels explained. "If an elf thought that it would be funny to tear you into a thousand bloody chunks he would do it – instantly. Think about how many times humans have powerful impulses – to kill, to rape, to steal – and multiply it a million times over. That is an elf and your half-blood friend will have inherited those impulses and the power from his father. You might go out on a date with him and halfway through he decides that turning you into a statue would be hilarious, or worse."

"Oh," I said. "And is there no way to stop them?"

"If you want to stop them from doing something, you have to make them swear by their names not to do it," Master Revels said, reluctantly. I got the feeling that he knew I was considering accepting the offer of a date. "And you have to be careful. They're very good at spotting loopholes and jumping right through them. Their names are the only thing they regard as sacred."

I said nothing for the remainder of the walk, thinking hard. It hadn't really dawned on me that magical creatures would have their own rules and laws. I'd known people from many different cultural backgrounds in school and I'd had problems understanding them...and they had been human. We had shared the same biology. How different might an elf be to a human, or a dragon, or a werewolf, or...who knew how many childish monsters truly existed in the magical world? There could be everything from ghosts and demons to monsters under the bed.

"Here we are," Master Revels said, finally. I looked up in surprise. We were standing in front of a police station. I'd only ever been in a police station once and that was after I had been arrested for underage drinking, along with several of my friends. There were no charges, thankfully, but it had still been an alarming experience. "Just keep your mouth shut and follow me."

He waved a hand, casting a glamour-spell of his own, and then he pushed the door open, walking right into the station. I followed him, and then stopped dead. The police station was populated by ghosts. I saw a man holding a chainsaw, his hands dripping with blood, leering towards a policewoman at the desk. There was a girl with Asian features, her hands cuffed in front of her, staring down at the floor as if she were trapped in a nightmare she couldn't escape. There was an older man who cast a very long and dark shadow. I shuddered as the ghosts turned to look at me, their cold eyes seeming to dig into my very soul, before I managed to start walking again. Three policemen nodded to me as they emerged from the rear of the building and headed out onto the streets, one of them followed by four ghosts who seemed to be constantly attacking him. I didn't want to know what *that* meant.

"Detective-Inspector John Smith," Master Revels was saying, as I came up behind him. "This is my assistant, Penelope Creighton-Ward. I believe that you have a set of files reserved for us?"

The policewoman didn't look surprised by the request. Perhaps she'd seen it all before, or perhaps it was the fact that she was clearly tired and nearing the end of her shift. She would have been pretty, were it not for the ghostly scars I could see covering her face. I looked into her eyes as she glanced up at me and knew part of her story. Her family had abused her and she'd set out to join the police to ensure that no one else was abused in quite the same manner.

"You're booked into room seven," she said, finally. Her voice was tired and worn. She sounded as if she were reciting from rote. "The files will be brought to you. Do not attempt to take any of them from the station. You will be searched upon departure."

I opened my mouth to complain, but Master Revels gave me a sharp look and I shut it again. Another policeman appeared and led us into the rear of the station, past a long line of holding cells – populated by ghosts, as far as I could tell – and into a small office. I took the seat he pointed to and watched as he left, clearly heading off to pick up the files. Master Revels touched his lips and I stayed quiet, waiting impatiently for the moment when I could speak again. Finally, after the files had been delivered and placed on the table, Master Revels cast another spell into the air and smiled at me.

"What did you think of the ghosts?"

I shuddered. "How many ghosts are there in this place?"

"I have no idea," Master Revels said. "Some ghosts are little more than psychic imprints on the surrounding area, created when a person is stressed or terrified or dying. Others are the remains of a mortal soul, trapped on the earthly plain. No one knows why."

He shifted into lecture mode as he opened the files. "Some believe that the ghosts have business left on Earth and refuse to leave until it is done," he said. "I saw a wife's ghost remaining with her husband until he died a few years later and then they both vanished. Others think that the ghosts are terrified of what they will meet in the world beyond and choose to cling to our world rather than face the unknown country. Pick whichever theory you like."

I shrugged. "All right," I said. "Why are we here?"

Master Revels passed me one of the files. I opened it and read through it quickly, struggling to decipher the jargon and legalese that seemed to take up more pages than were strictly necessary. It seemed that Jenny Dover, the twelve-year-old child of Mark and Rose Dover, had vanished two weeks ago after a field trip to the National Art Museum. She had had a happy life, according to her friends and family, and there had been no reason for her to run off and hide. There had been no abuse, no fights with her family or friends, no bullies at school...it looked as if Jenny had had pretty much the perfect life. That suggested that someone had abducted her, perhaps with very dark intentions, but the police had been unable to turn up any leads. I assumed that they'd already searched the houses of every known paedophile in the vicinity. A photo fell out of the file and I picked it up, scowling. Jenny was blonde, with an enchanting smile; a girl right on the edge of blossoming into womanhood. She looked innocent and harmless.

"Summarise it for me," Master Revels ordered. I did as he asked, condensing the entire file into two lines. "You may be unsurprised to discover that all of these files hold a similar story."

I picked up the next file and skimmed through it. Aisha Patel had vanished a week before Jenny, also after a trip to the museum. She was eleven, with the same sense of childlike innocence on the verge of bursting into flower. There were fourteen other girls, with ages ranging from ten to fifteen, who had vanished...after taking a trip to the museum. They had little else in common. Five of them attended schools with one of the other vanished children, seven of them came from Christian families, three came from Muslim families, one came from a Jewish family...the only things they had in common was that they were all female and had all gone to the museum before they vanished. I had some difficulty imagining a paedophile being interested in both sexes, which might mean that his victims would always be female. Or perhaps I just wasn't vile enough to comprehend their line of thought.

"I'm sure the police would have noticed that after the third or fourth abduction," I said, finally. I had never been too impressed with the police, yet anyone could have noticed that pattern. "Didn't they think to search the place?"

Master Revels shrugged and passed me another file. The police *had* noticed the pattern and requested – and received

– warrants to investigate everyone who was even remotely connected to the museum. They'd searched the place from top to bottom, interrogated everyone who worked there and found nothing. Nothing relating to the investigation, that was; they'd found several stolen artworks, a missing handbag that had been reported lost in 1967 and discovered that one of the cleaners was supplementing his salary by selling drugs to local teenagers. They'd thought that they'd found their man until they discovered that he had an airtight alibi for most of the abductions. And, worst of all, they'd found no trace of the girls.

"I see," I said, finally. I felt a shiver running down my spine as I contemplated the girls and their possible fates. I knew that there were plenty of mundane horrors in the world, yet...this was something worse than a vampire or a werewolf. "I assume that we're going to do something about it?"

"You assume correctly," Master Revels said, dryly. He finished skimming through the files, allowed me to read through the summaries quickly, and then stood up. "The police found nothing and there are signs that suggest that magic was somehow involved. The girls may have blundered into the magical world, but the pattern suggests otherwise; they have almost certainly been abducted. I think we'd better take a field trip to the museum."

I looked up, surprised. "There are people who abduct children from the mundane world?" I asked. "Why the hell would they want to do that?"

"You don't want to know," Master Revels said, flatly. I stared at him until he nodded ruefully. "You can use humans as sacrificial offerings; the younger the better. There's an entire world that is fond of abducting young women as slaves, although normally they prefer to take someone older and sexually mature. And then the elves have a habit of abducting children and leaving behind a Changeling in the nest."

He stood up. "Come on," he said. "We're off to see the museum."

Leaving the police station, it seemed, was harder than

getting into it. A grim-looking policewoman searched me quickly and efficiently, before pushing me out to wait for Master Revels. The ghosts seemed to have realised that I could see them and started to cluster around me, leering into my face and dripping translucent blood on my clothes. I found myself stumbling backwards and I nearly fell over, just before the ghosts fled. Master Revels had emerged from his inspection, doing up his coat. I guessed the policeman had taken longer to search him.

He said nothing as we walked back towards the Mound, leaving me to my thoughts. If the girls had been abducted, how could we help them? Could we not use magic to find them? Who would have taken them or why? I remembered the family of slaves I'd seen in the market and shuddered. Somehow, the thought of seeing Jenny, or Aisha, or any of the others being sold as slaves was inconceivable. Who would do such a thing? I remembered Master Revels and his warnings about elves; surely, even *they* wouldn't take humans as slaves?

I shook my head. Humanity's long history is one of man being inhuman to man. If humans didn't treat their fellow humans very well, how could we complain if other creatures treated themselves badly? How could we justify ourselves when we had so much of our own blood on our collective hands? I was still musing when we finally reached the museum and entered through the side door. Not entirely to my surprise, parts of the building were glowing with magic.

"It's been a long time since I was here," Master Revels said, softly. I nodded. I hadn't been to the building in ages, ever since I had been a child. It wasn't a comforting thought. Had someone looked at me and decided not to abduct me? "Let's see what we can find, shall we?"

We wandered through the building without a real plan. I found myself enjoying it more than I had expected, even though some of the displays were boring. Eventually, we found ourselves on the top floor, wandering through a very different exhibition. The Scottish Arts Council had been giving out grants to young and talented artists and the results of their work lay in front of us. There were a surprising number of visitors, much to my surprise; I thought the artists should have spent a few more years learning their trade.

And then I saw it.

One of the collections was of tiny statues, barely larger than my hand. Something about them caught my eye and I leaned over, picking one of them up. It was heavier than I expected and I had to use both hands, yet as I peered down at it something seemed to shimmer away. The statue had been protected by a glamour-spell and the new face...

I swore. I was holding Jenny Dover – or the statue she had become – in my hands.

CHAPTER SEVEN

"Excuse me," Master Revels said, as soon as he saw Jenny, "who made this statue?"

"That would be...ah, we don't have a name for him," the assistant said. "He calls himself Mr Pygmalion, sir. It's a stage name."

"Why am I not surprised?" Master Revels asked, dryly. If nothing else, it was proof that a magician was involved somewhere, for I was sure that the institution would have insisted on proper proof of identity if magic wasn't involved. "How often do you get a new statue?"

The assistant, it seemed, was a groupie when it came to artists, for she was happy to answer all of his questions. It seemed that the elusive statue-maker only came in when the crowds were all gone, where he would produce a new statue and sometimes take away one of the older statues to be sold. I felt a chill running down my spine as I realised that some of the girls might already have been sold and were adorning someone's mantelpiece or garden, with their new owners having no idea that they had once been human. I looked down at Jenny's statue and shuddered. Did she know that she was trapped, or had her mind been lost within the stone? I wanted to try a restoration spell at once, but Master Revels was still chatting to the assistant. She seemed to like him and I found myself wondering if he was going to ask for her number afterwards.

I shook my head and turned back to the statues. There were nine on the table, all surrounded by a protective glamour. I could guess why. The police would probably ask a few questions if they discovered statues shaped like the missing girls, although they would probably be unable to imagine the truth. Just for a moment, I wondered what would happen if the statue maker was to be taken to court. The law doesn't recognise the existence of magic, so the police would have a hard job proving that he abducted and transformed the girls. The bastard might walk free.

And some of the statues were already missing. We were looking for sixteen girls, which meant that seven of them had gone onwards to new owners. I looked down at Jenny again and silently promised her that we would get her out of it, although I had no idea how we could do that. A restoration spell might not work properly outside the magical world.

"And he's due to come in tonight," Master Revels said. The assistant nodded. "Would it be possible for us to meet with him?"

"He doesn't see guests, sir," the assistant said. "He only sees some of the staff and…"

"I intend to offer him a long-term contract," Master Revels said, smoothly. He held up a card in front of her face. It was charmed to support his story. "We feel that his work has considerable promise and that we could offer him funds to continue creating remarkable statues. They are certainly the most remarkable things in this building and…"

"I can take your number and pass it on to him," the assistant said, regretfully. "Or you could wait in the cafe and I can ask him if he would like to speak to you, but I could not allow you to remain here once the building is closed to visitors."

Master Revels shrugged, passed her a card with his number and beckoned me away from the statues. I came reluctantly, unwilling to leave Jenny behind, but I had no choice. He led me into an alcove and pulled a spell around us, making it impossible for anyone to see or hear us, whatever happened.

"I had a look at the spell binding them," he said, before I could say anything. "I might be able to break it, but that would mean that the person behind all this would get away, along with the remaining victims. We need to wait for him."

I stared at him. "Can't we free them now and put illusions in their place?"

"He's got a ward wrapped around the statues," Master Revels explained, flatly. "If the spell breaks, he'll know about it at once and vanish. We'd never be able to catch him. If the girls are still alive in there, we will be able to free them once we catch him and find out where the others have gone. If not...it won't matter how long we wait."

"Ok," I said, reluctantly. I remembered being a frog and how easy it would have been to lose myself in the frog's mind. I guessed that it was even worse as a statue, because there would be no movement and perhaps not even any other senses as well. "I don't understand; why did the bastard do that to them?"

"I have no idea," Master Revels admitted. He leaned back in the alcove and started to relax, checking his pocket watch thoughtfully. "Maybe he just wants the power of warping a person, body and soul. Maybe he thinks the girls need to be preserved rather than allowing them to grow up into adults. Or maybe he's just a sick bastard."

I frowned. "Could he be an elf?"

"I doubt it," Master Revels admitted. "The magic didn't *feel* as if it had come from an elf. It felt more human. No, whoever we're dealing with is human. I'd bet good money on it."

He twiddled his watch and time went funny for a long moment. I discovered later that it was possible to speed up time in a small area, allowing us to pass through several hours in a handful of minutes. When he took his hand off his watch, darkness was falling outside and the building was lit up...and nearly deserted. The tourists, and schoolchildren, and whoever else came to look at old train engines and artworks were gone. The assistant had closed the doors and let her hair down, literally. I knew that she couldn't see us watching her, but I still felt ashamed of myself, as if I was spying on her undressing herself.

"Stay here," Master Revels muttered in my ear. The sound seemed so loud that I almost jumped. "We'll watch and see what happens."

The door opened, revealing a short fat man with a big smile and a taller figure, wearing a top hat not unlike the one

Master Revels wore. I couldn't make out his face, no matter how much I stared, but the assistant clearly recognised him. She was definitely a groupie, I decided, just from the way she fawned on him. It wasn't uncommon, I was told later, for someone who was good at something to be followed by people who recognised genius when they saw it.

"Ah, Polly," the fat man said. "I'll leave Mr Pygmalion in your capable hands, shall I?"

"Yes, sir," the assistant said. She *did* look a Polly. "If you'll come right this way...?"

She led Mr Pygmalion over to the table and watched as he uncovered his latest creation. Either he was using magic to help him lift it or he was stronger than he appeared, for he didn't seem to have any trouble carrying the statue and placing it on the table. It was yet another girl, her features hidden behind another glamour-spell. Polly cooed over it, congratulating him on his latest masterwork. I had to remind myself that she had no idea that magic existed, let alone that it had been used to make the statues. Her flattery would have been disquieting otherwise.

"There was a couple in asking about you and your work," Polly said, once she had finished admiring the statue. "They were offering to pay you to produce..."

"I am not interested," Mr Pygmalion said. His voice was soft and whispery, as if he was older than he seemed or was using a charm to disguise his voice. "I care only for my art."

Polly practically swooned. "Of course, of course," she said. "I told them that you would contact them if you were interested and..."

Master Revels stood up and strode into the room, holding his cane ahead out him. "I'm afraid that we cannot wait for your call," he said. His voice echoed in the room, firm and resolute. "This has gone quite far enough."

Mr Pygmalion swung around. "The Thirteen have finally decided to take a stand?"

"They have ordered me to stop you," Master Revels said, holding up his cane as if it were a sword. "You can come with me peacefully or I will bring you by force."

Polly, of course, had no idea what was going on. I was

almost as ignorant myself, even though I hated to admit it. Who were the Thirteen and why had they ordered Master Revels to do anything – come to think of it, why was Mr Pygmalion concerned about them? Who were they to order my master to do anything?

"This is an outrage," Polly said, finally. Both magicians ignored her. "You can get out of here right now or I will call the police."

"I am the police," Master Revels said, calmly. He pushed some Compulsion into his tone. *"Polly; walk over to the seat by the window, sit down and remain silent. You will stay there until given further orders."*

I shuddered. Compulsion was an unpleasant trick and part of my training had consisted of teaching me how to resist it, not an easy task at the best of times. Polly had no defences at all and so she walked, robotically, over to the seat and sat down. I saw the horror in her eyes as her body refused to obey her and shuddered again. At least she might be out of the way when the fighting began, *if* the fighting began.

"How many girls have you taken from their parents?" Master Revels demanded, calmly. "How many lives have you ruined for the sake of your art?"

Mr Pygmalion glared at him. "Who cares about a mundane girl or two when their lives are nothing?" he demanded, angrily. "You will allow me to leave this building and walk free."

"The Thirteen want you," Master Revels countered. I couldn't help, but notice the terrified expression on Mr Pygmalion's face. The Thirteen, whoever they were, had to be something dangerous and daunting even to a powerful magician. "If you don't come peacefully, I will have to use force."

The two men stared at one another. "You wouldn't risk a battle here," Mr Pygmalion sneered, finally. "You couldn't..."

Master Revels snapped his cane hard down and threw a spell. Mr Pygmalion deflected it with his own wand – which he had somehow hidden up his sleeve – and counterattacked with his own spell. The two combatants went at it, their powers clashing in a dozen different ways, leaving me standing on the sidelines watching helplessly. Polly was far worse off, I realised suddenly; she couldn't even move. I swore as a burst of magic struck one of the lights and brought it down right on top of the statues, shattering and sending glass flying everywhere. The two fighters hadn't realised, but they were damaging the room and what would happen to the girls if their statues shattered? It could kill them outright!

I scrambled forward, keeping my head low, and reached the table. Ignoring the glass scattered on the floor, I reached out for the first statue and picked it up. I almost dropped it on the floor as a bolt of green light shot out over my head, but somehow I managed to carry it back towards the corner. I muttered what reassurance I could to the statue – just in case the girl could hear me – and went back for the next statue. The two fighters were still going at it, curses and spells flying everywhere. I kept my head down as I recovered the next statue and then the one after that, trying to keep them out of the fight. I turned, about to head back to the table, when a curse blasted it into a hail of sawdust. The statues went flying everywhere.

The shock somehow unlocked some of the magic in me. I reached out, using powers I hadn't known I had, to snatch the statues out of the air and bring them over to me. One of them landed hard, shaking the floor, but it had survived intact. I was tempted to try to restore them, yet I knew better than to bring them out into a battlefield. Mr Pygmalion and Master Revels were still fighting and there was no sign of a winner, not yet. I erected wards over the statues to protect them and stood up. I knew some spells and I could help Master Revels. I threw a curse at Mr Pygmalion, but his wards deflected it back towards me. I ducked sharply as bits of broken stonework cascaded down onto the statues.

Mr Pygmalion paused for a moment and threw a second spell at me. This one struck me directly, burning through my wards and reaching into my mind. I stumbled forward, my head a jumble of thoughts and feelings that seemed to contradict themselves, as if I wanted to attack my master in the back. *You've been hexed, you fool,* a voice said in the back of my mind. *Do something about it!* My hand was lining up to toss a spell when I finally fought off the compulsion and relaxed. Mr Pygmalion couldn't catch me that easily.

He looked astonished as I stood up and threw a second curse and then a third, trying hard to break through his defences. With two of us to fight, his position was weakening; if he turned his attention to me for longer than a second, Master Revels would break through his wards and get him. If he kept his attention focused on Master Revels, one of my curses – weaker though they might be – would break through and hurt him. It wasn't a good position to be in and he clearly recognised it. Using a word that sounded like broken glass, he disintegrated the floor below his feet and plunged down into the next level. Before we could follow him, he was running past a whole array of adult statues. I found myself hoping that they were not magical as Master Revels lowered us down and gave chase.

It was a nightmare. The statues were coming alive and lashing out at us, stone hands reaching out to crush our skulls. Master Revels blasted each of the living statues – I hoped that that meant that they were not living humans – as we passed, wrecking statues that had cost the building millions of pounds. Mr Pygmalion was still ahead of us, but unless I missed my guess we had blocked him from reaching the exit. I realised, almost too late, that as an artist he would probably know about the backrooms used by the staff, including the emergency exits. I ran forward and blocked his escape, gasping in pain as one of his curses sank red-hot needles into my body. The pain was excruciating, yet somehow I managed to stay aware. I couldn't afford to collapse now.

Mr Pygmalion stopped, pressing his back to the wall. I could feel powerful magic shimmering through the air, but I couldn't understand what he was doing until I felt the building itself began to shake. His power seemed focused around stone and the entire building was made from stone! Master Revels stepped forward, holding up his cane. There seemed to be no way to prevent him from bringing the entire building down on us.

"It's over," he said, quietly. Mr Pygmalion snorted. "Your time is up."

Master Revels threw a blistering series of curses, one after the other. I watched in horror as Mr Pygmalion struggled to counter him, shifting his wards to provide protection...and uncovering his back. I saw the opportunity and threw a reflecting curse of my own, backed with all the power I could muster. It reflected off the wall and struck Mr Pygmalion's back. He screamed as his wards collapsed and failed and, a second later, collapsed to the ground. Master Revels was on him at once, casting binding spells to hold him in place before transporting him into his jacket.

"We'd better get the statues as well," he said, heading back towards the stairs. I followed him, wondering if anyone would notice the changes in the building. How badly had Mr Pygmalion damaged the foundations before we'd stopped him? "And then we have to get out of here before all hell breaks loose."

I laughed. "And what are you going to say to the building's owners?"

"Nothing," Master Revels said. He grinned. "The whole thing will be blamed on a gas explosion, or maybe terrorists; terrorists are popular these days. The insurance will pay for the damage. Polly will be the lucky girl who escaped being killed, which will explain her blurred memories of the incident. She'll get paid a few hundred thousand pounds worth of compensation. The girls will be found somewhere safe and well and our statue-loving friend will be explaining himself to the most suspicious and paranoid minds in the magical world. They won't be too pleased that it got so messy, but they'll be glad of the conclusion. This guy could have caused a lot of trouble."

"The Thirteen," I said, thoughtfully. It was an unanswered question and I hate those. "Who *are* the Thirteen?"

"Don't say their name out loud," Master Revels said. He cast his eyes heavenward. "They'll hear you."

I glared at him until he relented, slightly. "I'll explain once we've finished clearing up this mess," he said, finally. I wasn't sure I believed him, but given how much care magical folk took with their names, maybe they *could* hear if someone spoke their name out loud. "It's a very long story."

Chapter Eight

The house was an ordinary suburban one in Morningside, towards the edge of Edinburgh. There was a small garden – complete with garden gnome – a pair of cars parked outside and an atmosphere that suggested that the owner of the house was very fond of housework. I walked up the path, checked the gnome to make sure that it wasn't one of the transformed girls and then rang the doorbell. A moment later, a sour-faced woman peeked out. Somehow, I had no difficulty in guessing who wore the pants in that family. Her expression was unpleasant enough to curdle milk.

I held up my spelled ID card and smiled. "Mrs Evens?" I asked. "I am Sergeant Dorothy Woolworth of the Stolen Arts Department." The magic in the card would take care of any doubts she might have, although I had no idea if there even *was* a Stolen Arts Department. "I understand that you recently purchased a small stone statue of a young girl-child?"

Mrs Evens stared at me and then beckoned me into the house. I wasn't too surprised. She struck me as the kind of woman who spent most of her time spying on the neighbours and gossiping about them to her circle of friends and she wouldn't want to give the neighbours something to chatter about to *their* friends. The interior of the house tended to confirm my first impression. It was filled with china knickknacks and decorations and they had all been carefully placed exactly where she wanted them to go. I doubted that a dust speck would have a long lifespan in her house.

I caught sight of two young boys and smiled at them, suspecting I saw a pair of teenage delinquents in the making.

They reminded me of boys I'd known at school, whose parents had been so strict and confining that they'd rebelled against them as soon as they grew old enough to understand what that meant. I wondered, absently, what the two boys would do; drugs, smoking, girls, rock and roll...there was no way to know. And besides, it was hardly my problem.

"Now," Mrs Evens said, as she invited me into the kitchen and closed the door firmly, "what is all this about?"

"The artwork you purchased was stolen from its rightful owner," I explained, patiently. It was even true, in a sense; the girl's childhood had been stolen to produce the little statue. "I am here to recover it."

Mrs Evens stared at me for a long moment. I watched various emotions battling it out over her pinched face. Anger won. "We paid good money for that statue," she said, sharply. "We have original documents and everything proving that the status belongs to us..."

"Forged," I said, calmly. I held out a sheet of paper that had also been spelled. It would be very convincing to anyone who was reading it, without any little errors that might cause embarrassment later down the line. "I'm afraid that I will have to take it with me now."

Mrs Evens stood up. "I have never heard such nonsense in my life," she said, clinging desperately to false hope. "If you want to remove the statue, you can pay for it and..."

"The statue does not belong to you," I said, firmly. I held her eyes, willing her to believe me. "If you refuse to hand it over now, I will have to go to the local police station, round up a team of policemen and return to search your house for the statue. Should we fail to find it, you will be held on a charge of receiving stolen goods until the statue is produced. There is still time to avoid dragging the police and the media into this."

She stared at me for a long moment. I kept my expression blank. She didn't know it, but if she refused to hand over the statue, I would have to use magic to take it by force. It would be difficult and it would risk her remembering something that might be dangerous later. On the other hand, we couldn't bring the mundane world's police into the affair. I willed her to believe me.

I could have used Compulsion, but judging from her appearance, she would be very resistant to it unless I applied it heavily, which would be impossible for her to forget. Even if she never worked out the truth, it would risk drawing attention towards the magical world and we couldn't allow that to happen. Master Revels had been very insistent that the statues were to be recovered peacefully, if possible. Towards that end, I had a final incentive to offer.

"I understand that you paid two thousand pounds for the statue," I added. It struck me as proof that some people will buy anything if they thought it was exclusive enough. "We recovered the funds from the person who sold it to you and we are happy to recompense you now, in full, once you hand over the statue."

"It's in the living room," Mrs Evens said, finally. She stood up and strode through the door. I heard sounds that suggested that the kids had been trying to listen in before hearing their mother's footsteps and running for cover. She led the way into the living room – it was so fancy that I couldn't understand how anyone thought it was suitable for kids – and nodded to a small table. The statue – one of the missing girls – sat there, right in plain sight. I could see the magic surrounding it; Mrs Evens clearly could not. I had never met a more unmagical person. "Is that the one you meant?"

I pretended to compare it to the documents in my hand, but the truth was that I'd known it the moment I saw it. "Yes," I said, flatly. I picked it up, wincing at the weight, before putting it down on the larger table. It was covered in framed photographs and one of them, a beefy man with a florid moustache, leapt out at me. He had to be Mr Evens. He looked thoroughly unpleasant, but at least he didn't look as if his wife could walk all over him. "Do you want the money now?"

Mrs Evens nodded firmly. I reached into the briefcase and produced a bunch of notes. I had suggested giving them a cheque, but Master Revels had insisted on giving them the money in cash, pointing out that it would be harder for them to make a fuss later. They'd also have to explain where they got two thousand points in used banknotes. The mundane police kept an eye on such transactions on the grounds that most of them were used for drugs or terrorism. Mrs Evens stared at the pile of banknotes in astonishment, before her eyes lit up with greed and she started to count them. I had to smile watching her. It took her several minutes to count them all, partly because the kids stuck their heads into the room and she had to scream at them to get out.

I did the maths in my head. I'd given her two thousand pounds in ten pound banknotes. There were two hundred notes in all, but she lost count twice and then tried to argue over the results. I looked at her patiently and eventually she accepted the money, not very reluctantly. I passed her a sheet to sign, in which she acknowledged the receipt of two thousand pounds and gave up all claim to the statue, and then picked up the statue again.

"Thank you for your assistance," I said, piously. Mrs Evens glowered at me, although I was sure that with a little creative editing, she could turn the story into one she could be proud of. If she was like some of the other folks from the suburbs, she might be proud of her brush with a criminal, even though some people would probably call her a fool for accepting stolen goods. It hardly mattered, one way or the other. "I hope I will not have to call again."

Mrs Evens started to wring her hands together. "And what do we do if we want to buy a replacement piece of artwork from the original producer?"

I sighed, inwardly. "I'm sure that he will be happy to contact you if I give him your details," I said, truthfully. I had no intention of doing anything of the sort. "The statues are modelled on a particular child and cost upwards of a million pounds each."

Her mouth fell open. She had had no idea that the statue was worth that much. I left her and walked out the door, staggering slightly under the weight of the statue. The van was parked several meters away – parking had been a headache – and carrying the statue all the way was difficult. I bent down and whispered what reassurance I could into the statue's ear. I didn't know if the girl was aware in there, or if she could hear me or not, but I hoped that she could. Her ordeal was nearly over.

I put the statue in the back of the van and then climbed into the front seat, beside Master Revels. "Success," I said, with a grin. We'd spent the last two days going from house to house, recovering statues. The bastard who had transformed the girls had finally talked, giving us a list of names and addresses. Even so, it was a hard task. At least one of the purchasers had given him a false address, leaving us with an impossible mission. How could we recover the lost girl if she'd been taken into the mundane world and far from Edinburgh? "How many more do we have to find?"

"One more," Master Revels said, as he started the engine and guided the van away from the kerb. "And then we will have to free the girls and return them to their families."

I'd been wondering about that. "How are we going to do that without attracting attention?"

Master Revels grinned, unpleasantly. "There is a genuine paedophile in Livingstone, not that far from Edinburgh," he said. "It's actually outside the police borders for Edinburgh, so when the police searched the houses of the usual suspects, they didn't search his house. The girls will be taken there and restored, after which the police will get a phone call reporting that they're there. The paedophile will be arrested and charged with kidnapping them, although he won't have touched them. The girls will have been drugged, which will explain their blurred memories and loss of any time sense. They go back to their parents, the paedophile goes to jail and the magical world remains undiscovered. A handful of spells will see to that."

I looked up sharply. "You're talking about sending an innocent man to jail," I said. "You can't..."

Master Revels shrugged. "The man we're talking about kidnapped and raped a little girl seventeen years ago," he said, flatly. "He is not *innocent*. He deserves far worse than the ten years in prison he was given – which turned out to be seven for good behaviour. Does that make you feel any better about it?"

I honestly didn't know. I had never been molested as a child. My parents had been boring folks and I had often complained about them, never really understanding how lucky I had been. I understood the sexual impulse – I'd wanted sex myself once I matured and I knew that boys felt the same way – but to involve children? My lip twisted in disgust. I couldn't imagine using a child for sexual purposes. It was the most disgusting thing I had ever heard, even including the slaves and how elves treated their half-bloods.

"Yes," I admitted, finally. Some would say that the paedophile had paid his debt to society. The more I thought about it, the more I agreed that he hadn't done anything of the sort. Still...it bothered me. For all I knew, he hadn't touched another child since being released from prison. "And what are you going to do with the *real* kidnapper?"

"We have a place for him to go," Master Revels assured me. "He won't be threatening anyone again, ever."

I hoped he was right.

"How often does it happen?" I asked, finally. "How often does someone from the magical world start preying on people in the mundane world?"

"More often than you would think," Master Revels admitted. "There are people who exist in both worlds and try to maintain links between them, using magic in the mundane world to improve their lives. There are people who regard the mundane folk as barbarians, as somehow less than human, and consider that they have the right to do whatever they like to them. And then there are the people who learn to use magic by accident and cause problems..."

He shrugged. "Luckily for us, most mundane folk are willing to swallow any explanation that doesn't include magic," he added. I nodded, remembering glancing at a paper reporting a gas explosion at the museum. The reporter had been quite insistent that nothing untoward had taken place. "Even if the girls do remember what happened to them, no one will actually believe them and they will insist that they were drugged and hallucinating at the time." He snorted. "They can read all kinds of things into anything, if they try. Can you believe that they believe that a boy who doesn't wash is actually the victim of child abuse?"

I remembered the small boys I'd known at primary school and snorted. If any of them had washed outside a swimming pool, it was involuntary. I had always thought that boys hated to be clean and preferred to ignore their personal hygiene, at least until they discovered that clean boys got more dates that boys who stank of unwashed hair and filthy clothes.

"Anyway, forget that for now," Master Revels said, as we pulled up in front of another house. "You can go fetch the last statue and then we will deliver them to their destination."

***

Night was falling as we reached the home of the paedophile. I had been expecting a monstrous house, perhaps decorated with the skulls of unborn children, but it was surprisingly normal. It was also in a very poor neighbourhood, perhaps because few people would want a paedophile living near them. I found myself wondering if his neighbours knew who and what he was, before deciding that it was unlikely. No father worthy of the name would allow a paedophile to live near his kids, even if it meant going to jail for murder.

Master Revels cast a series of spells into the air, centring them on the bastard's house. One of them would ensure that no one would see us at work, or call the police before we were done; the others would keep him asleep and neutralise any burglar alarms he happened to have in his house. A quick tap of Master Revels' cane to the door opened it for us, allowing us to slip into the house and search it quickly. The paedophile himself, an astonishingly fat man with an unpleasant face – or perhaps I was imagining that because I knew what he was – lay on his couch, having drunk himself into an uneasy sleep. He was clearly having a nightmare. I hoped that his sins were catching up with him.

"Down here," Master Revels said. He'd found the doorway to the basement. It was a small unpleasant room, perfect for holding small prisoners. I could believe that the paedophile had been continuing his work even before I saw the ghosts. There was a young girl, staring up hopelessly into a nightmare given shape and form. There were two small boys clinging to each other...I guessed that all three of them were long dead. I wanted to go upstairs and kill their kidnapper myself, or perhaps feed him to Circe...who knew; perhaps being a pig or a sheep was too merciful for him. I could have turned him into a worm and stepped on him without the slightest shred of remorse. "Get the girls down here and we'll finish the work."

It took several trips to bring all the girls down into the basement, but once they were gathered it was easy to restore them to human form. Caught within the spells Master Revels had cast, they fell quickly into sleep, allowing him to drug them with a small needle he'd produced out of his hat. I watched their faces and shivered at the terror they'd felt in their last seconds as humans, even though their kidnapper had clearly used glamour-spells to make the statues more attractive. They deserved so much better than to be treated like that.

"Don't worry," Master Revels said, flatly. "They won't wake up until the police arrive and nor will the new kidnapper. I wonder how he will explain their presence to the police."

We headed back outside, careful to lock the door behind us, and made a phone call from the nearest call box. The police had to have been on alert, for the moment we mentioned the address they told us to wait for them to arrive. We ignored that, put the phone down and hid under an invisibility spell as three police cars arrived and parked right in front of the bastard's house. Ten minutes later, the paedophile was under arrest and the girls were on the way to hospital, where they would be reunited with their parents.

"That should be all the loose ends tied up," Master Revels said, with an evil grin. The handcuffed paedophile was being marched away into a police van, watched by several reporters who had turned up to film the event. "That was a very good day's work."

"Excellent," I agreed. Seeing the ghosts had dispelled all of my doubts. "And now..."

I looked up at him, firmly. "Explanations," I said.

"As soon as we get home and have a good night's sleep," Master Revels said. "All right?"

CHAPTER NINE

I didn't sleep comfortably that night.

Tossing and turning in the bed, slipping in and out of sleep, I dreamed of Mr Pygmalion and the paedophile and many other horrors, all blurring together into one terrifying nightmare. When I awoke, the bed was soaked in sweat and I felt tired, as if I hadn't slept at all. I tried to use a meditation trick I'd been taught to fall asleep again, yet nothing seemed to work. I just couldn't focus my mind. I kept thinking of the girls and how they could have remained statues for the rest of eternity – how one of them might well remain a statue, unless we found her before her mind blurred into the stone and was gone. Mr Pygmalion had told us that he'd transformed thirty-seven girls in all and despite our best efforts one of them seemed to be missing for good.

Around eight o'clock in the morning, I finally gave up on sleep and stumbled into the shower, cursing my ex-boyfriend under my breath. I could have done with someone holding me as I cried myself to sleep, someone who would have listened and held me as I screamed and never let go of me. I had even considered looking for Master Revels and inviting him to share my bed, before dismissing the idea as a thoroughly stupid and idiotic concept. He was my tutor and I was his apprentice. It wouldn't be *right* for us to share a bed. Somehow, I found myself thinking of Cardonel. Perhaps he *could* take me out for a night on the town after all.

The warm water from the shower helped to awaken me and I found myself feeling much better as I towelled off and found my dressing gown. I couldn't be bothered dressing properly, not before breakfast, for eating something always made me feel better. I tied up my hair, pulled the dressing gown tightly around me and walked downstairs to the kitchen. A flutter of wings announced Fiona's presence as she flew down and landed on my shoulder. I wrapped her up in a hug and held her for a long moment, feeling her heartbeat pounding against my cheek.

"You had a long night," the tiny dragon said, when I let her go. "You could probably sleep in for a few more hours if you want."

"I can't sleep," I admitted. I knew that there were spells and potions to ensure a proper night's sleep, but Master Revels had warned me that it was easy to become dependent on them to the point where I literally *couldn't* sleep without chemical help. I had no wish to spend the rest of my days as an addict. What I needed was a chance to relax and blow off some steam and I wasn't going to get that from potions. "I had bad dreams."

"That's never a good sign," Fiona said, gravely. "I hope that they were not precognitive dreams."

I looked up at her scaly face, with the uneasy sense that I was being mocked. "I don't know," I said, finally. "What's going to happen to Mr Pygmalion?"

Fiona twitched. "That's up to his judges," she said, "but unless I miss my guess, he will be pushed through the Dimensional Gate into the Dark Continent, where he will spend the rest of his days trying to avoid the Shadow Wraiths that will tear him limb from limb, before eating his soul."

I blinked. "What on Earth is the Dark Continent?"

"It isn't on Earth," Fiona said. "A few hundred years ago, some idiot of a sorcerer managed to open a Gate to a world that had become infested with a creature of living shadow. The shadows tried to get into our world, but luckily for us they cannot survive here for long, not without a human host. It was decided that anyone who broke the law and was too powerful or dangerous to contain in any other way would be pushed through the Gate and into the Dark Continent, from where they would be unable to return."

"Oh," I said. It seemed a pretty dire punishment after all.

"Who's going to be judging him?"

"Leave that for the moment," Master Revels called. I'd had a ghastly night, but he looked as if he'd slept well. He wore his suit and top hat while drinking a large cup of tea. "Come in and have something to eat, then we'll talk."

I knew better than to think that he would answer any of my questions before we'd both eaten, so I sat down and allowed his magic to fill my plate. At one time, I would have worried about putting on weight and refused to eat bacon, eggs, sausages and toast, but now I knew better. Besides, he made me sweat it all off during the day. I had never liked to drink tea at all – I had drunk coffee to wake me up in the mornings – but now I was quite used to it. It was, as always, an excellent breakfast. Master Revels had had years to learn his craft. My own magically-produced foods either looked good and tasted funny, or looked awful and tasted good. I hadn't yet worked out how to balance looks and taste.

"You might want to read the paper this morning." Master Revels said, as I munched my way through a piece of toast. He opened a mundane newspaper and read from the top. "Police in Livingstone yesterday evening arrested a paedophile and recovered thirty-six girls from his basement. The girls, who had been kidnapped over a period of weeks, were apparently not molested by their captor, although they were drugged in order to prevent them crying out or trying to escape. It is believed that their captor had links to an international ring of child slavers who would have eventually taken the girls out of the country. Further investigations are on-going, but a police spokesperson said that preliminary examinations of the house confirmed the suspicion that three other children met their dooms within its dark walls."

He looked up at me. "I told you that they'd come up with an explanation for it somehow," he said, with a grin. "An international ring of child slavers. What total nonsense."

I shrugged. "You don't think that people will think that it is possible?"

"Of course it's *possible*," Master Revels agreed. "It just happens to be very unlikely."

He waved his hand at his mug of tea and it refilled itself at once. "Still, all of the loose ends will be tied up soon enough," he added. "The wanker, who was certainly guilty of murdering at least three other children, will pay the price for his real and imagined crimes. The girls will go back to their homes, none the worse for their experience...and you and I have the satisfaction of knowing that we did a good job and that we get the credit."

"That paper says that the police are getting the credit," I said, wryly.

"You know what I mean," Master Revels added. He stood up, still carrying his cup of tea. "Finish your breakfast and wash up, and then meet me in the study. If you still want explanations, I'll be happy to give them to you."

I ate up as quickly as I could, before starting on the washing up. I had asked him, some weeks ago, why he insisted that I do it when he could use magic to do it, but he'd explained that it helped to teach me discipline and patience. Fiona fluttered overhead, stealing the remains of my bacon and chewing on it while I washed, leaving me to wonder what dragons normally ate in the wild. I remembered the far larger dragon I'd seen at the market and shivered. I had a nasty suspicion that the answer was human beings. I finished drying the last of the plates and headed into the study. Master Revels was sitting in his armchair, reading one of the books we'd recovered from the library.

"Take a seat," he said, absently. He peered down at a piece of text with a magnifying glass. "Do you think that this is meant to be a..."

Fiona cleared her throat. "I think you promised some explanations," she said, firmly. I blinked in surprise. I had never seen Fiona be so assertive before. "You can try to decipher the book later."

Master Revels scowled at her, but nodded, closing the book gently and putting it on the table. I couldn't help but notice that someone had carefully engraved a devil's head onto the book's cover, leaving me wondering if it was a threat or a promise. Some magical books had their own defences, from spells that made it impossible for one to see them to spells that cursed anyone who tried to touch them without taking the proper precautions. Master Revels had trained me to watch for the latter, after telling me a series of horror stories about people who had opened one only to find themselves trapped within a pocket dimension.

"I suppose I do owe you an explanation or two," Master Revels conceded. I got the impression that he wasn't keen to talk about it to anyone, even to me. "Where would you like me to begin?"

I hesitated. "You mentioned a number," I said, slowly. He'd warned me not to mention their name out loud. "What are they and what do they do?"

"You can speak freely here," Master Revels said. "The Thirteen...well, as much as anyone is, they're the rulers of the magical world."

I looked up, surprised. "I always had the impression that there weren't any rulers," I said, puzzled. "You certainly implied as much."

Master Revels sighed heavily. "The Thirteen are the most powerful human magic-users in the world," he said. "I should add that they're the most powerful *known* magic users in the world. They...they generally act to maintain the status quo."

He didn't sound as if he wanted to continue, but he seemed to feel that he had no choice. "The magical world has too many Beings of Power and suchlike – like Circe – for anyone to control them properly. If the Thirteen sought to assert real control, they would find themselves destroyed in short order. As powerful as they are, they are still outgunned by the combined power of every other human mage in existence...and that doesn't even count the elves, or the Walking Gods, or the hundreds of others who are so much more than human. The Thirteen's main task is preventing the magical world from bleeding too heavily into the mundane world, hence our assignment to stop Mr Pygmalion."

I frowned. "How did they know that a magician was involved?"

"Trade secret," Master Revels said. "Let's just say that a very powerful entity laid down the ground rules over one thousand and five hundred years ago and very few people dare to disobey. The mundane world is to remain...well, mundane. We are not allowed to operate openly in their world."

"Oh," I said. I remembered the slaves and shuddered. "Why don't they stop the slave trade then?"

Master Revels winced. "They are limited in what they can do because the last thing they want is their enemies banding together to destroy them," he admitted. "If Mr Pygmalion had been kidnapping girls into the magical world and leaving them there, or sending them out on the Fairy Roads of Happenstance with no hope of a return to Earth, the Thirteen would probably not have been able to do anything about it – if they cared enough to think that they *should* do something about it. Controlling humans is quite hard enough; controlling elves or goblins or demons is much harder. A year or so before you met me, I had to hunt down a vampire that had gotten loose into the mundane world and started to prey on ordinary humans. He could have caused a disaster."

I stared down at my hands. "But why would that cause a disaster?"

Master Revels considered it for a long moment. "There is a fundamental issue when it comes to magic, one laid down in the laws of the universe," he said, finally. "If you are born in the mundane world, you have to have a willingness to accept magic if you want to use it. You cannot just tell yourself that you believe in magic; you have to actually *believe* in magic. The mundane world doesn't birth many people who are capable of truly accepting magic into their lives."

"But that leaves them helpless against magic," I protested, remembering Circe and Mr Pygmalion. "They have no defence."

"Quite so," Master Revels agreed. "You can be harmed by magic even if you don't believe in it. Yet...what would happen if magical events became so common that the mundane world started to accept, *en masse*, the possibility of magic actually existing? It would completely destroy mundane society and probably ruin ours as well. The

Thirteen's task is to prevent that from happening. Mr Pygmalion's actions risked exposure."

"If one of the girls had somehow escaped from her spell, or if the spell had simply worn off," I guessed. Master Revels nodded. "What would have happened then?"

"Like I said, the mundane world is very good at averting its collective eyes from any suggestion of magic," Master Revels said, "but the results could still have been very bad. A few years ago, there was a reporter who actually managed to deduce most of the story behind a series of unfortunate events in Pendle, down near the Lake District. There have been witches there for generations. If he hadn't been...handled carefully, he might have exposed part of the magical world to mundane scrutiny and who knows what could happen then?

"And even if there was a successful integration between magical and mundane humans, what would happen when the mundane encountered the elves? Or demons or giants; all the other creatures who regard humanity as their rightful prey, to be hunted and toyed with and abused as they see fit? The law separating the mundane world from the magical world might collapse, or the being behind it might intervene directly. Either one would lead to disaster."

He shook his head. "No, we're better off maintaining the barriers between the two worlds," he concluded. "And that is what the Thirteen does."

I nodded slowly. "And what do *you* do?"

Master Revels smiled. "I work for them as one of their...let's just call me a policeman, for the moment," he said. "When someone breaks the rules, they send me to deal with it."

"He's a little more than just a policeman," Fiona put in, mischievously. By now, I was sure I could recognise a scaly dragon grin. "He is responsible for so much more." She fluttered her wings. "And all of this, one day, will be yours."

I stared at Master Revels, who nodded. "The reason I need an apprentice is because I cannot do this job forever," he explained. "I cast spells in the hope that I would get a perfect apprentice walking up to my door. You came."

"Oh," I said. I wasn't sure I liked the sound of that. Living in the magical world was so much better than the dull mundane world – I never wanted to go back – yet I didn't like the thought of someone casting a spell to summon me. "Why did you choose me?"

"The magic chose you," Master Revels corrected. "It is rarely wrong."

"Oh," I said, again.

"You have a sense of justice, you think quickly on your feet, you learn rapidly and you have a remarkable talent for unfocused magic," Master Revels added. "Do you think that just anyone could have thrown off Circe's spell so easily? You gained fame and renown for that throughout the magical world."

"It wasn't that easy," I protested, weakly. I didn't want to pass up on the praise, but I thought I should be honest, if nothing else. "I had to struggle."

"It should not have been possible at all," Master Revels said, firmly. "Even the Thirteen themselves are a little nervous whenever her name is mentioned, because they view her as powerful, dangerous and unpredictable. You broke her spell and walked away free and clear."

"And naked," I said, sourly. I hadn't forgotten that, yet. "I need to think."

"I understand," Master Revels said. He hesitated. "If it's any consolation, I felt the same way when my master taught me what I needed to know. I didn't understand that the job needed doing and that I was the best person for the job, perhaps the only person who could lift his burden from his shoulders. It took me time to learn and he was always patient with me. I owe you no less."

"Thank you," I said. I paused. I didn't want to ask him, but the question had to be asked. "What would you say if I went on a date with Cardonel?"

"I'd say that that has nothing to do with what we are discussing," Master Revels said, crossly. He smiled, humourlessly. "If you are planning to go on a date with him, make sure he swears by his name to leave you unharmed and safe. You cannot trust an elf, ever. Keep that in mind."

I swallowed, hard. "I will, sir," I said. I wasn't sure if I wanted to go on a date with him or not, yet I didn't want Master Revels thinking that I would do everything he told me to do. "And thank you. Thank you for this opportunity."

"You don't know the half of it yet," Master Revels said grimly. There was a note in his voice that suggested trouble and strife. It struck me, then, that I had no idea how old he actually was. "Don't be so quick to thank me for anything."

CHAPTER TEN

"So," I said. "Why are we here?"

"You have to learn to use your senses," Master Revels said, dryly. He didn't seem very patient with me, but then...I had a date in the evening. His response had been to make icy comments about half-elves and what they could do, given half a chance. "Open your eyes and look around."

I knew what he meant. Magic didn't exist in plain sight, not in the mundane world. It existed at the corner of one's eye. Just because I couldn't see the magic didn't mean that it wasn't there. I closed my eyes and felt out with my developing senses...there was a nexus of magic right *there*. I opened my eyes and smiled. A third path was shimmering into view.

"I can see it," I said, in relief. I always wondered, at the back of my mind, if one day I would be unable to see anything magical, like the mundane humans. Were there people who lived in the mundane world who had lost the ability to see and use magic? I hadn't dared to ask. "Are you coming?"

We stood at the top of a slope, heading down towards Blackford Pond. A second path led down a steeper slope towards the hill. The third path seemed to lead in a direction that defied purely mortal senses, tempting me to walk right out of the mundane world and into a very different magical direction. I started towards it and stopped in surprise when I realised that he wasn't following me.

"I cannot walk that path," Master Revels explained. He didn't sound too pleased about it and I didn't blame him. If he worked for the Thirteen, enforcing what little law there was in the magical world, having a place that was completely off-limits to him had to be galling. "Don't worry, Dizzy; you'll be perfectly safe."

I took one last look at him and started to walk, holding my head up high. The path seemed to shimmer and twist under my footsteps – as if I was walking on slippery ice – but it remained stable. The woodland surrounding us seemed to shift and change as I walked further, taking on a darker, more complex aspect. I felt great powers shifting in the air around me and, just for a second, the watchful gaze of an unseen eye. My entire body tingled as the environment changed yet again – if the defences had rejected me, so much power could have torn me apart or enslaved me permanently – before the path twisted around me and terminated. I had reached my destination.

Master Revels hadn't said much about what I should expect, but that was par for the course with him. Over the last few days, he had introduced me to a dozen of the most significant figures and groups in the magical world, ranging from demented old witches with a cackling problem to scrawny overweight nerds convinced that they could bridge the gap between science and magic. This time, I found myself standing on a warm grassy knoll, with the sun blazing down on me from high overhead. In the distance, there was a pool, with a handful of naked women either swimming or sitting around it chatting to their friends. It seemed so safe and tranquil that I hesitated to walk closer, but I knew that I had no choice.

"Well met," one of the women called, as I approached the small group. She was slight, yet stunningly beautiful, with dark brown skin and a smile that instantly drove away all my doubts and fears. Her long brown hair fell over her breasts as she stood up and held out a hand, before pulling me into a hug. I blushed in embarrassment as she held me and she giggled. It was a surprisingly charming sound.

"Welcome to Haven," she said, in an oddly-accented voice. I'd grown up in a multicultural environment and I couldn't place the accent. "You may call me Sister Varsha, Spokeswoman of the Sisterhood. You are welcome in this place."

"You may call me Dizzy," I said, recalling my manners. One lesson that my master had driven into me time and time again was to remember my manners at all times. The magical world had a habit of punishing bad manners; indeed, the Elves regarded any display of bad manners as an insult that could be punished a thousand times over. He'd warned me that, for a trivial impoliteness, I could find myself gifted with a donkey's ears or worse. "Thank you for welcoming me."

Sister Varsha laughed. "You don't have to fear us here," she promised. I had the odd feeling that she was nothing more than what she seemed to be. There was certainly no trace of a glamour-spell surrounding her, although I could pick up streams of magic running through the surrounding forest. It was the most magical place I'd visited. "We are not your enemies or those of your master."

"Come, don't tease the girl," another woman said. She was older, with pinched features and a gimlet eye that seemed to stare right into my soul. "This place is a refuge for all of womankind, even those who believe that their rightful place is by their man – or master. She can relax here and be one of us."

"We don't allow men here," Sister Varsha explained, with a wink. She indicated her nakedness with a single wave of her hand. "Very few men could even discover the path that leads here and those who walked it would find themselves without their manhood when they reached the end, if the other defences failed to deter them. The Great Powers were summoned and used to create wards that could never be broken, even if all the men were to combine their powers and try to break in."

Her gaze broadened. "We are a home for those women who have nowhere else to go," she added, softly. "They run from their homes, from their husbands and families and children, and eventually they come to us. We take them in, we love them and care for them and eventually they are healed, either to go back to the mundane world or to go onwards to one of the many other worlds. And some stay here with us."

She grinned. "Why are you still wearing your clothes?"

I flushed hotly and they all giggled. I had never liked undressing at school, even before I had turned sexually mature and discovered growing pains, periods...and boys. The 'in' crowd at school hadn't hesitated to make fun of anyone who didn't meet their exacting standards; the fat, the ugly, the small-breasted, the large-breasted...anything that could be used to draw a line between one human and another. Whoever said that girls were the gentler sex obviously never met a girl in his life. I didn't want to undress, yet it could be taken as an insult...reluctantly, I removed my top and jeans, followed by my bra and panties.

"Welcome to our world," Sister Varsha chanted. Her friends echoed her words. "We stand naked before the feminine principle, the source of life and light and hope. We ask for the blessing of the goddesses upon our new sister."

I stood before them, feeling the warm air brushing over my body. I had intended to strike an absurd pose, but there was something about the environment that made it unnecessary. They were all *comfortable* together and, somehow, that infected me. I felt comfortable too, even as I sat down on the grass and discovered that it was soft and warm, not scratchy at all. I figured out, afterwards, that they'd created the Sisterhood's pocket dimension without any of the pests that featured so prominently in the mundane world. Whoever talked about sex in the open air obviously hadn't tried it before talking about it.

"You are welcome," Sister Varsha said, finally. She clapped her hands together and I suddenly had a glass in my hand. "Drink; there is nothing here that will harm you, although you may not care for all that we have here. And then we will talk properly."

The conversation became relaxed, now that I had been welcomed into the group. I listened, without saying much, as they spoke, sharing their stories and tales of how they had found the Sisterhood. The Sisterhood itself was *ancient*, so old that it predated Jesus Christ – at least, assuming that one believed the very old women who ran it from behind the scenes. It claimed to have started as a cult worshipping various goddesses from afar, but later it had become devoted to the feminine principle, a super-goddess that represented the very core of what it meant to be female. I suspected, from what I had learned from books, that it was actually a representation of a concept. There was no way to know for sure. All that really mattered, as the women explained, was that they had the backing of a very powerful Great Power and the freedom to do their work without becoming involved in politics.

"You see, many women don't realise their true potential," Sister Varsha explained, between sipping her own drink. "They find themselves wrapped in chains of custom and convention, from the cradle to the grave. Those who pride themselves on breaking out of custom and convention often find themselves in the same boat, just expressed differently." She snorted as she took another sip. "It's all about power, really; male power over women and female power over women."

That made no sense to me. "Do you want to know," the crone asked, "why women aren't ruling the world?"

I considered it. Women were, on average, weaker than men. A woman who got pregnant would, in the later months of her pregnancy, be far weaker and unable to fend so well for herself. A woman who was born in one of the less-lucky countries in the world would be treated as little better than chattel. A tutor I'd had once had explained that female sexual regulation was necessary to keep society functioning properly. I had never found the argument convincing. Too many people had done ghastly things because they'd convinced themselves that they were necessary.

"It's because we don't work together very well," the crone said, and cackled nastily. "Why don't women band together to protest their treatment and demand better rights? We could be spending our time developing a system that would protect women from men, but instead we spend it swooning over handsome men and competing for their attention. Why, I remember..."

"I don't think Dizzy wants to hear about your long and

adventurous life," Sister Varsha said, quickly. I was fascinated, despite myself. I had assumed that the women who found the Sisterhood would all have been abused, but the crone didn't look abused. "You had six husbands and outlasted every one of them."

"I wore them out in bed," the crone said. She sat up and winked at me. "Men are good for something more than just helping us to make more women."

Sister Varsha coughed loudly. "You see my point," the crone said, returning to the issue at hand. "We spend too much time competing amongst ourselves. The men – the poor loveable darlings – do the same, but men have a sense of proportion. How many women do you know who don't?"

"Too many," I said, slowly. The girls I'd known at school had taken themselves far too seriously. They'd mercilessly bullied anyone who didn't wear the right clothes or had their hair done in a different style...I recalled one group of girls who tormented a newcomer who had caught the eye of the leader's boyfriend. There had been nothing fair about that, but...men bullied each other too. I wasn't sure that I believed her claims, even though they seemed to make logical sense at first. "I take your point."

The crone laughed, seeing right through me. "Ah, you do not believe," she said. "And who asked you to believe anyway?"

I shrugged and took a sip from my glass. It was a heady vintage, although after my head swam once it stopped affecting me. The pleasant glow that had come over me had more to do with the company than with the wine. It was odd, sipping wine while naked and with a bunch of other naked women, but there was nothing sexual about it. It felt more like coming home.

Sister Varsha sat up suddenly and looked suddenly serious. "We have little to do with the Thirteen," she said, flatly. "We do not bow to their authority within our world or outside it."

I nodded, although the sudden change of subject was disconcerting. "I was told that that was so," I said, neutrally.

I had been told nothing specifically about the Sisterhood. "I imagine that you would prefer to have nothing to do with them."

"The Thirteen are very male," Sister Varsha said. I was starting to understand what she meant when she called herself the Spokeswoman. The magical threads I had sensed earlier had converged on her, allowing something else to speak through her to me. Was it the essence of the Sisterhood itself or something far older – and perhaps more dangerous? There was no way to know for sure. I tried to open my senses, but there was too much wild magic floating through the air. "They seek power above all else."

"Power to win mates," the crone said. She too sounded very serious. "They know nothing of the subtle arts of female magic. They will never understand the Sisterhood."

I shivered in sudden understanding. When mankind had been young, men had scrabbled over everything from property to women, while women had been effectively enslaved. The women had had to learn a different approach to magic than the men, spells that required little power and far less preparation. A male magician was likely to match power against power in a desperate struggle; a witch was more likely to be subtle, carefully crafting her spells to weave every edge of advantage together before starting the fight. I understood, now, why so many cultures had produced witch-hunts and religious inquisitions. They had been reacting to a terror they might never have understood, but they'd been aware of, even if only dimly.

Sister Varsha smiled as her face suddenly became normal again. "You will always have a place amongst us," she said. "That is your right as a woman. Until the day you come to us ready to learn from the Sisterhood, go back to your master and tell him that the Sisterhood will remain uninvolved in political affairs. I do not imagine that he expects anything else."

"I will pass on the message," I said. I hadn't known what to expect. "Thank you for showing me this place..."

"Oh, you don't have to go yet," the crone said. "You are welcome to join us for dinner and then to share the feminine rites."

I laughed. I hated to admit it – although I wasn't sure *why* I hated to admit it – but I loved being in the enchanted glade.

"Here," Sister Varsha said. She pulled a small pendant out of nowhere and carefully placed it around my neck. "If you wish to enter our world at any time, use the pendant to open a gateway and just step through into our place. No male will be able to use the gateway and remain a man."

The crone snorted. "You should tell her about the robber who tried to steal the Orb of Athena from us a few hundred years ago," she said. She grinned at me. I suddenly realised that she had been there personally. "We told him that no man could enter our temple and remain a man...so we turned him into a woman and let him go. He – she – had quite a remarkable career until he died and the spell was broken. His poor husband had a heart attack on the spot."

I laughed. It wasn't really funny, but I laughed anyway. "One final point," I said, seriously. I *did* have a date in the evening, after all. "What do you think of half-elves?"

***

That evening, once we had returned home and Master Revels had debriefed me extensively about the Sisterhood, I dressed for my date. Fiona had been quite happy to offer advice, but once I saw what she thought I should wear I put my foot down hard. I wasn't going naked, nor was I going so covered up that he wouldn't even be able to see my eyes. Fiona explained, between sniggers, that dragon courtship was different and they found human sexual customs absurd. There were times when I wondered if they were right.

Finally, I settled on a modest green dress and a shirt that allowed me to conceal several magical items I'd decided to take with me, just in case. The first time I stood in front of the mirror, it revealed that the back of the dress was magical, charmed to allow a watcher to see through the fabric if he kept staring. It took several tries before I was able to cancel the charms and wear it as a normal dress. I had no idea who had created the dress originally, but it was clear that they had been comfortable with showing more of their body than I would on a first date.

"Here," Master Revels said. He passed me a silver ring, engraved with a dragon's head. "If you need help, use the ring" – I could feel a complex charm woven into the silver – "and Fiona will come to your aid."

"Thank you," I said. I meant it. "You're very kind."

"Just remember what I told you," Master Revels said, tightly. I knew that he wasn't happy about me going on a date at all, let alone with a half-elf. I had no idea how his master had treated him, but it didn't matter. I wanted a social life of some kind. "Watch your back."

Fiona snorted. "In that dress, everyone is going to be watching her back."

I was out of the door before he could come up with a suitable retort.

CHAPTER ELEVEN

Edinburgh is a beautiful city in the daytime, but at night it comes truly alive. The skyline of the Old Town is lit up for miles around, with the castle glowing brightly in ways both mundane and magical. The party never really stops during the Fringe; I walked past entire crowds of entertainers, pausing only to watch a man walking across a set of burning embers. As far as I could tell, there was no magic involved, only sheer grit and determination. The man who was playing with fire, including breathing and even eating it, *was* a magician, someone with a remarkable talent for controlling one of the four great elements of the universe. It struck me as remarkable that the crowd couldn't tell that it was real magic, but then...real magic had no place in the mundane mindset.

I had agreed to meet Cardonel in the market, believing that it wouldn't be fair or just to ask him to pick me up from home. The market was glowing with life as I slipped through one of the entrances and moved towards the bookstall, curious to see if there was anything new on the shelves. Now that I knew more about what I was being trained to do, I'd been told that I could keep an eye out for interesting or unique books and – if I found something unusual – I could ask for it to be held for inspection. At night, the market seemed to take on a more sinister aspect. I saw a line of humanoid bears walking through the market, each one carrying a gun slung over his shoulder and glaring menacingly at all and sundry. They didn't seem inclined to break the truce that held the market together, but their teeth and claws looked terrifyingly sharp and their eyes promised mayhem and murder to anyone who got in their way. It was a great relief when they were gone, followed by a horde of tourists babbling on about the right to arm bears.

They weren't the only sinister newcomer to the market. A spectre wearing a long black cowl – hiding any and all features from my eyes – seemed to drift through the crowd, emitting an aura of cold terror that seemed to affect everyone nearby. I felt, for a second, unseen eyes resting on me and cold terror stabbing deep into my soul, before the spectre drifted off into the distance. It didn't seem to walk out of the market; it just faded away. A pair of adult vampires, wearing garb that suggested that they'd just stepped out of an adult horror movie, were bragging about their success in Hollywood to anyone who would listen. According to them, vampires were now more popular than ever before and innocent young maidens were just lining up to be bitten and drained of their blood. I had always known that show business had teeth. I'd never wanted to act myself, but one of my friends had tried to become an actor and had left the business totally disillusioned, claiming that they'd seen her as nothing more than a pretty face and a nice pair of tits. They had probably been right.

One of the vampires came over to me and tried to make eye contact. It would have worked if I had been unprotected, but the wards I had developed to protect myself laughed at such basic hypnosis. The vampire stared at me for a long moment, then bowed and walked away, leaving me shaking with anger. It seemed that hypnosis – maybe even Compulsion – didn't violate the truce of the market. I walked towards the bookstall, putting the matter out of my mind. Perhaps I could convince Master Revels to go to Hollywood and start hunting vampires. I chuckled, despite myself. They could name a show after me and call it *Dizzy the Vampire Slayer*.

The bookstall was as brightly lit as ever, with the usual handful of would-be magic users inspecting the shelves and trying to pretend that the more interesting volumes were within their price range. Master Revels had told me that there were too many young magicians who believed that they could use the cheap books to gain an understanding of magic and then move onto the more advanced material without reading the books. If they were lucky, nothing happened; if they were unlucky, they killed themselves and anyone else in the general vicinity. Magic was not a very forgiving field of education.

"Dizzy," a voice said. It dripped liquid sex. Despite myself, I felt my knees go weak as I turned around to see Cardonel standing there. He looked glamorous – in all senses of the word. "I was afraid that you would not come."

I smiled, pulling myself back together. "I would not miss my first night on the town," I said, as grandly as I could. His smile could have competed with the sun. "I'm afraid that I am going to have to ask you to swear for me."

Cardonel didn't look abashed. Master Revels had insisted – as a condition of letting me go on the date, where I would be out of his sight – that I made Cardonel swear not to harm me. The Elves respected nothing human, but their names were woven into their very souls – if Elves had souls, although I understood that the jury was still out on that. Cardonel, as a half-elf, would be bound by the same rules as his father.

"Of course," he said. I'd been afraid that he would be offended. Any reasonable boy would be offended if the girl had asked him, prior to the date, to promise not to harm or rape her during their time together. Even if he had no bad intentions, it would still be insulting. "How would you like me to swear?" He winked. "I know damn, blast, fuck..."

I laughed, but I refused to be distracted. "Swear, upon your name, that you will not harm me on our date," I said. Elves, I had been warned, were tricky. The wider the oath, the easier it would be for one of them to find a loophole. And then, of course, they could refuse to swear at all. "Please do that for me."

Cardonel gave me a look of guarded respect. "I swear, upon my name, that I will not harm you on our first date," he said. I snorted. I'd have to make him swear again on the second date and every date after that – if there was a second date. The jury was still out on that too. "I trust that that will please your master?"

"It pleased me," I said, with a coy smile. "Where are we going for our date?"

Cardonel took my hand and led me out of the market, down towards a series of paths I hadn't seen before. The dimensions of the magical world were themselves magical, twisting and turning at the whim of a magician, or fate itself. We should all have been crammed into the old town, yet the magical world was a dimension unto itself. I had been told that once I comprehended how the magic itself shaped the inner dimensions I would be ready to learn how to teleport, an art that few magicians had mastered. Quite a number, Master Revels had told me, had died trying to master it. Their remains had been preserved as a warning to anyone else intent on trying to learn the dangerous and subtle magic that went into a teleport spell.

We stopped outside an old oak door and Cardonel knocked, twice. A moment later, an unseen force opened the door, revealing a dance floor and a band of alien creatures playing on the stage. The music was old, a strange mixture of Scottish and Irish dance tunes, but it wasn't that that held my attention. The players were...weird. They were wrapped in glamour-spells, yet I could see through them and I had no idea what they were.

Cardonel grinned at me as he pulled me through the crowd towards the tables at the far end of the room. The room itself seemed to be bigger on the inside than on the outside, with what looked like thousands of people drinking and enjoying themselves. The dull buzz of chatter was drowned out by the music, to which young couples were throwing themselves around on the dance floor. I tried to understand, at first, the steps of the dance before I realised that there were no rules. The dancers were dancing as they saw fit and, somehow, it all blurred together.

Many of the dancers were human, but some were quite clearly inhuman. I saw a pair of centaurs dancing past – the female of the couple topless, allowing her breasts to bounce in the air as she moved – followed by a yeti stumbling through the steps, partnered with a young Chinese-looking boy. A woman who looked old enough to be my great grandmother sat in the middle of the room, knitting industriously on a pair of knitting needles and ignoring the dancers dancing past her. In one corner of the room, a man wearing armour, a winged helmet and carrying a massive hammer was chatting to another armoured man, whose head was hidden in shadow, concealing everything but two red eyes. A pair of dwarfs shuffled past, each one carrying a heavy axe on their shoulders and eyeing the hammer-carrying man with cold, calculating eyes.

"I'd like you to meet some friends of mine," Cardonel said, as we reached a table. He waved a hand at a small group of young humans; at least, they all *looked* human. "Dizzy, this is Linux" – a short spotty boy who would have been attractive if he took more exercise – "Sparks" – a blonde-haired girl with a wry smile and an attitude that suggested trouble and strife – "and Robin."

I gave Robin a puzzled look. Her features were indistinct, as if they were permanently blurred, yet I could see no trace of a glamour-spell hiding her face. It was odd; I knew that someone could slip a glamour-spell past me, but normally a glamour-spell concealed or deceived. Spotting a glamour-spell was halfway towards breaking it outright.

"There was an accident," Robin said. Her voice was dull and atonal. "My master sold my appearance to the Queen of the Fair Folk. I am cursed to remain unseen until they sell it back to me, if they ever do."

I shivered, for there was nothing human in her voice. The Fair Folk was a very old term for the Elves. The Elves demanded respect from those they saw as inferior to them and wouldn't hesitate to punish anyone they thought had been rude to them or about them. Back in the olden days, before the Elves had been pushed into the magical world, they had heard whenever their name was spoken. If Robin had lost her face and voice, the chances were that she would never get it back. The Elves would enjoy her torment too much.

The other two were more normal, I was relieved to discover. Linux belonged to the Rationalists, the group that tried to find a unified theory of science and sorcery. Master

Revels had commented, back when we'd visited them a few days ago, that the Rationalists were doomed to failure because science failed to understand that some of the forces underpinning the universe – even the mundane world – were *people*. Sorcery, on the other hand, accepted that and worked towards placating and recruiting the personalised forces, but few scientists were prepared to accept that the laws of science could change at a Being of Power's whim. Those that did were generally laughed at by their fellows.

Sparks, on the other hand, was an apprentice magician like me. She explained, in-between teasing Linux mercilessly, that she'd worked in a herbal and medical shop where the owner had sold magical remedies for everything from the common cold to AIDS. Sparks had grown interested when the cures had been proven to *work* and had started to ask questions. She had finally asked one question too many and so the store's owner had shown her the magical world and offered her a chance to start a new career. Working as a brewer of magical potions, she explained, was far more fascinating than accounting – and besides, she had never been able to find a job since graduating.

"Working for her isn't too bad now that I finally got the hang of it," she said, when the boys had gone off to buy drinks. "The Mistress used to strap me every time I made a mistake – she'd go on and on about how many people could have been killed if they'd drunk a poorly made potion – but now I'm working towards my freedom. I haven't yet decided if I am going to continue working for her or start up my own business."

The next hour went very well, I was pleasantly surprised to discover. The three apprentices were good company, although I did keep glancing at Robin's forehead and wincing inwardly. Cardonel was the perfect gentleman, keeping the conversation going and occasionally offering a pointed comment on how the older generation of magicians kept the younger generation down. Robin's master, he added, being a case in point. He'd used her as a bargaining chip with the Elves.

I leaned back and caught sight of a fat nerdy man sitting on his own at a table, a thin superior smile covering his face. When I asked Cardonel who he was, the half-elf looked blank, but Linux had the answer and explained that the man was the founder of a web forum that had somehow extended itself into the magical world and taken on a life of its own. Somehow, in the process, it had granted its founder considerable wealth and power, ensuring that he would have a place and a reputation that would awe most challengers. I found myself shaking my head in amusement. The magical world never seemed to stop surprising me.

A few minutes later, Cardonel convinced me to come out onto the dance floor. I was nervous at first, but after several turns around the dance floor I felt surprisingly relaxed and confident about the whole thing. The music seemed to push us forward, directing the dance; I found myself wondering if the music was being played by the musicians or if the music was playing *them*. The more we danced, the more we seemed to be dancing in tune. Cardonel bent down to kiss me, during a sudden shift into a romantic tune, and I let him. His kiss sent another tingle down my spine as the music came to a stop and we stumbled back towards the table.

"Ladies and Gentlemen," a voice announced. I looked around to see a man standing on the stage – the magicians had vanished, leaving me to wonder if they had ever been there at all – illuminated under a bright globe of light. "For your delight, I have purchased the finest slaves from the market." I felt a chill running down my spine as the crowd cheered loudly, waving glasses of beer and other liquids in the air. "Now remember, all of the normal rules apply; no ordering them off the stage. Anyone who breaks the rule will be evicted from the club and barred for life."

He nodded towards the rear of the room, towards the oak doors. There were four men standing there, wearing white shirts that displayed their improbably large muscles. Master Revels had told me that some men used magic to enhance themselves physically, but it was the first time I had ever seen anything of the sort. They looked like comic book heroes come to life, men with muscles on their muscles. It wasn't a glamour-spell either, I realised; those muscles were real. It was a miracle that they could walk without toppling over.

The lights grew brighter as a drum roll echoed through the room, announcing the arrival of twelve men and women. I felt a sudden wave of nausea as I recognised some of the slaves I'd seen back at the market, an entire family that had somehow been sold into slavery. There were no children in the group, thank all the Powers That Are, but there were six teenage girls, two teenage boys and their parents. They all wore slave collars and had the same damned and hopeless expression on their faces. The crowd was cheering now, stamping their feet and demanding that the show begin at once. The speaker, who was clearly trying to milk every last piece of attention from the display, finally gave in and barked an order to the slaves. Against their wills, their faces revealing their silent struggle against the orders they had been given, they started to undress.

I had to struggle to hold down a sudden urge to be sick. The crowd didn't seem to notice – or care about – my torment. They greeted every removed piece of clothing with a loud cheer and a hail of obscene suggestions. I watched in mute horror as the teenage girls were ordered forward, once they had removed their clothes, and ordered to perform a sexual dance. The crowd didn't care about the tears rolling down their cheeks. They cheered and laughed at every motion, calling out suggestions...suggestions that the helpless girls obeyed. At a command from the manager, the boys stumbled forward to join the dance while their parents were pushed into...I couldn't watch. I stumbled backwards and started to make my way out of the room. I no longer cared what anyone thought of me. I wasn't going to watch.

Cardonel came after me. "Dizzy?" he asked, in genuine puzzlement. "What's wrong?"

I ignored him until we were in one of the backrooms and sure of some privacy. "That's sick," I said, finally giving in to the urge to be sick. Cardonel looked away as I threw everything I'd eaten up in a tidal wave of vomit. The experience crystallised my determination. "We're going to free the slaves."

Chapter Twelve

Cardonel stared at me. "Are you out of your mind?"

I had to smile, despite the churning deep inside. It was the most human reaction I'd seen from him. "We're going to liberate them," I said, firmly. I didn't know, really, if it was the right thing to do...no, I knew that it was the *right* thing to do, but I wasn't sure if it was the *legal* thing to do. Of course, as far as I could tell, the general rule in the magical world was *might makes right*. If we did it, and got away with it, no one would give a damn about it. "Where are they kept after the show?"

Cardonel looked astonished, and then grinned, even though I had found a basin and was washing myself clean. I was glad that I hadn't eaten too much before the dancing. It would all have come pouring out of me. The half-elf didn't look away, nor did he look disgusted with me, for which I mentally awarded him extra points. There are boys who would have fled a girl, no matter how pretty or sexy or desirable, if they saw her throw up in front of them. I won't even talk about the temporary deafness that overcomes most boys when any talk of women's issues is raised. Or perhaps the Elves were perverted enough to find it funny. After looking at Robin's face, I was prepared to believe anything of them.

"They will be kept in the basement, of course," Cardonel said, finally. He looked as if he had decided to grasp a very unpleasant nettle. "You do realise that it won't be remotely easy to break them out? You'll have to break the very complex magical spells binding them to slavery and then..."

I nodded. I'd been taught how to break most spells, although some of them were impossible to remove, particularly the ones that a person embraced voluntarily. I couldn't believe that any of the slave families had accepted the spells willingly, which meant they could be freed and returned to the mundane world. I doubted that their tales would be believed, but in any case I could cast a few spells of my own to confuse their memories and make it impossible for any rational mundane policeman to believe them.

"I can do that," I assured him. The sound of music was growing louder. I guessed, from the sound of cheering and loud whistles, that the show was finally reaching its climax. "All you have to do is help me get downstairs and into the basement."

Cardonel nodded, reluctantly. "Very well," he said. He looked up. I was suddenly struck by how *alien* he looked. It wasn't just the pointy ears, but the sense that something – everything – was subtly wrong. Magic seemed to twist and flow through his body, too much magic for a human frame to contain. It seemed to be slowly eating him alive, like a magical cancer. I remembered what I'd been told about half-Elves and I shuddered. The Elves themselves were effectively immortal – nothing could kill them, apart from cold iron and even then they could pull themselves back together in a few centuries – but their half-breeds lasted only a scant few decades. Cardonel was literally burning himself up right in front of me. I wasn't sure how old he was, yet I doubted he would live past fifty. "There will be a price, of course…"

I quirked an eyebrow at him, unable to conceal my amusement. "What kind of price?"

Cardonel grinned. "You come on a second date with me," he said, with a wink. I had a feeling that the second date would be more intimate than the first. "Don't worry. We won't come back here or anywhere else that involves slaves."

"Thank you," I said. I held out a hand. He could have demanded almost anything and I would have agreed to it, just out of desperation. I *had* to free the slaves. I couldn't have explained it to myself, let alone an outside witness, but what had happened to them – what had been *done* to them –

was *wrong*. It had to be put right. If no one else was going to take care of it, I had to do it. "I accept your terms."

Cardonel drew himself up. "You have just made an old man very happy," he said, dramatically. I rolled my eyes, even though I was giggling. "My love for you is as boundless as the seas themselves, blessed by the many Great Powers that roam through this universe..."

I laughed. "Would you like a side of eggs with that ham?"

"Only if they are cooked with your fair hands," Cardonel said, with amusement. I could tease him, I realised; the boys I'd known in the past had grown unpleasant when they realised that they were being teased. "And now I suggest that we return to our seats. We can put on our own performance after the show."

An hour passed slowly after we returned to the table. The dancing slaves kept dancing, although they looked as if they would rather be somewhere else, anywhere else. I endured the concerned glances from the three others at the table – I suspected that Robin understood, although Sparks and Linux seemed bemused by my attitude – and talked about nothing in particular for the rest of the show. Cardonel amused himself by pointing out the various famous figures in the audience, several of whom seemed to be sneaking glances at me. I was used to boys looking at me, but this was different. I was being trained to serve the Thirteen after all and they would have to deal with me professionally. Sexism, at least, didn't seem to be part of the magical world.

I was glad that I'd had time to grow used to it, because otherwise the sights would have overwhelmed me. There was a tall man with flame-red hair, sitting next to a woman who had covered half of her face with a metal mask; the man cast a very dark shadow into the human world. There was a man who bore an alarming resemblance to the President of America, chatting to a man who bore an equally-alarming resemblance to Stalin, or perhaps Lenin. I could never tell the difference between them. And, in the corner, the ghosts of Christmas Past, Present and Future were sharing a bottle and chatting about which miser they were going to visit next Christmas Day. It made me wonder how many mundane concepts took on a life of their own in the magical world and grew and evolved past anything their creators had considered possible. Which came first, I asked myself; the chicken or the egg?

"Why, the chicken, of course," Cardonel said, when I posed the question to him. "The egg needs a chicken before it can come into existence…unless you use a magical spell and…"

"That's not wise," Sparks interrupted. She winked at me. "You want to know how to create your very own cockatrice?"

"No," I said, quickly. She looked the kind of person who would be happy to demonstrate and cockatrices were dangerous. They might not have been the most dangerous creatures in the magical world, but even creating them used darkest magic and it could go horrendously wrong. The books had been quite specific on that subject, although they had also detailed the whole process step by step. At least it didn't include naked dancing in the moonlight. "I think I don't want to know."

"Very wise," Cardonel said. The enslaved dancers had finally been pulled off the stage to a mixture of cheers and boos from the watchers, who started to stand up and pull on their coats. Most of them, I guessed, would be either going back home or seeking other entertainment elsewhere. The party here was over…and it would be over permanently if I had anything to say about it. "You three go onwards. Dizzy and I intend to…entertain ourselves here."

I blushed, almost as brightly as Linux. "Just make sure he gets you home before you're supposed to start work," Sparks said, firmly. "Your master will not appreciate you being late. He might even turn you into a toad to teach you how to be punctual."

"I'll be careful," I promised. I liked them enough to hope that we'd be able to meet again, perhaps individually. I disliked large groups personally. One was either part of the group or on the outside looking in. Neither one was particularly fun for me. "You all have a good evening, you hear me?"

Cardonel pulled me into a side corridor as the remainder of the audience started to filter out the doors. "The owners of this place earn some extra money by opening up rooms for anyone who doesn't want to go home," he said. "I happen to have one booked and ready."

I gave him a sharp look. "Hoping to get lucky, were you?"

Cardonel shrugged. "Hope springs eternal," he said, dryly. "This is pretty much your last chance to back out and change your mind."

"No," I said, shaking my head. I was amused at his presumption at hiring a room. Did he really think that I would put out on the first date? Or maybe it wasn't as unwise as it seemed. He *was* handsome and I *did* enjoy his company and if I hadn't seen the slaves...perhaps I would have made out with him, if not a little more than just making out. It would have made a pleasant change from lessons and being introduced to the movers and shakers of the magical world. "I have to do it."

"I hope you can live with yourself afterwards," Cardonel said, shortly. If I had been wiser, I might have followed up on that statement. He opened a door with a key made from human bone and beckoned me inside. The room was very basic, with a bed, a washbasin and a mirror hanging on the otherwise bare wall. It was clearly meant for sex and little else. There were strange ghostly images centred around the bed, although I couldn't see them clearly for once, which made a pleasant change. Perhaps there were just too many ghostly images and they all blurred together. "So...how shall we entertain ourselves for the next hour or so?"

It was clear what he had in mind, but I was too keyed up to indulge him. "Tell me about you," I said, instead. Cardonel looked up in surprise. "Where does a half-elf come from, anyway?"

He affected a droll tone that didn't quite manage to mask his amusement. "Daddy went walking in the mundane world one day and found a winsome young lassie who took his fancy," he said, in a sing-song voice that couldn't quite hide the pain behind it. "He showed himself to her and invited her to the Land below the Hill. He grew bored of her quickly and eventually threw her out, pregnant with his child. In the time she had spent in his home, three hundred years had gone by in the mundane world. She was completely lost in a world that included cars and marvels she had never dreamed existed. She still thought the world was flat."

Cardonel's voice darkened as he spoke. "The mundane world didn't understand her, of course," he added. "They thought she was mad and locked her up when they discovered that she was pregnant. They thought that she'd created the whole story about meeting the Elves and being born so long ago to hide a darker truth. By the time I came bursting out of her – almost killing her in the process – she had nearly lost her grip on sanity. She never found her own place in the mundane world and died not long after I was born.

"I didn't know what I was at first. My ears" – he touched them with one long finger – "weren't apparent at first. I was using magic to hide them from prying eyes without realising what I was doing. It took me several years to realise that I could see things that other people couldn't see. I was just so *aware*, far more than any mundane child. My mother's ghost whispered to me when she thought I was asleep, telling me about my father and…and promised me that one day I would return to the Elves. I should have known better. When I was old enough, I went to find my father – and they rejected me. I was lucky to escape with my life."

I put a hand on his shoulder. Cardonel had never asked to be born to such a family – if family was the right word. I couldn't understand how anyone could just abandon a child, but it wasn't unprecedented in human history. White men who had fathered half-black children had a nasty habit of abandoning them before interracial marriage had stopped being taboo…and they had had purely human children. The Elf-Human half-breeds belonged to neither world.

"So I spend my days here in the magical world," he finished, sadly. "I have no dreams and no hope for a future. I can have sex all week and there is no chance I can get anyone pregnant. I used to hope that I would be able to amass the magical knowledge necessary to drive into the Kingdom of the Elves and demand my place among them, or perhaps to tear them down, but it was an impossible dream. I belong nowhere, trusted by no one. Your Master warned you about me, didn't he?"

I hesitated, and then decided to be honest. "Yes," I said. There was no point in discussing the unflattering way Cardonel – and half-Elves in general - had been described. "I'm afraid he did."

"They don't like creatures that cross the barriers," Cardonel admitted. "My very existence is dangerous to them, yet I am something they can hit. I am not a Being of Power to be placated – if even talking on human terms is possible – or an Elf who has ties back to the Kingdom and the ability to call on support from the King and Queen of the Land below the Hill. They prevented me from gaining access to any of their libraries. I sometimes wonder why they haven't killed me outright."

He snorted. "Perhaps they think that my father and his court would go to war to avenge my death, once I am safely dead," he added. He chuckled, bitterly. "That isn't going to happen. My father would rest easier once he knew that I was dead."

I frowned. "If that is the case," I said, "why didn't he kill you?"

"The Elves don't have many children," Cardonel explained. "They don't breed as easily as humans, so killing one's own child is taboo to them, even a half-elf child. Daddy Dearest would probably be delighted if another Elf killed me, or one of the human magicians caught me and used my blood as an ingredient for a spell, but he couldn't kill me himself."

He leaned back on the bed and smiled. "Are you sure that you don't want to join me tonight?"

I blinked in surprise, before realising that it was his way of changing the subject. "Not tonight," I said. I hadn't realised, until I had said it out loud, that I had implied that I would sleep with him one day. I looked down at him and considered it. He was handsome, I did like him…and I felt sorry for him. The chances were good that he wouldn't live anything like as long as a mundane human, let alone a magical human with access to good rejuvenation spells. "Maybe I'll join you one day."

"Tease," Cardonel said, without heat. He sat up and stretched. His body contorted oddly as he moved. I found myself suddenly fascinated. His bone structure couldn't be human, not if he could move like that. "Are you ready to move?"

I looked up, sharply. "Is it time to move?"

"Just about," Cardonel said. He looked sharply at me. "Start by feeling out the security spells and then determining how to fool them."

I sat down, crossed my legs and focused my mind. Master Revels had trained me well and I could enter the searching trance quickly. All magic had an effect on reality, even if the effect was minimal and carefully hidden. I could feel out the defences surrounding the building and found myself smiling. Thanks to Cardonel, we were *inside* the main defences already. The wards were focused around keeping unwanted people out, not preventing someone from moving around inside the building. I was less amused to discover that one of the security spells seemed configured to spy on the people who hired rooms, including us. If anyone had been looking through it, they would have seen us chatting rather than making love. Angrily, I tinkered with the spell, forcing it to report that we were still in the room rather than sneaking out to free the slaves.

Outside the room, there were fewer security measures, although there was at least one security spell covering the basement. I studied it carefully and realised that I could fool it, given enough time and preparation. It would be relatively simple. All I'd have to do was convince it that I wasn't there.

"All right," I said, finally. I made my preparations and pulled a glamour-spell around me, a simple 'I'm not here' spell to fool casual observers. If I was lucky, I could walk past the manager and his goons and they wouldn't see me. "It's time to move."

Cardonel frowned. "Are you absolutely sure about this?"

"No," I said. There was something in his voice I didn't like. I wasn't sure if it was his reluctance or something else. "I'm not sure about this, but I am doing it anyway. It has to be done."

I reached for the door and pushed it open. "Come on," I hissed. "Let's go."

CHAPTER THIRTEEN

Cardonel followed me as I stepped out into the hallway, pulling a glamour-spell around his own body too. I took a moment to confirm my earlier check for security spells and then started walking. I knew spells that would allow me to see in the dark, but thankfully the halls were illuminated by a dim glow that seemed to shine down from high overhead, lending the building a vaguely creepy appearance. I suspected that we wouldn't get into trouble if we were caught here – the people who hired the rooms had to go home afterwards, after all – yet the further we went into the building, the greater the chance of being caught. I didn't want to know what would happen if they found us trying to free their slaves.

"This way," Cardonel hissed, pulling me down a darkened corridor. The light was fading now, leaving us in the dark. Cardonel muttered a charm under his breath and a ball of light appeared in his hand, illuminating the way forward. I smiled, impressed despite myself. The spell only provided light to the caster and those the caster chose to add into the spell. Anyone else wouldn't be able to see us using the light. "We need to move quickly."

A moment later, we pressed ourselves into a doorway as four of the muscle-men walked past, yawning with obvious exhaustion. Up close, they stank; a uniquely male scent that made me want to throw up again. I watched the muscles moving under their shirts and found myself wondering what spells they'd used to enhance themselves. The chances were good that they, like Cardonel, were burning the candle at both ends, shortening their lives in exchange for power. They tramped off into the distance, pushing and shoving at each other, and I found myself smiling. They had no idea how close they'd come to catching the pair of us.

Cardonel waved to me to follow him as we reached a staircase leading down into the basement. The half-elf was almost invisible in the gloom, despite the light he carried, leaving me to pick my own way down the steps. I almost ran into him at the bottom and he caught me before I could step forward. The door ahead of us was protected by a concealed charm, one that would have entrapped us both if we had touched the wood without proper preparation. The magician who had created it was amazingly confident or stupid, I decided as I examined it carefully; normally, such a spell would have a list of people it wasn't allowed to bite, but this spell had no safe list. The owner of the building could find himself entrapped as easily as a thief. It was odd, to say the least.

I focused my mind and muttered a charm under my breath, focusing a spell that was just enough to counter and deactivate the security spell. It resisted being deactivated for a moment and then collapsed, too easily. Even if the person who had established it had done it by rote, it shouldn't have been that easy to push it aside. I checked, my suspicions aroused, and discovered a second – nastier – spell hidden in the stonework. This one would have turned us both into statues until the owner came along and discovered what had happened. We would have been helpless prisoners. I deactivated the second spell too and pushed the door open with a finger. Nothing else rose up to greet us.

"Come on," I hissed, and slipped into the slave chambers. I wasn't sure what I was expecting to see, but it looked like a stone dungeon, complete with manacles hangings from the wall. They were empty, yet I could see crusted blood around them that suggested that they had, at one time, been used frequently. The stone walls played host to another security spell, although this one seemed configured to prevent anyone from teleporting in and snatching the slaves. I deactivated it anyway, on general principles, before we slipped further into the dungeons. We had to find the slaves before it was too late.

"In here," Cardonel hissed. I followed his gaze. There were four men standing in the room, all wearing slave collars. The door was unlocked, which puzzled me for a moment until I realised that the collars would prevent them from leaving and escaping. The defences were designed to keep people out, rather than keep them in. "I cannot see the women."

"They'll be here somewhere," I said. It was more of a hope than absolute certainty. If we couldn't find them before we had to leave, we would have to escape, leaving them in enemy hands. I could imagine just what could be happening to them, right now, and shivered at the thought. How badly would I treat someone who had no choice, but to do as I ordered? "Help me open the door."

Master Revels had lectured me quite heavily on slave spells and what they actually did. The slave had no choice. He or she had to show absolute and unquestioning obedience to their owner, no matter what they were ordered to do, but they maintained a considerable amount of free will. The men in front of me were still as smart and capable as they had ever been – if they had ever been smart and capable, as they had been enslaved – and they could be dangerous. The slave instructions they'd been given after they'd been fitted with the collars probably included a command not to obey anyone, but their master.

The door slid open and I stepped inside. The slaves gaped at me and then opened their mouths and started shouting for their master, screaming that they were being kidnapped. I cast a freeze spell at once, shutting them up quickly and brutally; they might have had no choice, but the racket could have brought the security team down on our heads. In the sudden silence, I could hear nothing apart from the beating of my heart. The sound hadn't alerted anyone, I hoped.

"Don't worry," I said, as I studied the first slave's collar. It was a nasty little thing. The spell concealed in the iron collar looked as if it wanted to bite me. It was more complex than I had expected – the result, I guessed, of the commands given to the slaves and ingrained within the spell – but it was fairly easy to dismantle and neutralise. "I'll get you out of here, one way or the other."

Once the first slave was freed, I worked my way through the others, before releasing the freeze spell. The slaves collapsed at once, although more because of the effects of the spell than because of any lingering after-effects from their enslavement. Cardonel helped them to their feet and pointed to the door, ordering them out into the basement. I left the collars there – after rigging them with a spell of my own to give anyone who picked them up a nasty surprise – and followed them. The men were free. Now all we had to do was liberate the women.

"Thank you," one of the boys said. He was around seventeen years old and would have been quite handsome, in a manner of speaking, if his face hadn't been so haunted by everything he'd seen over the last few days. He looked bitterly vulnerable and distraught. I had been told that slave spells could be addictive at times, with people choosing – as insane as it seemed – to be enslaved and give up their own free will to someone else. It was enough to make me feel sick. "Who are you?"

"No names," Cardonel said, before I could say anything. "We're not out of the woods yet."

I nodded and resumed the search for the women. It took us several moments to find them and, when we did, it became apparent that rescuing them was going to be harder. They were all gathered in a cell, not unlike the men, but they were protected by layers of more complex spells, each one carefully designed to keep out intruders. I wasn't too surprised. Female slaves, it seemed, were worth more than male slaves.

"I'll stay on guard," Cardonel hissed. "You concentrate on the spells."

"Understood," I said. My heart was pounding away as I started to dismantle the first set of spells. It was far harder than anything I'd done before, because the first set was interlinked with the second and third set, but I had no choice now. I felt sweat running down my back as I isolated the first set, cut the links between the second and third set and then started brushing them away. The owners hadn't wasted their money on this set of wards. I doubted that anyone else could have brought the wards down quicker. "Hang on…"

The fifth and six sets of wards collapsed, almost like a giant spider's web. I caught and isolated them with my mind, realising that the spell was alarmingly complex and likely to start trying to rebuild itself. Unless it was shattered beyond hope of self-repair…I pulled it apart completely and absorbed the traces of magic into my own magical field. I opened the door and cast the freeze spell at once, without waiting for the women to start screaming. Once was quite enough.

"Don't worry," I said, as I slipped through the door. "We're here to get you out of this nightmare."

The women were bound by the same spells as the men, although some of them had more complex spells than others. I guessed that they'd been given different orders, although there was no time to read the spells and find out what they had been…and besides, I didn't want to know. I was undoing the last set of wards when disaster struck and I broke a ward I hadn't realised was there. I should have known – the girl was stunningly pretty, yet far too young for trouble and strife – but there was no time to waste in recriminations. The wards would already be sounding the alarm.

"We have to get out of here," I snapped, as I broke the last slave spell and pushed the girls towards the door. A thought crossed my mind as I felt, rather than heard, doors slamming closed above us. I felt the wards around the building coming alive and starting to hunt for the intruders. They'd discover that I'd dismantled too many of them for safety. The owners would have to rebuild everything before their base was secure again. Not that it would matter to us, one way or the other. I heard the sound of heavy footsteps above us and knew that the muscle-men were on their way.

"There's only one way out," Cardonel said. I didn't hear any recriminations in his voice, but I knew that they were there. God alone knew what the owners would do to us if they caught us. "How do you think we can get past an army?"

I smiled as a thought occurred to me. I could get the women out, at least. I pulled the Sisterhood's pendant from below my shirt and held it up, triggering it with a single thought. The pendant grew brighter and a Gateway started to form, leading outwards in a direction that seemed to exist at right angles to reality. Human minds were not built to comprehend the true nature of the multiverse. I'd been told that those who looked too closely went mad. It sounded quite believable to me.

"Get the women through the Gate," I ordered. Cardonel looked surprised, but did as he was told. The women were reluctant to leave their male relatives, yet they had no choice. When they hesitated, I pushed Compulsion into my voice and compelled them into the Gateway. The Sisterhood would take care of them, I hoped. At the very least, they wouldn't return them to slavery. "Everyone else…"

"We could go too," one of the boys protested. I wondered at his attitude and then realised that he wouldn't understand the price. "Why…?"

"You can't walk that path and remain a man," I said, tartly. I had no idea what it would do to Cardonel, but I knew what it would do to a pure human. "We have to fight our way out of this."

The doorway burst open and a stream of muscle-men marched down towards us, cracking their knuckles in tune with their walk. Cardonel stood up and extended his hands, growing claws and sharp teeth; I prepared what magical tricks I could, wishing that I'd had more training in self-defence. The wards were pushing in now and they would help protect the muscle-men from my magic. I wasn't keen to see what would happen if I had to fight them hand to hand.

They stopped as a hooded figure appeared behind them. "Give up now and be enslaved, or be beaten and then enslaved," the manager said. He didn't sound too happy. I guessed that he'd realised that the women were beyond his reach. Well, apart from one woman; me. "There is no way that you can escape."

"Get fucked," I said, tartly. I was not going to go out without a fight.

"What she said," Cardonel said. He held up his claws and the light glittered off them, daring the muscle-men to move forward. He looked very inhuman and yet, somehow, truly magnificent. Absurdly, I found myself wondering where he'd hidden those claws. "Come and have a go if you think you're hard enough."

The manager's face, what little we could see of it, turned an alarming shade of purple. "Capture them and bring them to me alive," he ordered. The muscle-men straightened and started to advance towards us. "Do not kill them."

Magic flared from my fingertips and lashed out towards the advancing men. Three fell dead on the ground – part of me was shocked, even though I had no time to think about what I'd done – and two more staggered backwards before the wards started to press in on me. The muscle-men stepped over their dead comrades and kept advancing, pressing their hands together in an unholy benison. Cardonel leapt forward, howling a chant in a language that hurt my ears, and started to lash out at the men. He moved with blindingly inhuman speed, too quickly for them to catch or hurt, yet I knew that it couldn't last forever. The more he called on his gift, his heritage from his unwanted father, the more the magic would burn away at his human form. How many years of his life was he throwing away for me?

Two muscle-men bypassed him and advanced towards me. There was something frighteningly inhuman about their faces, as if they weren't quite connected to what they were doing. There was no sense of emotion at all. They were neither driven by duty nor sadism. They just were. I lifted my hands, trying to draw on my magic, yet the wards were pressing down too hard. I was trapped. I'd led them all to their deaths. At least I'd gotten the women out. Perhaps the thought would console me afterwards, if there was an afterwards.

A thought struck me and I snatched at the ring I'd been given. The dragon-face lit up at once. A moment later, space and time twisted around us – so badly that my head screamed in pain, unable to comprehend how the universe was being pulled out of shape – and a full-sized dragon was in the room with us. It roared loudly, blowing a wave of fire towards the muscle-men, who simply evaporated and disintegrated in the heat. The wards, which hadn't been prepared to handle a dragon, faded away as the dragon lunged forward. My head threatened to explode again. I couldn't understand how the dragon could fit into such a confined space, let alone spread its wings. Bright red eyes shone out and focused on me. I realised, far later than I should have realised, that Fiona had come to my rescue. She was no longer tiny.

"Get onto my back, all of you," she ordered. She blew another fireball up towards the top of the stairs to make her point. A series of explosions started to tear the building apart. I realised that the stockpiles of alcohol must have caught fire and started to explode. "Hurry up!"

I pushed the men towards the dragon – they had been rooted to the spot, unable to take their eyes off her – and shouted for Cardonel. He abandoned his last victim – a muscle-man whose head had been sheared off by his claws – and came flashing over to us. He helped me climb onto Fiona's back and then joined me. I clutched at her scales desperately, feeling the pounding heartbeat and heat even though my trousers. A moment later, space twisted around us and we were flying over Edinburgh, gazing down on the castle from high above. It seemed unbelievable that the entire mundane world wouldn't see the dragon, yet I knew that no one would even notice her.

Cardonel put an arm around me and I found myself sagging against him in relief. We'd made it, barely; we'd freed the slaves. The men looked terrified as they stared down at their city, yet they were...I looked around as it suddenly grew warmer and stared in horror. The two older men, the fathers of their families, had burst into flame. Before I could do anything, they had both burned to ash in front of their sons, their remains drifting out on the breeze. There was nothing left of them, but the smell of burning human flesh.

Fiona seemed unconcerned by the sudden outbreak of spontaneous human combustion. "We'll drop off your friends at the market place," she said, slowly, "and then we will go home. You have to face the music."

I shivered. I wasn't looking forward to that at all.

CHAPTER FOURTEEN

"I would advise being completely honest," Fiona said, as she settled down in front of the house. The two boys on her back took one look around, saw that they were in the open and ran for their lives. I silently wished them well when they returned to the mundane world, although their lives would have been completely ruined and their fathers were nothing more than piles of ash. The ash shifted as Fiona's body seemed to twist and she returned to her more normal size, settling on my shoulder like a giant parrot. "The Master will not thank you for lying to him."

"I understand," I said. I had hoped that no one would know that I – that we – had tried to free the slaves, but there was no hope of keeping it a secret now. Fiona had come to our rescue after all. I didn't understand the link between her and Master Revels, yet I knew that they communed in some manner I didn't understand. Come to think of it, if Fiona could become the size of a bus with very little effort, why did she fly around as a large bird most of the time? "What do you think he will do?"

Fiona twitched her wings, a dragonish shrug. "I imagine that he will not be happy," she said, as we reached the door. "Beyond that...well, there are a wide range of precedents. If you tell the truth, Dizzy, at least you won't get into worse trouble."

Precisely how much trouble I was in became clear as soon as I entered the house and closed the door behind me. My body started to move on its own, walking right towards the study and the single glowing square of light in the semi-darkness that informed me that Master Revels was present within his private room. I wanted to try to resist the pull, but my body adamantly refused to be deflected from its new course. It left me feeling terrifyingly vulnerable – I'd been taught how to resist Compulsion, yet this was different – and helpless. My hand moved to the doorknob, despite my fervent mental struggles, and opened the door. The warm light streaming out of the study seemed to welcome me as I stepped inside and closed the door, standing in front of the desk with my hands at my side. I couldn't move any further. My breathing seemed abnormally loud in the confined space.

Under other circumstances, I quite enjoyed looking around the study. Master Revels had decorated it in a fashion that seemed to suggest a combination of a serious scholar and a teenage boy. Books, some of them very old and valuable, were scattered everywhere, while toys and magical artefacts of all kinds seemed to be everywhere in the room. It was not a place for visitors. Every chair in the room was covered in piles of books and papers, leaving only one useable seat. I'd tried to move some of the books the first time I'd entered the room, but Master Revels had reprimanded me and warned me never to disturb the order. It was a very strange order, I thought, yet I kept my peace. My own room was far neater, or so I told myself.

I'd never seen Master Revels genuinely angry before, even when we'd been tracking down the missing girls. He looked as if he was having difficulty concentrating on his work, yet he was reluctant to look up at me. I wanted to swallow hard as I took in his face and realised that he was concentrating on calming disciplines, but even that was denied me. The spell that held me frozen, if it was a spell, was beyond my ability to perceive, yet alone break. I'd read about such spells in the books, spells that couldn't be detected by anyone who had actually become their victim, but I'd never thought that it could happen to me. It had been a stupid thought. In the magical world, anything could happen to anyone. If someone could be turned into a statue just by looking in the wrong dish of cooking supplies, who knew what could happen to me?

"Dizzy," Master Revels said, finally. I braced myself, as best as I could, for a world-class row. "Tell me something.

What were you thinking?"

His eyes narrowed. "I assume that you were actually *thinking*," he added. "Do you have any idea just how stupid you have been?"

I found myself suddenly able to speak. "Yes, sir," I said. I didn't trust myself to say more. After everything I'd been though in the night, which wasn't over yet, I wasn't sure if I would start screaming at him or break down in tears. A thousand arguments floated through my mind, the ones I had researched long before we'd snuck down into the basement to free the slaves, but they all seemed pale and weak in the cold light of his gaze.

"I very much doubt it," Master Revels said, sharply. He crossed his fingertips together and peered up at me. "Tell me; what were you thinking when you decided to follow the half-elf's lead?"

Surprise broke the paralysis. Master Revels clearly blamed *Cardonel* for everything. The idea of liberating the slaves, convincing me to join him, risking my life and freedom to save a handful of mundane humans...he thought that it had all been *his* idea. I told myself that I wasn't tempted to let him take the blame. It wasn't fair to get the half-elf into additional trouble. No one would come to his defence.

"It wasn't his idea, sir," I said, as calmly as I could. "It was mine."

Master Revels blinked at me. "Are you out of your mind?"

I took a breath. "I saw the slaves and how they were being treated," I said, keeping my voice as level as I could. If I was about to die, or be tossed out onto the streets, or forced to spend the next few weeks as a toad...I might as well go out after saying my piece. "No one could have seen them and not done something to free them from bondage."

Master Revels didn't smile. "Do you know how many attempts there are to free slaves by force?" he asked. I shook my head. "There are very few such attempts, Dizzy, so your claim is nonsense. The vast majority of magicians and others in the community would not have risked their lives or their freedom to save the slaves from slavery. Do you dispute that?"

I wanted to tell him that he was wrong, but cold logic suggested otherwise. There hadn't been anyone else at the club, at least as far as I could tell, who had objected to watching the slaves performing. They had watched the dances and the other entertainments without a care in the world, or a thought for the slaves. I had been the only one.

"You got most of them out of bondage," Master Revels said, when I said nothing. "Did you not see what happened to the two who signed the contracts?" I remembered the two men bursting into flame and shuddered. "They signed their lives away and those of their families when they signed that contract, Dizzy. They knew what was at stake."

"They sold their own families into slavery?" I demanded. "Is that even legal?"

"It is perfectly legal in the magical world," Master Revels said. "They signed the deal, so they were bound by the deal and the deal was enforced by powerful magic, the magic that makes up the borders of the magical world. Their wives and children, at least, will be unaffected. They didn't sign the contract."

He smiled humourlessly at my expression. "There are...interests that operate straddling the mundane and magical worlds," he added. "Those interests focus on mundane men and women who are...shall we say overextended? They offer money and support, with a rather unusual penalty clause. I'm afraid that most of their mundane victims don't take the clauses seriously until it's too late and if they cannot make their payments they are sold into slavery, along with their families."

I shivered. I had learned about loud and flashy magic from Master Revels, but the subtle magical tricks could often be more dangerous. A person who signed a magical contract with his true name – the magicians never shared their real names, choosing to go by assumed names to prevent their true names being used against them – would be bound by it, according to rules laid down by the universe itself. The universe had run out of patience when the two men had escaped and removed them from play. It wasn't a pleasant thought.

"That's not fair," I protested. "Don't they know what they're getting into?"

"The world is not fair," Master Revels said, flatly. "They signed the contracts. They should have known to take them seriously."

"And they were picked because they *wouldn't* be able to make their payments," I said, cynically. "Can't the Thirteen stop them?"

"They're not breaking any rules," Master Revels said. His voice had gone quiet, something I knew to be a bad sign. "And you, on the other hand, broke the rules quite badly."

I tensed. This was going to be bad. "Do you have any idea what they could have done if they'd caught you?"

He continued without waiting for me to answer. "If they'd caught you, they could have killed you and your half-blood friend and no one would have been able to complain," he said, sharply. "No one would have stood up in your defence, because you violated their building and stole their property. The Thirteen wouldn't allow me to punish them for it. Do you understand me?"

I nodded. "And what would have happened," he added, "if they'd taken you alive?

"They would have been within their rights to enslave you and put you on the stage to replace their lost property. Or, if they felt that you merited worse treatment, they could have sold you to the Elves, or the Dark Cabal, or the Rationalists. The Elves would have amused themselves by taking you apart and putting you back together in the wrong order. The Dark Cabal would have used your body for their research into the darkest of dark magic. The Rationalists would have used you as a living subject for their experiments. They never have enough magicians willing to be dissected while they're still living. Do you understand what could have happened to you?"

"Yes, sir," I said, shaking. The fury in his voice was terrifying. "I understand..."

"And, while you were at it, you would have destroyed *my* position," Master Revels snapped. "Or didn't you think of that? The Thirteen rely on me to serve as impartially as possible and if my apprentice had been caught stealing property from its rightful owners, it would have made it impossible for me to continue to serve them! My career would have been shattered. I would probably have had to leave Edinburgh and live somewhere else."

He pressed his hands down on the table. "And then there is Fiona," he added, tartly. "Did you think about what might happen if she'd been caught and killed?"

I hadn't thought that anything could stop a full-sized dragon, but I didn't dare open my mouth. "She would have been cut apart," Master Revels said, angrily. "You can use dragon skin as a shield against most magical charms. You can use dragon's blood as a key to unlocking deeper levels of magic within a person's mind, or opening Gateways to alternate worlds. You can rend down a dragon and use every last particle of its body. You could have gotten Fiona killed because you had to go off on a quixotic rescue mission!"

His voice lowered, back to more normal levels. "I understand how you were feeling," he said, softly. "I understand, probably better than you think, but you cannot change a world by striking out at the merest injustice. You would need to tackle the underlying problem and that would have been impossible if you'd been killed, or enslaved..."

I felt tiny under his gaze. My body was still locked, but the trembling was involuntary. I had been shouted at before, by my mother before I'd left her, yet somehow receiving a lecture from Master Revels was far worse. I could still feel Fiona on my shoulder and I wanted to pull her into a hug, if only to console me, but I couldn't move. I found myself hoping and praying that it was over, yet knowing that it was not. It might never be over.

"The good news," Master Revels said, more calmly. "Everyone who might have seen you is dead. Fiona torched the building so the remainder of the staff were occupied in trying to get everyone out and fighting the fire, rather that coming down to see what was going on. The slaves, apart from the fools who signed the contracts in the first place, are alive. Sending the female slaves to the Sisterhood was a good idea. The Sisters won't be too pleased to have them bursting in, but they will help them and make sure that they get safely back to the mundane world. The males...well, when they started running, they were on the path that would let them fall back into the mundane world. They will be fine, I hope, now that their fathers are dead."

His eyes darkened. "Fiona was not entirely unnoticeable," he added. "That may not be a complete disaster. Dragons have been known to pick fights for unpredictable reasons and Fiona might just have been mistaken for a rogue dragon. I'll try and spread rumours of a new dragon war just over the horizon, which should help concentrate a few minds.

"And the club owners will take weeks to repair it and reopen. I suspect that they will add stronger charms against dragons and perhaps do a little more work before they can open for business. You may have dodged a bullet."

"Thank you, sir," I said, and meant it. It was a weight off my mind. "I'm sure they won't be taking in any more slaves..."

"I highly doubt it," Master Revels said, sharply. "The last thing you want or need is for someone to draw a link between the slaves and someone burning the club down. This isn't the mundane world. You never know who might be watching or have access to a precognitive talent that could give someone an advance warning. You have to be careful for the next few days."

He pressed his fingertips together. I knew what was coming. "You disappointed me tonight," he said. There was no emotion in his voice, yet I felt it biting at me. I had wanted his respect, but instead he was angry and disappointed in me. "You did well when you had to break through the club's defences, but you chose your battle very poorly and could have lost everything; you *would* have lost everything, were it not for Fiona. She saved your life."

I felt my body jerk into life as he stood up. I turned to face a small table, one I hadn't noticed before. Lying on top of it, strangely alone, was a simple thin cane. I picked it up, my hand moving robotically, and passed it to him. Merely touching it sent unpleasant feelings running down my spine.

I knew, beyond all doubt, what was about to happen. The spell holding me in place broke, yet I couldn't move. I knew that I deserved what was coming. Or was it the spell, still in place? There was no way to know.

"Bend over the table, Dizzy," Master Revels said. I obeyed. He didn't use Compulsion, yet something pushed me forward. I had never felt so exposed in my life. Fiona fluttered off my shoulder and over to a perch on the wall. I caught a glimpse of her golden eyes and felt a sudden burst of reassurance. "I wish I didn't have to do this."

I wished he didn't have to do it either, but it wasn't my choice. I squeaked as cold hands lifted up my dress, then reached into the wristband of my panties and pulled them down to my knees. A cold breeze seemed to blow through the room, a chilling reminder of my vulnerability. My parents had never chosen to punish me in such a manner.

"You put your life in terrible danger and risked everything," Master Revels added. He took a position next to me and I cringed. It occurred to me suddenly that he had to be seeing absolutely everything I had, right on display, and I fought the urge to giggle. "If it is any consolation, my master punished me too...and my mistakes were far worse than yours."

I struggled to speak. "What did you do?"

"I'll tell you when you're old enough to take on an apprentice of your own," Master Revels said, flatly. I got the feeling that he didn't want to talk about it and that he'd only mentioned it to help reassure me. He needn't have bothered. "Suffice it to say that I thoroughly deserved the thrashing I got for it. I could have killed myself and a thousand other people."

There was a moment's pause, and then he lifted the cane and brought it down hard on my exposed bottom. For a second, there was no pain, and then I felt as if a red hot poker had been laid across my bum. I screamed, unable to help myself, and reached back to rub my rear end. He gently, but firmly pushed my hand back to the table and brought the cane down again, and again. The pain just kept growing worse. I tried to concentrate on one of the disciplines, yet every time I tried to focus, the cane struck me again.

The caning lasted only five minutes, if that, but I was sore for hours.

CHAPTER FIFTEEN

I'd read in stories, back when I'd been a young girl, about girls who had taken six of the best from their teachers – and school prefects, and sports mistresses, and governesses – and had carried on as if the thrashing hadn't caused any permanent harm. The young and impressionable girl I had been had believed that – if only because my parents had never spanked me – yet now I knew that it was nonsense, total nonsense. I had inspected myself in the mirror as soon as I had been released and allowed to go to my room and discovered that my aching buttocks were covered with no less than ten ominous red stripes. It hurt to walk, to touch them or to sit down. I lay face down on the bed and started to cry.

Sometime afterwards, I fell asleep, still lying on my chest. My dreams were strange things, images of the slaves, the desperate rescue and the cane looming over me blending together to produce a surreal nightmare. I couldn't sleep well at all, if only because every time I twisted in bed my aching bottom rubbed against the sheets, snapping me awake. I was grateful when Fiona flew into the room and settled down next to me, one scaly paw holding my hand. When I finally awoke, it was eleven o'clock and I felt dreadful.

My bottom was still a mess – the red lines had sharpened, even though the rest of my skin had faded to its normal pale colour – and my face was terrifyingly blotchy. It didn't hurt to move so much, although I didn't dare risk having a shower or even putting on some proper knickers and jeans. I donned my dressing gown – it was made of silk and gentle to the touch – and muttered a spell under my breath. The pain slowly faded, though it would be back. I'd been warned that spells like that always have a price. The pain would come back soon, doubled. Fiona fluttered down and settled on my shoulder as I finished tying up my hair.

I looked up at her. "How can I go down to face him now?" I asked. I suddenly wanted to cry again. Last night, I'd been stupid, nearly gotten myself and others killed, and then...I froze, horrified. I had killed last night. I had terminated people's lives. "How...?"

"Don't worry about it," Fiona said. She sounded amused by my predicament. "I'll tell you, between you and me, that you're not the first person in this house to be caned for stupidity."

"Stupidity," I repeated. In the cold light of day, what I'd done did look pretty stupid...and the aching behind didn't help. I understood, now, why schoolchildren had been so terrified of the cane before it had been banned. I was an adult, legally at least, and they were just kids. "How long have you spent in this place?"

Fiona blew out a tiny puff of smoke from her nose. "You should know better than to ask a lady her age," she chided, lightly. "For your information, Dizzy, I have been here for over four hundred human years."

Her mouth lolled open, a dragon smile, at my expression. "We dragons live a very long time," she added. "I know dragons that are older than your entire race, dragons that flew over the Earth before the human race was brought into existence, and dragons that fought with gods and demons back when the universe was young."

I frowned. "Our years must go by in a flash for you," I said. "Why are you here? I like your company, but why are you working here?"

"I like the human race," Fiona said. She winked one glowing eye at me, leaving me unsure if she had told the truth or not – or perhaps only part of the truth. There was no way to know. "I knew your master's master and his master and trust me; they all got the same treatment if they screwed up. You should consider yourself lucky. There are many problems one can get into in the magical world that cannot be fixed with a sore bottom."

I thought about it as I walked down the stairs and into the dining room. I knew just how badly it could have gone, so I should be grateful, right? I was unsure how to feel; part of me was glad that the matter was over, if it was over, and the other part was outraged. How dare anyone, even Master Revels, do that to me?

"Take a seat," Master Revels said, from where he was sitting. He passed me the newspaper with one hand and smiled. "You may want to look at that."

I sat down...and jumped up again, cursing. It still hurt to sit down, spell or no spell. I glared at him and spread the paper out over the table, ignoring the cup of tea that had materialised in front of me. It had amused me to discover that the magical world had its own newspaper, although it was very bland compared to the newspapers back in the mundane world. It seemed that all of the reporters had sworn magical oaths to tell the truth, the whole truth as they understood it and nothing else. There were no snarky comments, few political slants and a surprisingly limited amount of gossip. I guessed that when a magical celebrity could curse a reporter for spreading lies about her – or even for reporting inconvenient truths – it would limit the damage a reporter could cause.

The lead story concerned a sighting of a dragon near the market. The reporter had got some of the facts of the case right – at least he'd noted Fiona's presence – but after that he went off on a rant about the dangers of dragon raids and how dragons were a major danger to life and limb in the magical world. It ended with a proposal to start a dragon patrol to watch for dragons and keep them away from human settlements in the magical dimensions.

"That won't ever get off the ground," Master Revels said, when I looked up, horrified. "That ass is full of bravado, but very few magicians want to battle a dragon, even a young hatchling straight from the nest. Dragons are tough and very dangerous. Besides, there are so many of the Roads of Happenstance leading to the market that sealing them all would be an impossible task."

He looked down at his half-finished plate and picked up his knife and fork. "Get some breakfast," he said, mildly. "You have to make a call afterwards and then the Thirteen has seen fit to give us a new assignment."

I blinked at him. "You're taking me along with you?" I asked, astonished. "After last night..."

My hand rubbed my bottom as he snorted. "You'd probably blow up the magical world if I left you alone," he said, dryly. I flushed. "Dizzy..."

I looked up, reluctantly.

"I know how you're feeling now, but I don't hold anything against you any longer," he said, quietly. "You have remarkable promise and I don't intend to allow that to go to waste."

His words echoed in my ears as I ate my own breakfast, standing up. Fiona settled next to me and chattered absently about dragon society, reassuring me that most dragons wouldn't even notice the newspaper article, let alone care about it enough to hunt down the person responsible and burn them to death. Being so long-lived, dragons rarely bothered to take notice of humans as individuals, which made Fiona's presence so unusual. I suspected, after some thought, that I knew the answer. Humans might pose a threat to the dragons one day – if we developed even more powerful magic – and we might turn on them. Fiona's real job might be to keep an eye on us and make sure that if we developed anything threatening, the dragons would know about it well in advance.

Once I finished my breakfast, I used the pendant to make a call to the Sisterhood. The woman I spoke to was unfamiliar, but she was clearly familiar with the case and reassured me that the former slaves were being welcomed into the Sisterhood, having decided not to return to the mundane world. Their sons, she promised me, would be contacted and even though they couldn't enter the Sisterhood's pocket dimension, they would be taken care of by the Sisters. The woman had the nerve to congratulate me on liberating the women and promised that if I needed personal help, the Sisters would be there. I was rubbing my bottom again as I ended the call. If the women were free and happy – and it seemed as if they were – it had all been worthwhile. At that thought, the knot in my chest untangled itself and faded away.

"Get a proper dress and make sure that it reaches down past your knees," Master Revels ordered, once he had finished his own breakfast. I nodded, although I was surprised by the instruction. It made no sense to me. "There's no hurry. Take your time."

I'd inherited most of the female clothes in the house – at least until I left, or so I had been told – but there were so many it was hard to choose what I could wear. I eventually settled on a long blue dress that fell down to my calves. It looked demure, particularly when I checked it in the mirror for unexpected surprises, and it hid the fact that I wasn't wearing panties. I couldn't put any underwear on without feeling as if my bottom had just been caned again.

"Not bad," Master Revels said when he saw me. I had to laugh. I think that was the first time that he ever noticed my appearance. Fiona winked at me again. "Grab your coat and let's go. Idle hands are the devil's workshop and we have work to do."

I was nervous when I stepped outside, wondering if the whole of the magical world had heard me screaming last night, but no one paid us any special attention. It still hurt to walk, yet I discovered that if I gritted my teeth and kept going, the pain slowly faded away to manageable levels. The tourists thronging through Edinburgh, exploring the Royal Mile, paid no attention to us as we slipped back into the mundane world. I was used to the effect by now, but it still struck me as uncanny. There was an entire hidden world that they would never see.

Master Revels stopped at the top of George the Fourth Bridge for a moment, allowing me to pick up a copy of a newspaper from a street vendor. There was nothing about a fire anywhere in Edinburgh, thankfully, which suggested that the flames had been contained within the magical world. I had trusted in the spells masking our presence from the mundane world, yet I had been nervous. It would have been ironic if my determination to rescue the slaves had become the day that the magical and mundane worlds collided.

"Come on," Master Revels said, and started to lead me down the Royal Mile. I followed him obediently, wincing at the feeling of sunlight striking my back. It was a stunningly warm day for Edinburgh. He led me down towards an old church and paused, waiting for me to catch up with him. "What do you make of that?"

I followed his gaze, studying the church thoughtfully. The Tron Kirk had been built after the Bishops War – a war that most people had forgotten these days – when Charles I had tried to alter the structure of the Scottish Church by placing a Bishop in Edinburgh, or something like that. I had always had a good memory for facts and figures, but I had only heard the history of the very old Kirk once. The Scots had commissioned another church and worshipped there instead, daring Charles to do anything about it. Charles had had his head cut off shortly afterwards by Oliver Cromwell, although the two events might not be connected. These days, the Kirk was both the site of historical excavations and a tourist information centre. With the Fringe in full swing, it was clear that it was doing a roaring trade.

"It's busy," I said, slowly. I had no idea what I was looking for, unless it was traces of magic. I opened my mind carefully and sensed...nothing. The Kirk wasn't glowing with magic, not like the Castle and a hundred other buildings along the Royal Mile. It was an ordinary mundane building. "Why are we even here?"

Master Revels said nothing. I followed him into the building and through the tourist's section, into a vast room that showed us the remains of the archaeological exploration program. I found myself studying information plaques in puzzlement. The Kirk had been linked to Edinburgh's famous underground city – the Town below the Ground – yet the research had been halted a year ago, for no apparent reason. Master Revels was still distracted, so I wandered over to one of the staff members and gave him my best smile.

"This is a fascinating place," I said, seriously. As I had

guessed, he began to launch into a long history of the building and how it related to Edinburgh's history. Some of it was quite fascinating, all the more so because I knew about the magical world and could guess at links that he, for all of his knowledge, couldn't even imagine. The magical world and the mundane world had interacted more than anyone could have guessed. "Why did they stop the research here?"

The staff member looked left, then right, and then back up at me. "They were talking about ghosts," he said, quite seriously. "They said that they encountered ghosts."

A year ago, I would have laughed in his face. Now, having seen ghosts myself – both real ghosts and the afterimages of particularly traumatic events – I believed him. He didn't believe himself, however, and was giving me the dressed up version he saved for the tourists. I couldn't believe his cheek; I might not have much of a Scottish accent, but I didn't sound as if I came from England, let alone overseas. Still, I listened carefully, and a picture started to form in my mind.

The workers had started to feel chills soon after they began work, followed by strange accidents that seemed to have no real cause. They'd suffered a couple of injuries when power surged unexpectedly, followed by several more who'd been hit by flying objects...objects that had been thrown by an unknown and unseen hand. At first, they'd believed that students from the nearby University of Edinburgh were playing jokes on them, but as the incidents continued to mount, it seemed impossible that students could have organised them. The site security had been doubled, to no effect.

And then the sightings had started. The workers had seen ghosts – small children, older boys and girls – in the building. At first, they had only been glimpsed out of the corner of their eyes – not unlike the magical world itself – but as the days and weeks had passed on, the ghosts had gotten stronger and more visible. The workers had eventually convinced their superiors to halt the work. Unwilling to miss a chance to boost their funding, their superiors had leaked the news to the local papers and charged for access to the site.

"So as you can see, the place is haunted," my helpful tour guide concluded. "Fair sends a shiver down your spine, doesn't it?"

I shrugged. Try as I might, using all the tricks I had been taught, I could sense no sign of magic within the building. All ghosts, even the afterimages, left behind some traces of their presence, even if they were unwilling or unable to manifest fully. The only trace of magic I could sense was the faint blur surrounding Master Revels, something that was clearly not part of the building. It was strange...

"Ah, you're not a believer," the guide said. I smiled to myself. Does it count as having faith if someone actually *knows* that ghosts exist? "You should come to the tour this night. We've been allowing people to actually spend the night in the Kirk, where they actually see ghosts and all manner of strange things."

"I'll think about it," I promised him. It was an impressive story, although I had no idea how much of it was actually true. The absence of magic suggested that none of it was true, yet...*something* had clearly happened in the Kirk. Edinburgh's magical field should have infested the building, even if none of the mundane tourists could sense anything. "I just have to work late tonight."

I wandered over to Master Revels and filled him in, quickly. I'd never seen him looking disturbed before, even when we had discovered Mr Pygmalion's handiwork in the museum. He looked as if he'd seen a ghost, which was ironic seeing that ghosts were the last thing we could see here.

"Interesting," he said, when I had finished. "I wonder what it all means."

I looked up, sharply. "Didn't your masters tell you anything, or did they just send you to see what you could sniff out?"

Master Revels smiled. "They never tell me everything," he said, dryly. He looked up sharply before I could say anything. "I know you are there, by the way. Why don't you come out and join the party?"

One of the shadows in the room took on shape and form, disgorging a human magician. None of the mundane humans noticed anything amiss. He was tall, with dark skin, a neatly trimmed goatee and a pair of gold-rimmed glasses. He wore white Islamic robes and a skullcap on his head. Under his arm, instead of a cane, he carried a book.

"I wanted to know what you found," he said, in a lightly-accented voice that suggested that English was not his first language. "I found nothing, you see."

He chuckled and I found myself liking him at once. "It's the ghosts," he said. "The ghosts are all gone."

CHAPTER SIXTEEN

"I fear that I have neglected to perform introductions," Master Revels said, dryly. He'd noticed my puzzlement. "This is Dervish of the Unseen Words of Allah."

Dervish bowed to me, politely. "I always liked your master," he said, seriously. His brown eyes twinkled as he spoke. "Very little gets past him."

I smiled back, thinking hard. Was Dervish his *real* name, or merely an assumed name like Dizzy? "It's good to meet you," I said, sincerely. "You may call me Dizzy."

"A good choice for a name," Dervish assured me. "There are few links to the higher powers or to Allah Himself; the name is nothing, but what you make of it. You have chosen well."

Master Revels smiled, rather dryly. "Returning to the subject at hand," he said, "what do you know about the ghosts disappearing?"

Dervish winked at me. "He hates it when someone else is ahead of him," he said. "I know that this place was so infested with ghosts that even mundane people – those poor innocent mundane people – could sense their presence." He looked over at me for a moment. "Even mundane people can sense ghosts, if the ghosts are powerful and persistent. Ghosts really hate being disturbed, so if they were pulled from their slumber they would have started to try to push the mundane intruders away. Unluckily for them, the mundane people have thick skulls and it takes a lot to get a message into their heads."

"Such as *go away and leave us to sleep*," Master Revels injected, dryly.

"Quite," Dervish agreed. "So there were a vast number of

ghosts here, despite all the mundane world could do, until two days ago. And now they are all gone."

I blinked. "Gone onwards to their great reward?"

"Ghosts do sometimes fade away," Master Revels said. "We don't really know what happens to them. Some believe that they finally complete their mission on Earth and go onwards, others believe that God finally gets tired of them hiding on Earth and removes them...and some believe that they just fade away and disappear completely."

"Allah may be harsh, but he is never unjust," Dervish said, firmly. "We believe that sometimes he grants the ghosts mercy, or allows them to reincarnate in another body and try again. To suggest that a soul can be destroyed is...unpleasant."

"And yet they have all gone," Master Revels said. "The reports on this place warned of the presence of hundreds of ghosts, enough for even the mundane world to notice...and now they are all gone and all of the magic that should have been in this building has gone with them. Do you know anything that can do that?"

"There was an incident in Mecca a few years ago...but that was at Allah's command," Dervish said. He sounded uncomfortable, as if he didn't want to talk about it or even *think* about it. "The ghosts were allowed to reincarnate as a group after condemning themselves to wander the Earth after their deaths. The Merciful One granted it as a special case."

I frowned. "Could that have happened here?"

"I don't know," Dervish admitted. "The circumstances are very different, but this *is* a place of worship and Allah would have been watching over it. It wasn't as if this place was built to show off the wealth and power of men who choose to squander what Allah gave them."

Master Revels shrugged. "If the Higher Powers or even the All-Highest had intervened here, so close to so much of our population, we would have sensed it all across the country," he said. "If an angel had come to carry the souls to Heaven or Hell, we would have sensed it and all of us would have been hiding under our beds until it had departed.

A devil could not have taken their souls without their permission, freely given."

"Unless their life choices condemned them to Hell," Dervish said. I realised, suddenly, that they were old friends and would cheerfully argue for days if they were allowed to do so. "If the devil got impatient and sent one of his servants to collect them..."

"A few hundred years is nothing to those who walk in eternity," Master Revels countered. "He could wait until doomsday for them if necessary."

"Unless he thought they could redeem themselves and escape his grasp," Dervish said. "Or perhaps they were the victims of a spell used to trap their souls here, which finally snapped."

I cleared my throat and both men glanced at me. "You've actually seen angels?"

"Very few people have seen angels and lived to tell the tale," Master Revels said, darkly. "Angels have always given me the creeps."

"An angel makes the most fanatical fanatic look uncertain," Dervish added. "They have nothing but conviction that they are doing the right thing, whatever it is. They are great shining beings of light, Allah's messengers and his soldiers in the war against evil, powerful beyond measure or hope of reason. To look upon an angel in its natural form is to be transmuted to salt, as happened to Lot's wife after the fall of Sodom. It was an angel that destroyed the city and everyone who lived within its walls."

"And another angel that saved Lot and his family from the fires," Master Revels said. "They would have all been saved if she hadn't looked back and seen the angel standing over the city, bathing it in holy cleansing fire. It is not in the nature of an angel to accept excuses. One is either a saint or a sinner, with no room in-between for the vast majority of the human race. To encounter an angel is to risk certain death at its hands."

I closed my eyes. I hadn't been raised in a very religious family and I had never been to Sunday School, but from what little I recalled, angels were benevolent servants of

God. The story they were telling me was different, of angels that were so powerful and dangerous, if only because they *knew* that they were right. I wondered, suddenly, if angels had free will. Did fanatics have free will?

"That's a matter of opinion," Dervish said, when I asked. "Some believe that an angel that learns to think for itself will slide towards evil and fall into Hell. Others believe that the angels know the truth of the universe and serve Allah willingly. Some long time ago, before the Final Messenger of Allah, a man summoned an angel to ask it that very question."

I blinked. "And what happened?"

Dervish gave me a toothy grin. "Did you ever wonder where the Sahara Desert came from?"

Master Revels chuckled. "We're getting off track here," he said. "I found no trace of the ghosts and I assume you found nothing likewise. What does that tell us?"

"That the tourists who are coming here this evening are going to be disappointed," Dervish said. He winked at me when he saw his friend's expression. I wouldn't have teased Master Revels, not with my bottom still aching from last night. Still, it was good to know that Master Revels had outside friends. "They won't see a single ghost here."

I shrugged. I had never been on one of the famous Midnight Tours, but I had heard about them and I suspected that most of the ghosts they saw were actually created by mundane science and trickery. Given time, the tourist company would probably create a whole new legend for the Kirk, even if the real ghosts were all gone. It might even be safer than toying with the first set of ghosts.

"Apart from that, it tells us that someone has managed to destroy the ghosts or to capture them," Master Revels said, firmly. He didn't look as if he was prepared to be distracted any longer. "And, whoever it was, it has nothing to do with Heaven or Hell."

"It seems that way," Dervish agreed. "Fascinating, isn't it?"

I couldn't help myself. "Are you telling me that we're looking for kidnapped ghosts?"

Master Revels grinned. "It looks like it," he agreed. "So, my old friend, what happened at Mecca?"

"It wasn't the same," Dervish said. He stopped, as if he was listening to a voice far away. "If you wish to know, I would feel more comfortable discussing it behind a set of wards. Please will you allow me to share the comforts of my home with you?"

Master Revels glanced at me and then nodded. "We would be honoured," he said. "Besides, Dizzy needs to expand her mind a bit."

Dervish shrugged and led us out of the Kirk, pausing only to pick up a tourist brochure from one of the stalls. Once we were outside, he led us down the street, down towards Edinburgh Central Mosque. It was a strange building, a glimpse of Arabia in the midst of Edinburgh that clearly didn't fit in with the rest of the city. Dervish pressed his lips together and walked towards a bare stone wall. A moment later, as we followed him, the stone parted and allowed us through, revealing a flight of stairs leading down into the mosque's basement. It was no surprise to me that the stairs just kept going down, well below the official levels. We had stepped into another part of the magical world.

"A bunch of infidels put up the money for the mosque," Dervish said, bitterly. I blinked in surprise. I knew very little about Islam, but I couldn't understand why one Muslim would consider other Muslims infidels. I thought that that was reserved for Christians and Jews. "This place wasn't built out of the sincere love of Allah, or even out of a sincere desire to create a place to serve as both community centre and prayer hall, but out of the need to show off their money and bolster their Islamic credentials. If we were allowed to interfere in the mundane world..."

We stepped into a surprisingly large room. There were no tables or chairs, merely a set of cushions on the floor surrounding a sheet of plastic. It looked like a picnic ground and I realised, suddenly, that that was exactly what it was. Dervish waved us both to sit on the cushions and headed off through another door. Silence fell, broken only by the eerie sound of a preacher calling the faithful to prayer.

"Like most religions, Islam takes a very dim view of magic," Master Revels explained. He seemed perfectly at ease on the cushions. I was merely grateful that they weren't hard wooden chairs, ones that would have hurt my rear end. "The mystics who founded the Unseen Words of Allah were often persecuted by their fellow Muslims before they went underground and became part of the Magical World. They maintained their links to secret societies and groups within the Islamic World, but mostly they do nothing more than try to defend it against mystical threats. It's not an easy task. The deserts used to be home to a great many mystical creatures and they're waking up."

I nodded, looking around the room. There was a painting on one wall that caught my eye, so I stood up and looked at it. It showed a man wearing Muslim clothes – with a very long beard and holding a bottle in his hand – confronting a blue-brown creature with flaming eyes. I had seen something like it before, but not in the magical world. It was very like the Genie from *Aladdin*, yet it looked far darker and unpleasant, with long claws and very nasty eyes. The caption at the bottom was in Arabic. I couldn't read it at all.

"That's one of the most famous paintings in the magical world," a voice said, behind me. I turned to see a young girl, standing just behind me. I couldn't understand how she had crept up on me until I realised that she was barefoot. Her feet had made no sound at all on the carpet. "The painting is called *The Confrontation of King Solomon, Beloved of Allah, with the Lord of the Jinn*. According to legend, King Solomon was charged by Allah to capture the powerful Jinn – what you would call Genies – and imprison them in various magical containers. Once they were bound, the spells holding them prisoner charged them to perform three wishes for whoever released them before they could go free – and, as long as the third wish was always for the Jinn to return to the lamp, it worked perfectly."

She smiled. It was a pleasant open smile. "And sometimes the person who released the prisoner was not smart enough to order the genie to return to its prison," she added. "The genie broke free and wreaked havoc over the world. They have no sense of human morality to curb their antics. Or so legend has it."

"It's not legend, but simple fact" Dervish said, as he re-entered the room. A tray was floating in front of him, hovering over to the plastic sheet. I felt my mouth start to water as I smelled the curry and rice. "This is my daughter, Jewel of My Heart."

I blinked at the name, and then understood. They wouldn't want to share her real name with anyone, not even his friends. "I am pleased to meet you," I said, formally. "You may call me Dizzy."

"If you want to see something really special," Jewel of My Heart said, "look over there."

I followed her pointing finger. There was something there, yet it was cloaked behind an unusually powerful glamour-spell. I felt myself walking towards it, staring into the haze...and suddenly it snapped in front of me. There was a sword, its blade plunged within a cube of black rock, just waiting for someone to reach out and draw it from the stone. My hand crept forward before I realised that I was not worthy. I couldn't even touch the hilt.

"That sword belongs to all of us," Dervish said, quietly. "According to legend, Allah gave it to humanity, promising us that whenever it was truly needed, it could be drawn from the stone. It is powerful enough to destroy one of the Great Powers, if used in Allah's service. The last time it was used, many years ago, it destroyed a devil some fool had unleashed upon the world. And then, once it was returned to the stone, it was brought to Edinburgh. The last person to use the sword was granted a vision, warning him that the sword would be needed here."

"The legend states that the last task of whoever holds the sword is to put it in place for his or her successor," Master Revels said, as he beckoned me back to the cushions. "Whatever the sword is needed for, it will be needed in Edinburgh, something that has caused a great many sleepless nights among people here. The person who carried the sword hasn't always succeeded in saving the world or even saving themselves."

I blinked. "But the world is still here," I pointed out. "Why...?"

"You can look up the legends later," Dervish promised me. He waved a hand towards the bowls of curry. "Please, eat; it is given freely and without obligation."

The curry tasted great, I decided, after two bites. The chicken was nicely spiced, with the rice cooling it down just enough to make it palatable. Dervish took several bites of his own curry and then leaned back, looking up at the ceiling. I realised that he really didn't want to talk about whatever had happened in Mecca, even though it was important. Master Revels didn't press him. He just ate his curry and waited, so I did the same. I couldn't help glancing back towards the painting though. Was it my imagination, or was the Jinn changing position every time I looked?

"A decade ago, a number of girls died in Mecca," Dervish said, finally. I realised, finally, what he was battling with. He was *ashamed*. "Because of the circumstances of their death, they renounced Islam and cursed Allah in their last moments. They earned themselves a sentence to Hell, but Allah, the Most Merciful, allowed them to remain on Earth as ghosts. They haunted the city for years before He finally relented and allowed them to reincarnate in new bodies. He punished their tormentors most thoroughly."

I sensed, more than heard, part of his underlying emotions as he spoke on. He was ashamed of what had happened, ashamed...just as I had been ashamed when I'd seen the slaves. It might even have been worse for him because he hadn't done anything to try to save the girls while they were still alive. Even if he hadn't been there at the time, he still felt guilty and shamed of his failure. It wasn't his failure, yet...I knew exactly how he felt.

"The same could have happened to the ghosts at the Kirk," he added. "They could have been taken from their resting place and reincarnated."

"Perhaps," Master Revels said. "If so..."

"This isn't the place to seek answers for them, I suspect," Dervish admitted. He winked at Master Revels. "I just wanted to invite you for lunch."

"For which we are grateful," Master Revels assured him. I finished my curry and put the bowl aside. "If we need further assistance…"

"You are welcome to call on me," Dervish said, seriously. He stood up and I realised that the meal was over. "If someone is actually kidnapping ghosts…well, there's no reason why they couldn't use something like a Jinn bottle, is there?"

He waved a hand towards the painting. "And if they are," he added, "you know where you have to go look."

"Holy Corner," Master Revels agreed. He held out a hand and Dervish shook it firmly, before bowing to me. "If you will open the door for us…"

"Of course," Dervish said. "May Allah go with you."

CHAPTER SEVENTEEN

"That was a waste of time," I said, once we had started to walk back towards the Meadows. I felt warm because of the curry, but otherwise I felt as if we had wasted an hour. "Why didn't he tell us that he knew nothing right from the start?"

Master Revels smiled, humourlessly, and smacked my bottom. It wasn't a particularly hard smack, but it hurt my bruised behind and I yelped. "A word of advice," he said. "No one in the magical world ever tells everything they know about anything. Finding our friend there was a lucky break, the more so because he was willing to help us eliminate possibilities and steer us towards a possible suspect."

I rubbed my behind angrily. "What kind of suspect is Holy Corner?" I demanded. "Come to think of it, why did your masters want you to investigate in the first place? Why are we even bothering to stick our noses into this business if we're not going to do anything about it?"

Master Revels sighed. "My superiors – *our* superiors – are always interested in new and unusual forms of magic," he said. "They maintain their supremacy by always being in control of new magic, or at least understanding it completely. It wouldn't do to have some young whippersnapper develop a whole new form of magic and use it to replace one or all of them, would it?"

He tapped me firmly on the shoulder. "They exist to maintain the status quo, Dizzy," he reminded me. "Anything that threatens the stability of the magical world, regardless of if it seems good or bad is a possible threat. It has to be investigated by us. Does that make sense?"

I nodded, reluctantly. "And besides, you did have lunch and got to see a different aspect of the magical world," he added, dryly. "Did you like studying the painting?"

It was, I realised, a more pointed question. "The genie was moving in the picture," I said. I was sure of it now. Master Revels wouldn't have brought it up unless the painting was important, somehow. "That painting is one of the genie traps, isn't it?"

"So we have been told," Master Revels said. "The Unseen Words of Allah are the heirs to King Solomon and his magic, Dizzy. They know things that we have forgotten, if we ever knew them in the first place. Displaying the painting like that is a way of reminding the rest of the world that they have secrets and a rather less than subtle threat. A genie is a very dangerous enemy."

I smiled. "Are they worse than the Elves?"

"They grant wishes," Master Revels said. "They grant *any* wishes, any at all, which is why they are so dangerous. If I had one, I could wish for vast magical power, or to become one of the Great Powers, or to destroy the magical world...oh yes, the genies are feared and hated because of their power. And when one manages to break free...they have no sense of anything, but hatred for the human race that dared to imprison them. A very long time ago, back when Atlantis was a thriving city, one broke loose and destroyed the city in a single night."

"Oh," I said. I remembered watching all three of the *Aladdin* movies. The friendly blue genie had made the street rat a prince, before his lamp had fallen into the hands of the evil villain. The genie had turned him into the most powerful sorcerer in the world and then transported the palace to the top of a mountain. "How many genies are left in the world?"

"Very few, for which we are all delighted," Master Revels said. "There are occasionally legends of genie lamps or bottles being discovered and causing havoc before vanishing again, but no one has seen a genie for a long time. The one in the painting may be the only one left in the human world."

He sighed. "Dervish, for all of his faith and devotion to Allah, is cut off from the mainstream of Islam," he added. "The Unseen Words must serve and never be appreciated. The price he paid for his power is far greater than anything *we* ever paid. You should pity him."

We walked the rest of the way in silence, allowing me a chance to concentrate on the healing disciplines. The pain in my rear end was fading away, although I still felt bruised and I was certain that it would be a very poor idea to sit down on anything hard. Master Revels said nothing as we left the Meadows and walked back onto the main road, heading down towards Holy Corner. Like so many other places in Edinburgh, it glowed so brightly with magic that I couldn't understand how the mundane world couldn't see it. It was far brighter than many other buildings.

Holy Corner had picked up the nickname because it was a crossroads with a church at each corner. One of them I knew from a famous book sale that took place every year, but the others were new to me. It wasn't the visible churches that held my attention, though; it was the glowing ghostly church in the centre of the crossroads. It seemed to shimmer, right on the edge of visibility, seemingly unconcerned about the cars passing *through* it as their drivers drove up to Church Hill. Master Revels took my hand as the cars slowed to a halt, muttered a charm into the air and led me forward. The church suddenly became clear – the cars took on ghostly forms – and we stepped into the doorway. Inside, the noise of the cars suddenly vanished. It was the most spiritual place I had ever entered.

"This place is supposed to have been built by Deacon Brodie, one of Edinburgh's more colourful characters, although others say that it is actually far older and dates all the way back to the early Christians," Master Revels said, as the doors closed behind us. "It is maintained here by the faith of the monks who run it, creating a place for true faith to flourish in the magical world."

I looked up as an elderly man appeared in front of us. He wore a simple brown monk's dress and a heavy cross, which seemed to pull him into a permanent stoop. His eyes were dark and very knowing, as if he'd seen all the sins of the world and forgiven them.

"I bid you welcome in the name of Christ our Lord," he said. His voice was accented, an accent that would have been seductive in other places. Here, it just seemed to fade away in the silence. "We welcome you to the Silent Cathedral of Holy Corner. How may we be of service to you?"

"There were ghosts in the Tron Kirk that have vanished," Master Revels said. His voice seemed pale and weak compared to the silence. It seemed to smother all sound within the building. My ears felt weird, as if the silence was pressing down on us all. "I am charged with investigating them for..."

"Your masters," the monk said. He bowed, slowly. "You do realise that we have little to do with your masters?"

"Our interests are one in this matter," Master Revels countered. He bowed himself, equally slowly. "We can share information without compromising ourselves."

"Says the unbeliever," a new voice said. The newcomer wore purple robes and a golden mask that covered his face, hiding him from the world. His eyes seemed to focus on me before moving back to Master Revels. I shivered. There was something inhuman in that gaze, something that chilled me to the bone. "We of the Order do not wish to deal with those of magic."

"And yet you are here, within the magical world, because you feel that you are called to the duty," Master Revels said. He looked at me. "Officially, the Church – the Vatican – doesn't believe in demons and magic, at least not in the literal sense. Some of the Orders know better and regard themselves as charged to fight for Christ in the magical world. It is a very dangerous place to stand. Raw faith can be turned against anyone by someone sufficiently devious to do so."

He shrugged. "There are many secrets in the Vatican Library, Dizzy," he added, "and very few of them have anything to do with any form of Christianity you'd recognise. The secret scrolls of Saint Jude, Patron Saint of Lost Causes;

the true story behind how Christianity came to these islands; the secret records of deals made with the Great Powers, trading on God's name to bind the Great Powers to remove themselves into the magical world; hidden arts and spells that were once used by the Popes to try to secure their position..."

"Enough," the newcomer said. I realised that Master Revels had been trying to irritate him. It had clearly worked. "We have to uphold the edicts laid down by His Holiness in Secret Council."

"The ghosts were Christian ghosts," I said, suddenly. I wasn't sure what had made me say that, but it was true. "Don't you have a duty to find out what happened to them?"

There was a long pause. "We have a ministry to the ghosts inhabiting Edinburgh in the hopes that they can be redeemed from their suffering and pointed towards Heaven," the first monk said. "The ghosts that have drawn your attention are not the first to have vanished."

Master Revels gave me a sidelong look and then looked up at the masked monk. "Why are you not investigating further?"

"We examined the location of the first missing ghost," the masked monk said. "We found traces of magic, Elfish magic. The ghost was not destroyed, or taken, by any art known to us. They were taken by the Elves."

I felt my eyes go wide. "We are unable to follow them into the Elfish Kingdoms," the masked monk added. "Your masters may not allow you to follow them yourselves. We believe that the Elves have been snatching many ghosts over the past few months. How long has it taken for this to come to your attention?"

Master Revels ignored the dig at him. "Did you sell any of your artefacts to the Elves?"

"No," the masked monk said. "The Elves are no friends to humanity. Soulless tricksters; godless immortals...they have no place within our world. We are forbidden any intercourse with them." He looked at the other monk. "You may show them the artefacts and then they must leave."

He turned and vanished back into the inner recesses of the church. The first monk nodded after him and turned, leading us into a side chamber where there were tables strewn with various wooden artefacts. He chattered happily to us about the church's duty to confront the more dangerous aspects of the supernatural world, even though the vast majority of the mundane world didn't believe in magic or ghosts any longer. The Silent Order had freedom to go wherever they needed to go to confront devils and other malign entities. It was a dangerous duty.

"Don't ever walk into a mental hospital without heavy protection," he said, indicating a line of crosses and small containers that – I realised – were intended to capture and hold demons. "If you have the sight, you'll see the demons at their backs, urging them onwards to commit more and more atrocities. Hag-ridden, we call them; men and women who no longer have minds of their own or any sense of right or wrong. We try to trap the demons, but demons are clever and very wary of being trapped."

I frowned. "What do you do when you capture them?"

"We seal the container and then put them in a vat of holy water," the monk said. He didn't smile at the thought. "No one with impure intent can reach into the water to recover the containers, while contact with the water would be enough to destroy the demons completely."

Master Revels shrugged. "Could you adapt a demon trap to capture a ghost?"

The monk considered it. "It would be possible, I suppose," he agreed. "The demons provide most of the power to trap themselves, while ghosts cannot really be used as a source of power, so the trap would have to be adapted...yes, in theory it could be done. I've never heard of anyone actually doing it."

"I see," Master Revels said. "Can we borrow a couple of traps for experiments?"

"If you wish," the monk said. He passed Master Revels a pair of jars. They looked like sealed jam jars to me, although I could sense the spells crawling around them and waiting for their victim. If they fed off demonic power and used it to keep the demon imprisoned, the only way out would be for the demon to exhaust all of its power, which would destroy it completely. Or so we believed. At least they never came back, which was the important matter. "Just be careful with them. You can't get the wood these days."

He lifted his hand, there was a blinding flash of light and we found ourselves standing back in the mundane world. Master Revels checked the two jars quickly and then smiled at me, leading me back towards the castle. I hoped that we were going home. I wanted to rest and inspect my wounds in the mirror.

"Elves," he said, thoughtfully. "Why would elves want to kidnap ghosts?"

I looked up at him. "We could always ask...?"

"Don't ask that half-elf anything to do with your work for me," Master Revels snapped. I realised that, for some reason, it was a line he was unwilling to cross. I felt a twinge from my rear end and decided not to push it. At least I hadn't been forbidden to see him ever again. "You have to learn to keep secrets if you live in this world."

He tossed one of the jars in the air and caught it neatly. "Why *would* the Elves kidnap ghosts?" he repeated. "There's no power in them, no real way of tormenting them worse than they torment themselves and very little fun in it. Even if they want to experiment, they normally prefer to experiment on living humans or animals. Why would they bother with ghosts?"

I frowned suddenly, remembering something from a fairy tale I'd read back in childhood. "Can an Elf even enter a church?"

"Only if they were invited in, just like vampires," Master Revels said. "Back before the Elves left the human world, the only safe places from them and their malice were the churches and the handful of Places of Power in the world. Some people believe that God granted them an exception so they wouldn't be seduced into worshipping the Elves instead, while others believe that Elves are inherently evil and couldn't enter a church without permission from God

Himself. There's no way to know."

"Can't you ask them?"

Master Revels snorted. "People who ask questions of Elves on matters they consider sensitive are lucky if they *only* get killed in a terrifying manner," he said. "The Elves will not answer questions like that, Dizzy. Don't even think about it."

He shook his head. "But we will have to walk into the Elfish Kingdoms to ask them about the ghosts," he added. "The deals they struck with the Thirteen should allow us to do that."

We walked on for nearly an hour before we finally reached home. "You go inside, wash yourself and let Fiona know what is going on," Master Revels said. "I have to go talk to my superiors and then see if they will let us investigate further."

I pushed open the door and blinked as I saw the letter on the floor. It was addressed to me and was – I found myself laughing as I puzzled out the name – from Cardonel. It thanked me for a lovely evening and invited me out again in three days, hopefully for less exciting diversions. At the bottom was an elaborately scrawled, and charmed, signature that I could use to get in touch with him. The magical world wasn't a place for mobile phones.

Fiona fluttered down to greet me as I entered the main body of the house. "He asked me out again," I said, unable to conceal my delight. After everything that had happened that night, I would have forgiven him if he had never wanted to see me again, although I doubted that anyone would have caned him for his role in the great escape. "He likes me!"

"If you go," Fiona advised, "try not to get into trouble this time."

I laughed as I ran upstairs to my room and lifted my dress. The marks had faded, although I could still make out the lines on my buttocks where the cane had struck. I still didn't dare wear underpants, but at least I could get a proper wash and shower before redressing and walking downstairs for a mug of tea. I used the signature to call Cardonel and told him that I would be delighted to meet him and the gang again, if they would have me. The chat should have taken five minutes, yet somehow it ended up taking over an hour. Cardonel kept me laughing until Master Revels returned home.

"I have good news and bad news," he announced, once he'd gotten himself a cup of tea and sat down by the fire. "The good news is that we're going into the Elfish Kingdoms. The bad news is that we're going into the Elfish Kingdoms."

He shrugged. "Listen very carefully," he added. "A single mistake there could mean certain death, or worse. It won't be a simple caning this time."

CHAPTER EIGHTEEN

"I want you to be clear on one point," Master Revels said, the following morning. "While we're on the Fairy Roads and in the Elfish Kingdom, you follow the rules I told you. Do you understand me?"

I nodded, mutely. My initial excitement at visiting another world, even the one belonging to the Elves, had faded overnight. I'd read a handful of books on the Elves and I knew that, even if we followed all the Rules, the visit could still go horribly wrong. The Elves made the touchiest human culture look weak and permissive. Even sleep hadn't come easily and I'd had to resort to a Dreamless Sleep potion, which had knocked me out for several hours. Fiona had made a number of sarcastic comments over breakfast, reminding me that using potions to sleep was dangerous. Master Revels hadn't commented.

"Good," he said. He stood up and picked up his hat and coat. He'd ordered me to dress in my best, the finest clothes in the wardrobe I had inherited. I felt like a cross between a princess and a whore, even though I'd lost my breath when I looked at myself in the mirror. The Elves would probably not appreciate it, but I certainly did. The golden dress, the pair of glass slippers and the jewels hanging around my neck produced a stunning effect. I would never have dared to wear such an outfit in the mundane world. It was a walking invitation to a mugger. "Follow me."

I'd expected him to lead me out of the door and onto the streets, but instead he led me downstairs and through a series of corridors I had never explored. The strange interior dimensions of the house - Master Revels had never explained just how large it was, or who had created it in the first place – concealed hundreds of miles of rooms and storage space, some holding artefacts and books that were long forgotten. I promised myself that when I succeeded him and the house was mine, I would map it out in my head, if that were possible. It sometimes seemed to me that the dimensions altered themselves when no one was looking. I had no idea how Master Revels and Fiona navigated themselves so perfectly. One could live in the house and never come out into the rest of the world, both worlds.

We passed through a portcullis and then a secured trapdoor, dropping down further into the lower dimensions, if they *were* the lower dimensions. I had a hazy idea that the house had been built *into* the magical world, with the building in the mundane world merely the gateway to the *real* building. Master Revels had promised to teach me how to construct my own buildings one day, but that required thought and careful planning. A single mistake could prove disastrous. He'd told me, probably remembering when I'd freed the slaves, about a group of magical thieves who had extended their own buildings so that they intersected the locations of other buildings, bypassing the wards in a single moment. After that, the magical world's denizens had grown a great deal touchier about several buildings occupying the same space and time.

Master Revels stopped in front of a large wooden door and pressed his hand against the wood. It was absolutely *crawling* with magical spells, each one designed to keep out intruders and woven together in a manner that seemed to defy analysis. I reached out with my senses and picked up wards, change spells, freeze spells, time stops, death spells and other unpleasant surprises. Unpicking them all would be impossible, at least for me. I doubted that even one of the Great Powers could have done it quickly. Master Revels concentrated, working his magic, and the security measures started to unlock. He removed his hand and stepped back, waiting for them to finish unlocking. I realised, suddenly, that if someone pressed the spells beyond a certain point, they bit anyway. They had to unlock, once the process was started, on their own.

"Dizzy," Master Revels said, calmly. "It isn't too late to turn back."

I was tempted to flee back to Fiona and safety, but I shook my head. "No, thank you," I said, through a suddenly dry mouth. "I'll stay with you."

Master Revels smiled. "Brave girl," he said, and shook his head. "You might be very foolish at times, but you are certainly brave."

I flushed. "Thank you, sir," I said, and meant it. "I'd still have to go one day, wouldn't I?"

"True," Master Revels agreed. He placed a hand on my shoulder. "This door isn't part of the building, Dizzy. It's actually something far older. Just because it looks like a wooden door to us doesn't mean that that is what it *is*; it takes on a form that we would understand. It is probably the single most dangerous thing in this area."

I nodded. "So I want you to understand something else," he added. "You *don't* come and play with it while I'm not around. It's far too dangerous to allow anyone to tinker with it without permission. If you do, I will cane you hard and then dismiss you from my service. There is a point where courage becomes foolishness. Do you understand me?"

"Yes, sir," I said, feeling my throat constrict. Naturally, I was curious, but in the magical world curiosity often killed the cat, while satisfaction didn't always bring it back. Besides, I didn't want another caning, not then and not ever. "How did it get here if it isn't part of the building?"

"No one knows," Master Revels admitted. "There are stories that suggest that one of the Elfish Kings brought it here and gave it to the original creators of this building, allowing them access to the Fairy Roads in exchange for services rendered. There are other stories that suggest that the human-born King of Faerie placed it here so that he could return to the human world without running afoul of the physical laws that govern contact between the human and faerie worlds. No one really knows for sure."

The spells had finished unlocking and the door stood ajar. Master Revels held up a hand to stop me from walking in and waved his other hand at the door, tracing out a complicated pattern in the air. The door opened slowly, leaving me to realise that there was a security spell left on the golden handle, just waiting for some ignorant fool to come along and try to open the door. It was a final trick intended to snare anyone good enough to unlock the outside spells. It was completely unfamiliar and I couldn't imagine what it would do to anyone who triggered it.

"Now we step inside," Master Revels said, flatly. I followed him into a small room. Standing at the end, positioned neatly on the stone wall, was a mirror, one large enough to reflect my entire body. I found myself puzzled, even when I realised that there were *two* mirrors, set up facing each other. The effect created an illusion of two corridors stretching away to infinity. It took me a moment to realise that it was no illusion. Master Revels took my hand and led me over to the mirrors, positioning us between them. The world seemed to shimmer...

...And then we were standing on the opposite side of the mirrors. I felt myself swoon as my senses tried to cope with the new dimension. There were endless stone corridors, all decorated in an eerie gothic fashion, stretching away to infinity and beyond. I sensed strange figures walking along the stone floors, humans and non-humans and creatures that could never be mistaken for humans. It all poured into my brain and I staggered, falling against Master Revels as he caught me and held me gently until I recovered. Time itself seemed to be breaking down around me and I caught sight of my past, present and future. I was a young girl, riding a pony at the travelling fair; I was learning from one of the greatest magicians in the world; I was wearing sorcerer's robes and preparing for a duel...all at the same time.

I struggled to focus my mind, concentrating on the here and now. Everything seemed to slide alarmingly as it fell out of focus – I had the bizarre feeling that I had fallen *into* my body from a great height – and then the world stabilised around me. I was clutching Master Revels for dear life, hard enough to bruise him, as we stood together in the stone corridor. Embarrassed, I let go of him and stumbled backwards. I still felt as if I was drunk, but at least I could stand upright without collapsing.

"Don't worry," Master Revels said, as he rubbed his arms where I'd held him. I didn't want to know how badly I might have bruised him. "It hits everyone that way the first time."

I stared. "Why didn't you warn me?"

"You have to learn to adapt on your own," Master Revels said, flatly. "If I had tried to tell you what to expect, it would just have hit you worse. Quite a few people have stepped through the mirror into a looking glass world and discovered that their minds couldn't cope with it at all."

He took my hand and gently squeezed it. "Don't worry," he told me. "You're doing fine."

I allowed him to lead me through the strange stone corridors, unable to believe my eyes. It felt as if we were walking through endless underground catacombs in perfect silence, like some of the underground passages in Scotland's castles. The silence rapidly became oppressive, yet nothing we said seemed to echo back to us. The stone walls were decorated with carvings and strange etchings that seemed to change every time I looked at them. They started out as fairly mundane images, yet they rapidly became either disturbing or incomprehensible. I couldn't make head or tail of them.

There was one etching that started out as a scene from history, a group of humans bowing down in front of an elf. I assumed it was an elf, although it looked more like Mr Spock with more exaggerated pointy ears. It changed as I watched, becoming a scene where the humans were enslaved by the elf and then tortured to death, before disintegrating into total incomprehensibility. It became an image of a sinister octopus-like creature with staring eyes and a mouth filled with sharp teeth. I shuddered and looked away, towards the images on the other side. They were no better.

As I followed them, they showed a brother and sister who had somehow found their way onto the Fairy Roads and reached one of the Elfish Kingdoms. They were tricked by the Queen and pushed into eating something, becoming trapped in the Fairy Court. The Queen enjoyed their company for a time – there was no way to judge timescale in the images – and then grew tired of them, handing them over to the lesser members of their court to use for experiments. The boy was warped into a horrible monster; the girl was made beautiful, so beautiful that to look on her was to love her, yet given a sociopathic personality, one that drove her to use her charms for evil. The Elves had released them back into the mundane world and laughed to watch the chaos. It had kept them amused for weeks.

I shivered as a cold wind blew down the stone corridors. We had reached an arch that led to a widening stone chamber...and a bridge over a dark river that flowed silently onwards to an unseen destination. I clutched Master Revels' hand tightly as I took in the bridge. It was tiny, barely large enough to allow a single person to cross at a time. Down on the river, I caught sight of a hooded figure pushing a boat along, with a handful of passengers. I couldn't make out the passengers' faces, but they didn't seem human. There was something so sad about the scene that I felt tears trickling down my cheeks. I watched the boat vanish into the distance and looked up at Master Revels. He was frowning.

"They've changed it again," he said, grimly. I looked up at him in surprise. It should have occurred to me that the Fairy Roads shifted as often as other constructions in the magical world. There was something timeless about them, but they still moved. "I'm going to cross the bridge first. Once I am at the far end, you can follow me, carefully. If you fall into the water, you will never be seen again."

I nodded, feeling my body tremble. I had never been scared of heights before, yet the more I looked, the further the fall seemed...and then there was the eerie dark water below. I stared down at the river, hoping to see fish or even a riverbed, but there was nothing apart from the darkness. I found myself wondering if it was even water. It might have been something else, something far stranger. Master Revels gave me a quick hug and started to cross the bridge.

It was terrifying to watch him moving, step by step, into the distance. I didn't want to watch and yet I couldn't take my eyes off him. The bridge seemed to get longer and longer, thinner and thinner, until it looked almost as if he were walking a tightrope. I had a sudden overwhelming urge to run to the toilet, as if I hadn't been for hours, or maybe just to run. If I ran back into the corridors...I turned to look. Not entirely to my surprise, the corridors were gone. There was just a stone wall. The only way out was to cross the bridge. I turned back and bit down a word that would have shocked my mother. I was now standing on a cliff face, with barely any room to move. The bridge seemed thinner than ever.

Master Revels had finally reached the far end and I took comfort from that. He waved at me and I stepped forward, reaching the start of the bridge. My body locked up and refused to go any further. It wasn't a spell of any kind, merely outright terror. I told myself that I could do it, but my body refused to listen. I glanced to the side and saw that my space had been reduced, again. Soon enough, I would find myself falling to my death if I didn't move now. It took everything I had, but I stepped onto the bridge and started to walk. It seemed to twitch and bend under my footsteps, as if it wanted to throw me off. I felt a wave of dizziness and looked down, towards the waters. The sight made me stumble and I collapsed forward onto the stone bridge. I nearly wet myself. If I'd fallen just a little to the right or the left, I would have fallen into the water.

Somehow, I kept inching forward, step by step. I was crawling along the bridge, feeling the cold brushing against the dress...the dress that was probably ruined already, before the Elves saw it. The stone seemed to seep into me, yet every time I made to stand up, the entire bridge shook. I closed my eyes and kept moving forwards, to the point that I nearly screamed when I bumped into something soft and warm. I had reached the end of the bridge and crawled right into Master Revels. I forgot any sense of dignity and grabbed onto him, holding him tightly.

"Don't worry," Master Revels said, as he held me. "You made it."

There was a dull rumble from behind us. I turned, just in

time to see the bridge disintegrate and fall into the water below. I almost fainted. If I'd stayed on the bridge for any longer, I would have fallen with it...Master Revels turned me back and pointed me towards another arch at the edge of the stone wall. This one was glowing with life.

"The Gateway to the Land under the Hill," Master Revels said. He waved a hand at my dress. I felt magic shimmering over me and looked down to see that the dress was mended. "Do you remember the rules?" I nodded. "Come on, then. We have to get it over with."

The moment we stepped through the arch, we found ourselves standing on a grassy knoll. I glanced behind me and discovered that the arch had already vanished. In front of us, there was a road leading onwards into the distance. Master Revels, still holding my hand, started to walk down the road and I followed him. One of the rules of visiting the Elfish Kingdoms was never to step off the road. The Elves would delight in making me their prey if I fell into that trap. I looked into the distance and saw a band of Elves, riding massive horse-like creatures, going out hunting. I wondered, suddenly, what they hunted in their own dimension.

I didn't dare ask as the universe seemed to shift and change around us. We found ourselves in the middle of a dining hall, with thousands of Elves gorging themselves on food and drink, served by humans with suffering eyes. My nose twitched as the aromas awakened hunger in me, but I forced myself to ignore the smells. Eating Elfish food, unless it was given freely and without obligation, was another way to get trapped within their kingdom. There were too many stories about men and women who had eaten their food and then been returned home, to discover that hundreds of years had passed.

The room shifted again and we found ourselves in a Throne Room. It was a remarkable room, but I couldn't see anything apart from the person on the Throne. She just pulled everyone's eyes towards her.

I was looking directly at the Queen of the Elves.

CHAPTER NINETEEN

She was beautiful.

She was terrifying.

She sat on a golden throne and stared down at us imperiously. I couldn't take my eyes off her. She was naked, but there was no sense of vulnerability around her. Long flame-red hair cascaded down her back and over her breasts, teasing anyone looking at her with the promise of seduction. I couldn't help looking between her legs and I winced. There was no vagina or pubic hair, just smooth skin. Her proportions were perfect, yet inhuman. I found myself wondering what the celebrities, the ones who pushed themselves until they had the most perfect bodies in the world, would make of her. She was what they wanted to be.

It was her eyes, though, that caught my attention. They were cold and dark, utterly inhuman. There was something about them that sent a chill down my spine. They seemed to suggest that I was nothing; that I only existed to please the Queen and if I failed to please the Queen, the results would not be good. The Queen had no doubts about her superiority – no, her supremacy – and her absolute right to do as she pleased. After I looked into her eyes, I knew that I would never be seduced by her body, or by the air of glamour that seemed to shimmer around her. I knew what she was.

Even so, her presence was overwhelming. I wanted to kneel in front of her; I wanted to run for my life. Somehow, I remained still. I knew that, deep inside, she was laughing at the humans who had entered her world. We provided an immortal and jaded race with amusement and that was all that mattered to them.

The other elves pressed in around her. They were magnificent in their own way, yet they were far less human than the Queen, with odd bodies that seemed to move in odd directions. Their eyes were piercing, digging into me as if they could see right into my very soul; their faces were twisted into odd leers, as if they were looking forward to my pain and humiliation. I remembered the painful days when the boys at school had matured and suddenly found themselves confronted with desirable girls and shivered. The elves were looking at me in the same way, yet there was a cruelty about their gaze that left me shivering deep inside. I held myself up by force of will, somehow. Showing weakness in front of the Elves would be disastrous.

Behind the elves, there were the human slaves. They were naked, male and female alike, with suffering eyes and hopeless faces. I recalled the slaves I had freed and knew that they, abused as they had been, were far better off than the prisoners of the elves. They had all come into the elfish dimension, broken one of the rules and found themselves prisoners, compelled to serve for a very long time. The elves didn't care if humans didn't know their rules, or didn't mean to break their rules; the people who broke the rules were always enslaved.

I recalled what Master Revels had said and shivered. They might look human, but the elves were composed of pure magic. The laws governing magic governed them...and creating any form of obligation, deliberately or accidentally, had to be balanced or punished. I had been warned that the elves might offer me a gift. Unless it was given freely, or without obligation, I dared not accept it. They might use it as an excuse to enslave me.

The Queen switched her gaze to Master Revels, as if she had seen me and was unimpressed. "You have entered through the Lost Gate," she said. Her voice was chilling, both remarkably seductive and utterly inhuman. The elves fell silent and clustered in around her. They seemed less human with every second. "You come before us under the Compact. Do you serve the Thirteen Who Rule?"

"I do," Master Revels said. His voice seemed weaker in

the Elfish Kingdom, but somehow it seemed warm and welcoming. "They send me here to ask you a question."

"The Compact does not reflect well on questions," the Queen observed. Her mouth twitched into a cruel smile. Just for a second, I saw razor-sharp teeth hidden under her full lips. "You trespass where you are not wanted."

"The Compact allows us to ask questions about Elfish activities in our world," Master Revels countered. The Queen's voice had chilled me, yet he seemed unflustered. "The Thirteen seek their answers from those who can give it to them."

The Queen looked down at him, her dark eyes boring into his. I found myself wondering just what was happening and why. There had been no mention of a Compact between the Thirteen and the elves, unless it had been mentioned and I hadn't realised what it was talking about. The books hadn't been too specific about what the elves had done when they'd walked away from the mundane world and entered their own pocket dimension, one they controlled absolutely. Perhaps the Compact referred to something older than the split between the magical and mundane worlds.

"By the terms of the Compact, we may not answer unless there is sufficient payment," the Queen said. A dull rustle of amusement ran through the elves. "A payment will buy you one answer, Servant of the Thirteen. What payment do you offer us?"

"I offer myself to face the Ordeal," Master Revels said, firmly. He stepped forward, closer to the throne. "I will give you hours of amusement, provided only that you return us to the mortal world alive and unharmed, at the moment we left."

I stared at him. I hadn't expected him to offer himself to them. I'd read about the Ordeal in the books, although none of them had gone into details, perhaps because the authors hadn't known any details – or because they'd been too scared to write them down. The elves would test someone, somehow, and if they failed the elves would enjoy their suffering as they died. I wanted to protest, to offer to go in his place, but the words froze in my mouth. He had warned me to say nothing unless I was asked a direct question.

The Queen seemed to sense it. Her eyes bored into mine, forcing me down onto my knees. "And your apprentice wishes to go in your place," she said. I realised suddenly that the Queen could read minds and tried to block out the other thoughts that threatened to betray me. "She is a girl who daunted the Mistress of the Island, Circe herself. She will provide us with many hours of amusement and then we will answer your question. We swear it upon our Royal Name."

Master Revels looked horrified. I realised that he hadn't intended for me to take the Ordeal. He stepped forward, ignoring the protocol, and caught my hand. "Dizzy," he said sharply, "you don't have to do this."

The Queen laughed, a harsh inhuman sound, and her Court echoed her. "You wish the answer to your question?" she asked. "We have named our price. Your apprentice will face the Ordeal."

I looked at him and nodded. "I accept," I said. I had no idea what I was getting into, but I couldn't help thinking of the disappearing ghosts. I had to do whatever it took to find out what had happened to them. "I'll be fine."

"So shall it be," the Queen announced. Her body *twisted* suddenly, as if it was suddenly so much more than human, and then the world went away in a flare of bright light. "Welcome to the Ordeal, fool!"

I found myself standing in absolute inky blackness. I couldn't even feel something under my feet. I thought of a basic illumination spell and ran through it in my head, but nothing happened, not even the sense of magic working around me. The darkness seemed somehow claustrophobic. Anyone could be out there, waiting for me. I risked stepping forward and nearly lost my balance. I was standing in a room, I realised suddenly, with countless bottomless pits. In the darkness, I could stumble and fall to my death at any moment. I had to stay still.

It reminded me of reading about sensory deprivation in a thriller novel sometime ago, but it didn't seem very dangerous. Or perhaps that was the point. Given time, I would go mad in the darkness, or whatever was holding me up would collapse and I would plunge to my death. I had the sudden absurd feeling that countless elves were watching and sniggering at my discomfort and then it occurred to me that it wasn't such an absurd thought. The elves would drain every morsel of my suffering and probably record it for replaying when they were bored.

A light shone through the darkness, revealing a humanoid figure walking towards me. I strained my eyes and saw my mother, her cold eyes fixed on me. I felt a twinge of guilt flourishing within me, for it had been years since I had spoken to my mother. She had ordered me out of her life, yet...she was still my mother. I could have gone back to her, just to reassure her that I was alive and well. I had chosen, instead, to run into the magical world and not look back.

"You failed me," my mother said. Her voice seemed to cut into my very soul. "You're a worthless piece of trash, a useless piece of shit. You could have made something of your life. You could have been a doctor, or a teacher, or even a scientist. Instead, you threw away everything I gave you and wasted your life. You're a failure and I hate you."

I shivered and shambled backwards. "You're a stupid fucking cunt," another voice said. I turned to see my father standing behind me, as he had been in the handful of photographs I had saved, back when I had hoped that one day my father would save me from a humdrum existence. It was a female dream that, perhaps, I was a princess and my father a king. Absurd, of course; my father had been an abusive husband and a drunkard. When he'd left us, my mother had been delighted, even though she'd been left to raise a child on her own. "I should have washed out your mother's cunt just to prevent you from being born. You were never mine just the child of one of the men she let fuck her in exchange for money. She was never a very good lay. The best of him trickled down her legs, leaving you to be born from the refuse. You were never mine."

"You're lying," my mother shouted. Her voice rang in my ears, her face contorted with rage. "Look at him, Dizzy;

that's your father! How can you be surprised at your shitty life when you came from such poor stock? I could have fucked Bruce Wayne or someone, but no – I had to settle for Prince Fuck-Up! He could never keep a job longer than a week or two because the fucking managers discovered that he kept fucking it all up!"

"Bitch," my father shouted back at her. "You didn't do a good job of raising her, did you? Just look at her, all puffed up because she can recite a handful of spells and thinks that that makes her Wonder Fucking Woman! She's got herself into a trap she cannot escape, thanks to you!"

I found myself on the ground, holding my hands over my heads, but I could hear their words in my head. My father and mother, screaming at each other about how useless I was, how terrible I had been as a child...I wanted to block them out permanently, but there was no escape. Their words dug deep into my soul. A hand caught my arm and yanked me to my feet. I found myself staring into the face of my first boyfriend.

"You were never much of a lay," he sneered. I'd opened my legs for him because I had felt that he was on the verge of leaving me for my then-best friend. Mandy, who was a bitch if ever there was one, had been making eyes at him, so I had allowed him to fuck me one afternoon in his flat. It hadn't been a great experience for me, although he'd seemed happy enough. Virginity was nothing these days. "I pissed inside you and you thought I had come!"

I shuddered, feeling bile rising up in my throat. I had feared that, back when I had first learned about the birds and the bees, a boy would do that. It had been an immature joke, yet it had remained at the back of my mind, hidden away until the Ordeal had dragged it out of my memories. Dave kept attacking me, slicing away at my self-esteem, mocking everything about me. I had been a useless girlfriend, a poor cook, and a worthless bed-mate...it just rolled on and on. He told me that he had been cheating on me, with Mandy, with Tami, with a hundred other girls...and I believed him. There had been all those unexplained absences, mysterious messages on his mobile phone and photographs he kept hidden in his flat. I felt tiny, as if there was nothing left of me.

"Damn you," I shouted, trying to muster myself. "Get away from me!"

Dave leered at me, so I slapped him, but my hand went right through his face. A moment later, my hands were caught and pulled behind me, just before I felt the handcuffs placed on my wrists. I knew who I would see before I turned and looked. It was the cop who'd arrested me once – three years ago – for shoplifting. I had been lucky not to be formally charged with theft and sent to prison, or so Dave had told me, afterwards. I had only wanted something I couldn't pay for.

"You should have been locked up for the rest of your life," the cop snapped. He'd been decent enough in real life, but inside the Ordeal he was terrifying. His hands searched me roughly, lifting up my dress to feel inside my knickers. I screamed in pain as every inch of me was exposed and searched. "You're just another worthless girl with no sense of right or wrong. You're just useless. You should have been executed because you would never amount to anything."

He kicked me to the ground, my hands still cuffed, and I began to cry. It hadn't happened that way, not in real life. The cop had been polite, but firm; I certainly hadn't been searched so roughly, yet now...the dress was torn away and I heard the sound of snapping plastic gloves.

"She was always worthless," another voice said. It was Neil, my second boyfriend. He was a worthless sack of crap. I'd been taken in by his glamour and the fact that he always seemed to have money in hand. He'd bought me food, drink, clothing...and he hadn't been too bad in bed, but then he'd expected me to start paying him back by selling myself for money. I had tried it once, after he'd talked me into it, yet it had been the most disgusting and degrading experience of my life...and it hadn't happened that way! I'd dumped him, hadn't I? I'd escaped before he'd forced me into anyone else's bed. "Useless in bed, useless out of it, useless at selling herself...men would prefer to sleep with an AIDS-infected whore than her."

The cop leered down at me. "Who knows what she might be hiding inside her," he said, with a cruel leer. "Shall we look and find out?"

His hands were changing, flickering every time I looked at them. He wore gloves, and then a pair of translucent scissors, and then a surgical probe. I stared as they closed in on me, remembering...I was in the Ordeal! Everything I was seeing wasn't exactly real. Their chant of 'worthless, worthless, worthless; was just another trick. I fought to concentrate as they rolled me over in preparation for a search, remembering...

I had freed the slaves. It had been my idea, right from the start; I had freed them when everyone else in the magical world had been content to ignore their slavery. I had done well - even if it had cost me an aching bottom - and it had been my idea. No one had made me free the slaves, or risk my own life and freedom for their sake. I was far from worthless. I pulled my hands around – the handcuffs melted away as I no longer believed in them – and pulled myself to my feet. The figures stopped, staring at me. They no longer looked invincible; they no longer looked *real*.

If we shadows have offended, I thought, suddenly, *think of this and all is mended*. I had studied the play back in school, although we had never been allowed to actually act it out. How had the rest of it gone? *You have, but slumbered here, while these visions did appear...*

I had hated reading the Bard in school, but now his words gave me something to cling onto as the shadows started to close in again. My mother, my father, my boyfriends, the cop and behind them, other shadows, pulled from the back of my mind. All powerless, unless I chose to grant them power. I walked forward, certain that I would not fall, and they melted away. The world went white and I found myself in the Throne Room, standing in front of the Queen.

"Your Majesty," I said, with a bow. I had no idea where the new confidence had come from, but I resolved to enjoy it as much as possible. "I defeated the Ordeal. I believe that you owe us an answer."

CHAPTER TWENTY

The Queen seemed amused, although the same couldn't be said for her Court. The elves, the male elves in particular, looked...unhappy. I caught sight of one of them who looked vaguely like Cardonel and I wondered if he was his father. There was no way to know for sure. I had been warned, in the strongest possible terms, that Cardonel was *not* to be mentioned. Besides, the elves could change their shape and it could be nothing more than a mere coincidence.

"You have indeed beaten the Ordeal," she said, calmly. "And so you may ask your question, secure in the knowledge that we will answer one question truthfully."

I had the uneasy feeling I was being mocked. I glanced over at Master Revels and saw, to my surprise, that he was shaken. I'd been in danger and it had terrified him. Oddly, it didn't bother me that much now. I felt far more confident and secure, as if I could take on the entire world and win. The elves seemed to sense it and reacted harshly, their cold inhuman eyes boring into me. The humans...were no longer in evidence. I wondered what that meant. Maybe the elves thought that anyone beating the Ordeal would encourage them, although I didn't know why they would care. It wasn't as if the slaves could break free.

"Thank you, Your Majesty," Master Revels said. He sounded badly shaken too. I was surprised. I'd never seen anything daunt him before, even when we'd walked into the Fairy Roads and had to cross the narrow bridge. "We have one question. Are the Elfish Kingdoms kidnapping ghosts from our world?"

There was a long pause, pregnant with possibilities. The Queen seemed to be stroking her chin, considering her answer. The entire Court seemed to be holding its breath. I found myself wondering just what was going through her mind. The Elfish Code – the law bound into magic itself – insisted that they had to give a honest answer, but the elves could be relied upon to warp the answer somehow, giving one that was factually accurate and completely unhelpful…if they could. Master Revels seemed prepared to wait as long as necessary for their answer. I felt as if the Queen was stretching out the moment as long as she could, purely for her own amusement.

"No," she said, finally. The Court rustled with amusement. We had eliminated one possible suspect, but who did that leave? It left no one, as far as I could tell, unless there were other elves who didn't answer to the Queen. No one really understood how the elves organised and governed themselves. The general theory seemed to be, like the magical world as a whole, that might made right. "The Elfish Kingdoms are not kidnapping ghosts from your world."

Master Revels scowled, before slipping into a bow. "Thank you for your time, Your Majesty," he said. I heard the edge in his voice and shivered, knowing that the elves would be able to hear it too. "With your permission, we will take our leave."

"Don't go," the Queen said. She smiled a smile that would have been warm and attractive, if there was any human feeling behind it. "You are welcome to join us at our tables and eat with us this midsummer night."

Master Revels smiled. "And is the food given freely and without obligation, Your Majesty?"

The Queen smiled back. The smile suddenly became much less human – if that was even possible – revealing something *other* behind her smile. I caught a glimpse of something so large, something so alien, that I cried out in shock, sensing the waves of power rippling throughout the Court and converging on the Queen. She was very far from human and there was something, no less terrifying for being half-seen, behind her. She was vast, beyond human comprehension; what I was seeing was only the tip of the iceberg. The Court faded away around us and we were standing together on the path, which was leading off into the distance.

Master Revels caught my arm as I staggered. "Don't worry about it," he said. I had the feeling that he wasn't talking about the Queen. "We just have to walk home and then we can collapse in peace and safety."

I nodded. Walking down the path felt as if I was walking through knee-deep mud, but the more I walked the easier it became. It was a chilling reminder that the elfish world was very different from the mundane world, even the magical world. We were walking through pure dead magic, the magic the elves had used to build their paradise. I had, in a sudden flicker of inspiration, an insight into how they'd built their world. They had used their magic to open a Gateway to an empty dimension and programmed the underlying fabric of the universe to reflect their wishes. A human being who walked into the universe, lacking the connection of the elves, would be at their mercy. The only thing keeping them from abusing everyone unlucky enough to stumble into their world was the rules…and it was easy to break them and find oneself trapped forever.

Faerie spread out in front of us as we walked. I saw strange buildings that seemed to move in dimensions the human eye was unable to follow. I saw a small village made of mushrooms and another set within the branches of a tree. The entire scene was dominated by another tree that seemed to rise up to heaven itself and down to hell, the roots being set somewhere within the fundamental base of the universe. The sight reminded me of old legends I'd read, back when I'd been a child, yet I couldn't place it properly. It was just…familiar.

"Everyone has that feeling when they stumble into the Land of Always Summer," Master Revels commented, when I remarked on it. "The world reminds them of racial memories, of when the world was much younger and the human race lived in paradise. Being here, being armed with the ability to manipulate one's environment…it would either allow you to develop or destroy yourself. You could find anything here."

He snorted. "There's a dimension, not too far away, that is full of magic," he added. "A sorcerer who found himself there would discover that reality itself coincided with his thoughts – all of his thoughts. The universe destroys anyone stupid enough to remain there for more than a few minutes. They get torn apart by the monsters of their minds."

I nodded in silent understanding, concealing my awe as a line of tiny figures marched past, heading somewhere deeper into Faerie. High overhead, a bee the size of a large dog flew overhead, buzzing cheerfully as it came closer to us. It looked almost friendly, although by now I knew better than to take anything for granted in Faerie. The bee, for all I knew, was a dangerous predator. Mundane bees died when they stung someone, and their sting was hardly lethal to a human, but who knew if that was true for a magical bee?

"The bees probably slipped though a Gateway back when the world was young," Master Revels said. He sounded more relaxed now that we were away from the Queen. "If they stayed here, they would be exposed to wild magic and be mutated into something else. The elves might have experimented on them as well. And now they could never return to the mundane world."

I nodded, not trusting myself to speak. A scaled-up insect could not fly, not in the mundane world, any more than a dragon could fly or breathe fire. The magical bees would be dependent on raw magic to help them fly, using magic that simply didn't exist in the mundane world. The dragons, it seemed, could generate magic for themselves, but I had no idea if the bees could do the same. They would probably collapse under their own weight.

"Over the years, as magic started to go sideways out of the mundane world, most of the magical creatures came here to live," Master Revels added. "There are Unicorns and Centaurs and Talking Beasts and all manner of creatures that now exist only in legend, back in the mundane world. None of them can survive without high levels of magic; many believed that magic was going out of the world permanently, while others knew that humanity would eventually drive them to extinction. They all came here through the Fairy Roads and found a new home.

"Some people believe that the elves built the Fairy Roads as a way to move between the dimensions, which accounts for how they treat unwary visitors. Others believe that they were built by a far older race that has since vanished, leaving the Roads behind and allowing the elves to move in and take over. No one actually knows for sure – apart from the elves and they're not talking."

I grinned. "Which way would you bet?"

Master Revels considered it as the world started to shift around us. "I have no idea," he said, honestly. "It would take vast power to create the Roads within the warp and weft of the universe and the elves definitely have that kind of power. On the other hand, creating and maintaining the Roads requires a very different mindset to the one the elves show everyone, which suggests that someone else built them. I have no idea."

The world turned white, then red. I had a sudden sense of a wall of blood washing towards us and had no time to do anything before it struck us, leaving a foul taste in my mouth and ruining my dress. The suit that Master Revels was wearing was completely ruined by the wave. I saw blood dripping off his top hat and couldn't help a giggle, even though I felt awful. A moment later, the blood vanished completely, leaving us both clean and dry...and standing in a white void. The only thing we could see was the path in front of us.

"We don't always see the blood," Master Revels said. He sounded unperturbed by the experience. "It symbolises something, although opinion is divided as to what."

I wanted to spit, but instead swallowed hard. Even the taste of blood had vanished from my mouth. "Does anyone know anything for sure in this world?"

Master Revels laughed, not unkindly. "Dizzy, this is the magical world," he said. "There is no such thing as objective fact here. Haven't you figured that out by now?"

I flushed. A moment later, the world turned even brighter white and then we were standing together in front of the mirrors. I realised that I was clutching his arm and let go of it, turning to walk out the wooden door. He pulled me back, wove a complicated charm with his hand, and then allowed the door to open without triggering any of the security spells. I realised my mistake a moment later. A door, by its very nature, is both an entrance and an exit. If there were dangerous creatures roaming the Fairy Roads, one of them might find its way out through the mirrors and escape into our world.

Fiona fluttered down to meet us as soon as the door closed behind us, locking and sealing itself automatically. I cringed as I felt the security spells shimmering back into place, feeling a weird tingle passing across my body. If I had been any closer, the spells would have reached out and caught me. Master Revels nodded to me, chatted briefly to Fiona, and then led the way up to the kitchen. I think we both needed a mug of tea.

"Tell me something," I said, as we reached the kitchen. "Does anyone ever get onto the Roads by accident?"

"More than you would think," Master Revels admitted. "There were once millions of Gateways scattered across the Earth. Over the years, many of them – even most of them – were closed down by the elves, or by the various magicians who wanted to prevent intruders entering the magical world. Even so, there are quite a few Gates that open and close seemingly at random, sucking in anyone unlucky enough to blunder into them. They generally get lost on the Roads and end up trapped somewhere, if they're unlucky."

He told me a story about a pair of twin girls who had somehow found their way onto the Roads and ended up travelling from world to world with a group of magicians. I listened absently, although my head was spinning. The reassuring solid nature of the human world was a comfort, yet coming out of Faerie hurt, in a manner I couldn't fully explain. It felt as if I had been torn away from my mother's womb. The thought was a bitter one. I had treated my mother badly and the Ordeal had brought that home to me. I resolved that, when I had the time, I would return to my mother and try to make amends with her.

"I failed," Master Revels said, afterwards. I was shaken by the sudden change in subject. "I didn't expect them to challenge you to undergo the Ordeal."

"Hey," I said, as reassuringly as I could. "It was no big deal."

My trembling voice gave the lie to my words. Back in the human world, the memories refused to fade. Sure, I had beaten the Ordeal, but it had left permanent scars on my psyche. The bad memories it had dragged up, only to throw them in my face to amuse the elves, were resounding through my mind. Master Revels knew that I had lied, but he didn't call me on it. I think he understood more than he was prepared to admit.

In hindsight, I understood the Ordeal a little better. It had reached into my mind, pulled out all the nagging doubts and insecurities and pushed them at me, trying to use them to overwhelm my soul and – in the elfish realm – it would have destroyed me. Or, perhaps, I would have made a bargain with the elves just to make the pain stop. It was nothing as simple, or understandable, as physical torture, yet it was chillingly effective. If I had undergone it a year ago, before I dreamed that magic still existed in the world, it would have killed me. I would have been destroyed by my own mind.

"And then I asked an imprecise question," Master Revels continued. He didn't sound pleased with himself. "I asked about the Elfish Kingdoms, not the elves in general. There are some independent elves out there."

I frowned. "Like Cardonel?"

"Cardonel is a half-elf," Master Revels said, darkly. I knew that he was still unreasonably prejudiced against half-breeds. "They wouldn't consider him a *real* elf, Dizzy; they'd consider him an abomination. I told you that, didn't I?"

"Yes, sir," I said. I had already decided not to tell him that I was going on another date with Cardonel and his friends. It would only upset him. "So...what do we do now?"

Master Revels considered it. "We know that the Kingdoms are not involved, which is something of a relief," he said. "The Thirteen may want us to continue investigating or they may give it up as an unsolved mystery.

Perhaps the ghosts did fade out of our world and go onwards to their final reward. It would be unlike them to leave the matter alone, but you never know."

He shrugged. "And I am sorry about putting you through the Ordeal," he said. "I didn't expect that to happen."

"Don't worry about it," I said. It hadn't been his fault. Besides, I had walked away from it stronger and better. The elves hadn't had the last laugh at all. "You know, I meant to ask you...if elves and humans are different races, how can they have half-breed kids? Dogs and cats don't produce kids if they mate, do they?"

"I have honestly never considered the question," Master Revels said, dryly. He looked up at me, sharply. "Are you considering having sex with the half-breed?"

I flushed. There was something penetrating in his gaze, a suggestion that I had asked a question that had been far too revealing. "I don't know," I admitted. On one hand, I found Cardonel attractive – and yes, he had helped me free the slaves. On the other hand, I recalled the claws growing out of his hands and the glamour-spell he had used when we first met. "Could he get me pregnant?"

"Dizzy," Master Revels said, "this is the magical world. It isn't bound by mundane laws and science. Anything can happen here."

He shook his head. "If you and he have unprotected sex...yes, he could get you pregnant," he said. "I have no idea what any quarter-elf child would look like, but there is a good chance that it would kill you outright when the child was born. And then there is the fact that your child would be neither human nor elf. He wouldn't have a good life in the world."

"Oh," I said, embarrassed. I hadn't wanted such a discussion. Master Revels seemed to sense that and snorted. "I'll be sure to use protection."

"I'll teach you some protective spells, if you like," Master Revels said. He looked oddly embarrassed himself. "There are spells that can halt your menstrual cycle and prevent you having periods, but some witches prefer to ride their cycle and use it to power their magic. It was something I was going to have a friend teach you later on."

I smiled at him. He looked cute when he was embarrassed. "It's all right," I said. If nothing else, I could ask Sparks or Robin. They'd probably know who I intended to sleep with, but you couldn't have everything; besides, they seemed more composed than the average teenage girl. "Thank you for everything, really."

"You're welcome," Master Revels said. "Promise me one thing." I looked up. "Be careful."

CHAPTER TWENTY-ONE

"So...interested in Cardonel, are you?"

I flushed. Sparks had agreed to have a girl-to-girl chat with me, but she'd sussed me out right from the start. I didn't think that I could have hidden it from her. She had a talent, I had discovered, for seeing right to the heart of any issue at once.

"Yes," I said, and hoped that she wasn't interested herself. "Can you help me?"

"Maybe," Sparks said. She looked down at me, seriously. "And what can you do for me in exchange?"

I flushed again, trying to cover my embarrassment. No one did anything for nothing in the magical world. Even Master Revels had his motives in teaching me; he wanted an assistant and later a successor, something I wasn't sure if I wanted or not. I had no idea what Sparks might want and I wasn't sure how to ask. I shook my head. When in doubt, be direct and see what happens.

"It depends," I said. "What would you like?"

Sparks made a show of considering her options. "Well...how about some potion recipes from your master's collection?" she asked. "He's supposed to have books that no one else does, even the Potion Masters Guild, and I would like to try something new and interesting."

I considered it. Knowledge was power in the magical world, something that Master Revels had drummed into my head time and time again. There was no single school of magic, not even a shared agreement on what young magicians should be taught by society, with the result that bits of magical knowledge were lost, rediscovered and lost again repeatedly. It made little sense to me, but then I was a child of the mundane world, where knowledge was written down in mass-produced books that were made available to all, mainly through public libraries. If there was a public library in the magical world – and I had certainly never heard of one – it wouldn't include anything that wasn't already common knowledge.

"Something you haven't tried before," I said. I knew nothing about Potion Masters, apart from the obvious fact that they generally made potions and nothing else. "How do I know what you haven't tried before?"

Sparks shrugged. "Bring a list of possible potions, the older the better, and I will choose from the list," she said. She grinned at me. "Should we shake on it?"

I hesitated. Forming a contract in the magical world was very different from forming one in the mundane world. Breaking a promise, no matter under what conditions, could have dangerous consequences. The underlying nature of magic saw to that. But really, I asked myself, what harm could teaching her a single potion do? I could ensure that I didn't offer her anything truly dangerous.

"All right," I said, and extended a hand. Sparks took it and shook it firmly. I felt a tingle as our respective magical fields acknowledged the agreement. "Now...how do I protect myself from pregnancy?"

"Don't have sex," Sparks said, and laughed. I stared at her in astonishment as she leaned back in her chair, chuckling. "You must admit it works perfectly."

"I didn't promise not to turn you into anything," I said, angrily. Sparks had just taken advantage of me and I was furious! I would cheerfully have strangled her at that moment. "You utter..."

Sparks grinned mercilessly. "Ah, the look on your face," she said. She stuck a hand into one of her bottomless pockets and produced a small vial. "This potion is one of the simplest potions we are taught to make and it ensures perfect protection against both pregnancy and STDs for several days. Repeated doses can extend the effect, but taking it for longer than a few months can render you permanently sterile. I suggest that you learn charms if you intend to have children one day."

I nodded as I took the vial. It looked rather like a capsule of paint. Carefully, I opened it, sniffed it and recoiled. It smelt rather like paint too, or a drink made of pure alcohol and only a tiny amount of flavouring. I tasted it, very carefully, on my tongue and winced. It could probably be used as paint-stripper.

"Just swallow it in one gulp," Sparks advised. "That's what I do, if I can't be bothered to maintain a contraceptive charm…"

I poured the vial down my throat and swallowed, hard. The taste was appalling, as if I had swallowed poison instead of a simple potion. I gagged and choked, somehow forcing it down my throat. The taste seemed as if it would never fade away, but as I kept swallowing it somehow started to disappear. I felt as if it had permanently damaged my teeth.

"How…" I broke off, gasping. "How do people take this stuff on a regular basis?"

"My master says that anyone can get addicted to anything," Sparks said. "He tells us to make sure that potions taste bad to ensure that only people who need them drink them. I once told him that if potions tasted better, he'd have more customers. He wasn't too pleased."

I nodded. After everything that had happened to me, I could guess at what form his displeasure had taken. Sparks had pretty much confirmed it herself back when we'd first met. I suspected that her master had a point, even though it seemed counter-intuitive; people would pay for treatment, not for sweet-tasting liquid. If the potion worked, no one would question the person who'd made it; if it failed, they would have other things to complain about. And besides, I knew who to blame if the potion I'd taken failed. There were no vast chemical companies in the magical world.

"So," Sparks said, as my throat slowly recovered. "What do you think of our friend then?"

I flushed. This time, rather than go out clubbing, Cardonel had invited me, Sparks, Robin and Linux to his apartment. It was surprisingly mundane for a person who lived within the magical world, although there was no TV or DVD player. The apartment held a surprising number of books, mainly on the elves and how they related to other magical societies, and a set of comfortable beds. As far as I could tell, Cardonel lived alone, which raised the question of who the other beds were meant for. Come to think of it, I added to myself, who was paying for the apartment?

"I think he's attractive," I said. I wasn't about to discuss freeing the slaves. Master Revels had made it clear that discussing that little exploit with anyone else was asking for trouble. The slave owners might have survived the fire and come looking for revenge. The newspapers were still chattering about a new dragon war, although no dragons had been sighted for several days. "What do you think of him?"

Sparks considered it carefully. "He's good company," she said, finally. I settled back to listen. I hadn't had any proper girl talk since I had entered the magical world. Talking about boys was, after all, entertaining. "I've never actually done anything with him beyond being friends. I know he can't control the glamour-spell surrounding him, but it bothers me. It suggests that he wants to influence people even though he doesn't."

"Oh," I said. Truthfully, I was glad that she wasn't interested in him, although my own thoughts and feelings were a confused muddle. "Do you know if he had any other girlfriends?"

"He had a couple," Sparks said. "The Witch Poison and Cardonel were an item for a few years. It ended about as well as you would imagine with a witch who called herself Poison. After that, he had a brief affair with a mundane that didn't last long. I'm not sure why it fell apart."

I snorted. "She called herself *Poison?*"

"It was a very accurate name," Sparks said, dryly. "She wasn't a very nice person at all."

I would have asked more questions, except I heard Linux shouting for us both, inviting us back into the main room. Cardonel had set up a table and produced a deck of cards, although in typically magical fashion the deck was enchanted to produce odd results. I listened carefully as they explained the rules of the game – they called it Black Five Magic – and how the magic in the cards actually worked. Cheating, it seemed, was legal as long as someone didn't get caught. A cheater who *was* caught faced punishment at the hands of the deck, a punishment determined by how they held their cards. One combination meant missing a turn – by being frozen magically until their next turn came around – and another meant spending a turn or two as an object. With careful timing, one could even turn someone else's cards against them and trick them into triggering some of the magic within the cards.

"You should see some of the weirder games there are out there," Linux said, when I commented that mundane card games were more…mundane. "There's a version of Monopoly that does all kinds of things to the players as they move through the game."

"And there's a gambling house where you can sell yourself into object slavery, at least until someone raises the money to free you," Robin said, sharply. I got the feeling that she disapproved of such places. Given her missing face, it made a great deal of sense. "The people who run them lure in people from the outside world and give them enough slack to get into debt, and then take them for their own. You should know by now not to treat magic lightly."

Linux didn't look abashed. "We have been exploring magic for the last hundred years," he said. I blinked in surprise – he didn't look that old – until I realised that he meant the Rationalists. "We know most of the rules governing the use of magic. If those rules are followed, and honoured, the dangers are minimised."

"So you have said," Robin said. I got the impression that it was an old argument. "I suggest that we have the first game without magical surprises, just so that Dizzy can learn the rules."

Cardonel seconded this opinion and we went through a slow game. I was glad of her suggestion, because the game was deceptively simple. At first, I thought I understood the rules, but the more I played the more I understood that there was an element of strategy in it. Taking the easy way out tended to result in being snared and dragged back into the game. Every so often, just to confuse the issue, the cards shifted randomly. The winner was normally the player who adapted rapidly to the cards the game gave him.

"We don't normally bet money on our games," Cardonel explained earnestly, when we had finished the first game. "There's too much chance of causing bad feeling."

Everyone laughed. "What he means," Sparks said, "is that he keeps losing money that way."

Robin snorted. "One day he will lose everything that way," she said, as she dealt the cards. She had one great advantage over everyone else. She had a perfect poker face. Staring into her blank face was creepy as hell. "Gambling is too dangerous if you cannot afford to lose."

"But then there would be no fun in gambling," Cardonel countered, as he picked up his cards and made a show of gloating over them. I picked up my own cards and examined them. There weren't any really good or bad cards within the set, sadly, which might work out in my favour. No one could deprive me of something I didn't have. "You need to learn to live a little."

I smiled behind my cards. Did that explain his willingness to help me free the slaves?

The objective of Black Five Magic was to get rid of one's cards as quickly as possible. The fewer cards one held, the fewer options the game had for punishing cheating behaviour or allowing other players to get at you. At the same time, the fewer cards one held, the harder it was to get rid of the remaining cards. And that didn't include how other players could attack – tactically – players who seemed to come close to winning. At first, I played without a killer instinct, but as the game continued, I realised that that was a foolish position. Everyone else was determined to stab the other players in the back.

"You'd think that people would be keen to perform experiments to get their hands on more magic," Linux said, as he put a pair of cards down in the centre of the table. The cards rebounded onto Robin, who countered by putting down a card of her own that neutralised the attack. "But no, we are not allowed to risk experiments that might reveal how the Great Powers operate. Heaven forbid that we annoy them in any way."

"I would have thought that that was a wise decision," Sparks said. She put down a card of her own, reversing the flow around the room. I felt magic twitching around me and looked down at my cards. They had changed...and I suddenly held two of the most powerful cards in the deck. I understood, now, some of the underlying issues in the game. I could build up to using them, only to lose them just before I used them. "You do know how powerful the Great Powers are, don't you?"

"That's my point," Linux said, as Cardonel put down his cards. I recognised it as a gamble at once. "If we could learn how they do what they do, we could deal with them as equals, perhaps even control them. What could we do for the world if we learned how to control the snow demons?"

"We could destroy it," Robin pointed out. She stood up, leaving her cards on the table, and walked over to get a bottle of coke. I'd discovered that none of them were willing to drink alcohol while playing cards. "The snow demons are part of nature and tinkering with nature is never wise. Don't you remember the Chinese warlock who managed to create a drought in his native...?"

Her words bit off as she sat down. There was a flash of light and, where she had been, there was a tiny silver button. "Sorry," Sparks said. She didn't sound sorry. In fact, she sounded positively delighted. "You were the only real target."

A round later, Robin was restored to human form. "As I was saying," she said, as if she hadn't spent time as a button, "tampering with the weather is not wise. Are you sure that you would know what you were doing? I doubt it."

The discussion wore on, as did the game. I spent a turn frozen solid after missing a chance to pick up a card; Sparks spent three turns as a button after Robin, working with Linux, managed to deliver a real smack down. I guessed that she had wanted revenge, although it seemed that being transfigured so briefly did no real harm. If it did, no one except extreme gamblers like Cardonel would have played.

I listened as Linux and Sparks outlined their problems. Their masters were reluctant to experiment further than they should, even the Rationalists. I couldn't understand why – after all, even the Thirteen didn't control the magical world. Robin seemed more inclined to be conservative, but her master treated her badly and no one seemed to care. I started to understand their point – the senior magicians were keeping the younger ones down – yet I rather understood why. It hadn't been *that* long since I'd nearly killed myself trying to use magic to sort books.

The game finally ended with Sparks as the winner. "There are places where I could have you all as my toys for a few hours," she said, with an evil leer. I flushed. One of the places where the magical and mundane worlds interacted – largely unknown to the mundane world – was the BDSM community. There were people with the strangest perversions out there, including men who wanted to be transformed into bras and panties. After learning that, I'd made Master Revels swear that none of the clothes that had been passed down to me had started lives as men and women. The thought had just made me feel sick. "You should consider yourselves lucky that all I want is a glass of something strong.

"As you wish, mistress," Cardonel said, with a wink. He waved a hand in the air and an unmarked bottle floated over to the table, along with four glasses. The liquid in the bottle was clear, flowing almost like water. Cardonel poured it out and passed me a glass. I sniffed it carefully. Whatever it was, it was not water. It smelled more like very strong wine. "My friends, I give you the future."

I sipped carefully. It tasted better than it smelled. The others drank theirs in one gulp and then prepared to leave for their own homes. Sparks winked at me when no one else was looking, knowing that I intended to stay a while longer. If Linux or Robin noticed, they gave no sign.

"I don't understand," I said, when the three of them had gone. The question had been bubbling in my mind since Linux had started talking. "What's holding researchers back from exploring the deeper nature of the magical world?"

Cardonel blinked at me. "The Thirteen," he said, flatly. My eyes opened wide. "They don't want anyone exploring the deeper secrets of magic. That might undermine their power, you see."

He leaned forward. "Your master, the one who took you in and gave you a home," he added. There was something in his voice I didn't like. His reluctance to speak his name out loud was worrying. Master Revels might hear if his name was spoken. "Your master, Dizzy, isn't their policeman. He's their *enforcer*."

CHAPTER TWENTY-TWO

I stared at him, all lust gone.

"He's their *enforcer*?" I repeated, shaken. I didn't know what to think. "What do you mean?"

"Your master is the Thirteen's enforcer," Cardonel said, calmly. He seemed unfazed by my puzzlement. "He enforces their laws on everyone else, the remainder of the magical world. What do you *think* he does for a living?"

I hesitated, unwilling to say anything. I still didn't know what to think. Master Revels had presented himself as a form of policeman, all the while admitting that policing the magical world – where might made right – was an impossible job. He'd certainly been willing to do whatever it took to return the lost and transfigured girls to their homes...and throw a paedophile in jail while he was at it, yet he hadn't been able to do anything about the slaves. I wasn't sure that he had even *wanted* to do anything about the slaves.

Cardonel pushed forward, putting one hand on my leg. Normally, I would have wondered if I should allow him to continue advancing towards me, or if I should back off and make it clear that I wasn't interested in sexual intercourse. Now...I was too busy thinking about the latest rebellion. It made a great deal of sense, but then...a policeman would probably look like an enforcer to a person at the bottom of the heap.

"The Thirteen are the closest thing the magical world has to a government," Cardonel said. "They're the ones with the clout, the agreements with the Great Powers and the Dragons, the ones with the power to get things done. What do they do with it? They do nothing with it, but maintain things as they already are - where they are comfortable.

They think that maintaining the status quo is everything."

I frowned. "I was with him when he defeated a person who was threatening the mundane world," I said. He was so close now. Part of me wanted to surrender to him; the remainder kept warning me that part of the attraction was magical, rather than genuine attraction. Cardonel was glamorous because he was partly magical. The fact he couldn't help it didn't make it any easier to bear. "I don't think that he is a bad person."

Cardonel shrugged. "I don't know that he *is* a bad person," he said, flatly. "I just know that he works to enforce the status quo and stamp on anything new. What do you think keeps the Rationalists from performing their more interesting experiments? The Thirteen do. They send their enforcer around to shut them down whenever they start planning a new experiment. Who do you think prevents open contact between the magical and mundane worlds? The Thirteen prevent it because maintaining their own covert links between the magical and mundane worlds allows them to profit in both worlds."

He touched his ears. "Who do you think condemns half-breeds like myself from joining society?"

I swallowed. I knew that Master Revels seemed to maintain an unthinking prejudice towards Cardonel and half-elves in general, although I saw no basis for it. The elves might have been unpleasant stuck-up bastards, but their children weren't their parents. It hadn't occurred to me that there were other half-breed children out there – dwarfs and goblins were roughly humanoid, after all – yet it made a certain kind of sense. The magical world's senior members certainly seemed to exclude them from any serious position. I had to remind myself that I actually knew very little.

He sat back and stood up, pacing the small apartment. "They've been running things for a very long time," he said. "The Thirteen invite newcomers, strong and powerful magicians, to try for a space on their council. It helps ensure that potentially dangerous newcomers are either co-opted or neutralised. They're quite happy to rig the contests if the newcomers allow them to do it, just to keep them from

214

reaching heights they could use to threaten the Thirteen."

I frowned. "How can they control the Great Powers?"

"They don't," Cardonel admitted. "They seem to have made deals with most of the movers and shakers among the Great Powers. That gives them a surprising amount of power, more than you would expect, and allows them unanticipated advantages. Do you know that the Thirteen are the only ones who are allowed any precognitive visions?"

"No," I said. That actually made sense. I'd never been able to figure out how we'd known about the missing children – or that their disappearance had a magical connection – but if the Thirteen had access to a source of knowledge about the future, they'd know that their kidnapper was risking revealing the existence of the magical world. "How do they do that?"

A second question occurred to me, but I held it to myself for the moment.

"They made deals with the Great Powers," Cardonel said, tightly. He sounded as if he didn't want to talk about it, yet felt as if he had no choice. "The older Great Powers are not...as linked to the present day as we are. As I understand it, they're dislocated within the time vortex and can catch glimpses of the future or the past, which they can relay to the Thirteen. They don't do anything for free, Dizzy. The slaves you and I freed, once they had been worked to death, would have been sent to the altars and sacrificed to the Great Powers."

He stopped pacing backwards and forwards and turned to look at me. "Do you understand what is at stake?" he asked. "The Thirteen control the magical world."

The comment puzzled me. "Tell me something," I said. "How do you know all this?"

Cardonel tapped his ears. "My ears are far sharper than they look, my dear," he said, with a thoroughly lecherous grin. "I hear everything."

I scowled at him. "And the truth is...what?" I demanded. "I don't think that the Thirteen meet in dark bar rooms or discuss their plots while sitting in a smoke-filled chamber."

Cardonel smiled, rather wanly. "We've been putting it

together for a long time," he said. He leaned forward, staring into my eyes. "There's a...group of people who have been working towards making a far better world for ourselves. They believe that they can convince the Thirteen to move away from their rule and start opening up the possibilities for newcomers. I'm part of that group."

I blinked. I hadn't expected a bald-faced confession, although I doubted that he could have hidden it from me. "You want to overthrow them," I said, in shock. "Why?"

Cardonel grinned. "Why did you want to free those slaves?"

I remembered the feelings that had driven me onwards, the conviction that slavery was morally wrong and enslaving people who had done nothing to deserve it was unacceptable. In hindsight, I suspected that Master Revels agreed more than he wanted to admit, at least to me. He hadn't quibbled with my reasoning, even as he caned me for risking both my life and his career.

"Because I believed that it had to be done," I said. "I wouldn't have been able to live with myself otherwise."

"Exactly," Cardonel said. "And now you understand why I feel that the Thirteen need to be curbed, if not overthrown."

I found myself caught in a mental trap. I knew nothing about the Thirteen; I certainly didn't know how much of what Cardonel was telling me was actually true. I could ask my master, but that would risk exposing Cardonel and his conspiracy...and if the Thirteen was truly evil, where did my loyalties lie? I wanted to learn more, yet I suspected that Cardonel would eventually ask me to swear to keep it to myself...it wasn't the evening I had planned when I had asked Sparks to help with contraception!

Cardonel took my silence for a wish to know more and kept talking, telling me about various enforcement missions Master Revels and his predecessors had carried out over the years. A group that had intended to join the Second World War and use magic to win a victory had been destroyed, its members scattered to the ends of the Earth, leaving behind nothing but rumours about an occult connection. Another group, one that had intended to conduct unauthorised worship of various gods, had been mercilessly destroyed. The children from a marriage between two of the most powerful – and unaffiliated – magicians of their day had been taken away from their parents and sent to live with various other magicians, for no apparent reason. The parents themselves had been banished into another dimension and lost forever.

I listened, unsure of what to think. Part of me wanted to believe him; part of me knew that I had no real reason to distrust Master Revels. He'd been the one who had taken me in and taught me...and started to groom me to be his successor, when I knew almost nothing about the job. I knew I needed to find out more, yet...

"Enough," I said, finally. I didn't want to reveal just how confused I was. "Why are you telling me all this now?"

"I wanted you to understand," Cardonel said. "You're not in a very good position and you could use a friend or two."

He smiled at me. His inhuman face seemed to light up and I felt my heart melt. I pulled him towards me and kissed him as hard as I could, feeling – after a moment – his tongue slipping into my mouth. There was an oddly familiar taste to him, the taste of cold iron. I almost smiled. No wonder the elves disliked their half-breeds when they tasted of the one thing that could destroy them, even if it only had power outside their private dimension. My hands went around his back, feeling oddly-constructed bones – he didn't seem to have a spine – and I gasped as his hands went to work on me. They felt weirdly inhuman, both perfectly sensitive and yet demanding.

I pushed him down and climbed on top of him, kissing him deeply as his hands slipped down my back and into my pants. I shivered as they slipped inside my panties and started to work on my bum, wincing slightly as I felt his fingers stroking the scars left on my bottom. I rolled off him as he pushed me over and started to undo my shirt, revealing my breasts, and then shuddered in delight as his mouth started to work on my nipples. It was suddenly very hard to undress without tearing anything.

The sight of his body shocked me, even though it was growing harder and harder to think clearly as his fingers worked their magic on me. It was strange, almost like a plastic mannequin, without chest or facial hair. Curiously, I reached up and ran my hand over his chest, feeling – instead of a ribcage – a tiny lattice of bird-like bones. Naked, Cardonel seemed oddly vulnerable; I could have thrown a punch and broken through into his chest. He leaned down and I felt his cool skin brushing against mine as our lips met again, and again. A moment later, I leaned back as I felt him enter me, pushing deep inside my body. I cried out...

I could feel magic spinning around us as Cardonel started to thrust inside me. The entire room seemed to be lit up with eerie blue light, shimmering through our bodies and flaring out into the room. His form seemed to dissolve in my eyes, revealing nothing but a haze of magic. I felt him pushing deeper and deeper into me, harder and harder, and I felt myself start to lose control. My magic was brushing against his and driving us both wild. I pulled him close, feeling his arms wrapped tight around me, and the last remnants of my control vanished. There was a final flare of magic and delight and we both lay still.

Afterwards, we lay together for a long time. I felt completely drained, almost shattered by the experience. My body seemed to ache, yet it was a warm ache, a reminder that I had just had an orgasm. Cardonel was still inside me, just lying on top of me, exhausted himself. I had to smile. Falling asleep after sex was a male habit that seemed to cross races. I wondered if his father had done the same back when he had been impregnating his mother. My last boyfriend had been just like him, although he was a druggie, which had sometimes made it hard for him to get hard. He'd blamed it on me, of course.

Eventually, Cardonel rolled over and fell out of me. I had to giggle at the look of surprise on his face, even though – without lust burning through my body – looking at his naked body was rather creepy. It raised all sorts of associations in my mind and none of them were very good. I tried to push that thought out of my mind. Cardonel didn't deserve to start thinking that I'd allowed him to sleep with me out of pity.

"I trust," he began. He broke off as I started to giggle. He sounded absurdly pompous. "I trust that that was good for you too?"

I was tempted to keep him waiting for an answer, but that would have been cruel. "Very good," I said. I felt so drained that I could hardly move. "Is that what sex is always like in the magical world?"

"Only with me," Cardonel said. My giggles became chuckles and finally outright laughter. My ex-boyfriends had said the same. "I used a few charms to intensify the experience."

I started. The thought wasn't an amusing one. "A few charms?"

Cardonel seemed to sense my sudden change of mode. "Nothing harmful," he assured me. "A charm to ensure that neither of us hurt the other, a charm to allow our pleasures to build together and a charm to ensure that neither of us would hold back when the time came to unleash ourselves."

"Oh," I said. I didn't like that thought very much; no, I didn't like it at all. Maybe it hadn't been a spell designed to push me into bed – however expressed – but it still wasn't a pleasant thing to do. I remembered how some of the other magicians had acted and shuddered. No, I didn't like it. "Please don't do it again."

Cardonel didn't understand. "You came," he said, dryly. I flushed, unable to shake my head. "I felt you come. You shouted and screamed and everything."

"That's not the point," I said. It was an effort to move, but somehow I managed to sit up and swing my legs over the side of the bed. Somehow, without me noticing, we'd ended up in his bedroom. Had his charms assisted with that, or had I just missed the teleportation spells while I'd been kissing him? "I don't like people tinkering with my mind."

"What about people beating you?" Cardonel asked. I realised – and flushed again – that he could see the marks on my bottom. "If we were able to convince the Thirteen to share power, we would ban beating apprentices and workers..."

"I'm sure you would," I said, as I stood up. I finally remembered a charm to draw on power and chanted it under my breath, accepting the wave of energy it brought. Like all such spells, there was a price to pay, but by then I would be in bed and fast asleep. "Point me in the direction of the shower, please."

Cardonel followed me, still naked, as I waddled towards the shower. As he moved, I was struck again by his alien nature. It would have been less disturbing, I told myself, if he had been a full-blooded elf, even though sleeping with a full elf would have had its own dangers. Cardonel looked so human that it was alarming to see hints of a more disturbing nature.

"I'm sorry if I have offended you," he said, as I stepped into the shower. A moment later, he stepped inside and triggered the water. "Allow me to make it up to you."

I wanted to protest, but his hands went to work and I decided that I'd postpone the protest for a few hours, or maybe a day. He was *very* good, even without the charms...

***

I considered his words as I walked home and stumbled into bed, feeling the rejuvenation spell finally catching up with me. If there was more to the Thirteen than Master Revels had implied...what did that mean for me if I took service with them? I wanted to ask him personally, yet...if I did, it would reveal that I'd spoken to someone who opposed them. It might have explained his prejudice against Cardonel if he knew that Cardonel was on the opposing side, but then...this was the magical world. Nothing was ever that simple.

Master Revels had gone out, I discovered, when I finally dragged myself out of bed and stumbled downstairs for breakfast. Fiona, who rarely seemed to care about my appearance, looked concerned. She was concerned enough to order me back to bed and have my food transported up to me by magic. I had only myself to blame. The rejuvenation spells always extracted a price. Master Revels returned by late evening, by which time I was feeling better and determined to find a way of asking pointed questions. I wanted to know just what was going on.

He didn't seem inclined to talk at first, though. "Go get dressed for a walk in the cold," he ordered. "Wear dark clothes and a scarf."

I blinked at the instructions, but headed off to comply. I knew better than to keep him waiting, so I was dressed in ten minutes and headed back downstairs to find him pacing impatiently in the lobby. He'd changed his suit for a set of working clothes, suitable for a joiner or plumber. He had never looked less like a magician.

"Come on," he said, as he opened the door. "We're going hunting."

Chapter Twenty-Three

"Stay close to me," Master Revels ordered, as we headed out into the darkness. "We're going to walk the Wizard's Freeway."

I nodded, studying his back and watching as the first tendrils of magic started to curl around him. The Wizard's Freeway was a complicated spell that created a path between two places – often places that were very far apart in geographical terms – and linked them together, allowing a magician to walk from one to the other relatively quickly. I'd been taught the basics of the spell, but I'd also been warned in no uncertain terms that I was not to use it without desperate need or supervision. The magic was deceptively simple. A magician who lost his train of thought in mid-cast would be lucky if he managed to return to the normal world.

The roads seemed to flicker around us, blurring down into a single path, which we walked as quickly as we could. Master Revels set a hard pace, for which I didn't blame him; walking the Wizard's Freeway felt rather like walking on ice, when one didn't know just how thin the ice actually was. And, of course, there were worse monsters under the ice than fish or even sharks. Everything went black for a second, but before I had time to panic the world returned and we found ourselves in Morningside. The mundane people walking in the darkness, perhaps heading home or into town to a party didn't even notice us shimmering into existence.

"Come on," Master Revels said. "We have to get to the hospital before it's too late."

I followed him, stumbling a little, for he was setting a fast pace. In the darkness, I could barely see him, yet I could sense the magic surrounding him. I wondered, as I studied his back, just how much of his job was still a mystery to me. Which side was actually right? And, if I didn't know that, which side should I be on? I looked away from him as we passed through the gates into the hospital. I hadn't been to a hospital since I was a kid, when I'd had to have my tonsils removed, and I hadn't enjoyed the experience very much. The nurses had been kind, but harassed; they'd had no time to play with a young girl. And then my throat had started hurting and...

The thought was a surprisingly less painful one now, after the Ordeal. I'd been through much worse, after all. I caught sight of a set of cars parked at one corner of the hospital car park and frowned in surprise. The people who could have afforded such cars could have afforded to go private rather than use the NHS. There was something about them that suggested that they were – vaguely – connected to our reason for visiting the hospital. It didn't actually suggest any reason *why* we were trying to get into a hospital.

I'd wondered how Master Revels intended to gain entry, but in the end it was very simple. He breezed though the main doorway as if he owned the place, held up a card for the bemused security guard to see and kept walking, as if he expected any opposition to just melt out of his way. The guard sent me a reassuring expression as I stumbled after him, as if the hospital was used to seeing arrogant consultants and their interns striding everywhere, but said nothing. I guessed that he was bored and underpaid for his job.

Inside, the hospital stank of disinfectant and something else, something I couldn't quite recognise. Master Revels showed no sign of discomfort as he found the stairs and led me up two flights and into a hospital ward. It was surprisingly quiet to my ears, as if everyone had decided to flee. There were ten beds in the ward and all of them were empty, but one.

Master Revels indicated the bed with one hand and I followed his finger. A young girl was lying in the bed, her hands clasped in front of her as if she were praying. An angelic haze of blonde hair surrounded her, drawing attention to her fine cheekbones and closed eyelids. She couldn't have been more than twelve years old, a girl on the verge of blossoming into a woman. I felt a sudden burst of envy for her. She was innocent and unmarked by the world.

And she was completely alone. I glanced around, puzzled. There were no other patients - which struck me as odd - and there were no staff. There were no nurses checking on the girl, no doctors moving from patient to patient...there was no one else around. Anyone could have walked in and done anything to the girl, or any other patient for that matter. Hell, *we'd* walked in and no one had tried to stop us.

"I pulled a few strings," Master Revels said, by way of explanation. "This part of the hospital has been evacuated. The vast majority of patients were shipped elsewhere, along with their staff. Dawn here" – he indicated the girl with a wave of his hand – "was left alone. If anything should happen to occur there will be fewer people to get in the way."

I stared at him. "Why are we here?"

Master Revels grinned at me. "Look at her," he said. "What do you sense?"

I turned back to Dawn. Of course; I had looked at her with my eyes, not my magical senses. I concentrated and peered at her, seeing nothing...no, there was a tiny trace of magic, unfamiliar magic. I studied it, trying to see how it worked, and realised that it was concentrated around her neck. I reached forward, following the magic, and slowly pulled back her collar. Two nasty red marks jumped out at me at once. Someone – or something – had bitten her hard, leaving twin puncture marks in her skin.

"She was found four days ago in a park," Master Revels said, "after she went wandering off on her own. The doctors who examined her said that she'd caught a chill, but she refused to awaken despite everything the mundane world could do for her. There was no sign that she'd been attacked, apart from the marks on her neck. The mundane world decided that she'd been the victim of a dog."

I shook my head. "No, sir," I said. I *knew* what the marks

were, all right. I'd seen them in countless horror movies. "She was bitten by a vampire."

Master Revels nodded. "The mundane world is far too fond of vampires," he said, disapprovingly. "They suck blood, which is enough to make them heroes to some; I guess they think that the vampires are more honest than the political leaders they have. They also infect someone they bite with vampirism, with the result that some of the people they bite turn into vampires themselves."

I looked up, sharply. "*Some* of the people they bite?" I asked. He nodded. "And Dawn – this girl – is going to become a vampire?"

"Perhaps," Master Revels said. He shook his head sadly. "The mundane world gets quite a bit wrong about vampires. There's always a few days between the bite and then...the victim either fights it off or gives into the bloodlust and accepts the curse. This girl has been in a coma for several days, which suggests that the vampire drained her energy as well as blood. She will either rise tonight as a vampire or recover and live a normal healthy life."

He shook his head. "And the mundane world thinks that vampires are sexy," he said. "Whatever will they think of next?"

"They keep putting out films about vampires," I said, feeling oddly stung. They'd been some of my favourites when I'd been a child. "They get good press."

"I could write a book or direct a movie where a child molester is a hero," Master Revels said, darkly. He found a chair and settled down to wait, waving for me to sit on the opposite side of the room. "That wouldn't make it right."

The hours ticked by slowly and I found myself looking away from the girl, up towards the clock on the wall. If the sun rose before she awoke, she would live as a human being; if she awoke earlier, she would be a vampire. I'd read enough to know that the vampire curse was incurable. The only way to deal with her would be to kill her and burn the body, destroying it completely. Master Revels seemed untroubled by the wait, leaving me to wonder what he was thinking as he watched the girl, never taking his eyes off her.

He could have killed her right away and made certain that she could never rise as a vampire, which suggested to me that he wasn't a bad person. But then...what was the Thirteen's interest in all of this?

"Every time the mundane world gets all excited about fictional vampires, we see a resurging infestation of *real* vampires in the magical world," Master Revels said. He shrugged. "The two worlds are linked in ways that most people don't even begin to grasp, with events in their world affecting ours and vice versa. I think it has something to do with the uncertainty principle, but I'm not quite certain what that is."

I groaned at the pun.

"And sometimes the vampires manage to create nests within the mundane world and start bringing in new victims," Master Revels added. He looked up at me and winked. "The average vampire isn't very clever. He just wants to suck your blood. A very few vampires, however, are smart enough to get organised and that's when we start having problems. A vampire isn't just stronger or faster than the average human; he's capable of hypnotising and controlling anyone unwary enough to be caught by him. Have you ever heard of the mafia?"

I nodded. "There were a handful of vampires who took over the organisation and used their powers to create a secure base for themselves," Master Revels said. "Their headquarters was accidentally bombed during the invasion of Italy in the Second World War and the survivors scattered. Their great defence is that no one really believes in vampires..."

He looked back at the bed and swore aloud. It was empty. I jumped to my feet in shock, realising that the girl had somehow woven a spell around us – us – and used the distraction as a chance to escape. Master Revels was on his feet, holding up one hand as he reached out with his senses, looking for the vampire. A moment later, I saw her, her angelic face contorted with fury as she lashed out at him. He caught her blow on his cane and drew back his hand to throw a spell, but she was gone, moving so quickly that she was a blur.

"This way," he snapped. I followed him as he ran down the corridor, wondering how many vampire powers the girl was going to be able to access quickly. If she ran outside and just fled for her life, she would be halfway across the city before the sun started to come up...but then, would she be able to find shelter? Vampires couldn't enter a house without permission from the people inside. "I took a few precautions..."

The interior of the hospital seemed colder somehow, although I told myself that I was imagining it. It was hard to concentrate on probing the building while I was running, but I kept picking up traces of her presence. She seemed to be shimmering in and out of existence, as if she were transforming from human form to mist, all the while remaining within the building. It made me wonder what she was thinking, or even if she was thinking at all. We plunged down the stairs after her, heedless of the danger. Whatever the Thirteen wanted with her, she had to be stopped before she started tearing her way through mundane children.

"Stay alert and keep checking everything," Master Revels ordered, as we reached the basement. It was colder here, cold enough to make goose bumps rise on my arms, even though it wasn't as cold as winter. Something touched my nostrils and I winced. I could smell blood. "She's already found one victim."

I had a spell prepared in my mind before we turned the corner and looked into the morgue. The girl was sitting on one of the tables, her lips burrowed into the throat of a handsome young man, whose eyes were wide with shock. I saw immediately that he wouldn't be coming back as a vampire, if only because her jaws were burrowed so tightly within his throat that he would die the moment she pulled away from him. She turned around, the hospital gown tearing as she moved, to stare at us, her red eyes dark and cold. I could see nothing human within her gaze. Her face had warped unnaturally. Blood dripped from around her lips and onto the floor.

"Put him down," Master Revels said, calmly. I looked at

him in surprise and then realised that he was trying to calm her down. It felt like a waste of time, but perhaps it would make capturing and destroying her easier. She moved so quickly. "Is there anything in there that remembers being human? Do you remember your mother, or your father, or your pet dog...?"

Dawn lifted her lips from the young man's throat, one hand holding his body upright effortlessly. I watched in horror as his head tumbled over and fell towards the ground, spilling blood everywhere. It should have clotted, but there was something in vampire saliva that prevented blood from clotting. It was a very efficient design in its own way. I wished I knew how vampires had come into existence originally, although it was probably some kind of curse. The centaur folk's mere existence was the result of a particularly nasty curse, way back before the birth of Jesus Christ.

"Food," she said. There was nothing human in her voice. Her red eyes bored into mine and I felt her mind reaching out, trying to dominate me. My legs trembled, but somehow I held my own and broke the connection. She wasn't going to get me the same way twice. "I need food."

"I know you need food," Master Revels said. I shuddered as I saw her tongue flicking out to lick at the headless corpse. "We can give you food, but we need you to put him down and come with us quietly and..."

She moved like lightning, her hands shifting into claws as she came right at me. I panicked and threw a fireball into her face, but it seemed to have no effect on her. She landed on me and knocked me over backwards, her jaws opening wide and reaching for my throat. I felt raw magic boiling up within me and flaring out, throwing her right across the room. Her form shifted, became a haze of mist, and moved back towards me. I summoned a second spell and threw it right through the mist. There was no effect.

"Here," Master Revels said. He was holding a tiny container, one of those we had picked up from the Silent Order. A single word and the magic in the jar blossomed loose, reaching out towards the mist and pulling her into the container. I thought that we had her for a second before her physical form suddenly congealed and she came right at us. Master Revels ducked and her claws sliced through the air above his head; I was less lucky. A hand slammed into me and sent me flying across the room. My head banged into one of the tables and I saw stars spinning in front of me.

Dawn span towards me, reaching out for my throat again. A second later, her form glowed with magic and burst apart in flames, ashes falling down on the floor. They mingled with the blood and seemed to spin again and again before finally collapsing into dust. Master Revels didn't take chances. Muttering spells – as I lay there on the floor, stunned – he swept up all the bloody remains and consigned them to a pocket dimension. Blood could – sometimes – allow a slain vampire to reconstitute itself from nothing. This time, there would be no room for her to reanimate.

My head was still unsteady and I felt sick. I tried to focus my mind enough to perform a healing spell, yet nothing seemed to work properly. Blood seemed to be rushing through my head, blurring my vision...or perhaps I was just imagining it. It was so hard to focus...

I felt soft hands touching my head. I groped for a name. "Cardonel?"

"I'm afraid not," Master Revels said, dryly. I was too dizzy to flush. "You're concussed, among other things. Don't try to cast any spells in that condition. Just relax and let me work on you."

Slowly, the pain faded away, leaving me shaky, but able to stand upright. He held my arm until my legs agreed to support me, although they kept threatening to go on strike at any moment. I hoped that he hadn't drawn any conclusions from what I'd said, but it seemed unlikely. I told myself that it was none of his business who I allowed into my bed and tried to push the matter aside.

"You did all right," Master Revels said, as we staggered together down the Wizard's Freeway. I hated to think about the hospital staff coming into work and discovering the mess. Somehow I managed to mumble something to that effect. "I'll ask Dervish to take care of it. He owes me a favour..."

A wave of heat struck us as we stepped back into the magical world. A building was burning, right in front of us. And then there was someone shouting in my ear as a new wave of dizziness ran through me.

"The Rationalists," he was shouting. His words seemed to rattle around my skull. "Their building is on fire!"

CHAPTER TWENTY-FOUR

"Be quiet," Master Revels ordered, sharply. My head was still spinning and I could barely think. The heat was tearing away at my mind. "Get her a healing potion, now!"

My mind swam. The next thing I felt was a pair of hands holding me and a vial of some kind being pressed against my lips. I drank and a warm feeling shimmered through my body. A moment later, my head cleared and I opened my eyes. I hadn't even realised that they were closed. Ahead of us, a building was burning brightly, with strange hints of magic pouring through the fire.

"That was a healing potion with sufficient power to heal death itself," a voice said. I looked up into the calm face of a middle-aged lady with grey hair and brilliant blue eyes. I liked her on sight, if only because she reminded me of an ideal mother or aunt. "How are you feeling?"

"Much better," I said. It was true. The aches and pains that had plagued me since the brief battle with the vampire had faded away to nothing. "What are the side effects?"

The aged witch shrugged. "Get some sleep as soon as possible and don't try to wake up," she said, dryly. "Let your body recuperate on its own and then wake up. Get plenty of rest and relaxation over the next few days. You should be fine."

"Thank you," I said, pulling myself to my feet. I felt better than fine. I hadn't felt so sharp since...I couldn't remember ever feeling so good. At the back of my mind, there was a little voice reminding me that feeling so good was probably an effect of the potion, but I ignored it. "That was a very good potion."

The witch smiled. "My small reputation as a potions

brewer is confirmed," she said. There was an alarmingly loud crackle from the building and I turned to see part of it collapse into the flames. The flames themselves were far from natural. There was something truly eerie about them. "Your master is over there, if you wish to speak to him."

She pointed one long finger towards Master Revels, who was standing some distance away, his hands clasped behind his back. He was staring up at the fire, his features illuminated oddly in the flickering light. I started to walk over to him, glancing from face to face in the crowd. There was no one that I recognised, but in the fire I could make out just how many of them wore illusions to conceal and protect their inhuman natures. Several of them, I realised with a shudder, were vampires. I wondered if they knew that we had killed one of their own only a few hours ago. Or perhaps they didn't really care. I had no idea how the vampires organised themselves within the magical world. Maybe the ones who hunted in the mundane world were their renegades.

And besides, the vampires weren't the weirdest creatures who had come out to watch the fire. There were a group of mermen and mermaids, floating inside spheres of water that surrounded and protected then; werewolves hiding their natures behind illusions, a pair of centaurs watching from the edge of the crowd and a strange-looking little man wearing an Irish costume. There was a woman wearing a veil and I wondered if she was one of Dervish's people, until I looked and saw her eyes. Whatever she was, she was very definitely not human. I looked away quickly and walked over to Master Revels. He smiled at me – he was relieved, I thought – when he saw that I was walking upright without help.

"If you feel bad, tell me and you can go home to bed," he said, shortly. I shook my head. I had never seen a large fire in my life and besides, it was bringing all kinds of life out onto the streets. I watched in some astonishment as a gargoyle started to move as the flames threatened to spread further, dropping feathers from its gaping mouth as it clambered down the side of the building and into the night.

It, I realised, ate the city's population of pigeons and seagulls to sustain itself. "Tell me what you make of the fire."

I turned and looked towards the fire. There was something odd about it, something I knew I ought to recognise, yet I couldn't make head or tail of it. I could sense magic flaring through the fire, with bursts of raw magic flickering through my awareness – the crowd made noises as the bursts of magic passed over them – and then fading away, only to be renewed seconds later. I leaned backwards and gasped in astonishment as the picture fell into place. The flames themselves were alive. I was staring up at a massive demonic face hidden within the flames.

"A fire demon," Master Revels said, when I told him. He sounded more excited than I would have expected. I was starting to realise that part of him lived for the challenge of encountering and overcoming new and dangerous threats. "I've never seen a fire demon before, not even when I was caught up in the Hellfire War."

I blinked. "What was the Hellfire War?"

"I'll explain later," Master Revels said, shaking his head. "The fire demons cannot live on our plane for long, which means that some idiot managed to summon this one and bind it to this location. We know that because if they had failed to bind it to one location, half of this part of the magical world would be on fire by now and it would probably spread into the mundane world. On the other hand, unless they managed to construct the wards just right, it isn't going to remain bound there forever."

"And that means that it can escape," I finished. Master Revels nodded. I'd read about demons getting loose on Earth and countless other worlds in the books and very few of those stories ended well. The demons had no sense of human morals and were terrifyingly powerful. Entire worlds had died because of their antics and several dimensions were demonic kingdoms, in all but name. "How do we send it back to hell?"

"Carefully," Master Revels said. He reached out and beckoned to someone standing at the other side of the fire. The target of his gaze stepped forward, moving as if he would rather be facing the dentist than Master Revels, and stopped in front of us. He was a short overweight man wearing a stained white lab coat and a pair of eye-protectors. It was a shame that he hadn't managed to protect his face, for parts of it were marked and scarred. Whatever he had looked like when he had started as a Rationalist – he had to be a Rationalist, no one else would wear lab clothes as a uniform of sorts – he was forever marked now. I could sense strange magic woven into his clothes, providing a form of protection. It was clearly imperfect.

Master Revels ignored his appearance. "So, Calculator," he said, calmly. "What were you trying to do that brought a fire demon to this world?"

Calculator looked as if he didn't want to answer any questions, but something in Master Revels' gaze convinced him to talk. "We weren't running any experiments," he said, slowly, as if every word was being forced out of him. There was no Compulsion involved, I realised; Calculator just didn't want to talk. "There were no experiments in progress when all the alarms started to sound and that...thing appeared in our private world."

Something clicked in my head. The building was far larger on the inside than on the outside, a common feature of buildings within the magical world. No wonder it was taking so long to burn down, even though it seemed to be completely enveloped in flame. I looked up and saw the eyes of the demon, staring down at the puny humans surrounding it and laughing. There was nothing human – or sane – in those eyes. It seemed to laugh at us, even though it was bound, a chilling reminder that if it broke free it would never be contained again. Whoever had summoned it to our world was mad. A demon might have to keep whatever bargains it made with the human who summoned it to this world, but the devil was always in the small print. You'd have to be a fool to bargain with a demon and expect to come out of the deal ahead, or even alive.

"I don't believe you," Master Revels said, coldly. I swung back to him, staring as his eyes bored into Calculator's very soul. "I think you're lying about something."

"I swear to you, on my name, that we were running no experiments," Calculator said. He sounded almost as if he were pleading, although I wasn't sure what he was pleading for. To be believed, perhaps. "Do you think that we are mad enough to do...*that*...to our own people? Do you know how many people are caught in the blaze?"

"No," Master Revels said. It sounded a convincing point to me. "How many have been killed by the fire?"

"At least ninety-seven researchers," Calculator said. I shuddered. The population of the magical world had never been counted, but I'd had the impression that it wasn't that high. "There was absolutely no warning. It just broke through our wards and set fire to everything."

"Interesting," Master Revels said. "Very well; I believe you."

"Thank you, thank you," Calculator said. He sounded as if he had thought that his life had been in danger. I wondered if that were true. "What are you going to do now?"

Master Revels turned to look up at the flames. "I'll call the Silent Order and get them to come and back us up, if necessary," he said. He sounded reluctant to ask for help, but there was no choice. Trapping a demon, particularly one that had already manifested in the material world, wasn't easy. Demons were smart, capable of seeing their way out of any trap and hell-bent on malice. "We'd better start setting up the wards now."

I watched from a distance as Master Revels and a number of other magicians – I recognised Dervish among their number – pushed the crowd back and started setting up new wards. The fire demon howled its fury in a language that seemed to be composed of smouldering ash, ranting and roaring as it directed streams of fire towards anyone foolish enough to step too close. A river of flames surged out, spinning towards the magicians, only to be held back by their personal protections. The heat seemed overwhelming. I was sure that it would only be a matter of time before everything collapsed and the fire demon was free. Just how large was the building anyway?

I asked Calculator and he shrugged. "We never measured

it," he said. He didn't seem to be as scared of me as he was of my master. "We just built it and secured it with magic, and then we started carving out rooms for our experiments and sharing information. All of the records have been destroyed in the fire and we will be a long time rebuilding everything. This may be the end of the Rationalists."

It made a certain kind of sense. Knowledge was power in the magical world and so far too much magical knowledge was hoarded by the magicians, rather than shared for the benefit of all. The elder magicians hadn't wanted to see the up and coming younger magicians reaping the benefits of their work and expanding on it, no sir! They would sooner force the young men and women to relearn all the secrets for themselves, perhaps sharing only a handful with their apprentices. It was confirmation, if I needed it, that magicians were human too.

The Rationalists, on the other hand, had concentrated on sharing information among themselves, claiming that by sharing knowledge they could also share the risks – research into magic, as I suspected that someone had just found out, didn't promise a long and healthy life. Master Revels had once told me that people who tried to figure out the underlying roots of magic – how magic actually worked – often came to grisly ends. It hadn't made them popular among their peers, if only because their peers feared that the young upstarts would learn something they could use to change the magical world.

I remembered Linux telling me about it, while we'd been playing Black Five Magic. He'd said that some of the younger Rationalists were convinced that the older Rationalists – never mind the rest of the magical world – were holding them back. It had struck me as absurd at the time, but now I wondered. Calculator had claimed that there had been no experiments underway when the fire had begun, yet that really only meant that he *knew* of no such experiments. Had someone been trying to summon and control a demon and it had gone horribly wrong?

Master Revels and his team of magicians had started chanting, using their voices to bind their magic together and strengthen the wards. The fire demon let out another howl of outrage as the building started to collapse completely – a wave of heat billowed out at us, causing the mermaids to teleport away before their water started to boil – and turned into a burning pile of debris. The fire demon raged forward, free of its bonds, only to strike into the wards and rebound sharply. I cringed as I felt heat pushing me back, knowing that none of us could expect any mercy if the demon broke free, just before there was a final flash of light and it was gone. The remainder of the fires vanished, leaving smouldering embers.

"Don't go into the wards," Master Revels called. I frowned in surprise before realising that the fire demon was bound to flames...and there were still burning items within the pile of dust and debris. It might still be there, playing games with us and hoping that someone or something would set foot inside the wards. Or it might be gone, heading back to hell and sniggering to itself at the thought of us watching the remainder of the building burn, never daring to step into the wards and trying to save something. "We'll have to wait until morning to see if we can summon rain and put the fires out."

I yawned and a number of spectators joined me. "Go home and get ready for bed," Master Revels ordered. "I'll join you there once I have finished securing the building."

"Yes, sir," I said, with another yawn. I felt tired and battered, despite the healing potion. The edge it had given me had worn off. "I'll see you back home."

The walk back was slower than I had expected. The magical world seemed to have decided that the fire would be a good time for a party, so parts of the market had opened up, selling – much to my amusement – marshmallows and sausages on sticks. Several of the Rationalists were shouting angrily about this, but others seemed to find it hilariously funny and were buying food and drink to partake of while they watched the flames and the recovery effort. I avoided a man with a food tray who was trying to sell me suspicious-looking pies and reached home, fighting to keep down another yawn or two. Fiona greeted me at the door and helped me up the stairs and into the shower. I didn't bother to undress. I just allowed the cold water to wash over my body and wake me up a little. Afterwards, I managed to undress, get into my pyjamas and stumble back downstairs.

"You need your sleep," Fiona said, firmly. I wasn't in the mood to listen to her, so I ignored her words. I wanted to know what had happened and the only way to find out was to ask Master Revels when he came home. "Get upstairs and go to sleep now."

I started to reply, but I was cut off by a yawn. It was probably for the best. I had forgotten that she could breathe fire and what I had intended to say would have annoyed a saint. Besides, Fiona had saved my life and freedom once. My head swam again, but I refused to fall asleep. I knew that once I fell asleep I would be sleeping for hours – I felt as if I would be sleeping for days – and my curiosity was too strong to allow me to fall asleep. I wasn't sure how much time had passed when Master Revels returned home, looking as tired as I felt. He'd changed back into his normal suit, but without the top hat. He didn't seem to be carrying it when he came home.

"You should be in bed," he said, when he saw me. I gazed at him blearily. "Come on. I'll help you to bed."

"What happened?" I tried to say. My voice refused to work properly and it took me several tries before I said it in a way he could understand. "What happened...?"

"I don't know yet," Master Revels said, as he reached out for me and picked me up. It seemed to be almost effortless for him, even though I wasn't a light girl. I had known that he was stronger than he looked, but I hadn't known he was *that* strong. My thoughts – I felt like I was almost drunk – ran in strange patterns. He hadn't needed a cane to set my bottom on fire. "I'll have to find out, although...I confess I don't like the timing. Some idiot summons a fire demon on the same day I'm outside the magical world..."

His voice trailed off as darkness gripped my mind. I was barely aware of him carrying me upstairs and putting me to bed, just before I fell into sleep and unpleasant dreams.

CHAPTER TWENTY-FIVE

"So," Fiona said, sometime later. "Who's a sleepy head, then?"

"Oh, shut up," I growled. I never liked people who were bright and cheerful in the morning, although – come to think of it – I wasn't sure that it actually *was* morning. I felt rather thick-headed, which suggested I hadn't slept for as long as I should. "What time is it?"

"Four o'clock in the afternoon," Fiona said. Her mouth lolled open into a dragonish leer. "You'll be pleased to know that you didn't oversleep."

I ignored this attempt at humour and staggered into the bathroom. Once I had relieved myself – and showered in the vain hope it would help me wake up completely – I pulled on my dressing gown and stumbled downstairs. Fiona, perhaps sensing that I was too tired to carry her, flapped along above me, making sardonic comments about my state of mind. Given that my head felt as if it were made of cotton wool, I had some difficulty in thinking up suitable retorts. I had expected to see Master Revels at the breakfast table – I always saw him in the morning – but he wasn't there. It took me several minutes to remember that it was actually mid-afternoon and he was probably working elsewhere.

A shimmer appeared above the table as I sat down, rapidly forming into a miniaturised version of Master Revels. "Dizzy," he said. He sounded as tired as I felt. "I have been called away for a few days. Continue with your studies and wait for me here. If you feel the urge to go out and socialise, fine; just don't bring anyone, and I mean anyone, back home with you. Make sure you get lots of rest. That was a nasty blow on the head you took."

The image vanished before I could say anything. "He's gone out and left me here," I said, in surprise. I grinned up at Fiona. "I could invite everyone I know and have a massive party."

"And then spend several days rubbing your bottom and moaning," Fiona said, darkly. I flushed and she laughed. "I think you might discover that the punishment for inviting others into the building is worse than a simple caning. Do you know the expression that a magician's home is his castle?" I shook my head. "Well, it's true...and invading a magician's home without his permission is something that no magician will take lightly. No one will bat an eyelid if he kills you for having a party without his permission."

I looked up, surprised. "They take it that seriously?"

Fiona nodded. Her oversized snout bowed towards the table as she moved. "Every magician in the world got that way through study, research and practice," she said. "The more powerful the magician, the more likely he is to have figured out something that relatively few other magicians have figured out. Most magicians, particularly the young and impatient fools, have a habit of trying to spy on the older ones and steal what they can in the way of knowledge. You never know what piece of knowledge will allow some young upstart to displace you, to beat you in an open duel or silent assassination in the shadows of night, to drive you from your home and take your books and Objects of Power for their own..."

"I understand," I said. I'd been joking, really. "I won't even dream of holding a party."

"That would be wise," Fiona said, gravely. She winked at me. "I'd suggest studying instead, at least for the first couple of days. He may decide to test you when he comes home."

I shrugged, waved my hand in the air and triggered the kitchen spells. The magic, when it wasn't directed, had an uncanny gift for producing food that suited my mood. A plate of sausages, scrambled eggs and toast appeared in front of me and I discovered, somewhat to my surprise, that I was famished. Or perhaps it wasn't that big a surprise. I hadn't eaten anything apart from the healing potion for over twenty hours. Fiona watched me carefully as I started to eat – it hadn't occurred to me, until afterwards, that perhaps I shouldn't be eating so much – but nothing happened. I finished my meal, clicked my fingers to banish the remains of the meal and the plate back to the magic field and started to return to bed. All of a sudden, I felt tired and worn out again. This time, of course, there was no one to carry me to bed.

The thought kept me warm as I settled back into bed – Fiona watching from her perch at the side of the room – and fell straight asleep. This time, I slept far more peacefully, untroubled by dark and threatening dreams. When I awoke, several hours later, it was six o'clock in the morning. I didn't need to get up so early, but I didn't feel like remaining in bed. I ate breakfast, got dressed in my work clothes and walked into the library. It was the same mess as it had been back when I'd first seen it – somehow, it felt as if I had spent my entire life in the magical world – yet at least it was a more ordered mess.

I sorted through the piles of books until I found an old potions book that seemed to date back all the way to the 9th century, although it was impossible to be sure. Master Revels had once commented that there were people who made books that *looked* old, in order to ensure that the suggestion of ancient – and perhaps forgotten – magic helped their sales. Given that the magical world never seemed to have heard of the printing press, let alone computers and modern printing methods, I sometimes wondered why they bothered. There was something charming about the old-style books, yet there were plenty of unreliable spells within them...

Potions tended to have all kinds of effects, depending upon the intent of the person producing them. Sparks had to have more patience and discipline than I had if she was intent on manufacturing potions for a living. Some of them required very precise handling, including making them only at set times of the year, and others required strange, weird and wonderful ingredients. One potion, which revolted me, required a unicorn's horn and the fur of a mouse that had never mated with another mouse. The penalty for getting it wrong, it seemed, was a colossal explosion. It was claimed to have been invented by a French druid and gave the drinker superhuman strength, but not for very long. It seemed that drinking too much could turn the drinker into stone.

"That one hasn't been made for years," Fiona commented. I looked up in surprise, before remembering that Fiona had been around for far longer than I had, or even Master Revels. "You just cannot get virgins for love or money these days and only a virgin woman can ride a unicorn, or convince the poor beast to give up its horn. I believe that there are reports that several hundred unicorns were taken into the Sisterhood's pocket dimension and allowed to roam free there, but I don't know for sure."

Sparks, I decided, would have liked the recipe, but not if she couldn't find the ingredients. I started to read onwards, shaking my head at some of the recipes, including one that claimed to grant anyone who drank it remarkable endurance in the bedchamber. The writer of the book seemed incapable of discussing sexual matters openly and used so many euphemisms for having sex that I had to read it twice to be sure of what it was saying. The ingredients were remarkably common, so I guessed that it was actually a potion that was common knowledge. Magicians might have been devoted to power more than sex – or at least most of the older magicians I'd met were – but they would definitely have liked the potion. I made a note of it anyway and read onwards. There was a potion that promised dreamless sleep, a potion that promised a form of telepathy and a whole series of love potions. I found myself studying them with interest, remembering when I was a young girl and some of the older boys just wouldn't *look* at me. I would have sold my soul for a love potion.

Reading onwards, it struck me that many people had done exactly that. The basic love potions were comparatively harmless – they created a feeling of love and affection in the victim – but some of the stronger ones were dangerous.

The victim could become fixated on the object of their desire, to the point where they would do absolutely anything for the person who had slipped them the love potion. If the mild potions were a harmless prank – well, I wouldn't have been laughing even though most of the magical world would probably have gotten the giggles – the stronger potions were just on the far side of rape.

"I hope you're not thinking of trying to produce one," Fiona said as she fluttered down to see what I was looking at. "Far too many young witches and wizards have ended up in hot water by producing love potions and then giving them to the wrong people. Do you want to know how they were punished? They were given a very strong form of love potion and bound to their former victims."

I snorted. "I didn't want to know that," I said. It struck me as odd that anyone in the magical world would ever consider the concept of crime and punishment. Most of them seemed to accept that the strongest were in charge, at least until they were displaced by someone under them. "I wouldn't dream of giving someone a love potion."

Fiona landed on the table and looked up at me. "That's what they all say," she said, darkly. "The people who wander into the magical world discover its temptations and then they start thinking that magic can solve all of their problems. They are of course wrong, as they discover when karma starts catching up with them or someone bigger and nastier than they are destroys them. Magic is a living force and it isn't safe to trifle with it."

"Yes," I agreed, remembering the elves and the stories I'd heard about the Great Powers. "I won't tinker with love potions. I promise."

Fiona gave a dragonish shrug. "If you never learn anything else from anyone," she said, "learn that you should never make promises in the magical world. Breaking them can have...unpleasant consequences."

I flushed. "It was a figure of speech," I protested, although I knew that that wouldn't matter. In the magical world, ignorance was no excuse. After chatting to some of the others who had entered the magical world, I had realised that I was definitely one of the luckier ones. There were people who found themselves enslaved, trapped into agreements they hadn't realised were binding, or worse. "I wouldn't do it anyway."

"I should hope not," Fiona countered. "Love spells can be very dangerous."

I stopped for lunch and ate sandwiches and crisps, and then went outside for a long walk. The fresh air helped clear my head, allowing me to think clearly again for a few hours. The remains of the Rationalist building were being explored by a dozen Rationalist magicians and their apprentices, including Linux. I caught sight of him and he waved. A moment later, I waved back. It didn't look as if anything could be saved from the wreckage, but they might have been lucky. The fire demon might have merely broken the connections between the pocket dimension and the magical world.

Sparks had told me that she worked in a health food shop on North Bridge and so I walked there, enjoying the chance to forget about the magical world. The health food shop itself was remarkably expensive, although it seemed to be very popular nonetheless. The woman at the counter gave me a very unpleasant look when I walked in – she reminded me of one of the women who had bought Mr Pygmalion's statues – but didn't argue when I asked if I could borrow Sparks for a few minutes. Sparks looked reluctant as she followed me outside, at least until we were out of the old crone's sight. She started to giggle and, after a moment, I joined her.

"She's going to be wondering what kind of connection we have now," Sparks said. She winked at me as I stared at her in puzzlement. "Your master is one of the most important men in the magical world. She may start wondering if she should pay me more."

"I hope she does," I said, sincerely. I passed her a sheet of paper and allowed her to read the list of potion names, although I'd held back the ingredients. I'd see which one she wanted first. "Which one would you like?"

Sparks considered the list for a long moment. "The

painkiller one is probably one of the ones we have already," she said, finally. "Even if it isn't, there isn't any market for new painkiller potions, not when the old ones work more than well enough. I rather like the thought of the dreaming potion" – she smiled; the potion, drunk before sleep, guaranteed a lucid dream – "but I'd have to test it to be sure that we didn't already know it."

She ran down the remainder of the list. "There's nothing world-shaking here," she said, reluctantly. "Didn't you see anything really odd?"

I shrugged. I wasn't about to discuss love potions with her or anyone else. "Those are the most exotic I could find," I said. "Which one would you like?"

"The dreaming one, I guess," Sparks said. She leaned back and shook her head as I produced the recipe from my handbag and passed it over to her. "I sometimes wish that the old crone would drop dead and leave me to run the business on my own. She treats me like a slave."

"You don't have to tolerate it," I said, puzzled. "Why don't you just leave her?"

"The agreement I made with her doesn't allow it," Sparks said, bitterly. "I have to remain working for her until she releases me or until I can buy myself out. Producing and selling an unknown potion...it should work, if I am careful."

"Good luck," I said, sincerely.

I watched her go inside and then stood up myself, heading back home. A shadow fell over the land and I looked up to see a pair of dragons heading towards the market, leaving me to wonder if one of them was Fiona. There was no way to know. I heard some of the mundane people around me talking about rain coming, utterly unaware that two fantastic creatures had just passed over them. I shook my head. I'd spent months in the magical world and had been through so much, some deserved and some not, yet I would never consider going back. I belonged in there now.

Fiona greeted me at the door as I came in and passed me a note. It was from Cardonel, inviting me to dinner with him in a couple of days. I sent a reply to say that I accepted and then went back to my studies. There were relatively few books on the Thirteen – and how their workers related to them – but reading between the lines I found a surprising amount of data that confirmed Cardonel's words. The Thirteen acted more like a cartel, co-opting or locking out the newcomers, than I had realised. It made me wonder, as I finally headed off for dinner and bed, which side I should be on.

***

The four days passed slowly. Fiona watched as I worked my way through a series of magical problems, learning how to cast spells that were rarely used unless the shit had already hit the fan. I'd been warned not to try to actually cast them myself unless I was in grave danger or under supervision, but at least I knew – in theory – how to use them. I wouldn't know for sure until I actually tried and by then it might be too late. There were some magical spells I couldn't perform at all, something that wasn't exactly uncommon in the magical world. Some people just couldn't pick up certain spells.

I met Cardonel for a dinner date at a fancy eatery in the mundane world, danced for hours with him and then allowed him to take me back to his apartment and make love to me. This time, he stayed away from politics and chatted about nothing, making it a far more agreeable date for me. He even offered to come help me study, but I'd taken Fiona's warnings seriously and chosen not to invite anyone home. Cardonel shrugged, yet he clearly understood. Even though he was a half-elf, he had a kind of freedom denied to most humans and non-humans in the magical world.

Fiona seemed worried about something when I returned home, although she said nothing to me and concentrated on supervising my practice in the various disciplines. I slept and spent most of the fourth day on my studies, learning more about vampires and just how dangerous they could be. Master Revels had been quite correct, I decided, to insist on destroying the new vampire as quickly as possible. It – I couldn't bring myself to think of it as female – would only have grown more dangerous if we'd risked leaving it alone. The day passed slowly without a sign of Master Revels. I went to bed convinced that he would return home and I would see him in the morning. He had always been punctual before.

When I arose, he still had not returned. Fiona and I were alone.

CHAPTER TWENTY-SIX

"So," I said, to Fiona. "What do we do?"

The tiny dragon looked nervous, if dragons could be said to look nervous. It was another reminder that there was a great deal I didn't understand about the relationship between her and Master Revels – between her and the person who held his post. Fiona had clearly been around for much longer than any single human, even the ones who used magic to prolong their lives to unnatural lengths. It made me wonder what could make her nervous. As best as I could tell, dragons were almost indestructible, even by magic.

"The master said that if there was a time when he didn't return home, the Thirteen would have to be alerted," Fiona said, reluctantly. She didn't sound happy about it, although I couldn't understand why. The Thirteen would surely help their lost servant. "He issued those orders before you joined him and issued no others since."

"Oh," I said. I understood – he clearly didn't consider me ready to succeed him yet – but it was still galling. "How long should we wait before we start calling the Thirteen and asking for help."

"Oh, you cannot *call* them," Fiona said, evading the question. "You have to visit them and ask for assistance. And even then they might refuse. I don't know where Master Revels was going when he left or who we might ask to find out."

I scowled. I was certain, somehow, that Master Revels had run into trouble. He would have called to let us know if he was going to be delayed, or simply returned home for a night's sleep and a chat before heading back out again. It was possible that he had a girlfriend somewhere in the magical world – just because he'd shown no sign of interest in me didn't mean that he had no sexual urges; hell, for all I knew he was a homosexual – and was staying with her, yet surely he would have said *something*. Logic suggested that I shouldn't panic just yet, but the cold feeling running down the base of my spine suggested otherwise. Even in the mundane world, woman's intuition was nothing to laugh at. It was a very subtle form of magic.

Fiona fluttered over to me and landed on my shoulder, offering what comfort she could. "I understand how you're feeling," she said. "Wait until lunchtime. If nothing happens by then, we'll go speak to the Thirteen in person and ask for their advice."

I frowned. "Don't you think that they will want to give me orders?"

"Perhaps," Fiona said, with a dragonish shrug. "On the other hand, you haven't actually sworn loyalty or obedience to them, so they have no actual right to give you orders. Not that that would actually stop anyone if they thought they could get away with it."

The three hours until lunchtime passed slowly, too slowly. I tried to concentrate on reading various magical texts – including the instructions for creating a pocket dimension large enough for a palace within a tiny room – but my mind refused to focus. I just *knew* that Master Revels was in trouble and that I had to save him, which would have been fine if I had any idea where to start looking. I had no idea where he had gone and, when I tried to go into his study to find a note he might have left for me, I discovered that it was locked and sealed with powerful security spells. They *growled* at me when I tested them lightly and I decided not to try risking a break-in. Ending up as a toad, or statue, or even dead would be no help to Master Revels, would it? I asked Fiona if she knew how to enter the room, but she shook her head. Most magicians liked to keep their secrets. I had never been in the room without him.

I had soup and bread for lunch – I couldn't eat anything else – and checked for a message from Master Revels. There was nothing; the silence was almost deafening. I beckoned to Fiona, who fluttered down from where she had been having a nap. I envied her the ability to sleep even when worried, but perhaps she wasn't too worried. Dragons lived so long that our lives were little more than eye-blinks to them. Fiona couldn't bring herself to care too much about a man she knew was a mayfly compared to her. It would be dangerous for her mental health.

"Come on," I said. "We're off to see the Thirteen."

Fiona settled on my shoulder and waited for me to unlock the door and step outside the house. The security spells on the outside, at least, responded to my commands and sealed the house, rendering it impossible – I hoped – for anyone to break in while we were out. Master Revels had told me that the security spells were complex, but any security system could be broken, given a determined attacker and enough time. He'd also told me that there were a handful of wizards who had accidentally managed to lock themselves out of their houses and never been able to regain entrance. Magic was fond of little jokes and surprises for the unwary user.

Master Revels had constructed his house – after buying the property in the mundane world – in the shadow of Edinburgh Castle. The Thirteen had actually occupied the castle itself, although they had created pocket dimensions and other magical accommodations to hide their presence from the mundane world, which resolutely refused to forget that the castle existed. Distraction and diversion spells have their limits, even when used against mundane people who don't have the slightest idea that magic exists. There was a pile of rubble somewhere in the north of Scotland, I'd been told, that was actually a hidden castle, belonging to one of the oldest magical families in the country. The mundane world thought that it was just a ruined building, too old and uninteresting to be worth exploring. That had always struck me as amusing. How many other ruins hid magical complexes?

I walked up towards the castle, ignoring the tourists thronging around to pay a vastly-inflated charge to get into the public areas, and found the path into the magical side of the castle with ease. The air seemed to shimmer in front of me as I stepped onto the path, expanding into a complex that existed in many dimensions at once, beckoning me onwards. I felt security spells buzzing at the back of my mind, interrogating me and alerting their masters that I was coming, spells so powerful that I couldn't imagine anything being able to fool them for long. The spells had reached into my mind and read my thoughts directly. If I'd harboured angry feelings about the Thirteen, they would have known...and with so much power bound up in the castle, they could have squashed me like a bug.

Fiona twitched as the wards washed over her and then allowed us both into the magical zone. I guessed that the wards didn't probe too far into a person's mind, or the Thirteen would have known about Cardonel's odd comments to me about power-sharing. Or maybe they already knew what he and his friends had in mind and just chose to ignore it. If Master Revels had held half-breeds in complete contempt, I was sure that the Thirteen would share the same attitude. And besides, it wasn't in the character of supremely powerful magicians to believe that anyone could be their equal, let alone their superior. Confidence – the absolute confidence that comes from self-knowledge and determination – was one of the foremost tools in the magician's arsenal. A magician who went into a duel convinced that he would lose definitely *would* lose.

The stone corridors of the castle expanded around me. I shivered as the magic pulled us along, leaving me no longer in full control of my legs. I had to admit that it was a very neat security system – no one would be able to do anything the Thirteen didn't want them to do – yet it felt creepy, putting me firmly in my place. That, I guessed, was the whole idea. The Thirteen would want their visitors feeling awe, respect...and maybe just a little fear. They were, after all, the most powerful magicians in the world.

My legs kept walking forwards until I found myself in a chamber. It was richly decorated, with fine tapestries hanging from the ceiling and covering the walls. Ahead of me was a table with thirteen seats, allowing the people placed at the table to glare down at me properly. Behind them was a roaring fire, one that wasn't burning wood, but magic. I could feel the presence of additional security spells settling around the room as the door slammed closed behind me. My body dropped to one knee in front of them.

I wasn't sure what I had expected when I saw the Thirteen. Men like Master Revels, perhaps; powerful, dignified and in control. Instead, I saw thirteen different illusions, each one blatantly absurd. One of them was a naked woman with oversized breasts, another was a strange cross between a human and a crocodile and a third looked far more like a typical wizard, with a long white beard, a pointy hat and a staff in one hand. They were all hidden behind their illusions and it took me a moment to realise that it was another way of putting people in their place. The absence of deceit was, after all, common courtesy...and they were making a *point* of how rude they could afford to be.

"You may stand," a voice said. Try as I might, I couldn't figure out which one of them had spoken first. They seemed to be wrapped in their own private web of spells, allowing them to communicate with each other without me – or anyone else – overhearing them. I was intensely grateful for Fiona's presence on my shoulder. She was a comforting reminder that I wasn't entirely alone. "Why do you wish to speak with us?"

It occurred to me, as my body stood up on its own, that I might not be talking to *all* the Thirteen. There were so many security spells in the room that my ability to see magic, particularly the more subtle kinds of magic, was untrustworthy. It was like staring into a blinding light and trying to see what lay beyond it. It hurt to look too closely.

"Master Revels is missing," I said. I couldn't tell if they responded to that or not. The illusions surrounding them were too strong. "I need to know what to do now that he is gone."

There was a brief flurry of magic between the different members of the Thirteen. I couldn't make it out, or even tell what it was doing. I guessed – I hoped – that they were sharing information with each other. There was no way to know for sure.

"He was doing some research for us," the voice said, finally. I still couldn't tell which one of them was doing the talking. "The destruction of the Rationalist Building is a matter of grave concern to us, as is the disappearance of a vast number of ghosts. We ordered him to investigate."

I blinked in surprise. *Other* ghosts had gone missing? Of course; the Silent Order had said as much, back before we'd walked into the Elfish Kingdom and I had undergone the Ordeal. The thought gave me an unexpected burst of confidence and I stood up straighter, peering into the illusions. I found myself wondering just what they had to hide. Most magicians wouldn't be satisfied with power, or at least power on its own; they'd want the entire world to know that they were the most powerful magicians within it. If the Thirteen wanted to hide their identities, what did it mean? I thought of the *Wizard of Oz* and smiled. The Thirteen might not be as powerful as they claimed to be. Pay no attention to the men behind the illusions indeed!

"He did not report back to us," the spokesperson continued. "We are most concerned about his well-being."

I blinked. "But you don't know where he is or where he went?"

"We do not monitor his every move," the spokesperson said. I picked up a hint of…unconcern from the voice. It was so hard to know for sure. "We have found that the best agents are those who operate on their own, without support or supervision from us. They use our name and call upon favours we have earned and deals we have signed."

I stared at the illusions. "I have to find him," I said, sharply. "You have to tell me where he might have gone!

The room's atmosphere shifted, becoming more dangerous. "You do not make demands of us," the spokesperson said. I felt my body tremble at their command, a reminder of their power. Just like the elves, their inner world was theirs and, within it, they were all-powerful. Of course, given that the membership of the Thirteen was supposed to change regularly, they were very far from unassailable. It dawned on me that the system was designed, not to keep the Thirteen on top, but to prevent wars and uncontrolled duels between wizards who wanted to dominate the rest of the magical world. "You are our servant, for your master is our servant."

I felt red-hot rage flaring through me at the thought, but somehow I managed to control my anger. I didn't dare lash out at them, not now.

"Please tell me where I can start looking," I said. I knew I sounded weak, but there was no choice. "I have to find him."

"We will begin investigations," the spokesperson said, grudgingly. I had the feeling that, like a mother who said 'maybe' to her child, they really meant that they weren't going to bother. There were probably hundreds of magicians who would be willing to try to replace Master Revels, which meant...I found myself wondering, hopelessly, what would happen to Fiona and myself. "If we find him and we can recover him, we will do so."

I knew what that meant, all right. The Thirteen were far from all-powerful in the magical world. If Master Revels was a prisoner of the elves, or one of the Great Powers, or even a coalition of other magicians, they weren't going to risk their own position by trying to free him. I supposed that I understood a certain reluctance to tangle with the elves – and the Silent Order had mentioned that elfish magic was involved – but still...it was a poor reward for a man who had served them loyally.

"As for yourself, you will report to Master Dervish," the spokesperson continued. It was very definitely an order. "Should we be unable to locate and recover Master Revels, we will arrange for someone to take over your apprenticeship, if that is what you wish. Master Revels would have wanted it that way."

"Perhaps," I said, unconvinced. My determination to find Master Revels myself was undiminished. "Thank you for your time."

My body turned of its own accord and marched through the door, back out into the stone corridors. I fought the controlling spell as best I could, but I couldn't break it until it snapped itself, just after I reached the mundane sections of the building. The ancient castle had disappointed me when I'd seen it as a schoolgirl, for reasons I couldn't really explain, even to myself. Now, with the benefit of hindsight, I wondered if I'd sensed the presence of magic and had been frustrated because I'd been unable to see it. No one, not even a pair of Japanese tourists who were taking hundreds of photographs, saw my appearance. A girl appearing out of nowhere just wasn't part of their worldview.

Fiona left me when we reached the house, allowing me to walk back to North Bridge on my own. I didn't want to report to anyone, even Dervish, but once I had reported in I could do as I liked – or so I told myself. The parts of the magical world I could see appeared to be disturbed, not entirely to my surprise. It wasn't every day that a fire demon appeared and destroyed an entire building. They'd be talking – and worrying – about it for hundreds of years, probably. I'd looked up the records and discovered that while minor demons appeared all the time, the major demons – the really powerful and dangerous ones – were very rare. I suspect that the entire human race, even the ones who worshipped demons, was grateful for that small mercy.

The Mosque looked slightly different to my eyes this time, although I wasn't sure why. I found the magical doorway easily enough and stepped through it, ignoring the puzzled glances I received from a pair of young men who were clearly waiting for prayers. Their eyes seemed to glaze over as I vanished, both from their sight and from their minds. I found the stairwell and walked downstairs, feeling Dervish's security spells brushing against my mind. The doorway at the bottom of the stairs was open, waiting for me.

"Welcome," Dervish said. He looked as if he had aged overnight. His beard, which had been neatly-trimmed the last time I'd seen him, now looked as if he hadn't bothered to cut it. "I'm afraid I have made a dreadful mistake."

I blinked. Magicians very rarely confessed mistakes. The mundane world considered it a sign of maturity, but the magical world regarded it as a sign of weakness. Besides, allowing someone to know about your mistakes could give them an insight into how your magic worked.

"You see, I may be responsible for his death," Dervish said, before I could say anything. "I sent him to see the Nameless Elf and I haven't heard anything from him since."

CHAPTER TWENTY-SEVEN

I felt a shiver running down the back of my spine at the name.

"There's an elf in this world?" I asked. I'd always had the impression that the elves normally stayed in their own dimension, with only half-elves like Cardonel living in the human part of the magical world. Of course, with the market being here, there was no reason why some elves wouldn't want to visit the more crowded parts of the universe. "Why...?"

Dervish shook his head. "Master Revels and I talked about the missing ghosts," he said, grimly. I had the impression that he hadn't worried about it at all until the Thirteen contacted him, which had suddenly convinced him that he'd sent Master Revels to his death. "We were studying the remains of the fire, you see; it started in the records section of the Rationalist Building. Whoever summoned the fire demon wanted to destroy the records of every experiment they'd conducted over the last year."

I didn't see how the fire and an elf without a name went together, but I resolved to wait and see what he said. "Some of those experiments included research into how ghosts and elves and other magical creatures could exist," Dervish continued. "You see, humans – even magical humans – are flesh and blood, with a little magic infused into their skin. Creatures like vampires or werewolves have stronger magic infused into them, but they don't control it; in a sense, it controls them. A vampire's nature, in particular, is determined by the strength of the magical infection.

"But that isn't true of creatures like elves and sprites and lesser demons," he added. "You see" – I was getting sick of hearing him say that – "they're composed from magic and the solid matter we think we see is an illusion. A ghost, particularly an intelligent ghost rather than a psychic impression of something traumatic that happened long ago, is a human that somehow became converted into a magical form. The Rationalists were very keen to discover if they could do it deliberately."

I frowned. "They wanted to see if they could die and yet remain in the world?"

"Allah is not so easily cheated," Dervish agreed. "The Rationalists were unable to create ghosts at will. There is something that we humans have – a soul – which the magic-based creatures lack. When we die – when we lose the anchor of our bodies – our souls go onwards to heaven or hell, as Allah wills."

"But there are ghosts who are allowed to remain on Earth," I said, puzzled. "Why do some remain and others are forced to go onwards?"

"We don't know," Dervish said. "Sometimes it is an act of mercy; sometimes there seems to be a reason for the ghost to remain behind on Earth. We don't know for sure. Certain parties within the Rationalists, however, wanted to push the experiments far further forward and may have enlisted the aid of the Nameless Elf."

"I see," I said, slowly. The name – or lack of it – meant nothing to me, yet somehow I was sure that it was important. "Who is the Nameless Elf?"

Dervish studied me for a long moment. "I hope," he said finally, "that you're not considering anything dangerous?"

I said nothing. In truth, I had no idea what I wanted to do or say.

"The Nameless Elf was tossed out of the Elfish Kingdoms a few hundred years ago," Dervish said, when I said nothing. "The Queen told him to leave and stripped him of his name, the most important thing to an elf. We don't know what he did wrong or even if he did *anything* wrong. The elves aren't human, Dizzy; they forgive or condone things that horrify us and they have laws banning things that seem hilarious to a human observer."

I wondered, briefly, if the Nameless Elf was Cardonel's father, but the timing didn't work out. Cardonel had claimed to be younger than that, barely older than me. Besides, the elves seemed to blame the half-breeds for existing, rather than blame their parents for bringing them into the world. They reminded me, far too much, of aristocrats disowning bastard children and denying that they had ever existed. Even so, it sounded odd. The elfish society is very different from ours.

After going through the Ordeal, I'd read everything Master Revels had had on the elves. Their society made little sense to us. Elves had been known to commit treason and get away with it, provided that they did it in the proper and acceptable manner. Queens had been dethroned and sent into exile, only to return, overthrow their replacements and regain control of the elves. And yet, putting the merest foot wrong could produce a horrific punishment. The elves had an elfish criminal that, every day, they used as a source of magic, relying on his immortality to replace what they took from him. No one, least of all the elves themselves, remembered what he had actually done to merit the punishment. Or at least they wouldn't admit to it.

And then there was the way they treated human slaves...

"He found a place within the magical world," Dervish added. "His arrival excited much interest from various different parties, including the Rationalists and the Sceptics. They wanted to know what he knew, so they made deals with him. And what he did with those deals..."

Dervish shook his head. "Do you understand how rare it is for the entire magical world to unite around a single cause?" he asked. "The rumours got out and they spread, and they spread, until finally someone was moved to investigate. And what they found...the entire magical world was united in horror at what the Nameless Elf had done. They linked their power and confined him to a single place, trapping him there forever. They should have executed him, or confined him to the Dark Continent, but no one dared take that step. Who knew what the elves would make of it."

I couldn't see the elves caring about what happened to

someone they'd stripped of his name, but perhaps they would find themselves forced to take notice if one of their people was killed by the magical world. Master Revels – or his counterpart of that time – wouldn't have wanted to risk antagonising the elves too far, not when they could invade the magical world and wreak havoc.

"Since then, he's been a prisoner," Dervish added. "It isn't a harsh confinement – people can still go in and out – but he cannot leave. For an elf, used to running where he pleased, it is a suitable punishment. No one should enter, in my view, yet the others didn't listen when walling him up forever was suggested. And not everyone who goes in to talk to him comes out again."

I shivered. "And what happens to them?"

"You don't want to know," Dervish said. "The Nameless Elf performed experiments on some of his victims, using their flesh and blood to delve deeper into the mysteries behind how magic and humanity go together. For others, he merely killed them and ate the bodies, or performed horrendous acts on their living flesh. He is a monster and I sent your master to see him, believing that he was the link between the ghosts, the fire and the Rationalists. And he hasn't come back."

I felt icy resolve crystallising in my mind. I'd freed the slaves and all that had happened was a caning. I would gladly take another caning if it meant rescuing Master Revels from captivity. He didn't deserve to be left to suffer and I had the uneasy feeling that if the Thirteen realised that the Nameless Elf was involved, they would choose to let the matter drop rather than confront him. It wasn't as cowardly as it sounded; the Thirteen had bound themselves into treaties with the elves and threatening the Nameless Elf might break them. The elves just *looked* for an excuse to fuck with humanity.

"Right," I said. I stood up before I could think better of it. "Tell me where I can find the Nameless Elf."

Dervish shook his head, firmly. "No," he said, sharply. "Dizzy, even a fully-trained magician would have problems *escaping* an angry elf, let alone getting answers out of him.

You would have to put him in a position where he had no choice but to answer...and elves are very good at avoiding such positions. I cannot let you go to confront the Nameless Elf, not alone."

"I have to go," I said. I knew that it was going to be dangerous, yet...I felt as if I had no choice. Perhaps Cardonel could give me some advice on how to deal with the Nameless Elf. Perhaps I wouldn't have to fight him to convince him to give me honest answers. Perhaps...there were just too many possibilities. "You sent him there and now you're talking about abandoning him."

Dervish's face, already dark, flushed darker. I had the impression, just for a second, that he was going to hit me. I had, after all, insulted his courage and few men bore themselves well under that sort of insult. Of course, advising someone to stand up to homicidal maniacs, as Blackadder said to Baldrick, was the sort of advice that should be treated with extreme caution. If the Nameless Elf had been less terrible, dealing with him shouldn't have been a problem. And, in the magical world, power and the will to use it was the key to advancement.

"You don't understand what you're getting into," Dervish insisted. "The Nameless Elf is *dangerous*! If I am supposed to be taking care of you..."

I shook my head. "You have a daughter to take care of," I said, firmly. "I will deal with the Nameless Elf." I hoped I sounded confident, for I very definitely was *not* confident in the slightest. "Where do I find him?"

Dervish, reluctantly, gave me directions and wished me luck. I gave him a hug, much to his surprise, and walked out of the mosque, heading back towards the market. I'd had some ideas when I started to think about confronting an elf, for while elves were all-powerful within their own dimension, they were very much reduced in the human world. Still powerful, still dangerous, but they were hardly unbeatable. If the Nameless Elf had been invincible, the magical world wouldn't have been able to confine him. I told myself that as long as I remained calm and focused, the Nameless Elf wouldn't be able to bother me. In the market,

I bought a handful of vital supplies, including a pair of weapons the Nameless Elf wouldn't be able to touch. I might not have been allowed to take anything like it into the Elfish Kingdom, but I could use them in the human world.

I called Cardonel and asked him to meet me at his apartment. When I walked in, he kissed me at the door, his hands roaming all over my body. It was clear what he wanted and I surprised myself by feeling another burst of lust myself. I kissed him back hard and started to fumble with his trousers, allowing him to push me up against the wall and pull down my own jeans. I gasped in delight as he pushed inside me and started to move faster and faster, bringing us both to the boil. Afterwards, we just clung to one another, holding tight. I hadn't realised how much tension I'd been feeling until it drained away.

"I need your help," I said, once we'd undressed, showered and pulled our clothes back on. I like sex – one of the reasons my mother called me a slut and threw me out of her house – but I always feel unclean afterwards. Oh, not in a religious sense; I guess that, just like a cat, I like being clean. I didn't see any reason to make him wear a condom – I'd taken contraceptive measures – and he'd come inside me. "I have to visit the Nameless Elf."

Cardonel started. I was holding him and I felt the shock ripple through his body. It dawned on me, too late, that Cardonel probably hated the Nameless Elf. He might have been tossed out of the Elfish Kingdoms, but at least he'd once been part of them and a respected elf, rather than a half-breed who, through an accident of birth, had been condemned never to have a home. The Nameless Elf, at least in some ways, was what Cardonel wanted to be. He was an elf, with all of the powers and abilities, but without a home or even family.

"Look," I said, slowly. I seemed to have developed a remarkable talent for antagonising people. "I'm sorry if I…"

"It's not your fault," Cardonel said, sourly. He shook his head and then looked up at me. "Dizzy, my sweetheart, have you quite lost your mind?"

"No," I said. I knew that Dervish would probably

disagree. So would most of the magical world, if they knew anything about it. "I have to find Master Revels, whatever it takes."

Cardonel winced. "If you walk into the Nameless Elf's territory, you may not walk out again," he said, darkly. "I once went to ask him, when I was young and stupid, if he could help me become a full elf. I escaped by the skin of my teeth."

I smiled. "At least you escaped," I said. "How did you do it?"

"It wasn't a pretty sight," Cardonel admitted. "I'd tell you, but I might want to use the method again. In any case…it wasn't a pretty sight."

"Oh," I said. A number of possibilities leapt to my mind. I pushed them back down as far as they would go. "Cardonel, darling, I have to go."

"Do me a favour and stop talking like a romantic lead," Cardonel said. I laughed. "I understand what you want to do and why you want to do it, but it could kill you – or worse – for nothing. I ought to tie you to the bed and leave you there until you come to your senses."

I snorted. "You'd like that, wouldn't you?"

"Dizzy…"

"Yes, I know what you mean," I sighed. All the men in my life either seemed to be over-protective or intent on doing me harm and generally treating me like crap. I supposed I should be grateful that Cardonel was one of the former. "Now tell me…how do I deal with the Nameless Elf?"

"You don't," Cardonel said. "The Nameless Elf is completely insane. You cannot count on him to even follow the normal rules that elves have to follow. Because he lost his name, many curses and commands just slid off him. He is quite capable of tearing you in half for no other reason than it amuses him, or deciding that he wants to hurt you because he thinks he *shouldn't* hurt you. He spins between rationality – or a version of rationality – and absolute madness. If you come upon him while he's embracing madness, you're dead. He once skinned a pair of visitors alive and wore their skins as clothing for several years."

He shook his head. "If he's feeling rational, he may talk to you and agree to deal with you," he added. "You can make bargains with him then, but remember he's not bound by most of the rules of magic. You cannot trust him to keep a promise and you certainly cannot make him swear on his name."

"Because he doesn't have one," I guessed, dryly.

"Precisely," Cardonel said. "There are people here who believe that he actually *wants* to break promises in the hopes that the laws of magic will rebound on him and destroy him. He's been cast out from everyone like him – apart from me, nothing remotely elfish has visited him since his exile began." He held up a hand. "But don't go feeling sorry for him. Based on what we know he's done, ever since he was exiled to our world, he thoroughly deserved the sentence from his Queen and worse. He should have been executed and to hell with the possible consequences."

He reached out for me and held me close. "Are you sure that you have to go?"

"Yes," I said. I wasn't going to back down now. "There's no choice."

"Idiot," Cardonel said. He kissed me. It wasn't a passionate kiss, more of a goodbye kiss. I realised suddenly that he feared that he would never see me again and it almost broke my resolve. I kissed him back gently and turned away so that he wouldn't see the tears in my eyes. "While you're with him, remember that he still has most of the elfish powers. Watch your back."

I waved goodbye and walked out of the apartment, wondering if I would ever see it again. Dervish's directions had been very clear. Like many places in the magical world, the Nameless Elf's prison co-existed with a place in the mundane world, adding a certain additional power to the wards sealing him into place. The Nameless Elf was trapped within the Edinburgh Dungeons, a popular tourist attraction. I realised, in a moment of insight, that the mundane world had been encouraged to build their tourist attraction on top of the prison, just to tap their power and use it to keep him imprisoned. It was surprisingly clever. I sensed the hand of the Sisterhood somewhere within the spells.

"Well," I told myself. I was standing just outside the Dungeon. I could feel the Nameless Elf's presence now, a shimmering sense of insanity that threatened to contaminate anyone who touched it. I almost turned and walked away. I hadn't had so many doubts when I'd freed the slaves. There, I'd been secure that I knew that I was doing the right thing. Here…I felt terror, enough terror to weaken my knees and drive me away. "Here goes nothing."

Bracing myself, I stepped forward.

CHAPTER TWENTY-EIGHT

The stench hit me at once, a mental feeling that seemed to crawl through my eyes and into my brain. It was a warning, I realised, a field intended to warn anyone foolish enough to enter the building that they were confronting incredible danger. I braced myself against the feeling and kept walking, unwilling to allow myself to be deterred by the field. The aversion field was, I knew, the merest of the defences surrounding the building. As I walked on, feeling the building opening up in front of me, I sensed the presence of countless other defences. They were unlocking themselves one by one, allowing me to enter without trouble. They were so complex that I knew that, if they had been designed to keep everyone out as well as one specific person in, I would never have been able to unravel them.

I heard, or thought I heard, voices at the back of my mind as I pushed on. *Unless I mistake his nature quite, he is the merry wanderer of the night; may the lord have mercy upon our souls; what do you call an elf with no name...?* I tried to block them out as I walked onwards, unable to decide if the voices were warning me, taunting me or simply quite mad. I wondered, suddenly, if they were ghosts, impressions of others who had walked the same pathway and never returned. The Nameless Elf welcomed all to his domain, but rarely allowed them to leave. I thought, suddenly, that I was making a big mistake, yet I couldn't turn back. Something was pulling me onwards, deeper into the tangled web that served as the Nameless Elf's home and prison.

My eyes opened – I hadn't been aware that I had closed them – and I saw the interior for the first time. It was horrific. I felt as if I was walking through a human body,

splashing my way though pools of blood and avoiding pieces
of flesh and bone. Blood poured from somewhere high
overhead, pooling on the floor before being absorbed and
reappearing somewhere else. The smell was unpleasant and
I had to force myself to breathe through my mouth. The
stench might have driven me from the building, if I had
been able to flee.

Ahead of me, I heard high-pitched laughter, a sound that
sent chills running down my spine. It was joined, moments
later, by voices screaming for help, a symphony of the
damned. I realised that the Nameless Elf – not unlike
Robin's master – had stolen the voices of his victims and
pulled them all together into a hellish instrument. The howls
and shrieks echoed in my ears, reminding me that few left
the Nameless Elf's territory alive.

I stepped through a door and found an antechamber.
There were thousands of bodies within the room, all dead.
They were displayed in dozens of horrific poses, from
crucified men and women to bodies that had been cut open
and spread out on a table. It was a horrifying sight, all the
more so when some of the bodies came to life and started
pleading with me for help. Their maddened eyes showed
just how long they'd been kept at the mercy of the Nameless
Elf, always on the verge of death, but held back from the
final merciful release. I caught sight of a small boy and girl –
they couldn't have been older than seven – who had been
literally cut in half and joined together, creating two strange
hybrids. I couldn't understand how they were still alive, yet
somehow they lived and breathed, mounted on the wall like
a butterfly trapped within a specimen box. They had to have
gone completely out of their minds.

"I'm sorry," I said, quietly. There was nothing I could do
for them, at least not at once. Maybe there would be a way
to convince the Nameless Elf to free them, even though it
would mean their deaths and those of most of the other
people in the room. They wouldn't last long without his
magic to support them. "I am truly sorry."

A glint of stone caught my eye and I turned to see a statue
of a little girl. I swore aloud as I realised that it was the

missing statue, the final girl Mr Pygmalion had kidnapped...it felt like years ago now. We had never been able to trace her until now. Someone working for the Nameless Elf, someone capable of walking between the mundane and magical worlds, had bought her and brought her to his master. The Nameless Elf probably enjoyed looking at her and watching her staring back at him. Or maybe she was dead. Trapped and helpless for so long, her mind might have merged with the stone and effectively vanished.

There was another high-pitched giggle up ahead and I turned, feeling a presence at the back of my mind. Just by existing in the human world, the Nameless Elf warped it out of shape. I took one last look at his room of horrors – if only to remind myself not to fall into his hands, although I had the terrible feeling that it was far too late – and stepped out of the door. The blood-stained corridors seemed to be closing in as I walked further into the building. The sound of laughter didn't seem to grow any louder.

I jumped back in alarm as something burst out of the wall and slid past me. It was a giant worm, carrying what looked like a bazooka, followed rapidly by two more. Their eyes, almost human, looked focused and determined, but they completely ignored me. I wondered if they'd been human once, or if they were just another of the Nameless Elf's experiments, or if they were just another set of weird creatures in the magical world. The space where they'd come from had already sealed up neatly. The Nameless Elf had no intention of allowing me to go anywhere except where he wanted me to go.

The sound of laughter faded away as I kept walking, to be replaced by a sudden inhuman silence, broken only by a distant thumping noise. It took me a moment to realise that it was my own heartbeat, so loud that I was surprised the Nameless Elf couldn't hear it, or perhaps he could. The corridor came to an end suddenly and I found myself standing in a large room. The Nameless Elf – there could be no mistaking him – was standing at the other end of the room.

He was shorter than I'd expected, wearing an outfit that

appeared to have come from Revolutionary France, complete with tri-cornered hat and fancy jacket. His features reminded me of the male elves I'd seen back in the Elfish Kingdoms, but there was a strangeness to his expression...something in his eyes that sent shivers down my spine. His jacket appeared to be moving of its own accord, as if there was something hidden under his clothing. I doubt that he was pleased to see me. I suspected, rather, that he had another form that kept threatening to burst out into the open. The Nameless Elf was far more than he appeared.

His eyes locked on mine and it took everything I had not to run. The elves I'd met in the Elfish Kingdom had been arrogant, convinced of their own superiority, but the Nameless Elf was clearly insane. I could sense raw magic flaring out over him, bursting into existence like fireworks and then being absorbed into his body; the links he'd created to his prison, turning it into his own world. He hadn't been able to interfere with the spells holding him inside, thankfully, but what he'd done had been quite bad enough. The Thirteen of that time had probably just been relieved to have managed to seal him inside a prison, where he could only hurt people stupid enough to walk inside. People like me.

"Well, well, well," the Nameless Elf said. His eyes travelled over my body. It wasn't a sexual gaze, more the gaze of a scientist considering where to start the dissection. The men and women I'd seen earlier, kept alive and suffering by his magic, had to have been his test subjects. I wondered if that had been why he'd been stripped of his name and exiled to our world, but I doubted it. The Queen would probably have considered exterminating the entire human race to be a hoot. "Won't you come into my parlour, said the spider to the fly..."

He giggled again, an utterly inhuman sound. It was unsettling, but I held my ground somehow. I had no intention of running, if it were possible to run. He'd managed to gain control of the interior of his prison and he could probably turn it against me with little effort. His other form seemed to shimmer into existence, a strange translucent network of tentacles and eyes, before it faded away again. I saw enough of it to know that I didn't want to see it again. What I'd seen so far was already disturbing to the imagination.

"And you walked in of your own free will," he added. He let out a cackle that started to turn into a hiss. "You belong to me now."

He held out an inhumanly long hand and flexed, producing long claws and needles that seemed to be part of his body. "And we are going to have so much fun together," he said. He looked back at me. "I wonder how you would look with two heads."

I very nearly commented that two heads were better than one, but that metaphor wouldn't be so effective in real life. My mind was screaming at me to run, yet somehow I held my ground. The Nameless Elf hadn't attacked me yet, so maybe there was a chance to reason with him. Of course, being nameless, there was no force ready and waiting to punish him for breaking his word.

"I come in peace," I said. The Nameless Elf greeted this declaration with another giggle, which became a fit of high-pitched laughter. "My master visited you and vanished. Are you holding him prisoner?"

"Yes, no, three bags full," he chanted. His giggle was starting to hurt my ears. I could feel the magic in the room shifting, turning against me. The chances were good that he was planning to do something amusing to me. He had so much raw power that he could probably do anything he could imagine. "Why do you think I would help you? You're nothing, but a mere human. I can penetrate your reality at any point and alter it at my whim. What do you think I cannot do to you?"

He held out his hands, pressed them together and then pulled them apart, revealing a thread of life. I saw, to my horror, images from my past hovering in front of him. My birth, my first day at school and the first boy I'd kissed, moving in with my ex, being disowned by my mother...I realised, to my horror, that his madness gave him access to power beyond that of any normal elf. His view on the universe, shaped by madness, allowed him to do so much more than anyone who was even remotely sane. There was no way I could match him, at least in raw power. The only hope was to trick him.

I pulled back and studied him through my own senses. Staring at him was like staring into a blinding light – with the added danger that the madness that had infected him would jump across to me – but somehow I held my gaze. He was a blur of magic, enough magic to reshape the world if he ever managed to escape; a pattern that seemed to twist and turn in front of me. I understood, now, why there was only one weapon that could be used against an elf. I'd planned for it, yet...could I use it?

The Nameless Elf chuckled and started to poke at the thread of life. I felt my body change as he altered parts, giggling all the time. I was taller; I was shorter; I was black, Chinese or brown...just for a few seconds, I was a man. My hair grew long and then fell out. Old age raced through my system, only to be reversed and cancelled a split second before I would have died. There was no pain, just a growing sense of helplessness and dependency.

"You're no fun," the Nameless Elf proclaimed. He looked as if he'd bitten into a lemon. "For all of your power and potential, you're no fun at all."

I shrugged. The changes he'd wrought on my body weren't transfigurations, not in the sense that Circe had transfigured me when she'd encountered me for the first time. In a very real sense, the changes he'd caused in me had always been there; they hadn't been imposed on me. The Nameless Elf seemed to be twisting time and space into a pretzel in a manner that would have shamed Doctor Who, but he wasn't actually hurting me. Of course, that could change the moment he realised his mistake.

"I need answers," I said, as calmly as I could. My voice felt odd. I looked down and realised that I was standing on all fours; the Nameless Elf had transformed me into a donkey. I had no idea if that had been a possible course of life for me or not, but I forced myself not to let it get to me. "Are you the one holding my master prisoner?"

The Nameless Elf ignored me, still peering down at the thread of life. A second later, I was human again, just in time for the first of the false memories to hit. My mother had abused me as a child. My stepfathers had raped me when I started to mature. My first boyfriend had beaten me to within an inch of my life...the memories raged through my mind, confusing me and warping my grip on reality. It seemed to be less effective than changing my physical form, yet, given time, it would overcome me. And then the Nameless Elf would *really* start having fun.

He giggled and looked up at me. The false memories faded away, yet I would always remember having had them. Perhaps enough of them would remain to leave me wondering if they were real...his poisonous gift to me. I hated him at that moment, hated him for what he'd done to me and all of his other victims.

"So...you want answers," he said. "I can give you those answers."

The Nameless Elf smiled. I saw razor-sharp teeth inside his smile. The invisible form seemed to shimmer back into existence, casting an eerie shadow over his body. I recoiled in shock. He seemed to sense that and cackled in amusement, throwing back his head and laughing outright.

"All you have to do is stay ahead of me for an hour," the Nameless Elf said. He leered at me, somehow freezing me to the spot. "If you survive that long, I will answer all of your questions and free my captives into the bargain. If you fall...you will become mine."

He reached out and placed a hand on my throat. I would have flinched if I could have moved, but my body refused to obey me. His hand trailed down towards my breasts, stroking them gently and then down towards my crotch. There was nothing sexual in it, I realised in a flash of horror; he was inspecting his new possession. I knew that I had no choice, yet...if my plan failed I was going to die – or suffer a fate worse than death.

"Go," the Nameless Elf ordered. The universe seemed to tilt around me and I was somewhere else within his complex, stumbling as my body unfroze. There was so much raw magic around that all of my senses were useless. I couldn't even hear anything over the sound of mad laughter. A moment later, I heard his voice. "Ready or not, here I come..."

I plunged down a corridor and ran, knowing that he would be coming after me. I had to look like I was panicking – I was, a little – and I knew that he would enjoy it. The universe shifted around me again and I discovered that I was running right towards him. I almost fell over as I tried to slow down, only to find myself shrinking and flying through the air towards his mouth. I pulled magic out of my reserves and threw it at him. It didn't hurt him – most human magic couldn't hurt Elves – but it sent him tumbling backwards. I fell out of the air, suddenly restored to human form, and landed hard on my front. The impact knocked the wind out of me. Before I could recover, strong inhuman hands had rolled me over and I felt someone landing on top of me.

The Nameless Elf leered down at me. "I win," he said, and giggled. He placed one hand on my chest and I felt his magic interacting with mine. "Your magic is mine and then...oh, there are *so* many things we could do together. We're going to have so much fun."

I shivered helplessly as I felt my magic begin to flow out of me. The Nameless Elf looked as if he was devouring it somehow, perhaps enjoying the flavour. He held me down effortlessly – physically, he was far stronger than any human – and just kept draining my magic. I braced myself. This wasn't going to be pretty and it could go horrendously wrong. I'd never get a second chance either. He might kill me outright or simply transfigure me and leave me as an object forever.

There was a brilliant flash of blue light and the Nameless Elf began screaming in pain.

It had worked!

CHAPTER TWENTY-NINE

The trick had been simple and, to be honest, I'd never expected to get away with it. There was only one thing that could harm the elves – and only outside their dimension – and that was Cold Iron. I'd considered bringing an iron sword from the market, but that would have been detected and the Nameless Elf would probably have killed me out of hand – or forced me into a position where I had to kill him, if he was truly as suicidal as Dervish and Cardonel had insisted. I'd had to smuggle it in somehow.

On the face of it, transfiguration could be used to produce all kinds of elements – gold, for example – that could be sold in the mundane world. In practice, the transfiguration spells simply didn't last very long and when they expired, the gold returned to its original state. I'd taken iron dust and woven it into my clothing, before transfiguring it into something harmless. As long as I had my magic, it would *remain* harmless, but when the Nameless Elf had started to drain my power, he'd suddenly found himself surrounded by Cold Iron. The results had not been pretty.

I pulled myself to my feet and walked over to him. He was lying on the ground, twitching as if he were being assailed by a thousand invisible bugs. Elfish magic simply didn't affect Cold Iron at all, which meant that if he tried to escape – perhaps by turning immaterial or resuming his magical form – the Cold Iron would enter his body and poison him. Death would be prolonged and agonising. His only hope was for someone – me, perhaps – to remove the iron before the poisoning advanced too far and his form came apart. The Nameless Elf, simply because he lacked a name, might be *more* vulnerable to such an attack than the average elf.

He no longer looked even remotely human. His fine clothing had vanished, leaving an oddly-shaped body that reminded me of Cardonel, one that seemed to be constantly on the verge of shifting into another form. I recoiled slightly as I caught a glimpse of the invisible other form, threatening to break loose and consume him. I wished, not for the first time, that I knew more about where the elves actually came from. Generations of human researchers had speculated wildly – from a prototype for the human race to the last survivors of a dying world – but the elves refused to answer any questions about themselves. They tended to do horrific things to anyone foolish enough to ask, so very few people dared.

"All right," I said, carefully summoning my magic. Cold Iron didn't just harm, poison and eventually kill the elves; it also neutralised their magic, at least as long as the iron was touching their skin. I reached down and opened his mouth, flinching at the feel of touching something alien. The teeth that stared up at me, locked in an expression of agony, reminded me of a shark. I wasn't going to reach inside his maw with my bare hands. "Let's talk, shall we?"

The Nameless Elf seemed to struggle to speak. "What..." He broke off, coughed, and tried again. "What have you done?"

I ignored the question. "You sound remarkably coherent now," I observed. It was true. The pain seemed to be helping his mind to focus. "You're not quite the madman you appear, are you?"

"I find that pain is a wonderful motivator," the Nameless Elf gasped. I understood. His magic had been spinning out of control, burning through him, ever since he'd been stripped of his name. Now, in a rather amusing paradox, the Cold Iron was helping him to think clearly for the first time in years. "Take the remainder of the iron away from me and I will give you the world. I will make you the ruler of this world and set you on a throne above those of all the nations. I will grant you power and riches that will allow you to do whatever you want to do. I will make you a goddess."

"I don't want to be a goddess," I said. It was true. I'd

read up on the few gods and goddesses that still interacted with the human race and most of them were shaped by humanity in one way or another. Circe, the demigoddess I'd met, was bound to her role by human will. She might very well have no free will of her own. "I want you to answer my questions." I hesitated. "I also want you to free your captives."

The Nameless Elf turned to look into my eyes. "Do you know what the elves will do to you for what you have done today?"

I shrugged. "If they cared about you," I said, "why did they throw you out in the first place."

He managed to sneer. "You could not possibly understand," he said. He gasped in pain and I realised that some of the Cold Iron was pushing through his skin and into his body. "You're only human...how are you *doing* this to me?"

"I'm a genius," I said. I wasn't going to tell him what I'd done. If he didn't figure it out for himself, I might want to use the method again. "Try me."

The Nameless Elf snorted. "Could you explain democracy to a potted plant? Could you convince a bacterium to consider communism as a viable way of life? Could you define the existence and nature of the August Personage" – God, to the elves and other magical creatures – "to spiders and ants? There are concepts that your woefully imprecise language has no counterparts for, because you're not clever enough to invent them."

I smiled, although I never took my eyes off him. "Very well," I said. I wasn't going to risk allowing him to dictate terms to me. "You're going to answer my questions and then release your captives. If you refuse, or I think you're lying to me, I'm going to hurt you. If it gets pushed too far, you are going to die. Maybe your Queen will demand that I am punished, maybe she won't...but you will still be dead."

A thought occurred to me and I shivered. "I understand that your people have no souls," I added. "If you die, you die permanently and no trace of you will remain. Do you want to risk it?"

The Nameless Elf stared up at me, testing the bonds. "Very well," he growled. "Do I have your word that you will release me?"

I considered my words carefully. "Once you have answered all of my questions and released your captives, I will walk out of your...house and release you," I said. I wasn't stupid enough to release him while I was still in range. Truthfully, I had no idea how I was going to handle that, but I'd make it up when the time came. "Are those terms acceptable to you?"

There was a long pause. "Yes," the Nameless Elf growled, finally. "And I will not seek to harm you or anyone else while you are in my house."

I took that with a pinch of salt – after all, he could lie as much as he wanted – and refused to release him from the Cold Iron. He glared at me until he realised that I was not going to budge on that issue and then leaned backwards, trying to find a position that would allow him some comfort. It was not a pleasant sight. His form kept shifting, as if he had to devote more and more energy to remaining human – or at least humanoid. I had the eerie sense that if his physical form collapsed completely, the Cold Iron would pull him down and destroy him.

"Good," I said. "Are you holding my master captive?"

"No," the Nameless Elf said.

I stared at him. I'd been so convinced that Master Revels was his captive, even though I hadn't seen him among the other prisoners. I wondered if he was lying, yet I couldn't sense any attempt at deceit. It suggested that he was telling the truth, unless he was somehow hiding his feelings despite the Cold Iron. No one really understood how powerful and capable the elves truly were, yet...I could hurt him – torture him – or accept the answer.

"I will rephrase," I said, carefully. The elf might well find a way to twist my words. "Are you holding Master Revels captive?"

"No," the Nameless Elf repeated. I'd wondered if he might count someone else as my master, as unlikely as that seemed, but that was now proven false. "What is your next question?"

I gathered myself. "How many people are you holding captive within your home?"

"Two thousand, seven hundred and nine," the Nameless Elf said. He leered at me, a touch of the old arrogance returning to his voice. "And all of them are improved on the original. I reached into their weak mortal bodies and rebuilt them at will."

I stared at him, sickened. "Why?"

The Nameless Elf smiled. "Why not?"

Back in school, I hadn't studied much history, but one area we had been allowed to study was the Nazi Holocaust, how the Third Reich had attempted to exterminate the Jews. Their doctors, unhampered by concerns about morality and human rights, had performed gruesome experiments on Jewish captives, for all kinds of reasons. They'd been the worst kind of humans, utterly unconcerned about other humans, yet...they'd had a motive, no matter how awful, for doing what they'd done. The Nameless Elf had done it because it was fun for him, if not for his victims. Drinking in their fear and shame had probably been part of the fun.

I fought to control my temper and the desire to just push the iron into him and watch him die. "Can they all be returned to normal?"

"They would not *want* to return to normal," the Nameless Elf said. "They are vastly improved human beings."

He seemed to be telling the truth, but then, the most effective way to lie was to tell what one thought was the truth. The Nameless Elf might sincerely believe that his victims were better off after he'd worked his will on them. I pushed that thought aside and scowled.

"Tell me," I said. "Are you involved with the kidnapped or destroyed ghosts?"

The Nameless Elf shook his head. "No," he said. "What could pathetic shadows of weak humanity have to teach me?"

I wondered if that were true. The elves might have been immortal, but they paid for it by being soulless, with no guarantee that they would be able to live on after death. I could see the elves being desperate to learn what made some humans ghosts, just so they could use it for themselves and perhaps survive on after their deaths. Or perhaps not; they certainly didn't seem to think about the concept of dying very much, if at all.

It wasn't my problem anyway. "Right," I said, grimly. I bounced a few other questions off him, but they were all unimportant. "Do you happen to know anything useful at all?"

The Nameless Elf snickered at my frustration. "I know that sometimes what is hiding in plain sight can be the hardest thing to see," he said. I realised that he was deliberately trying to annoy me. He'd decided that he didn't know anything about what I was interested in and so he could bait me at will. "You really should question your assumptions."

I stared at him. "Do you know who summoned the fire demon that destroyed the Rationalist Building?"

"A fire demon is easy to summon if you have the right tools," the Nameless Elf said. That didn't quite answer my question. "I have no idea who might have summoned it. Anyone can summon a demon with the right preparations and then lose control."

"I already know that," I growled. I shook my head. I'd risked my life and freedom...for nothing. The people who'd told me not to confront the Nameless Elf had been right, damn them. "How do I release your captives?"

The Nameless Elf refused to tell me at first, claiming that he had to release them personally, which meant that I would have to release him from the Cold Iron. I refused, naturally; he'd be able to kill me before I could react, even if it meant risking his own death. It took several minutes and threats of outright torture for him to tell me how to start releasing them myself, a task that meant giving me some control over the house. Even touching the magical field his gaolers had created gave me a headache. One by one, the captives were freed. A handful dropped dead the moment they were released from their bindings, while the others simply ran for it. I saw the two – I couldn't imagine what someone called a person who was half male and half female – running for their lives, along with many others. They didn't realise that the Nameless Elf was helpless.

I wondered, briefly, how the magical world would cope with the sudden influx of refugees. The Nameless Elf had been trapped for hundreds of years. He'd had plenty of time to lure them into his domain and then toy with them, before freezing them in time and suspending them from his wall. The human captives would be stepping back into a world that had moved on in their absence. I hoped that the Thirteen would take care of them, or perhaps they would have friends and family who had remained in the magical world.

"There have always been those who have come to me," the Nameless Elf said, as the last of the captives made his escape. He didn't seem too downhearted by the defeat, if defeat it was. It occurred to me that he was too happy for someone who had just lost some of his possessions. "The ones you freed will remain touched by my work, bearing testament to my handiwork. There will be others who will come into my domain and offer themselves to me, or offer others to me in exchange for favours or knowledge."

I looked at him. Something had just clicked in my mind. "People sell slaves to you?"

"Of course," the Nameless Elf said. "The human race is a puny race. You have no spark of true greatness within you. The men you choose to lead your people would not hesitate to do whatever it took to maintain power. They bring slaves into your world of magic and then give them to me. I take them in delight and use them for my art."

"The *Thirteen* sells you slaves?" I asked. Who else could he mean? "They...?"

"Of course," the Nameless Elf said, again. "You don't think, do you?"

"No," I agreed, absently. I asked a question that had been bothering me, although I wasn't sure why. "Why did Cardonel come to see you?"

"He wanted me to turn him into a real elf," the Nameless Elf said. He laughed until I pushed the Cold Iron against his skin. "The very thought!"

I asked him several more questions, but he couldn't tell me very much, although I did learn that he had a handful of human allies who brought him items from the mundane world, including the transformed statue. I'd put that in my bag and I'd take it home and free her personally. The paedophile Master Revels had used as the fall guy for the whole scheme would be in jail, loudly protesting his innocence to a disbelieving world, but I could probably construct a convincing scenario.

"You have asked your questions," the Nameless Elf said, breaking into my thoughts. "You can now free me and depart."

I knew that he was right. Reworking the spell that had transfigured the Cold Iron was the work of a moment, although I had to set a timer to make sure he wasn't freed while I was still inside the wards that were keeping him prisoner. I looked down at him, shook my head tiredly, and started to walk towards the exit.

"You don't think," the Nameless Elf said, his words somehow echoing out after me. "What hides in plain sight, but is never seen?"

I stepped out of the door and waited long enough to ensure that the defences were resetting themselves, keeping him prisoner for the rest of eternity. I felt my spell trigger and remove the Cold Iron, followed rapidly by a chilling temper tantrum. Even outside the wards, I felt it; the Nameless Elf was furious. I wondered, with a cold heartedness that I hadn't known I'd possessed, if he would think to wash. The transfigured Cold Iron was still on his skin, after all, and my spell would run out of power soon. The results...would not be pleasant for him. I found it hard to care. The Nameless Elf was a threat to anyone unlucky enough to stumble into him.

But I'd hit a dead end. The Nameless Elf hadn't held Master Revels prisoner, nor was he involved with the fire demon or the disappearing ghosts. We'd visited the Elfish Kingdom and the Queen had confirmed that the elves were not involved, which left...?

Something shattered in my mind, a ward I hadn't known I possessed. No, not a ward; something else that had been interfering with my mind, a powerful and yet subtle glamour-spell. I looked out on the world with new eyes and swore aloud, just before I started to run. I knew who was behind the plot now, even if I didn't know why. And I had to stop him before it was too late.

And I felt like a fool. The Nameless Elf was right. What hid in plain sight and was never noticed? The answer was simple; the obvious. I'd overlooked the key to the whole mystery.

I'd been used and I hadn't even noticed.

Chapter Thirty

"You bewitched me!"

Cardonel regarded me with surprise. I'd come bursting into his apartment without even bothering to knock, a serious breach of the magical world's few manners. A magician's home was his castle, after all, and even a half-breed like Cardonel was entitled to his privacy. Bursting in was a clear way of signalling unfriendly intentions. He looked...oddly weak when I stared at him.

"The Silent Order found traces of elfish magic," I said. He'd tried to kiss me when he'd seen me and I'd pushed him away angrily. Any man would have found them offensive and worrying, but I suspected that his worries had a different foundation. It was easy to forget, looking at him, that Cardonel was older than me and probably more experienced in the ways of magic. Even as a half-elf, he had a connection to magic that no human magician could match. "We believed them and we checked with the elves and then with the Nameless Elf. They had nothing to do with it."

I stared at him, unwilling to take my eyes off his chest. Making eye contact would have been dangerous. "We knew that an elf was involved somewhere and yet I never thought of you," I said. I waved a hand at his pointy ears. "It never occurred to me that you were a half-elf and would have some ability to use elfish magic. Were you laughing at me when you told me that you were burning up because of your father's energies? I should have realised that you had access to some elfish tricks."

Cardonel's eyes narrowed. "Dizzy..."

"I never thought straight when I was with you," I snapped. In hindsight, it was chillingly clear. "I thought you were sexy; my knees went weak every time I looked at you. You exude a panty-dropping musk that would have a man-hating lesbian bending over for you. How much of that was nothing more than glamour-spells?"

I pushed on before he could say anything. "The Nameless Elf must have recognised your spell on me," I said. "He kept asking what was the only thing that was in plain sight, yet never seen. You, the half-elf, the one who might have a desperate need to understand the ghosts and where they go after they finally fade away. You, the half-elf, with connections and friends among the younger Rationalists, the ones who want to push ahead with experiments the Thirteen saw fit to ban. You, the half-elf, who talked about breaking the stranglehold the Thirteen had on the magical world and convincing them to share power...

"I never spoke to my master about your words. Why didn't I do that?"

"Maybe you liked me enough not to betray me?" Cardonel asked, angrily. His form was starting to flicker, just like the Nameless Elf had done. I wondered, with a sudden burst of insight, if I had ever seen his real form. Sure, he'd dropped one glamour-spell, yet there could easily have been a second hidden under the first. The elves were experts at disguising themselves and presenting a certain appearance to the world and Cardonel had definitely inherited that talent. He had to be physical, because his mother had been physical, yet...what did he really look like? I had the nasty feeling that I wasn't going to like what I found. "I helped you to free the slaves, remember?"

"Yes, you did," I said. His voice had been dripping molten honey. It would have been more convincing if I hadn't been able to sense, now, the tiny flickers of Compulsion within his voice. It was quite possible to tell someone that two and two made five and, if one used enough Compulsion, they would believe it and even try to justify it to themselves. My senses were on a hair-trigger. "And yet..."

I learned forward, pushing the Compulsion away. "You met me in the market and came onto me," I said. "That isn't typical in the magical world, yet you did it...and I liked you from the start. My master thought otherwise, but I thought that he was acting out of racism; he seemed to think that all half-elves were untrustworthy. Somehow, that urged me to go out on a date with you, where I met your friends. You helped me to free the slaves...and in doing so, I was grateful to you. Or did you think that I would be in your hands afterwards? The slave owners would certainly not be happy with me and you could have blackmailed me into compliance.

"And I found you attractive, and I slept with you, and ... how much of that was real feeling and how much of it was something that you inserted into my mind?"

Cardonel opened his mouth to speak, but I rode over him. "I'm the apprentice to the Thirteen's enforcer, to use your word," I said. "You had to have been delighted. If you could get me to spy on my master, you'd have the source you needed, someone who could help you on your grand plan. But I wasn't willing to commit myself and instead we started looking at the missing ghosts. And then my master went looking for the source of the fire demon."

Something clicked in my mind. "I bet it was Linux who summoned the fire demon," I added. "All the records would have been destroyed, apart from the ones he'd taken out and given to you, research into ghosts and how they could be used. Why did you even want them?

"Dizzy..."

"Don't you fucking Dizzy me," I shouted at him. "Take me to my master or I swear I will hurt you, here and now!"

Cardonel moved so quickly I barely had a second to sense the magical blast before it slammed into my wards. Blue fire, sparking with evil alien intent, flared out in front of me, burning through protections. I pushed it away and released the spell on the transfigured Cold Iron, hoping that it would knock him out or render him powerless, as it had done for the Nameless Elf. Instead, Cardonel came striding through the fire, utterly unaffected. He no longer looked human. I could see long claws stretching out of his hands and his face was something horrible, warped by magic.

"I have no vulnerability to Cold Iron," he said, his words

hissing in my mind. Like the full-blood elves, he was telepathic, at least to some degree. "My mother may have weakened me with her impure human blood, but she gave me a power that even my father didn't enjoy."

He pointed a long finger and clicked his fingers. There was a blue-white flash of light and the world went away. I felt, just for a long moment, as if I were drowning in inky darkness, as if my life was draining out of me. I heard voices all around me, calling out, although I couldn't tell if they were warning me or welcoming me. I saw an angel, with wings spread wide, looking down with an expression of absolute sadness. There was a pale woman, wearing a silver ankh around her neck, standing ahead of me. She lifted her hand and waved...

And then I was back in my body.

"Welcome back to the world of the living," Cardonel said. "I never meant to injure you."

I scowled at him. While I'd been out, he'd stripped me of everything from clothes to magical artefacts, leaving them piled up at the other end of the room. He'd cuffed me to a wooden chair, so thoroughly that it was almost completely impossible to move. The cuffs were made of silver, making it harder to use my magic, although my head was scrambled so badly that using any magic might have been horrendously dangerous. If I'd thought it would rebound on him, I'd have taken the risk, but there was no way to be certain.

"Bastard," I said, harshly. "What are you going to do with me?"

"Well," Cardonel drawled. He reached out with one hand and stroked my right breast. "I'm sure we could find some way to pass the time."

I recoiled. "You'd have to force me," I snarled. "I bet you get all your women that way."

He paced away from me, peering down at my clothes and then at a timepiece he had in his hand. "You'll be pleased to know that we don't intend to do anything to you," he said, darkly. "You're not important to us. Once the New Age has dawned, you will be released and you will be welcome to join us or find your own place within it. Until then, I'm afraid that we are going to have to keep you here." His voice became mocking. "I'm sorry for any inconvenience."

"I'm sure you are," I sneered. This wasn't good. I was naked, unable to move and completely at his mercy. I understood why he'd stripped me, far too well. Magic was often as dependent upon symbolism as much as anything else and being naked signified helplessness. The cuffs not only ensured that I couldn't move, but also that my ability to use magic – when my head finally cleared – was limited. Cardonel had put me into a position where a great deal of magical inertia would make it difficult to escape. "How long are you going to keep me here?"

"The New Age will dawn at midnight tonight," Cardonel said. He shrugged dispassionately. "It was never meant to be so soon, but your master was getting alarmingly close to the truth and he might have been able to rally the Thirteen to act in their own defence. The Great Powers of the Universe would certainly have acted to prevent the dawn of the New Age if the Thirteen refused and they might well have destroyed much of the world in the process."

"The New Age," I repeated. I concentrated on looking helpless. Like his father's people, Cardonel had a tendency to be overconfident and gloat; I'd seen that while he'd been playing cards. If I asked the right questions, he might explain everything. "What are you going to do?"

Cardonel leered at me. "Everything will change," he said. "There will be a new age of magic, where wonders will once again be common and we will rise to new heights."

"You plan to destroy the Thirteen," I said, slowly. "I don't think that that would bring about a new age of magic."

"My plan is far greater than that," Cardonel said. He leaned closer. "What is the greatest difference between humanity and the elves?"

"One is made of matter, the other is made of magic," I answered. It was hardly a hard question. "What do you intend to do about it?"

My mockery, as I had hoped, spurred him onwards. "The source of magic lies in a dimension very far from our own, and yet – for the right kind of person – right next door,"

Cardonel proclaimed. I realised, suddenly, that he was giving a political speech rather than anything else. "We can tap that magic and, properly filtered, use it to rise to a new level of being, a new form of magical creature. Humanity will shed its physical form and become a creature of magic, a creature far more powerful than any of the elves. We will rise to new heights and the elves will only be able to watch and weep as we leave them far behind."

He rounded on me, his dark eyes burning with alien fire. "We will puncture a hole into the afterlife itself, the source of all magic," he thundered. "We will use the magic to reform the entire world, mundane and magical. We will rise and the Great Powers, those who have held humanity at their mercy since the dawn of time, will be bent to our will. The whole of Creation will change forever."

I stared at him, appalled. I knew that the Great Powers were capricious, yet they were an essential part of running the universe. Destroying them, perhaps even controlling them, would have disastrous effects, assuming that it were possible. If they knew what was being planned, every great power in the universe would unite against him. It was quite possible that Cardonel's scheme would blow up in his face, which would have dire consequences for everyone in the magical world. Or maybe God would send an angel to stop them, whatever the cost. Entire cities had died in the past through God's will.

"You're mad," I said, finally. Why hadn't I seen it before? "You have to stop this..."

Cardonel laughed. "What do I have to lose?"

"Everything," I said, firmly. "You're half-human, Cardonel; do you have half a human soul?"

He studied me for a long chilling moment, as if he was on the verge of lashing out with his claws and slicing through my throat. "You're just the same as your master," he hissed. "You never think or dream of the vast possibilities beyond the devastation. And it never occurs to you that the people under your feet have thoughts or feelings of their own. Look at me, Dizzy; do you find me attractive now?"

The glamour-spells surrounding him popped and I

recoiled. For the first time, I was gazing upon Cardonel's real form. He was short, with aging skin and no hair...and blue fire burning under his physical form. I could see fires licking through his chest, slowly burning away at everything that anchored him to life. His father's magic had never been meant to be confined in a matter-based form and it was slowly burning its way out. When it completed the destruction of his physical form, Cardonel would die. The more he used his power, the sooner he would die.

And he stank. I smelt age, and burning flesh, and something eerily inhuman. I understood, now, why so few humans trusted half-elves. If I'd seen him like that, back when we'd first met, I would never have trusted him, let alone allowed him inside me. There were tales of men and women who allowed themselves to be seduced by sexual demons – a succubus was far better than any merely-human woman in bed, but the price was appalling – and woke up in the morning to discover what they'd permitted so close to them. Very few had survived the experience, at least with their minds intact.

"I have only a few days left at most," Cardonel hissed. "I stand here on the verge of total collapse. Merely holding my body together requires an act of will far greater than anything you could imagine. The only thing keeping me alive is my force of will. Tonight, I will know apotheosis and the entire human race will follow in my wake."

I understood, seeing how all the pieces fitted together. "The Rationalists figured out how the ghosts were linked to the afterlife," I said. "You worked out how that could be used to punch a hole though and then draw on the magic there."

"My body is partly magical, after all," Cardonel said. His form shimmered and he returned to his more normal appearance. I knew, now, that I would never look at him in the same way again. "I understand magic in ways that even the Rationalists will never understand. When the magic comes pouring through the hole, I will be there to give it shape and form. The influx of raw magic will transform me and in doing so the entire world will be transformed."

I found myself searching, desperately, for the words that would convince him not to do this. "You could surrender yourself into the mundane world," I said. "You'd be human there. You'd just blur away and live out a human lifespan."

"As one of the sheep," Cardonel said. "The humans of the mundane world are so happy, so distant and so small. They have no idea of the truth behind existence, of the Great Powers that manipulate events behind the scenes, or even how they can take some of that power for themselves. They run around, desperate to find money and a job and a partner and have kids and never realise the truth behind the universe. They kill themselves and others for the sake of the August Personage, struggle to impose their way of life on others...they're tiny!"

He looked down at me. "Would you choose to go back to the mundane world and spend the rest of your life there?"

I shook my head. "No," I admitted, "but I can look forward to a normal human lifespan or even a far longer one if I learn how to rejuvenate myself. You will die soon. Surely, life as a human isn't that bad..."

"My father showed me the gates of paradise and told me that I wasn't allowed in," Cardonel sneered. "The humans rejected me; the elves rejected me, even though they brought me into existence. I will make the human race rise up and the elves will be crushed."

I stared at him. "You will destroy them?"

Cardonel laughed. "I will force them to realise that there is something in the universe far more powerful than them," he said. "That alone will destroy them."

He sobered. "And all it will cost is one human life."

"If you're looking for a virgin sacrifice, I'm not qualified," I said, dryly. "Or did you merely make me *think* that you'd been inside me?"

Cardonel laughed. "No," he said. He reached into my clothes and pulled out the statue. "I thank you for bringing her to me. I intended to take someone from the streets, which might have risked everything. You may have ensured the birth of the New Age."

"No," I protested. "Use me instead!"

"You're not qualified," Cardonel reminded me. "The spell needs *innocence* and you are far from innocent."

He checked my bonds and then stood up, saluting. "The wards will keep you here, Dizzy," he said. "I will be back for you when the New Age has dawned and the world has forever changed."

With that, he vanished, leaving me alone.

Chapter Thirty-One

For a long moment, the rage boiled up within me and I struggled against my bonds helplessly. I'd brought the statue-girl with me, intending to free her as soon as I could, and instead I'd just turned her into a human sacrifice. I could see now what they intended to do. They would kill her and follow her soul as it slipped onwards into the afterlife, piggy-backing her death to open a permanent link between the afterlife and our world. I wasn't sure if I believed everything he'd told me, yet...it all hung together remarkably well.

"Damn it," I swore, as I struggled. I'd seen plenty of movies where the handcuffed criminals had been able to get free while the cops weren't looking. They'd clearly not bothered to consult a real cop, because I couldn't even begin to get free. The cold wooden chair began to press against my naked bottom, a droll reminder of my punishment...wait, a *wooden* chair? It was so simple that I found myself laughing out loud. Cardonel, after all, had never lived in the mundane world and saw magic as the answer to all of his problems. I knew better.

Using all the strength I could muster, I pushed the chair back as hard as I could. I was trying to overstrain the legs and break the chair. It all happened very quickly; one moment I was still seated on the chair, the next it shattered and I fell to the floor. I cried out in pain as I struck the floor – the chair had scratched me in several places and I was bleeding badly – but I was able to pull free. I might have had four pairs of handcuffs dangling from each of my arms and legs, yet I was free! I summoned magic and unlocked the handcuffs, and then concentrated on healing the damage. It looked worse than it actually was. Two minutes later, I had dressed myself and headed over to the door. It was locked and crawling with enough security spells to deter anyone. I studied them, wondering if I could pick my way out, but it was impossible.

Cursing, I went back into the apartment and searched for anything I could use. There was nothing. Cardonel wouldn't have owned many Objects of Power and he wouldn't have left anything in the apartment with me, just in case I did manage to break free. I checked the walls, wondering if I could simply blast through them and escape that way, but again there were too many security spells to risk anything. I scowled. I'd gotten out of one trap only to be trapped again. Cardonel was probably laughing somewhere, knowing that even if I managed to get off the chair I'd still be unable to escape. Or had he had some reason to think that I could get off the chair and be able to escape?

It clicked suddenly and I cursed my own stupidity. I still had the Sisterhood's pendant and Cardonel had seen me use it, back when we'd freed the slaves. He hadn't been able to take that from me, if only because men couldn't take the pendants without female permission. He'd been able to remove it from my neck and leave it with my clothes – I guessed his half-elf nature had confused the magic on the pendant – but he hadn't been able to put it outside my reach. I took it, allowed my magic to flow into it and opened a Gateway. A moment later, I was walking through the woods and down towards the pool I'd seen before, where the same women waited for me. In the distance, splashing around in the pool, I spied some of the girls I'd freed from captivity.

"We welcome you, sister," Sister Varsha said. She seemed unchanged from the last time I'd seen her, even though I'd pushed a handful of liberated slaves into her dimension. "Why do you call upon us?"

I ran through a brief explanation of everything that had happened since we'd last spoken, starting with the fire and then how I'd beaten the Nameless Elf, only to be defeated by his half-elf cousin. I didn't hide anything from them except one detail. I didn't dare explain the full nature of Cardonel's plan to them, not if my suspicions were correct. The Sisterhood had a patron, after all, and she might take a very dim view of his plan.

"You have been a credit to your sex," Sister Varsha said, when I'd finished. "What do you wish to do now?"

"Is it not obvious?" The crone demanded, from where she was lying on the ground staring up into the blue sky. "She wants to rescue her master and the poor transfigured girl."

"She has an obligation to try," Sister Varsha agreed. I nodded. I hadn't turned the girl into a statue and sold her as a piece of modern art, but I'd certainly been responsible for her falling into even worse hands. "We should assist her."

"Except our ability to interfere outside our own dimension is limited," another Sister said. "This sister" – she indicated me with a wave of her hand – "has already compromised our neutrality once. Should we allow her the chance to do so again?"

I flushed, but the crone spoke first. "We have assumed the responsibility to be there for women who have been abandoned by others," she said, sharply. "We have to live up to our obligation."

"Yes," the newcomer agreed, "but we still do not have the ability to reach out and rescue the girl."

"No, you don't," I agreed. I looked up at Sister Varsha, praying that I was right. "I need to speak to your patron."

Sister Varsha stared at me, just for a moment. "Our patron rarely speaks to anyone," she said, "apart from those who are given to her. She may not speak to you."

"I believe that we have already met," I said. "Please will you allow me to speak to her? I need her help."

She pointed to another pool hidden within the surrounding trees. "Go there, place your hands into the water and speak her name," she said. "If she pleases to talk to you, she will do so."

I nodded and walked away, towards the hidden pool. The trees closed in around me. I glanced behind, only to discover that the path I'd walked on was no longer there. Shaking my head, I turned back and walked onwards, praying that I was right. The Nameless Elf had been dangerous enough, but this person was far worse. And it would be even worse if I was wrong. I hoped my reasoning was correct...

The pool suddenly shimmered in front of me. I knelt down and pressed my hands into the cold water, feeling waves of magic flickering against my hands. The pool had a presence that awed me, the result – I saw – of magic pouring through from an unknown source and into the pocket dimension that played host to the Sisterhood. It explained so much about them. Their patron was a power that all men feared. I held my breath as I spoke her name aloud.

"Circe."

And she was suddenly there, rising from the pool. No water dripped off her, for the pool was, in some ways, part of her. Her eyes met mine and, just for a second, she winked at me. I could sense the endless strata of power surrounding her and plunging downwards towards infinity. There were some that whispered that she was merely an extremely powerful sorceress who had adopted an even older name, but I knew better. I was looking into the eyes of a goddess.

"My lady," I said. I felt oddly reassured by her wink. "I need your help, on my behalf and that of a lost girl."

Circe's voice hadn't changed, even as she floated above the water. "I may not interfere, save to punish those who are given to me or to repay debts," she said. "Do you feel that I can assist you, knowing that there may be a steep price?"

I took a breath. If I was wrong about this...there were far worse things than frogs to spend the rest of one's life as. Circe would definitely take it the wrong way. "I believe that you owe me something," I said, and braced myself for thunderbolts. "You transformed me without my permission."

Circe said nothing. She just floated there, waiting for me to continue. "I read about you after we first met," I said. "You're bound by your own nature. You can only harm men who have offended against women, like the men who would have harmed me if you hadn't interfered. I am not a man and I have not offended against women. Why did you transfigure me?"

I pressed my case, gambling everything on a single roll of the dice. "Before I was transformed, I had problems grasping the underlying nature of magic," I admitted. "My mind, influenced by the mundane world, had problems working magic. Afterwards, after you transformed me and I struggled to transform myself back, I found that magic flowed easily and I took another step away from the mundane. I think that you were...hired to transform me into something."

Circe's gaze flashed fire, literally. "No one hires me to do anything," she said. There were still no thunderbolts. I remained human. "Your master wished a favour and I obliged."

I nodded. I'd guessed that Master Revels, desperate for a successor whatever it took, had been willing to arrange for his apprentice to run afoul of one of the Great Powers, knowing that if she failed to save herself she would never be able to master the more complex magic used by the greater magicians. Circe had obliged, although I wondered why – and knew that I didn't dare ask. Come to think of it, perhaps I did know; she might well have been the person – or Great Power – who had informed Master Revels about Mr Pygmalion. Perhaps he'd been handed over to her for punishment, once the Thirteen had finished stripping his brain of anything useful.

"But I didn't grant you my permission to transform me," I said. "I believe that you owe me a favour."

Circe looked at me for a long moment. "Very well," she said. "I will answer three questions for you, as truthfully as I can, and then provide you with transport to wherever you want to go."

I frowned. "As truthfully as you can?"

"I am not the August Personage," Circe said, flatly. "I can and will answer questions, but I am not omniscient. And after this, we are even and I will owe you nothing."

"I understand," I said. I had to think quickly. I had to ask the right questions. "Where is the final kidnapped girl, the one who Cardonel stole from me, being held?"

Circe smiled at me. I understood, suddenly, that I'd asked the right question. "She is being held on Arthur's Seat, in the Hill Fort there," she said. I scowled. That made a great deal of sense. Arthur's Seat was one of the most magically powerful places in Edinburgh, but because of its strange nature no magician – even the Thirteen – had dared to set up a permanent home there. The hill had little to do with King Arthur, but far too much to do with Merlin, once the greatest sorcerer of his age. "You will need to be very careful."

"Yes," I agreed. "Are the other kidnapped victims being held there too?"

"Yes," Circe said. She sounded disappointed. I guessed that that hadn't been such a good question. "You may find your master and the ghosts there."

I thought hard. The final question had to be a good one. "What defences are there, waiting for me?"

Circe didn't smile. "There are so many there," she said. "They have summoned a demon and used him to man their defences. Even looking at him is hard for me..."

I had to remind myself that Circe was even less human than the Nameless Elf. What I was looking at was merely the tip of the iceberg, something she wore to allow us to see her and pretend that we understood her or what she was. The eyes of a goddess could see for miles, uncover secrets and learn great truths. In the past, we had worshipped the gods, giving them power through our supplications. Even now, strange things came into existence in the magical world, purely because humans believed in them. What came first; the chicken or the egg?

"Three questions, three answers," Circe said. "I will warn you to be careful, but then...I could give you a glamour-spell that would allow you to penetrate most of the defences without being detected. Would you like that?"

My eyes narrowed. "I want to know the price ahead of time," I said. I'd read too many stories of bargains with the gods going horrifically wrong. "What do you want from me?"

Circe didn't bother to play around. "I want you to do me a favour sometime in the future," she said. "I don't know what yet, but I give you my word that you won't have to betray Master Revels or anyone else. I may just need another agent in the mundane world."

I considered and then nodded slowly. "Very well," I said. "Give me the spell."

Circe leaned forward and kissed me on the forehead. Her lips were as cold as ice. "Be careful, Dizzy," she whispered. "You are not walking into a safe place."

The world went white and then faded away. I looked up to find myself standing in front of the Mosque. How had Circe known that I had intended to come here next? I found myself shaking my head in awe. No wonder primitive humans had called her and her kind gods and goddesses. They'd had no other context to look at them. And yet...did the gods exist because we believed in them, or did we believe in them because they existed?

Dervish looked relieved to see me as I walked into his apartments. "Dizzy," he said, in relief. "The entire magical world is chattering about you."

I blinked and then nodded. Naturally; I'd freed thousands of people from the clutches of the Nameless Elf. Everyone would know what I'd done. I wondered, suddenly, how the Thirteen would view it. They'd tolerated the Nameless Elf's activities and even concealed most of them. They wouldn't be able to claim ignorance now. The remainder of the magical world would know that they were lying. Master Revels might not be too happy with me.

"I know," I said. I wasn't about to discuss everything with him. After all, he'd sent me to the Nameless Elf. I didn't want to believe that he was a villain, but I still knew to be careful. Besides, Master Revels had considered him a friend...and I had considered Cardonel a lover. "I need something in your possession."

I looked around and saw the sword in the stone. "I think I have to try to take the sword," I said. "Please don't try to stop me."

Dervish twisted his hands together in agitation. "Dizzy, be

careful," he urged. "There are powers in that sword that haven't been dreamed of for hundreds of years. If you take it – if Allah lets you take it – you will be responsible for it until the time comes to pass it on to someone else. The responsibility has killed many people and sent others to hell. You're not ready to take the sword."

I reached out to the sword, ignoring him. Somewhere in the distance, I could hear voices singing, drowned out by the clash of battle. The world seemed to tilt and twist around me, sending eerie shadows flickering out into the normal world. The sword...was so much more than a sword. It was something far greater and far more powerful.

"The sword is made from a strand of His power," Dervish said. I barely heard him. "A mortal who wields it will eventually be destroyed by it. To use the sword is to be certain of everything, to be transformed into a fanatic. You will be consumed by it, the moment you lose your grasp on yourself. Don't..."

My hand closed around the hilt. I felt it then, a history that stretched back to before the dawn of time itself. I saw mighty angels clashing in battle, before falling down towards the fires and the darkness below. I saw the first humans climbing up from the water, only to be tempted into sin and rediscover war for themselves. I saw the sword passed from hand to hand, from mighty warrior to mighty warrior, from religion to religion, until it was passed to Dervish's ancestors, who took the sword and hid it away far from the Muslim Lands. I pulled and the sword came easily out of the stone. A moment later, there was a brilliant flash of white light and I felt as if someone had stabbed me in the heart.

And there was a voice calling my name.

"Dizzy," Dervish said. "Can you hear me?"

I looked up and smiled. My senses had never been so sharp, yet when I tried to stand up I felt another burst of pain. Moving cost me everything I had. "What..."

I cleared my throat and tried again. "What happened?"

"You drew the sword," Dervish said. I felt it now, like a splinter lodged in my heart. The sword was part of me now, at least until I passed it onwards. "You..."

"I have to go," I said. I could tell, now, that time had passed quickly while I'd collapsed. It was nearly midnight. "Thank you for everything."

"Don't thank me," Dervish said. There was something in his eyes I didn't like. He was afraid, afraid of me. The sword seemed to find it coldly amusing. No mere human ever lived up to his religion. "I will go, instead, to pray for your success and your soul."

CHAPTER THIRTY-TWO

I could feel the intricate traces of magic spilling out over Arthur's Seat as I ran towards it, silently cursing the needle in my heart. I wasn't sure if the sword had become something else or if it was somehow coexisting with my body, but it hurt to move. It explained, I decided, why so few people have tried to hold onto the sword after they'd accomplished their task; the sword's presence was a constant pain in the ass. If it had been a conventional sword, on the other hand, it wouldn't have been any use against a demon. I could feel the demon's presence too in the distance, a nexus of power I didn't dare look at too closely. It might have looked back.

The Hill Fort, to mundane eyes, was just another set of ruins. To my eyes, gazing into the magical world, it was a building built right on top of a nexus of wild magic. The Thirteen, or their Celtic predecessors, had tamed the magical nexus under Edinburgh Castle and learned how to use it as a source of power no one had ever succeeded in taming Arthur's Seat. The Hill Fort had been built, at least according to the magical world, to prevent an invasion of our world from the Fairy Roads. Several roads converged in the nexus of wild magic and not all of them led to friendly territory. Even if they had all been friendly, the roads changed at whim. Tomorrow, they might lead directly to a dimension of evil demons or monsters.

I paused, after staggering up the path towards the Hill Fort, trying to catch my breath. The climb had winded me more than I had expected, the result of complex and subtle magical wards designed to discourage mundane people from coming too close. Someone really didn't want to be disturbed. I opened my mind slightly and peered out towards the Hill Fort, feeling out the defences and booby traps. There were warning wards, backed up by defences that ran the gauntlet from freeze spells to change spells, followed by a handful of death spells capable of dealing with anyone that managed to get through the earlier ones. They were so powerful that they were actually bleeding into the mundane world. I hoped that no mundane people were walking towards the Hill Fort now. The results would not be pleasant.

Time to see if Circe is as good as she says, I thought. There was no way I could dismantle all those wards in time to prevent the sacrifice. I knew, somehow, that they would kill the girl precisely at midnight, when all the stars would be aligned. If Circe's promise of protection didn't hold I was about to walk right into a trap, without any way to escape. The sword's mere presence, as painful as it was, was a reminder that there was another option, but slicing through the wards would have warned everyone inside that they had an intruder. I knew better than to think that the sword, even if it was the most powerful Object of Power I had ever seen, would make me invincible. And besides, I had a feeling that drawing and using the sword too much would have its own side effects. Dervish had been terrified, with – I suspected – good reason.

I stepped forward and felt the first ward shimmer over me. I held my breath as it ghosted through me and onwards, choosing to ignore my presence. I let out a sigh of relief and took another step, passing through a second ward and then a third. They ignored me, although I felt as if I were being scrutinised right down to the molecular level. I shivered as the fourth ward flickered into existence. It was so powerful that it had been keyed to physical footsteps, not a magical presence. I suspected I knew who had designed that ward and it hadn't been Cardonel. Linux would have been smart enough to link a ward into the mundane world.

The next set of defences loomed up in front of me and I braced myself. The freeze spells should have been triggered at once, even though freeze spells were the easiest for a trained magician to dispel. I felt a wave of cold air blowing across me, but nothing else. I stepped through the wards and onwards to the next set of defences. The change spells flared out over me and accomplished nothing. Cardonel might have meant to transform anyone who got so close into a worm, a very helpless form, but they did nothing to me. I had to smile. If there were any spells Circe would know inside out, they would be change spells. I winced as the death spells loomed up in front of me, emitting terrifyingly bad vibes, yet they too ignored me. I just kept walking.

Up close, the Hill Fort was just as impressive as Edinburgh Castle and, like the Castle, it was far bigger on the inside than the outside. The people who had built it originally had known what they were doing, for rather than link it to a pocket dimension or a building elsewhere in time and space they'd hollowed out the space inside the hill and built their inner defences there. I had to admire what they'd done, although I wasn't sure I'd have risked it myself. They'd balanced the inner world on the magical nexus and if anything happened to the nexus their world would collapse and, as two things couldn't occupy the same space without powerful magic, probably explode out into the mundane world. The mundane world knew that the volcano below Arthur's Seat was extinct. I wondered what they'd do if the explosion took out the hill and unleashed a new volcano in the heart of Edinburgh. Or perhaps it wouldn't work like that. I knew very little about volcanoes.

I walked around the Hill Fort twice, looking for a door or a way in, but found nothing. The building was surrounded by stone walls, blocking all access. I cursed under my breath, knowing that time was running out, as I hunted desperately for the way in. The building was already within the magical world. There should have been no need to hide a doorway into the building, not unless Cardonel had been far more paranoid about his defences than I had expected. Unless...I looked over at part of the wall and frowned. It looked as if it had been in the wars, yet there was a curious regularity to it, something that rang a bell in my mind. It clicked suddenly and I swore again. Cardonel and his friends hadn't walked through a door into the Hill Fort; they'd clambered over the walls!

It had been years since I had done any climbing at school and this was far harder than wall bars, although there weren't any sadistic PE teachers either. I braced myself, put my foot on the first stone, and started to climb. The sword's presence was surprisingly reassuring, although I didn't dare look down. Sheer terror would have held me frozen until it was far too late. Years ago, I'd watched a demonstration by army climbers in Princes Street. The men had shimmied up the poles and sheer walls as if they had been monkeys. I had no idea how they'd made it look so easy.

A cold wind blew around me as I climbed higher, something I suspected was intended to discourage other climbers or maybe even blow them off if they didn't hang on tightly. Now I was so high, I couldn't go back down; it was hard enough concentrating on climbing higher and higher. I moved between the gusts of wind and just kept going. The higher I got, the more dangerous it became. I almost slipped on a rock that felt wet to the touch. I nearly didn't realise when I reached the battlements because I was so focused on the climb.

I collapsed as soon as I had pulled myself over the edge and onto the solid stone floor. I might have remained there for too long, had I not felt the roar in my bones. There was a single passage ahead of me, leading down towards the interior of the Hill Fort...and I could sense the demon's presence at the bottom of it. I forced myself to my feet, cursing the cold under my breath, and staggered down the passageway. I knew I needed time to gather myself, but time was running out. The hellish climb had consumed nearly an hour. It hadn't felt anything like so long.

There was another roar as I turned the corner and came face to face with the demon. I'd expected a humanoid figure, with horns and cloven hooves for feet, but instead I was gazing at something my mind refused to give shape and form. My head span and I knew, without the presence of the sword, that merely looking at the demon would have blown my mind into the furthest reaches of insanity. I knew that demons could take on more pleasing forms – they weren't allowed to make deals with insane men or women – but this one didn't seem to have bothered. I found myself wondering which demon it actually was. If I'd known its name, I would have been able to command it myself, yet a single mistake would have given me to the demon.

I stepped back as its breath – I hoped it was its breath – rolled out towards me. It stank of hellfire and damnation and burning sulphur. Two glowing eyes, burning with power, turned to gaze out upon me. I almost staggered under its gaze before realising that it couldn't actually reach out to catch me. It was bound inside a circle that would hold it securely, but in order to get past it, I would have to walk through the circle myself. I doubted that the demon would allow me to pass unmolested. The person who had summoned him had probably promised him everyone who walked through the circle without his permission.

"WHO ARE YOU THAT THREATEN MY SLUMBER?"

The words echoed in my head, sending me staggering backwards; they seemed to be made of fire itself. The demon spoke directly into my mind, rather than bothering with anything mundane and human like a normal voice. I recoiled as the words thundered through my mind, carrying the very taste of a demon with them. There could be no negotiations with this creature. Cardonel had bound it to his will and it would follow his orders without hesitation.

I stepped forward. "You have permission to return to the pit," I said. It was worth a try. If Cardonel hadn't been careful enough, I might just be able to dismiss it without a fight. "Leave now, taking none with you."

The demon laughed. "I AM BOUND TO THIS SPOT BY THE WILL OF THE HALF-MAN," it said. His voice didn't improve upon closer acquaintance. "DO YOU THINK THAT YOU CAN TRICK SUCH A ONE AS I? THE TORMENTS THAT WOULD BE FOSTERED ON ME WOULD ONE DAY BE FOSTERED ON YOU. ALL OF YOU CLEVER LITTLE CHILDREN OF THE

MUDMAN THINK THAT YOU CAN TRICK US. WE ARE AGELESS. WE CAN WAIT FOR ALL OF YOU. ETERNITY IS A VERY LONG TIME."

He was referring to Adam, I guessed. The stories about the War in Heaven were contradictory, but most of them seemed to focus around some of the angels refusing to bow to Adam and Eve, first of the human race. Depending on which version you believed, the War in Heaven had taken place before the Garden of Eden had been created, or afterwards, when Satan – then one of the most powerful and beautiful of the angels – had tempted Adam and Eve with the apple of knowledge. The story was a metaphor for a far deeper truth, a parable to use the Christian term, which hadn't stopped countless religious scholars – all male, of course – using it as a rod to beat their wives, sisters and mothers.

They were silly bastards, in my view. A merciful God wouldn't hold Eve's female descendants responsible for her crime, even if she had been the first one to bite the apple.

I drew the sword, somehow. I had no sense of it leaving a sheath, but suddenly it was in my hands, glowing with brilliant white light. Just looking at it made me feel a strange mixture of emotions; I was unworthy to even look upon it and I was the only one worthy to carry it. I understood, now, why Dervish had been so scared. The sword's mere presence made it hard to think rationally. The white light flared up and I saw the demon flinch back, yet somehow it was unable to leave the circle and flee. I had to move quickly. I doubted that Circe's protections would be able to conceal the sword's presence now I'd drawn it and started to call upon its power.

The demon's form congealed into a horrific monster, several times the size of a man, and breathed hellfire at me. The sword danced up in front of me and deflected it, much to my relief. Hellfire doesn't burn skin and bone; hellfire burns your very soul. Once a soul fell into hell, the demons set it on fire permanently, at least until the soul repented of its sins and cried out to God. I found myself stepping forward, right towards the demon – and right towards the circle. The demon's hands grew claws and its teeth grew sharp. It looked, I was suddenly amused to note, rather like a cross between a human and a raptor dinosaur. I'd actually met a handful of dinosaur-folk from the inner world back when I'd been studying – it seemed a lifetime ago – and they were decent people. The demon was a monster whatever form it took.

I lunged forward and crossed the circle. The demon let out a howl of delight and lashed out at me. I jumped into the air, allowing the sword full control, and landed neatly on its oversized arm. Before it could react, I was off again, slashing out with the sword towards the demon's back. It jumped forward and crashed against the invisible wall keeping it within the circle. I winced as it turned around, faster than I would have believed possible, and lunged at me again. This time, I held up the sword and slashed its arm right off. The demon howled as the sword cut through its physical form. The remains of its arm fell to the ground and faded away, leaving behind nothing but the faint smell of sulphur.

"YOU WILL PAY FOR THIS WENCH," the demon thundered. It had lost nothing of its arrogance, I noted. "I WILL HAVE YOU IN MY HANDS IN THE DEEPEST PIT OF HELL. YOUR BLOOD AND TEARS WILL BE DRAINED DRY. NOT EVEN THE HATED ONE WILL BE ABLE TO PUT YOU BACK TOGETHER."

I slashed out again, this time cutting through the demon's chest. The wound wasn't deep and the cut healed a second later. I cursed my own mistake as the demon breathed another wave of hellfire at me. The demon wasn't the monster it looked like and the only way to beat it was to cut it apart, destroying the underlying immaterial form. The stench of the hellfire rolled over me and I gasped, distracted just enough for the demon to land a mighty blow that would have killed me, were it not for the sword. Instead, it threw me back out over the circle and up the corridor. A little extra force would have thrown me all the way over the battlements and down towards the hard rocks below.

"YOU WILL NOT GET WHAT YOU WANT," the

demon proclaimed. "DO YOU THINK THAT HE HAS FEELINGS FOR YOU?"

Demons always lie, I reminded myself, as I pulled my aching body to its feet. The sword was still in my hand – it was part of me now, at least until I passed it onwards – and was pulling me back towards the fight. I allowed it to lead me onwards, realising – to my dismay – that the monster was concentrating on regenerating its lost arm. It paused to give me a look of utter malevolence and I shivered. The hell-kin were the embodiment of pure undiluted evil.

I kept walking forwards until I was back inside the circle. The demon howled and leapt forward, trying to come down hard on me. I ducked back and then stabbed up towards its chest. The sword went inside and, this time, I focused my power and will through the blade. There was a massive burst of white fire and the demon simply disintegrated. I found myself kneeling on the floor, shocked and a little stunned. Only the traces of magic ahead of me pulled me back to my feet and onwards.

No one stepped out to bar my path, or even to try to delay me. The passages opened up into a single vast chamber, right at the heart of the Hill Fort. I was standing on a balcony over a massive pool of boiling light. I knew, at once, that it was the nexus of wild magic. It bubbled and seethed under me, reminding me that going too close would be dangerous. Some of the odder magical races had only come into existence when they'd fallen into wild magic. I'd met intelligent cats, dogs, mice and hamsters, to say nothing of weird crosses between humans and animals. They could never have lived in the mundane world.

And, right at the centre of the chamber, high above the pool of magic, I saw Cardonel.

And, lying in front of him, I saw the girl.

Strong arms grabbed me from behind. "I'm sorry, Dizzy," Robin said. "I cannot let you interfere."

CHAPTER THIRTY-THREE

I struggled, but she was surprisingly strong and unworried by the sword. It was no longer in my hand. It took me a moment to realise that it had returned to its position inside me, although it was no longer painful. Robin had me in a grip that steadily made it harder to struggle, so eventually I had to relax. She pulled me over towards one side of the wall and pressed me against it. A moment later, my hands and feet were stuck in what felt like glue.

"Dizzy," a tired voice said. "I wish you had not come."

I looked over in surprise. There was an old man hanging beside me on the wall. I stared; the cheekbones and voice were familiar, but everything else had aged. I had known that Master Revels was much older than me, yet I hadn't realised just how many rejuvenation spells he'd been forced to use, not until I saw him with all of his power draining away. It was the only way they could have held him prisoner, but it had brought him to the brink of death.

"I had to come," I said. I had been determined to rescue both him and the girl. He was my teacher, the one who had tried to warn me about the danger of trusting a half-elf, and she was my responsibility. I didn't know her, but it was my fault that she was on the verge of being sacrificed. "I...what can we do?"

Master Revels shrugged. Even that took a great deal of energy from him. "How did you get into the building without being stopped?"

"I had help," I said. I wasn't going to name names, not here. "What happened to you?"

"I went to see the Nameless Elf," Master Revels admitted. "I figured that if elfish magic was involved in capturing the ghosts, he was the most likely suspect. I didn't get there. I was attacked by your friend the day I left you, after the vampire, and lost the ensuing fight."

My eyes opened wide. "He *beat* you?"

"A keen observation, Dizzy," Master Revels said, "And most annoying to my ego. Yes, he and his friends caught me by surprise and beat me. They knocked me out...when I woke up, I found that most of my power had been drained, leaving me with just enough to keep myself alive. Since then, I have been hanging here, waiting for the end of the world."

I stared. "He isn't going to destroy the world," I protested. "He just kept saying that he wanted us all to be magical and..."

"Don't you know anything about the fundamental nature of human desire?" Master Revels snapped. "You give everyone in the human race the powers of a god and we will rip ourselves apart like rats in a sack. We'll become worse than the elves, even if we don't start attacking the Great Powers. And if we do, we run the risk of blowing up the entire universe by interfering with the forces that keep it balanced. Your lover boy wants to save his life and, in doing so, is going to doom us all."

I shivered. "I know," I admitted. I didn't want to face it, even though I no longer had any illusions. I looked over towards the girl. She'd been restored to human form, but she'd moved from one nightmare to another. Cardonel had placed her on a stone table and tied her down with golden cord. She could barely move, yet alone escape her fate. "How long do we have?"

"The magic will surge at midnight," Master Revels said. "He will kill her then and follow her ghost."

As if the word had opened my eyes, I was suddenly aware of the ghosts in the room. There were thousands of them, all spinning through the air. I saw young plague victims from long ago, their staring eyes fixed upon the girl, perhaps hoping that her death and the torrent of magic would free them from their long imprisonment. Others, more aware of what was going to happen, were shaking their heads sadly. I saw a nun, wearing a black scarf, whispering to the girl. I couldn't tell if the girl could hear her or not, but I hoped that she would find some comfort in the nun's words. Soldiers, wearing uniforms that dated all the way back to the days of Robert the Bruce, were surrounding Cardonel. They wanted to fight, yet there was nothing they could do. They were helpless to affect the physical world.

I started to struggle against the glue, but it held me as securely as a pair of handcuffs, perhaps more so. I realised that if I managed to generate any magic, even with my hands and feet immobile, the glue would simply absorb it. I had to admire Cardonel's work, even though I hated him for everything he'd done. There was no way out of the trap. Even the pendant the Sisterhood had given me was daunted by the glue. Or was there another option? I felt the ring on my finger and shivered. I could call Fiona right into the heart of the Hill Fort.

Cardonel walked away from the girl, crossing the balcony towards us. I watched him come as dispassionately as I could. He was wearing a long white robe, decorated with mystical symbols and patterns my eyes refused to follow. His glamour-spells had faded away completely, leaving his face as it had truly appeared, but no one seemed inclined to abandon him. Everyone involved in his plan was committed now. Either they succeeded in opening up the gateway to a new age of magic or the magical world would tear them apart. There could be no mercy for people who had nearly triggered doomsday.

"You don't have to do this," I said, when he stopped in front of us. "You could spare her life and pass onwards into the mundane world and..."

"Be silent," Cardonel snapped. "I want you both to know that you have failed. There are only ten minutes before the clock strikes midnight. When she dies, we will open up the gateway and welcome the new age of magic. You will be the witnesses as the human race begins its rise to godhood."

"Oh, be quiet," Master Revels said, sharply. I think he recognised my distress and was attempting to divert attention to himself. "If you want to gloat, you really need a goatee and a white cat to stroke."

Cardonel opened his mouth angrily, but somehow managed to control himself. "The bad news is that your body and soul are too...old to contain the new surge of magic," he added, nastily. "You will be blown apart by the surge when it rages into you, as will the Thirteen and all the others who have sought to hold us back. Your energies will end up serving us."

He turned and stalked back towards the altar. I watched him go and then triggered the ring, praying that Fiona could get here in time. I was suddenly very aware of the mechanical clock at one end of the giant chamber, ticking away the seconds until the ritual began. The Hill Fort was designed to stop an invasion from alternate dimensions and realities. What if Fiona couldn't reach us in time? I tried to pull free of the glue again, but it was impossible. There was no way out.

Space warped madly in front of us and a full-sized dragon appeared from nowhere. Several of the people in the room ran screaming, even though Cardonel held his ground. Fiona blew a fireball towards him, which he deflected with ease, and then another wave of fire towards us. The glue melted under the heat and I fell to the floor, tearing the remaining glue away from me before it could cool. Master Revels fell to the ground beside me, coughing and choking. He was far too old to tolerate such treatment for long. Like me, he was gasping helplessly for breath.

Fiona whirled round, somehow floating in the air over the magical nexus without apparent trouble, and concentrated on Cardonel. The half-elf seemed to have no problem holding his own; he pointed a long finger at Fiona and blue fire flared around her snout. She howled in pain as his magic interfered with the magic holding her impossibly-bulky body in the air, twisting and turning in a desperate attempt to evade him. He ran forward, pushing her back with his blue fire, seemingly immune to the fireballs she spat at him. The entire chamber seemed to be unworried by the fire.

I ran myself, out over the nexus and towards the altar. The

girl was lying there, staring; I wondered if she'd lost her mind. I started to tear at the golden cord and pulled it free, despite the presence of a dozen security spells intended to keep the girl firmly bound and helpless. Somehow, all the magic in the room was being sucked towards Cardonel and Fiona. I freed the girl, pulled her into my arms, and thrust her down one of the balconies to Master Revels. He could get her out of the chamber...

Fiona howled in pain again and then fell, as if the laws of the mundane world had suddenly asserted themselves on her body. The dragon splashed into the pool of wild magic and vanished in a blinding flash of blue light, suggesting that she'd been completely disintegrated by the mere contact with wild magic. A tidal wave of magic rose up towards us, sending me collapsing to the balcony as my senses swam, just before Cardonel turned and saw me. I don't know what was going through his head at that moment; he had to know, somehow, that I'd just ruined his plan. The ghosts, all suddenly more physical because of the wild magic, were tearing at him. He muttered a word under his breath and there was a flash of light, sending the ghosts flying backwards. I swallowed as I saw him starting to walk towards me.

"It's over," I said. Master Revels had gotten the girl out, or so I told myself. Besides, the longer Cardonel stayed focused on me, the less time he'd have to find her and get her back onto the altar before time ran out. "Give up and..."

Something hit me from behind. I fell forward. If it hadn't been for the sword's presence in my body, I would have blacked out. As it was, I rolled over and realised that Robin had come up behind me. She pulled at me with one strong hand, as if she intended to pull me onto the altar. There was something about the scene that bothered me, even as I found myself laughing; I wasn't *innocent*, so I couldn't be used as the sacrifice. Yet...I had forgotten something. What was it?

Cardonel grabbed me from her and threw me aside, as easily as a man might pick up a baseball and throw it across the room. It struck me a second too late – as the clock began to strike twelve – that Cardonel had always had a back-up plan. He had told me that he'd intended to use a random person, perhaps someone snatched off the streets, as a sacrifice before the girl I'd rescued had fallen into his hands. Robin, whose faceless face was a reminder of the evil that a proud sorcerer could do to the person pledged to serve him, was another innocent. She could be used as the sacrifice!

I heard Linux crying out – perhaps guessing the truth at the same moment I did – when Cardonel hit Robin and threw her onto the altar. I felt, more than heard, the ghosts crying out in horror as he stabbed her chest with the stone knife. The altar shattered as she died and I felt her soul start to leech out of her body. The ghosts, pushed in by the magic Cardonel had created, found themselves following her as she fell away from her body and onwards to the next world. My senses seemed to follow her as well, as if I was being tugged out of my body and pulled onwards, forcing me to grab onto reality as the balcony appeared to heave and tilt under me. I had the terrifying impression that I was going to fall, like Fiona, into the nexus of wild magic and die in a brilliant flash of light.

"Yes," Cardonel was shouting. His magic was growing stronger all the time, stronger and stronger as he tapped the nexus below. He was glowing with brilliant blue light, his face changing as everything human was burned away, while everything immortal was transfigured. "Yes, yes, yes..."

"NO," a single voice said.

It sounded like the demon I'd defeated on my way in, but far – far – worse. The voice seemed to come from everywhere and nowhere. I wanted to be sick and only the fact I had the sword inside me prevented me from throwing up all over the balcony. The demon's voice seemed to grow stronger, as if it would never fade away. I heard it everywhere in my mind.

Everything clicked and I realised, in a flash of horror, just what had gone wrong. Robin hadn't been innocent at the end, not when she'd willingly taken part in a plan to kidnap and kill a child – and acted to prevent me from saving the girl. Cardonel had sacrificed her anyway, unaware – or unheeding – that her soul was going to hell. God might overlook some sins, or allow them to be punished in the mortal realms, but not others. Robin might have started life in the magical world as a victim, yet she had become a victimiser.

I looked towards Cardonel and shivered. His form was still glowing, but the blue fire was steadily being replaced with an eerie red glow. He was taking on the form of a demon, one who wouldn't be bound by the laws that defined Heaven and Hell. As a half-elf, he had enjoyed immunity to Cold Iron and some of the other elfish laws; as a half-*demon*, who knew what he could do? Perhaps he wouldn't be as powerful as the full demons, but he wouldn't share their weaknesses.

"KNOW THAT WE ARE PLEASED WITH YOU," the demon said. I pushed my hands against my ears, but I couldn't block out the hellish voice. "WORM THOUGH YOU ARE, YOU HAVE CREATED A NEW GATEWAY TO THE INFERNAL REALMS, ONE THAT MAY NOT BE BLOCKED OR BOUND BY THE MOST FAVOURED OF THE ALL-HIGH. WE ARE FREE UPON YOUR WORLD AND WE WILL NOT BE CHAINED AGAIN."

I tried to block my senses, but it was impossible. The demons were reaching out of Hell now – I couldn't even *look* in the direction of Hell – and reshaping the magical field to suit themselves. The ghosts were screaming as they saw their eternal damnation ahead of them. Robin's body was burning now as the demons reached our world, tearing through the walls of reality as if they were made of nothing more complex than tissue paper. I could hear them, laughing and cheering as they burned through, making humanity – and every other race – terrible promises of suffering to come. I could hear the Great Powers howling their fear and panic, I could see the Elves realising that there was something greater and more terrible than them on their way, sense the sudden outpouring of violence and horror into the mundane world. The forces that Cardonel had unleashed would never be contained within the magical world.

The sword spoke to me, mind to mind. A series of visions poured through my mind. I saw what would happen. I saw the demons tearing the magical world apart, killing each of the Great Powers and luring the magicians into sin. I saw the demons walking into the Elfish Kingdoms and burning them to the ground. I saw the Sisterhood and a thousand other groups wiped out in a split second. I saw the demons reaching into the mundane world and unleashing Hell on Earth. I knew that it would happen, unless it was stopped. I knew, also, that there would be a price. The price was my life.

I hesitated, just for a second. The world hadn't been good to me until the last year. If they'd asked me to give my life for the world a year ago, I might well have rejected it. Now...now I'd seen that there was so much more to life. There were good people in the world that deserved to live. Perhaps even the worst people deserved a fair chance at life. I had had my chance at a life less ordinary and now I had to die to save my world.

It hurt, but I pulled myself to my feet. Cardonel was floating ahead of me, his eyes staring at nothing as the demons reconfigured his body to serve as their gateway into the human world. I knew that he was still alive and aware; the demons wouldn't have been happy unless they were showing him just how foolish he had been, tormenting him endlessly with the thought that he'd gained the immortality he wanted, an immortality of never-ending suffering. It was unwise to make bargains with demons and even more unwise to fall into their hands without any protection. Cardonel had had none. They could do anything to him.

The sword was suddenly in my hands, glowing brightly, and the demons recoiled. I sensed them marshalling their power, to reach out through Cardonel and swat me like a bug, but it was already too late. His form changed, became far less than human, but the sword guided me towards my target. I ran forward and rammed the sword right into his body. The magic field surged around me, there was a brilliant flash of light and then the world started to fade away. The last thing I heard was Master Revels shouting my name...

And then I was gone.

CHAPTER THIRTY-FOUR

I awoke.

I was lying in my bedroom back home. I pulled back the covers and looked around. My old stuffed teddy bear, Mr Grumbles, was sitting at one end of the bed. I found myself wondering, as I swung my legs over and climbed out of bed, if it had all been a dream. Had I truly entered a world of magicians and witches and wizards, or had I dreamed it all. The door opened and my mother entered, carrying a breakfast tray. I felt myself burst into tears as I saw her again, as happy as she had ever been, and reached out for her. She took me into her arms and held me until my sobs had faded away.

"This isn't real, is it?"

My mother looked down at me. "It is as real as you want it to be," she said. "You are welcome here."

I shook my head sadly, staring down at myself. I could see, now, just how weird the room actually was. I was wearing my old nightgown, which had been too small for the seven-year-old child I'd been, yet it fitted perfectly. The bed, too, was too small for my adult form, yet I hadn't had any problems sleeping in it. Everything was perfect, but subtly wrong. I shook my head again and almost started crying. I should have known better. It was too good to be true.

"It is true," my mother said, quietly. "Everything is true in its own space and time."

"Oh," I said, wiping my face. "Who are you?"

She looked at me for a long second. "In terms your human mind can comprehend," she said slowly, "I am God."

I stared at her. There was something about her – a sense

of inhuman perfection, compassion and peace – that made it impossible to doubt her word. The more I looked at her, the more I became aware that there was far more to her than I could ever comprehend. She held up a hand and deflected my probes, smiling sadly. I realised that she'd done me a favour. If facing an elf or a demon could come close to destroying my mind, what would happen if I stared into the true face of God?

"You don't have to be scared," she said. "Trust me; I don't need your worship and I certainly don't need your starship."

I found myself giggling. "You've seen the movie?"

"I've seen everything," she said. There was something indefinably sad about her voice. "I've watched every last sparrow fall from the trees I created. I've watched the human race from the dawn of time until the final hour. I know everything about you and your family; I know everything about everyone. I've seen every movie your race has ever produced."

"Oh," I said, again. I was stunned. "Should I start apologising for every sin I have ever committed?"

"If you like," she said.

I frowned. "Would it make any difference?"

"Your race has the idea that I serve as judge, jury and executioner of every last person in history," she said. "It doesn't work that way. I created humanity so that you would lack the self-knowledge that is my curse, the objectivity that makes it impossible for me to be anything else than what I am. When you live, you lack objectivity; when you die, your souls are no longer connected to linear time and you see yourselves as you truly are. If you feel that you have sinned, you condemn yourself to a hell you create. I mourn every last fall and I wait for the purified souls to rise up to join me."

She smiled, anticipating my next question. "I don't interfere openly very often," she added. "I sometimes answer prayers, sometimes whisper in a person's ear; I do little else. Your race has to rise to heights you can barely imagine without me pushing you along."

I found myself struggling for words. "But there are people who do horrible things in your name," I said, slowly. "Why don't you stop them?"

Her face darkened. "There are those who think that I grant them sanction and forgiveness for their crimes," she said. "They can never forgive themselves when they die and realise the truth. I have often allowed such a soul to reincarnate on Earth rather than suffer in a self-imposed hell, granting them forgetfulness. They do better the second time around."

She smiled. "Are you going to ask the other question?"

I swallowed hard. "Am I dead?"

"In a manner of speaking," she said. She gave me a mischievous smile. "You chose to give up your life to prevent your lover from unleashing the apocalypse. You're currently floating in...let's call it the Waiting Room. You have several possible choices."

She grinned. "I don't often make such an offer," she added, "but you deserve to choose.

"You can choose to return to your life in the mundane world. You would be seven years old again, with your whole life in front of you. You'd have a second chance at life.

"You can choose to return to your life in the magical world, where you would have an eventful life that might well kill you earlier than your appointed time.

"Or you can go onwards to judgement."

I stared down at the floor. I didn't want to admit how badly I'd missed my mother and the first home I'd known, even though it had all turned sour in the end. Or maybe it hadn't. This time, with foreknowledge of what had happened in the past, I'd be able to change things. Instead of wasting my time at school, I could learn and gain qualifications and then live a better life. And yet...I loved the magical world. I wanted to be part of it.

"If I go back home," I said, slowly, "what would happen?"

She smiled. "You'd wake up back in your own bed, convinced that everything you'd gone through was just a bad dream," she said. "You'd hold your mother tightly in the morning and promise never to leave her again. You'd go to school and start studying desperately. You'd grow up as a studious girl, eventually qualifying to be a doctor because you still want to help people. You'd go on a field trip to North Korea after the blockade ends and meet your future husband there. You'd be married at twenty-seven and will have four kids, who will grow up into pretty girls and strapping versions of their father. You will be happy."

I looked up. "Do you promise?"

"I have never promised anyone happiness," she said. "I have merely given them the tools to become happy, if they chose to do so. You could throw away your second chance."

I looked back down. "But if I don't go into the magical world, the apocalypse is still unleashed..."

"It won't be unleashed," she said. She smiled at my confusion. "People assume that time is a strict progression of cause to effect...but actually, from a non-linear, non-subjective viewpoint, it's more like a big ball of wibbly-wobbly...timey-wimey...stuff."

I had to laugh. "You've watched that show too?"

She laughed too. "Take it from me," she said. "The apocalypse will not be unleashed because of you, even if parts of time have been rewritten to allow you to return to the mundane world. You saved the entire world."

I nodded. "One final question," I said. "What happened to Cardonel? Is he...?"

She held up a hand. "No one is told anyone's story, but their own," she said. "He has to find his own way out of where his choices have led him."

I thought about it. The thought of being back with my mother and having a second chance at life was tempting, yet...I wanted to remain within the magical world. I understood, somehow, that if I returned to the mundane world I would never be able to visit the magical world again. I realised now what Cardonel must have been thinking when he'd been reminded that he could put his elfish aspect aside and walk into the mundane world. He would have been happy and ignorant, unaware of the truth behind how the world worked.

And besides, I owed Master Revels an explanation.

"I choose to return to the magical world," I said, firmly.

She didn't try to discourage me. "Very well," she said. She reached out and gave me a hug. Just for a second, I was wrapped in the tenderness of undying love. She *was* love. "Open your eyes."

"My eyes are open," I protested.

She smiled. "Then close them," she said. "I will always be with you."

I closed my eyes. When I opened them again, I was lying in my bed at Master Revels's house. He was sitting by my side, staring down at me anxiously. Fiona was seated on her perch, preening herself. She was alive! I sat up and felt a stab of pain. The sword was still part of me. She – God – hadn't mentioned anything about that.

"Well, of course," Fiona said, when I got over my shock. "I'm a creature of wild magic. What did you think that more wild magic would do to me?"

"I thought you were dead," I protested. "I thought..."

"He managed to cancel most of the magic in my form," Fiona said. "It was a very ingenious attack, in its way. I fell out of the air and right into the nexus. A quick bath and I was as right as rain."

I rubbed my head. "What happened?"

"A cup of tea, first," Master Revels said. "And then we will tell all."

I listened and drank my tea as they talked. After I'd stabbed the half-elf – everyone was careful not to mention him by name – the gateway to hell had collapsed. Master Revels and a handful of others had rounded up Linux and the rest – I was relieved to discover that Sparks wasn't among them – and arrested them. They'd found me lying on top of the altar, completely out of it. Master Revels had taken me home, put me to bed and waited for me to wake up.

"You saved the world," Master Revels said. "There isn't a person or humanoid or Great Power in this universe that doesn't owe its life to you. You're a hero."

I rubbed my head. Everything seemed like a dream. Had I

really met God?

"I'm proud of you," he added. "And so is the rest of the world."

"Thank you," I said. I didn't want to know, but I had to ask. "What is going to happen to the other members of…of his conspiracy?"

"There's no room for losers in this world," Master Revels said, grimly. "They'll be interrogated under truth spells and then escorted to the gateway and shoved into the Dark Continent. After what they tried to do…we'd execute them, but it might not take."

"Oh," I said. I stared down at my hands. "I trusted him."

"Everyone makes mistakes," Master Revels said, flatly. "The thing that defines us is how we respond to those mistakes and correct them – if we're lucky enough to realise that we have made a mistake in time. You saved my life and that of my companion." He reached out and stroked Fiona's scales. "And you saved everyone else into the bargain.

"A wise man said that if you saved the world, it will reward you every day," he added. "I think that you are about to discover the truth of that statement."

He smiled as a letter appeared out of nowhere and dropped down into the table. "Let's see," he said, opening it. "There is a werewolf running somewhere in Newhaven, a report of a stranded mermaid in Portobello and a new and deadly vampire cult down near London. That should keep us busy until lunchtime."

Master Revels stood up and held out a hand. "Coming?"

"Of course," I said, pulling myself to my feet. I felt fine; great, in fact. "I wouldn't miss it for the world. I love this job."

The End

Elsewhen Press

a small independent publisher specialising in Speculative Fiction

Visit the Elsewhen Press website at elsewhen.co.uk for the latest information on all of our titles, authors and events; to read our blog; find out where to buy our books and ebooks; or to place an order.

Elsewhen Press

a small independent publisher specialising in Speculative Fiction

Bookworm
Christopher Nuttall

Elaine is an orphan girl who has grown up in a world where magical ability brings power. Her limited talent was enough to ensure a magical training but she's very inexperienced and was lucky to get a position working in the Great Library. Now, the Grand Sorcerer – the most powerful magician of them all – is dying, although initially that makes little difference to Elaine; she certainly doesn't have the power to compete for higher status in the Golden City. But all that changes when she triggers a magical trap and ends up with all the knowledge from the Great Library – including forbidden magic that no one is supposed to know – stuffed inside her head. This unwanted gift doesn't give her greater power, but it does give her a better understanding of magic, allowing her to accomplish far more than ever before.

It's also terribly dangerous. If the senior wizards find out what has happened to her, they will almost certainly have her killed. The knowledge locked away in the Great Library was meant to remain permanently sealed and letting it out could mean a repeat of the catastrophic Necromantic Wars of five hundred years earlier. Elaine is forced to struggle with the terrors and temptations represented by her newfound knowledge, all the while trying to stay out of sight of those she fears, embodied by the sinister Inquisitor Dread.

But a darkly powerful figure has been drawing up a plan to take the power of the Grand Sorcerer for himself; and Elaine, unknowingly, is vital to his scheme. Unless she can unlock the mysteries behind her new knowledge, divine the unfolding plan, and discover the truth about her own origins, there is no hope for those she loves, the Golden City or her entire world.

As an indie author, Christopher Nuttall has self-published a number of novels. *Bookworm* is his second novel to be published by Elsewhen Press. Chris is currently living in Borneo with his wife, muse, and critic Aisha.

ISBN: 9781908168320 (epub, kindle)
ISBN: 9781908168221 (368pp, paperback)

For more information visit bit.ly/Bookworm-Nuttall

Visit the Elsewhen Press website at elsewhen.co.uk for the latest information on all of our titles, authors and events; to read our blog; find out where to buy our books and ebooks; or to place an order.

Elsewhen Press

a small independent publisher specialising in Speculative Fiction

THE ROYAL SORCERESS
CHRISTOPHER NUTTALL

It's 1830, in an alternate Britain where the 'scientific' principles of magic were discovered sixty years previously, allowing the British to win the American War of Independence. Although Britain is now supreme among the Great Powers, the gulf between rich and poor in the Empire has widened and unrest is growing every day. Master Thomas, the King's Royal Sorcerer, is ageing and must find a successor to lead the Royal Sorcerers Corps. Most magicians can possess only one of the panoply of known magical powers, but Thomas needs to find a new Master of all the powers. There is only one candidate, one person who has displayed such a talent from an early age, but has been neither trained nor officially acknowledged. A perfect candidate to be Master Thomas' apprentice in all ways but one: the Royal College of Sorcerers has never admitted a girl before.

But even before Lady Gwendolyn Crichton can begin her training, London is plunged into chaos by a campaign of terrorist attacks co-ordinated by Jack, a powerful and rebellious magician.

The Royal Sorceress will certainly appeal to all fans of steampunk, alternate history, and fantasy. As well as the fun of the 'what-ifs' delivered by the rewriting of our past, it delights with an Empire empowered by magic – all the better for being one we can recognise. The scheming and intrigue of Jack and his rebels, the roof-top chases and the thrilling battles of magic are played out against the dark and unforgiving backdrop of life in the sordid slums and dangerous factories of London. Many of the rebels are drawn from a seedy and grimy underworld, while their Establishment targets prey on the weak and defenceless. The price for destroying the social imbalance and sexual inequality that underpin society may be more than anyone can imagine.

As an indie author, Christopher Nuttall has self-published a number of novels. *The Royal Sorceress* is his first novel to be published by Elsewhen Press. Chris is currently living in Borneo with his wife, muse, and critic Aisha.

ISBN: 9781908168184 (epub, kindle)
ISBN: 9781908168085 (400pp, paperback)

For more information visit bit.ly/TheRoyalSorceress

Visit the Elsewhen Press website at elsewhen.co.uk for the latest information on all of our titles, authors and events; to read our blog; find out where to buy our books and ebooks; or to place an order.

ABOUT THE AUTHOR

Christopher Nuttall has been planning sci-fi books since he learned to read. Born and raised in Edinburgh, Chris created an alternate history website and eventually graduated to writing full-sized novels. Studying history independently allowed him to develop worlds that hung together and provided a base for storytelling. After graduating from university, Chris started writing full-time. As an indie author, he has self-published a number of novels. *A Life Less Ordinary* is his third fantasy novel to be published by Elsewhen Press. Chris is currently living in Borneo with his wife, muse, and critic Aisha.